BREAK Free

PACIFIC PREP BOOK FOUR

R.A. SMYTH

Break Free
Brutal Lies Copyright © 2021 R.A. Smyth

ISBN: 9798769548413

Cover & Interior Design by Nikki Epperson. All Rights Reserved.
Editing by Lunar Rose Editing Services.
Formatting by Rachel Smyth.

He thinks they've broken me.
He thinks I'm nothing but an empty shell, ready to be molded into
their perfect soldier, his perfect wife, a damaged plaything.
He might be right.

I've never been so exhausted, beaten down, and wary. I'm so close
to giving up, so close to accepting my defeat and twisted fate.
The darkness is quickly closing in around me, but a sliver of light
appears when I read the note from my brother and my guys.
I will rise, like a phoenix from the ashes. I will be a catastrophic
force, one this compound trained me to be.
My guys are coming for me, and I almost feel bad for the carnage
we're going to inflict.

We'll burn it all down, right after I break free.

PACIFIC PREP PLAYLIST

Skin – Sixx:A.M.
We Care – Osatia
Castle – Hasley
You're Somebody Else – Flora Cash
Hurricane – Theory of a Deadman
Pavement – SayWeCanFly
Till Death – Fivefold
Hollywood's Bleeding – Andrew Baena, Johnny Ciardullo
Forever – Late Night Savior
This Is Our War – Halocene
Shivers – Ed Sheeran
Walk Outside – East Love
Love Alone – Thriving Ivory
Barefoot and Bruised – Jamestown Story
Hand Me Down – Citizen Soldier
Uncomfortably Numb – Arrows in Action, Taylor Acorn
Obsessed – Sam Riggs
Stay – Black Stone Cherry
…And many more

Play Now

TRIGGER WARNINGS

This book is a dark, contemporary, new adult reverse harem romance, meaning the FMC will end up with 3+ males.

TThis is the final book in the series, and if you've made it this far, you will be familiar with most of the trigger warnings, but just for clarity, here they are—physical abuse, psychological abuse, graphic violent and sexual scenes. One final one below is a spoiler so read at your own risk!!!

SPOILER WARNING FORCED STERILIZATION ***SPOILER WARNING***

If you are suffering from the very real effects of a book hangover, I offer a support thread in my facebook readers group—<u>Rachel's Rebel Rehab</u>—if you need somewhere to rant or yell. You will also be able to find some amazing bonus scenes under the files section, and information on the future of our favorite Pacific Prep characters.

The series consists of 4 books and will ultimately have an HEA.

PROLOGUE

Lawrence

Fifteen Years Ago

THE PARTY IS IN FULL SWING WHEN WE ARRIVE, PRECISELY AS planned. It took a while for everything to come together, but by the end of tonight, the Davenport name will be synonymous with grief and heartache.

"Ow, you're hurting me," the woman beside me hisses as she tries to tug her arm free from where it's linked with mine. I relax my shoulders enough so I'm not squeezing her arm, and scope out the room. Now that I've come this far, I just want it over with, but I have to play my part if I want tonight to go off without a hitch.

"Let's get a drink and mingle," I mutter, grabbing a couple of champagne glasses from a passing waiter. Handing one to my date for the evening, we make our way through the crowd, stopping every now and then to chit-chat with incessant suck-ups.

Just when I'm about ready to blow my brains out, Wilbert Warren shuffles his way through the crowd, the fat fuck already rosy-cheeked from too much alcohol.

"Lawrence, lovely party, isn't it?"

"It is." I return his too-wide grin with a tight smile and zero enthusiasm.

His glassy eyes move to the woman I brought with me this evening, carefully selected so she will blend in and get the job done.

"Who's your ravishing date?"

"Elise," she greets politely, introducing herself. "Pleasure to meet you."

"The pleasure is all mine." He reaches out to take her hand, kissing the back of it, and I have to bite my tongue to hold back my sarcastic comment. The idiot thinks he's so smooth, flirting with anything that's attached to a pair of tits, but it's beyond me how he managed to knock up not one, but *two* women. Money obviously speaks louder than good looks.

Elise emits a girly giggle that I know is all for show, but Wilbert eats it up like it's chocolate frosting, and the two flirt back and forth until Barton steps up to the front of the room, Maria dutifully at his side. Tapping the rim of his champagne flute, he speaks up, gaining everyone's attention.

"Ladies and gentlemen, we are honored to have you here to celebrate with us this evening. I still can't believe it has been five years since this wonderful woman agreed to marry me."

"If you'll excuse me, I need to use the ladies' room." Elise smiles softly, flitting her gaze my way before taking off through the crowd, just like we planned.

The second she's out of sight, Wilbert digs his elbow into my side to gain my attention, waggling his eyebrows like a pussy-deprived teenager. Sighing, I ignore him and pretend to focus back on Barton's pathetic speech. In reality, I'm with Elise, picturing her sneaking upstairs. All of our houses are built the same, so it wasn't difficult to give her directions to the nursery.

With everyone focused on Barton and distracted by the party, she should be able to sneak in unnoticed and take the girl, and we'll all be long gone by the time anyone realizes she's missing.

Elise returns by the end of Barton's boring speech, and I catch her eye. Knowing my unasked question, she gives a small, barely perceptible nod of her head, silently letting me know the job is done. She got the girl and has handed her off to one of my men, masquerading as our driver for the evening.

We mingle for a while longer, and I make a point of congratulating Barton and Maria, even though the words taste like poison on my tongue. The only reason I get through it with a straight face is knowing everything will change after tonight. While they are down here, showing off for their guests, their daughter will be on her way to the compound, where she will never see the light of day again.

As the night wears on, Elise and I get more explicit with our PDA, making it more than apparent that when we duck out early, and I can't be reached, it's because I'm too busy fucking her brains out. As anticipation thrums through my veins, that's *exactly* how I plan to fucking celebrate.

When we do finally stumble out into the cool evening air, we hurry to the limousine I hired. The driver tilts his head when he opens the door, and as I slide into the back seat, my eyes fall on the sleeping toddler lying across the leather seats.

Elise slips in beside me, and the driver closes the door, moving to the front of the car and starting the engine.

"What are you going to do with her?"

I don't know if she's second-guessing her decision, just curious, or simply trying to make conversation, but I don't care. She had no qualms about accepting my money in exchange for her role in tonight's plan, so even if she is rethinking her decision, it's too fucking late.

"That's none of your concern."

She shrugs it off, and we lapse into silence again until we pull up at the hotel I booked us into for the evening. The driver pulls open the door and helps Elise out. Sliding out behind her, I pause as I redo the button on my jacket and say in a low voice, so it doesn't travel, "Take her to the compound and come back in the morning."

"Will do, boss."

I stand and watch as the car leaves the parking lot, and only when the red lights have faded into the distance do I turn around, a victorious grin on my face. For the first time all night, I take in the slutty dress on Elise, noticing how her nipples are visible through the thin fabric and her long, toned calves in the heels she's wearing. My dick hardens. *Oh yeah, I'm more than fucking ready to celebrate.*

By morning, I'm sated and happier than I have been in a very long time. My phone has been going off for the last hour, but it's still early, so I don't answer it—after all, I'm meant to be in a sex-hazed cocoon.

The same limousine as last night pulls up at the steps, and the driver gets out as I open the door for Elise.

"My driver will take you wherever you want to go," I tell her. "I never want to see you again."

She doesn't say anything, all business, as she gives a sharp nod of her head and climbs into the back seat. I close the door behind her and turn to the driver.

"Any issues last night?"

"None. I have someone looking after her for now. When she's old enough, she can join the other recruits."

I nod in agreement, not giving a damn what the guards at the compound choose to do with the girl now. I don't give a shit about some useless child. I've achieved what I wanted, and now I get to revel in the fallout.

He moves to step away, and I stop him, gesturing with my head toward where Elise is hidden behind the blacked-out window. "Bowen, deal with this problem too."

I can't have any witnesses or risk her gaining a conscience and coming back one day. She needs to be dealt with, permanently.

Bowen grins maliciously. "Already done, boss."

As he walks round the limousine and climbs in behind the wheel, I walk toward my own car. Pulling my phone out of the inner pocket of my suit jacket, I dial the number I need and hold it to my ear. The phone rings twice before it's answered.

"You're going to get a call today from Barton Davenport. Whatever he offers, I'll double it."

"What do you want?"

"I want you to send him on a wild goose chase."

Hanging up, I slide into the plush leather seats of my Maserati. I fire off one final text, saying *'the job is done'*, and before I can put the phone away again, it starts to ring, Barton's name coming up on the screen.

Huffing out a sigh, I answer. He doesn't give me a chance to even spit out a greeting before his angry tone comes down the line. "Where the hell have you been? I've been trying to reach you all morning."

"Sorry, it was a late one. That girl I was with gave me quite the workout after we left the party."

I hear him huff on the other end. "Just get to the house. We need everyone from the board for a meeting."

"Why, what's going on?"

There's a second of silence before the angry snarl of his words hits me, warming me up like a glass of dark whiskey, and I mentally pat my back for a job well done. "Someone took my daughter."

CHAPTER 1

Hadley

The blasting of death metal music—loud enough to deafen me—jolts me out of my semi-dream state, and I groan. My eyelids are too heavy, refusing to do anything more than twitch, and I quickly give up on attempting to open them. The strobe lights I can see flashing through the closed lids are enough to make me not want to open my eyes, even if I could. My exhaustion is bone deep, and I'm too tired even to try and lift my arms to block out the screaming as it threatens to crack my skull open.

A pounding headache starts up behind my eyes, nausea churning in my stomach as I flop over onto my side. I manage to gather enough energy to blindly stretch an arm out and lift a piece of bread from my food tray on the floor.

They keep switching up their torture tactics. They'll starve me for a few days, and just when I think I'm about to die from dehydration, they bring me food and water and deprive me of sleep instead.

I can't do anything but merely exist. I force the bit of stale bread into my mouth, chewing and swallowing it, even as my stomach revolts. I know I'll need the energy, though. Hawk and the guys are coming, I *know* they are, and I need to be ready to do whatever I can to help them when they arrive. I refuse to be a dead weight for them to carry out of here. That thought ignites a fire in my stomach, and I manage to chew the last few mouthfuls of bread with more vigor.

Despite the amplified vibrations of the electric guitar and some dude screaming about how his heart was ripped out, I pass out. But when I next jerk awake, the room is oddly quiet. Deafeningly so. Or maybe my eardrums burst and I can no longer hear anything. I'd honestly accept that reality at this point—anything to not have to listen to that god-awful racket again.

Unfortunately, the sound of a shoe scuffing the floor confirms not only that I have *not* lost my hearing, but that I'm not alone in here. And in spite of my weakened state, my fight-or-flight response kicks in, and I jump upright, ready to defend myself as my ingrained instincts flare to life.

"Hey, hey," a guard hushes in a slow, soothing voice intended to put me at ease, yet does anything but. He raises his hands to indicate he means me no harm, except there's no way I'm buying that bullshit.

My eyes narrow, and I track his every move, ignoring the lightheadedness at my abrupt shift upright and the thrumming of the pulse in my neck as my heart rate skyrockets. Without lowering his hands, he points to a tray of food he left on the floor. *What the fuck? The guards never come in here to leave food.*

His weird behavior only makes my eyes narrow further as I try to suss out his motives. As far as I know, Lawrence hasn't given the *okay* yet for Bowen, or any of the guards, to touch me—beyond beating me. Even if he had, Bowen has already insisted on first dibs, and none of the guards would ever dare go against him. Lawrence might think he runs the compound, but really, it's Bowen. The only reason he hasn't done as he pleases with me is because this is what he truly gets off on—the infliction of pain. He's a sadist through and through. I also get the impression that Lawrence has told everyone I'm still a goddamn virgin—probably to ensure they don't disobey him. I don't even fucking care, so long as it keeps them away from me.

"Eat," the guard grunts, jerking his head toward the tray.

I scoff. Does he seriously think I'm that stupid?

"Why, so you can drug me and do whatever the fuck you want with me while I'm passed out? Yeah, no thanks."

The corner of his lip lifts in a small, barely-there smirk. *Who the fuck is this guy?*

"Not my thing. I prefer my girls to be conscious when giving them the time of their life."

I scoff again, sneering in disgust.

"Eat," he continues to persist, this time using the toe of his boot to shove the tray closer to where I'm sitting on the narrow strip of thin foam posing as a mattress. "You'll need your strength."

"For what? Whatever new torture method you've devised? I'd rather not be conscious for it."

He shakes his head and huffs out a sigh like I'm deliberately being difficult, but seriously, what the fuck did he expect?

"Don't be so morbid," he snarks. "The sun will rise on another day, and may it be better than the last."

His words freeze me in place, and I can't do anything except sit and stare at him. My eyes roam over his face, searching for something familiar, but the room is too dark. Maybe his nose looks like hers did? It's been too long. I try to bring her face to the forefront of my mind, but it's blurry, and I can't recall the finer details.

"What did you just say?" My voice is low, threatening yet unsure, and I notice he's watching me just as closely. A strange intensity replaces his nonchalant demeanor.

"You know that saying?" he questions, his tone sharp.

I hesitate before responding. "A friend of mine used to say it all the time."

He nods his head slowly, before lowering into a crouch. He's careful to stay on the opposite side of the small space in the cell so he's not crowding me.

"My mother used to say it to my sister and me when we were kids." My eyes dart between his, trying to piece together what he's saying. I feel like there's something significant in his words, but what? My brain's too dulled from lack of sleep and food to figure it out.

He continues to scrutinize me, and I can tell he can see my brain trying its best to think straight. "That was before she died. My sister and I ended up in foster care, and we were separated. I haven't seen her since she was five."

My stomach roils precariously as the penny drops, my breaths coming in uneven rasps.

"You're Marcus." My voice is nothing more than a whisper, and the second I say his name, his face collapses in pain, aging him in a split second. The heartache shines through his eyes, making me wonder how I hadn't seen it before.

"Meena was my sister."

I can't do anything but sit and stare at him, unsure whether I'm hallucinating or this is actually real. *Her brother.* I remember her telling me about him. He was the one who essentially cared for her—ensured she was fed and had clean clothes. Their mom was a druggie, too obsessed with getting her next fix to give a shit about her kids. When she died from a heroin overdose, the two of them were put into foster care, where they were separated. The day she was sent to a different home than him, was the last day they saw each other.

When Meena first showed up at the compound, she used to cry herself to sleep every night. Back then, all the recruits slept in the same large room, and some of the other kids would give her a hard time over it. I didn't really understand her sadness. I'd never cared about anyone enough to miss them that much, but I could practically feel the pain pouring off her, and could only imagine how difficult it would be to lose the one constant in your life. Never mind ending up trapped in this godforsaken place.

My eyes roam over his face. "I don't…" I shake my head, words failing me as I struggle to wrap my head around the fact that Meena's brother is here right now. "How?" The word is barely a croak, and even though my head is swimming with questions, I'm incapable of saying anything more.

He's still crouched in front of me, with his arms leaning on his thick, muscular thighs. At my question, his head drops to his chest, and he releases a heavy sigh, fraught with so much heartache it sucks the oxygen out of the room.

"When I aged out of the system, I went looking for her. I got the address of the last foster home she was at, but the people there told me she'd run away three months earlier." A pained expression crosses his features, and in frustration, he runs his hand over his short, buzz-cut hairstyle.

"I searched everywhere for her. I spent months trawling the streets, trying to find her or anyone who had seen her. No one knew who she was, or at least, they weren't willing to tell me anything if they did. I'd gone years without viable leads, and I'd all but given up, until I heard the whispers about kids being taken from the street. I knew it was a long shot, but I had nothing to lose. It took fucking forever to get any sort of proof, and even longer to find a way in."

"How long have you been here for?"

"Just under a year."

So he must have arrived shortly after I left.

"So you know…" I trail off, unable to say the actual words. Only I don't need to. He gives a quick jerk of his head, lowering his gaze so I can't see the grief that I have no doubt is swimming in them.

"I do." His words are choked, and it takes him a second to compose himself before he says anything further. "They told me you were friends."

I swallow around the lump clogging my throat, licking my already dry lips. "We were. She…" I pause, struggling to find the right words, before blurting out the blunt and honest truth. "She saved me."

"How…" He looks away, emotion again rendering him speechless as nausea churns in my stomach, and the memories of that day rush to the surface.

"No," Meena cries vehemently as tears stream down her face. She's on her knees in the middle of the ring, perched beside the unconscious form of a new recruit.

"Kill her, or I'll kill you," the guard snarls, growing impatient with Meena's stalling.

Every day, we have to get in the ring with each other and fight until someone can't get up again, but we've never been asked to kill our opponent before.

Meena sobs over the girl's unconscious form, shaking her head as the rest of us watch on with bated breath.

"Meena," I cry out, my own cheeks wet. Her head lifts to look at me through watery eyes, and the look on her face breaks some essential part inside me. "Please," I plead, ignoring the fact I'm begging her to kill someone.

Her lower lip trembles, a fresh wave of tears streaming down her face, however, she doesn't give in. If anything, the longer she looks at me, the more her resolve reinforces itself.

Her face hardens into a determined mask that only destroys me further because I know what it means. I'm shaking my head, silently imploring her not to do this, but the second the guard told her to kill the innocent kid in front of her, I knew she would never do it. No amount of pleading with her will ever change her mind because, unlike everyone else in this cesspit, myself included, Meena is pure. She's got the heart of an angel. She's been here for about five years, but she's never once let the scumbags in this place destroy the goodness in her. She's got something none of the rest of us have — integrity.

It's because of her that I'm still here, that I'm still human enough to know right from wrong, even though at this moment, I'm begging her with everything I have to do the wrong thing...just this once.

Please, Meena. I can't live without you. It's selfish of me because you're far too good for this place. If this is the life you're meant to live, then death is your only way out. You can spend eternity with the angels in heaven, where you belong. But, *please*, If you're not here to pull me back from the darkness, I'm scared of what I'll become.

"I don't have all day, girlie," the guard snaps. His harsh words break Meena's attention from mine and she lifts her chin when she looks at him.

"No." This time the word comes out strong, defiant, and even though I'm dying inside, I'm so fucking proud of her.

The guard doesn't appreciate her defiance though, and he takes a menacing step toward her, followed by another. Every time his heavy boot hits the floor, my stomach twists dangerously, and my pulse skyrockets. I'm not sure if I'm about to be sick or pass out.

Instead of watching him draw closer, Meena returns her gaze to mine, and I hold it, refusing to look away from her. "I love you," she mouths, even as tears flow steadily and fear shines in her eyes.

"I love you too."

It feels like it takes forever, yet no time at all, for the guard to traverse the distance to where Meena is kneeling, and his hand snaps out, slapping her across the face with enough force that she falls onto the mat, a gasp escaping from her.

He doesn't stop there, kicking out with his steel-toed boot next. The air rushes out of her as his foot connects with her stomach, and she curls in on herself. I don't even realize I'm screaming and trying to get to her, until I receive my own slap. Only then do I notice I'm being restrained by another guard. I barely register the sting in my cheek as I watch the scene unfold, Meena's cries of pain drilling into my mind. It's a sound I'll never forget. It'll haunt my nightmares for the rest of my days.

"Meena," I scream, still fighting off the guard. It's a futile attempt,

but it doesn't stop me from clawing at his skin, even as he threatens and curses me.

I don't know how long it goes on for, but eventually Meena's cries fall to whimpers before they just stop, and all that's left is the heavy panting of the guard still attacking her. The solid thud of his boot hitting her small body. Blood covers her face, making it impossible to tell if she's alive or not.

When the guard finally steps away from her, giving me an unobstructed view of her limp form lying lifeless on the mat, I stare pointedly at her chest, waiting on pins and needles to see if it rises or not. When there's no sign of movement, the last of my energy drains out of me, and I collapse in the guard's arms, sobbing and crying.

"Let me go," I cry, pushing against him again, but he still doesn't release his hold. The sick, fucking piece of shit guard who killed my best friend lifts his head, searing me with his ice-cold gaze that lacks any ounce of empathy. For every speck of emotion he's missing, I throw all the pain and devastation threatening to drown me right back at him. I glower at him as fiercely as he's scowling at me, and in the clashing of our gazes, I promise him the most excruciating of deaths.

One day, Major Bowen will be at my mercy, the way Meena was at his. He's going to beg me for amnesty; he's going to pray for it to end. Throughout it all, I'm going to soak up every pained scream and desperate whimper, and when the light dims in his eyes, he will look up at me and know *his death was of his own making.*

I CAN'T TELL HER BROTHER ANY OF THAT, THOUGH. "SHE DIED because she refused to be turned into a monster like the rest of us." A single tear slips down my face. "She was the best person I have ever known, and she held on to that until the very end."

He ducks his head, and I glance away, giving him a moment while he sniffs and wipes at his eyes. Tears still shine in them when he looks back at me, but there's a determined set to his jaw that reminds me so much of Meena. It has a fresh wave of tears threatening to break past my defenses.

"We've gotta get you out of here. I wasn't there for Meena when she needed me, but I can at least help you."

I have no idea what he can do to help, not without putting himself at risk, and I won't let him do that for me, but he can at least be on alert for when my guys come, which should be any day now, hopefully.

"I have people coming for me," I tell him, watching as his eyebrows lift in surprise. "I don't know when, but you might be able to help them when they get here."

He nods. "Anything I can do, I will."

CHAPTER 2

Beck

DESPITE BEING ON THE ROAD BEFORE THE FIRST RAYS OF LIGHT GRACED the horizon, it takes all day to drive to Black Creek, and I'm exhausted and disheveled by the time the urban wasteland makes its mark on the surrounding landscape.

Too much coffee and unappealing gas station food have me feeling both buzzed and groggy. The combination leaves me short-tempered and impatient as I park the car, throwing up a faint hope to whatever God above that likes to pull on our puppet strings, it will still be there when I return in a few hours.

Walking the streets of Black Creek feels both familiar and also like I'm seeing the place for the first time. It's been ten years since I was last here. Ten long years. And while the streets look the same, they also appear much more bleak and dreary than I ever remember. Walking past an alley, the stench of piss hits me like a freight train, and I can hear the telltale signs of homeless people farther down it, most likely scrounging for scraps and huddling together for warmth.

STAYING ALERT, I MAKE MY WAY QUICKLY DOWN THE STREET UNTIL I come to the first bar I've seen. It's the last unit at the end of a row, and the wild roar of a drunk crowd escapes the bar before I even open the door, which looks like it's barely hanging on its rusted hinges. The whole thing squeaks dangerously as I yank it open and step into the crowded, sweat-staunched room. As I push my way through the horde of perspiring bodies toward the bar, I scan my eyes around the room. After all these years, I thought I'd feel a sense of coming home when I stepped foot back in this rundown town, but taking in the scruffy riff-raff surrounding me, I have never felt more out of place. If I don't belong here, and I don't belong in the overprivileged world of Pacific Prep, where do I belong? A voice at the back of my head whispers *with Hadley*, and the rightness of those two words pacifies me. With that reminder of my girl, I push through the throng of people lining the bar with renewed energy.

"What can I getcha?" the bartender asks. He's an older man, in his fifties, with long gray hair pulled back in a bun. There's a cigarette sticking out of the corner of his mouth, and as he inhales, the tip glows, the ash growing along the end until it falls off, dropping into a glass in his hand.

I keep my features neutral as he exhales and smoke curls out from between his parted lips. The stink of cigarettes permeates the air between us and clings to my clothes.

"Beer. Eh, Bud will do," I grunt out, figuring something in a bottle is the only safe choice.

Grabbing a bottle, he uncaps and hands it to me. As he slides it across the bar, I lean in toward him. "And I need some information."

Lifting an eyebrow, he doesn't say anything, waiting for me to continue.

"I need to know where I can find the Reaper Rejects."

His eyes widen slightly, and I don't miss the way his gaze drops, taking in my clean, form-fitting t-shirt and jeans that aren't hanging off my ass like half the idiots in here. I deliberately dug out an old top and jeans from the back of my dresser, wanting to do my best to fit in here. But regardless of my casual attire, my scruffy beard that's grown out since Hadley disappeared, and my tattoos on display, it's obvious I'm not from around here. I look too put-together. I don't have that mix of vicious hunger and hopelessness in my eyes or the same haggard appearance as most of the people who have lived here their whole lives.

"They operate out of a house on River Street," he responds, his gaze lifting to meet mine.

River Street? *Fuck*. I've been skeptical about Mason's theory that Cain and Oliver are behind the quickly growing Reaper Rejects, but it's hard to deny the mounting evidence. Knowing their base of operations is River Street—the street all three of us grew up on, only makes it that much more likely that it's them. Why else would a gang set up there? There's nothing particularly appealing or strategic about that street. It's nothing more than rundown, dilapidated houses, half of which lay empty and had been claimed by the druggies and vagrants that roam this town in abundance.

Nodding my head, I lift the beer bottle, taking a long swig of the cool, frothy liquid. It's cheap and bitter, but it helps to calm my nerves. With one last once-over, the bartender moves to the opposite end of the bar to serve a newcomer, and I sweep my gaze over the rest of the room, not really taking any of it in as my thoughts drift to the friends I once knew. There's so much that could go wrong tonight. There's no guarantee the men that lead the Reaper Rejects are still the same friends I knew growing up. Time changes us all, and living here hardens you in this dog-eat-dog town. It makes you cynical and untrusting. Ten years is a long time, and for all I know, they saw my leaving—and the fact I never reached out to them—as an act of betrayal. By turning up unannounced, I could be walking into a fight, if not a bullet to the head.

Yet, as I finish the bottle, slap a few dollars down on the sticky counter, and push my way through the writhing mass of drunken bodies out into the dark street, there's no doubt in my mind. There's no second-guessing, or hesitation. It doesn't matter what greeting I receive from them, or how high the risk is, I still have to try. For Hadley.

I make it back to my car and drive over to River Street on the opposite side of town. Familiarity crashes through me as I pull onto what used to be my childhood street. The place where the guys and I played chicken with passing cars, where my mother would stand on the front porch and yell for me to get my ass inside and ready for bed. The place where our childhoods came collapsing down and everything changed.

As I gradually make my way down the street, I slow the car to a crawl, probably looking like I'm preparing for a drive-by shooting. I pull over to the curb, stopping opposite what was once my house. Staring out the window, I take in the narrow, two-story terrace house. The place is shrouded in darkness, not a single light on at this late hour. Everything about it looks the same as it did the day I left. White paint is peeling off the front door and window sills, and the front steps still look like a hefty weight will have them snapping in two. Patches of dead grass and weeds have pushed their way up through the concrete slabs lining the house, only adding to the derelict appearance.

With a heavy sigh and a nostalgic ache in my chest, I tear my gaze away from my old front porch, instead focusing on the place two doors down from where I'm parked. Cain's childhood home. Unlike the darkened houses on either side, light streams out from the front windows, lighting up the road in front of the house, and I can just about make out two men standing in the shadows on the porch.

Well, I didn't come all this way just to sit here. May as well get out and see if this guy really is Cain. I push open the car door and step out, striding confidently along the sidewalk with my head up, looking like I belong. As I reach the metal gate, I notice the guys by the door stiffen and stand upright, eyeing me warily.

"The fuck do you want?" one of them calls out.

"I'm looking for Cain," I shout back. "Does he still live here?"

The guy at the door hesitates for a second. "Who's askin'?"

"Beck Jacobs."

He silently assesses me for a long moment before jerking his head in indication for his buddy to go inside, hopefully to get Cain—assuming it is actually Cain in there and not some high-out-of-his-mind drug dealer that I'm about to piss off.

The two of us stand, facing off in silence for a long moment, until the screen door creaks open. With the light from the hallway behind him, it's impossible to make out the details of the man standing in the doorway, and I squint through the glare, trying to work out if the tall, broad, muscular man in front of me is the lanky kid I used to know.

"Fuck me. Talk about a blast from the past."

His voice is a deep rumble, nothing like the hoarse rasp I remember when it was breaking as a pre-teen boy. Regardless, there's a familiar ring to it, and for the first time tonight, a sense of rightness settles in me.

"What's it been? Ten years?" Despite not being able to see his features all that well in the dark, I can feel his eyes roam over me. "What brings you back to my run-down neck of the woods?"

"I heard about some thugs going by the name of Reaper Rejects. Had to come see if I needed to beat up some shithead kids."

He barks out a cold laugh, making it impossible for me to figure out if this is all friendly banter or if my being here has pissed him off.

"Guess you better come in then."

Nerves coat my palm as I push open the squeaking metal gate and walk up the short walkway of cracked and broken flagstones, climbing the rickety steps that protest under my weight to the front porch.

In the dark, with the interior light behind him, it's impossible to get a read on him, even this close. Not that he gives me much time to analyze him anyway, turning on his heel as my boot hits the porch, and pulling the screen door open so he can step inside.

I follow him into the once-familiar house. Growing up, the four of us spent a lot of time here. Eating in Mama B's kitchen and hanging out in the living room. While the interior looks the same, right down to the markings etched into the living room door frame, marking each of our heights, it's completely different. A haze of smoke floats in the air, and following the noise coming from the room on my right, I find a bunch of thugs lounging on sofas, their feet up on the worn coffee table, with beers and cigarettes in their hands as they watch me closely.

Cain gives them a brief nod as we pass, which they all return, still keeping their wary gazes on the intruder and potential threat—me.

"Where's Mama B?" I question as we move past the living room.

"Dead," he gruffs out sharply, and I can't tell if it's from emotion or a silent warning to drop the topic. I swallow my questions and ignore the pang of sadness at hearing of her passing, following him down the hall to the kitchen.

"Out," he barks as we enter the small kitchen at the back of the house. The few guys in the room quickly grab their stuff and scurry out, sparing me a glance as they move past me.

I hardly notice them though, as Cain turns to face me. In the harsh light of the kitchen, I can see everything that I couldn't make out in the darkness. I take in the tight set of his jaw and the hardness in his eyes that never used to be there. Combined with his unruly black hair, brushed up and stylishly tapered along the sides, and his dark stubble, he looks menacing and unapproachable. Tattoos cover his neck, running from his stubble-covered jawline to dip beneath the neckline of his top, and, dropping my gaze, I can see swirls of colored ink running down his arms and decorating his fingers. I can only guess that every inch of skin in between has been branded too. I can feel his eyes assessing me, the same way I'm scrutinizing him. He's got the same Reaper Rejects tattoo scratched into his skin that I do, except his is on his left bicep. Looking at his right one, there's a newer, more professional-looking tattoo that I'm guessing is his gang's insignia. It also says Reaper Rejects, only with a reaper's scythe cut across it.

Pulling my gaze away from the myriad of tattoos adorning every inch of visible skin, I instead notice how much he's filled out since we were kids. He's no longer the scrawny boy he used to be. Rather ropes of muscle make his biceps bulge against the tight fabric of his black t-shirt as he crosses his tattooed arms over his chest and leans back against the kitchen cabinets. He criss-crosses his feet at the ankle, drawing my attention to the dark denim jeans hugging his thick thighs and the black, steel-toed combat boots he's wearing.

My gaze returns to his face, taking in his hardened expression, and *fuck*, if that steely look in his eye doesn't kill a little something in me. What has he had to survive in the last ten years? Or is this all a consequence of that day?

After another tense moment of silence where he continues to take me in, his eyes lift to mine. Just when I'm beginning to think I might have made a huge mistake coming here, a wide grin splits his face and he shakes his head, releasing a chuckle.

"Fuck, man. It's so good to see you."

He closes the distance between us, clapping me on the back, and I sag in relief as I embrace him back, a nervous chuckle escaping me.

"You too, man. It's been far too long."

He steps back, his hands still on my shoulders as he studies me. "You look fucking good, man. Finally outgrew that beanpole body you had."

He laughs again, and I swear, every time he does, it sounds more like the old Cain I remember.

"Shut up, asshole. Look at you! You on fucking steroids or something?!"

He just laughs and shakes his head, pulling open the fridge

door and grabbing a couple of beers. He hands one over to me, and I twist the cap off.

"Is O around?" I'm suddenly dying to see him and get the three of us back together again. It wouldn't be like old times—too much has happened for that—but it would be fucking great to catch up.

"Nah." Cain takes a long sip of his beer before answering me. "Dude got himself caught up with The Feral Beasts after, you know…" He trails off, a darkness clouding his eyes, but he quickly shakes it off. "Ended up in prison last year. He's got about a year left of his sentence, and I'm hoping he'll join me here when he's released"—he shrugs—"but we'll see."

I nod my head, not altogether surprised by that news. Honestly, I'm just glad he's still alive. In this world, you never know. I'm sure plenty of the kids we went to school with are long dead and buried.

"So this is all really yours?" I gesture around the room, but we both know I don't mean the house.

"Yup." He beams proudly. "We're a small outfit, but we're growing. With the Beasts gone, we've seized a lot of their territory and started making a name for ourselves."

I nod. I've got a thousand other questions, but I don't feel I can pry into his operation here and, honestly, I might be better off not knowing the ins and outs of it.

"What about you? I bet you made something of yourself." A cocky smirk curls the corner of his lips. He's so damn sure I made it in life. "Bet you've got the whole shebang—white picket fence, two-point-five kids, and the perfect housewife."

I bark out a humorless laugh. He couldn't be further from the truth.

Rubbing the back of my neck, I grimace, glancing away before focusing my gaze back on him, fixing him with a determined look. "That's actually why I'm here. I need your help."

He doesn't say anything, watching me closely before nodding for me to continue. I move to the old, wobbly wooden table that I remember the four of us carving our initials into the underside of when we were seven years old and collapse into the chair, taking a deep breath before I catch him up on the last ten years—more specifically, all the shit that's come to light in the last twelve months.

The whole time, he leans against the kitchen counter, listening intently with an impassive expression that gives nothing away. When I finish, a weighted silence lingers in the air as I wait impatiently to see if he'll help—if he's even able to help. I didn't miss the tight lines around his eyes when I mentioned kids being lifted off his streets, and if nothing else, I'm hoping that threat to his town will be enough to incentivize him.

The kitchen door opens, and a young-looking guy pops his head in. "Sorry to interrupt, boss. We need you for a minute."

Cain gives a sharp nod, and the guy ducks out, closing the door behind him.

With a sigh, Cain runs his hand through his unruly black hair and fixes me with a look. "It's late, and I dunno how long this will take. You can have my old room for the night, and we can discuss what to do in the morning."

"You'll help us?" I question, half in surprise and half in relief.

He huffs out a breath. "'Course I will, brother. Not only are they taking kids from *my* streets, but they've got your girl." He comes closer to me on his way to the kitchen door, clapping me on the shoulder. "You love her, right?"

"I do."

He nods, having already known the answer before I confirm as much. "Then we're going to get her back."

Without another word, he leaves the room, and the extent of my relief almost has me keeling over. Suddenly, getting Hadley back doesn't feel like an insurmountable task. I have no idea what the fuck we're going to do, or how Cain and his guys can help, but the fact he's on our side and willing to try lights a fire within me, sparking hope and a newfound determination.

Exiting the kitchen, I grab a duffel bag from my car that I'd packed just in case and saunter up the stairs to Cain's room. I hear him and some of his men talking in a side room at the front of the house when I amble past, but whatever his gang is involved in is none of my business. I'm not about to shit all over his hospitality by getting caught eavesdropping, so I quickly walk past the closed door.

As I crest the top of the stairs, I pause, my eyes finding the closed door at the end of the hall. Swallowing around the lump of emotion clogging my throat, I head in the opposite direction, knowing my way to Cain's old room like I do the back of my hand.

Pushing open the door, I huff out a dry chuckle. It's not much different than when we were kids. He's upgraded the bedding, from Ferrari sheets to plain navy ones, but other than that, every-thing's exactly the same. All his childhood shit is cluttering the top of the dresser, and I move toward it when I notice a photo of the four of us. We were only five or six at the time. Oliver's got a black eye, and Cain's sporting a split lip. My head is thrown back while I laugh, and Evie is scowling at all of us. I run my thumb over her face, sighing heavily before setting it back on the dresser and moving to the bed. Dumping my bag on the mattress, I sit beside it, rubbing my hand down my face before pulling my phone out of my back pocket and firing off a text to the guys, letting them know I'm here and all is going well so far.

A second later, the phone rings and West's name pops up on the screen.

"Hey," I greet wearily, lying back on the duvet to stare up at the ceiling.

"How's it going?"

I know he and the others are impatient for good news. All of our hopes reside in getting Cain and his men on board.

"Good, I think. Cain's agreed to help us. We'll put together a plan in the morning."

"Good." Silence falls between us, and all I can hear down the line is the faint sound of his breath. Now that he's got reassurance that I haven't fucked everything up and that we're working on a plan to get Hadley back, I expect him to hang up, but to my surprise, he speaks again. "What's it like being back there?"

His voice is a smooth, deep rumble, and all of a sudden, I just want to be back in their dorm room with them all. *When the fuck did that happen?*

"It's weird. I have spent so much time thinking about coming back, and now that I'm here, I just wanna come home."

He doesn't respond at first, but the silence is comfortable, contemplative, unlike the usual tension that threads between us.

"Well, sort out everything in the morning and come home tomorrow. It'll, uh, be good to have you back."

He rushes out the last few words like they burn his tongue, but regardless, they still bring a smile to my face. We speak for another few minutes before hanging up, and I quickly strip and climb into bed. I drift off to sleep to the thought of killing every fucker keeping me from my girl.

WHEN I EMERGE FROM MY ROOM THE NEXT MORNING, I PAUSE AS MY gaze zones in on the door opposite the hall. It's inauspicious, and you wouldn't give it a second glance if you didn't know what was behind it. But I do know what's behind it—at least, what used to be.

I don't even realize I've moved, but the next second, I'm standing in front of it. My hand trembles as I reach out, wrapping my palm around the cool door handle. My stomach churns, but wild horses can't drag me away right now as I turn the handle with a clammy hand and slowly push the door open.

I'm not sure what I expected, but storage boxes and old furniture in a white-walled, nondescript room were not it, and some sort of weird half-whine, half-laugh chokes its way out of me as I peer around the bland room.

"I had it converted into a storage room," comes Cain's

emotionless voice from behind me. "Couldn't stand looking at it, knowing she'd never step foot in there again."

I nod, unable to utter a single word, as I tear my gaze from the room to look back at him. I can see the pain in his eyes; grief and vengeful anger pour off him.

He blinks and it's gone, an impassive slate replacing the emotion on his face. "No point in dwelling over shit we can't change. Your girl's still alive. Why don't we focus on saving her?"

I give him a tight nod, *still* unable to speak past the lump in my throat and, closing the door behind me, I follow him down the stairs. The house is quiet, and there isn't a soul in sight as he directs me to a small office.

He sits in the overstuffed chair behind a desk with disorganized piles of papers wedged into the small space, and I drop into one of the two chairs taking up the last remaining bit of space.

"Right, so to recap last night. Your dad and his cronies own Nocturnal Mercenaries, and they've been taking kids from Black Creek and forcing them to work for them." He waits for me to nod in agreement before continuing, "And one of them has kidnapped your girl and is holding her there against her will?" I nod again, my teeth gritting as anger flares within me over the whole fucked-up situation.

"Alright. I've told my men to be here in an hour so we can talk about what to do." He leans back in his seat, getting comfortable. "So tell me about this girl. You met her at that fancy school?"

I ease back in my chair. I'm keen to get on with the meeting and get a plan I can take back to the guys. But I guess, for now, there's nothing I can do but wait for Cain's men to arrive.

"Yup, she's a student there." I know he won't judge me, but I do suppress a smirk when his eyebrow quirks in surprise.

"Didn't picture you falling for some rich princess."

I snort, knowing Hadley would be furious if she heard him right now. I ignore the pang in my chest when I think of her. "She's far from that. She's more like someone from here." His other brow climbs up his forehead, and I decide to tell him the truth about her. It's best that he knows she's not some helpless girl who needs rescuing. Yeah, sure, that's what we're going to do, but I know once we get to her, she'll be more than able to hold her own.

"She grew up there. They molded her into a trained killer. She had the guts to escape, to try and make a life for herself. But this sick fuck is obsessed with her, and he dragged her back there. She's strong, *incredibly* strong, but I don't know if she will survive that place a second time."

I watch his expression change from surprise to shock to something much darker. Shadows roll in behind his eyes, and I know exactly where his thoughts have gone. *Evie*. Girls being taken against their will is a hard line for Cain. One he won't tolerate.

There's a hardness in his eyes that I only ever remember seeing once before, on the day Antonelli's men came and stole Evie from her own front yard, shooting up the street while they were at it. That day changed our entire lives. It ripped apart the safe bubble we lived in. Where, as children, we thought we were invincible, and it exposed us to the true horrors that exist in this world. That was the day we stopped being children and became adults, hardened to the world around us. It was a day I'll never forget.

He leans forward in his chair, resting his elbows on the wooden desk. His features are tight, and his nostrils flare as he says, "We're going to get her back, brother. Then we're going to make sure they can't steal another kid ever again."

An hour later, Cain leads me into the front room of his house where, at first glance, about twenty men are waiting for us. They're relaxed, lounging on the sofa, until we enter. Then they all straighten, their full attention on their leader. It's interesting to watch, to see the respect and power Cain has over these men. Long gone is his easy expression, instead he's wearing the impenetrable mask of a leader, ready to direct his men.

Cain slowly looks around the room, meeting each of their eyes and giving a few of them nods of acknowledgment before he addresses everyone.

"My brother, Beck, has brought a serious matter to my attention. He has informed me that kids are being stolen from our streets." He pierces each man in the room with a steely gaze. "Turned into soldiers; forced into being killers. All so some rich fuckers can line their pockets."

I'm watching his men closely, assessing them. While I trust Cain, I don't know any of the men in front of me. So I notice when their jaws clench and their eyes narrow in anger.

No one speaks, though, and Cain continues, "You all know I don't stand for children being taken against their will and used as pawns." A few men nod or murmur their agreements. "As if that isn't insult enough, they've taken Beck's girl."

All eyes fall on me, and I subtly straighten my spine and lift my chin, letting them see the parts of myself that are still very much Black Creek. I allow the darkness in me to rise to the surface and shine through my eyes. Let each and every one of them see that I will destroy *anyone* who gets in the way of me saving my girl.

After an assessing moment, one of the men focuses his attention back on Cain and speaks up, "We can't let them get away with that. Tell us what you want us to do."

The rest of the gathered men give sharp nods of agreement, and the room fills with determination and a willingness to fight as shoulders are pushed back, and everyone leans forward to hear Cain's plan.

Cain lets a small, prideful smile lift the corner of his mouth before he barks orders at his men. "The organization is Nocturnal Mercenaries. Beck here can give us a schematic of the compound where they are keeping the children and his girl. Still, we need to know as much as possible about their setup before we wreak havoc—guard changes, security systems, and any potential weaknesses. Reach out to your contacts, and see if you can find anyone who knows anything about them. We need to move quickly, so get it done, boys."

With renewed energy and the promise of impending violence, the men quickly get to their feet, pulling out their phones and talking to one another as they leave the room.

"What now?" I ask Cain, unable to sit still and do nothing, but not knowing what I should be doing.

"Now you go back to that stuffy school, and I'll call you when we know more."

"The guys and I are going with you when you go," I tell him in a fierce tone that brokers no argument.

He quirks an eyebrow. "The guys?"

I might have conveniently left that detail out earlier. "Her brother…and the other guys Hadley is…dating."

His eyebrows climb to his hairline, and I can see he's smothering a laugh. Questions dance in his eyes, but now isn't the time to get into any of it, something he realizes as he lets the topic go.

"They can handle themselves?" he asks, and I nod. "Fine. We could do with all the manpower we can get. You should get back though, before anyone notices you're missing. The last thing we need is them realizing you've been up here."

I agree. We have no idea how close of a watch any of our parents are keeping on us. Before I leave, I draw up a schematic of the compound, and Cain gives me a burner phone which he'll use to contact us when he's got more information, so we can all work on a plan. He promises it will take no more than a day or two, and I'm holding him to his word. I don't know how I know, but I can feel it in my very bones. My girl doesn't have much longer. It's like I can feel her giving up with each passing day. I *need* to get her back before she's irreparably damaged.

CHAPTER 3

West

"FUCKING HELL," I SNARL, BANGING MY FIST AGAINST THE TABLE AS I glower at the computer screen in front of me, ignoring the tired itch behind my eyes and the jittery adrenaline from too much caffeine. Ever since we got back from the open day, I have spent every moment trying to hack into the compound's security system. To have any hope of getting Hadley back, we need access to the compound's cameras and security, yet I can't find a back-door into either.

Huffing out a breath, I grind my teeth, and for what feels like the millionth time, change part of the code before grabbing my mug and going to top it up with a fresh cup of coffee. *God knows I'm going to need it.* We can't go after Hadley until we have a way into the compound, and we can't get a way in until I crack this fucking code. Until that happens, I won't be sleeping or doing anything else that takes time away from helping Hadley.

THE KITCHEN IS EMPTY, AND CHECKING THE TIME WITH THE CLOCK ON the oven, I realize it's only four a.m.—no wonder no one else is about. My sleeping pattern is entirely out of sync. Rubbing at my tired eyes, I brew a fresh pot of coffee.

Once it's done, I fill the mug to the brim, taking a long, much-needed gulp of its life-sustaining properties.

"What are you doing up?" Hawk's voice is thick with sleep as he pads barefoot into the kitchen. In his half-awake state, his eyes roam over my face, likely seeing the exhaustion from too many days of no sleep. "Ah, haven't been to sleep yet."

I rub my lids with my fingers and shake my head.

"Not having any luck with the compound's security?" The strain of being away from Hadley for so long is getting to him, evidenced by the fact he's awake at the ass-crack of dawn, but regardless, his tone is soft.

"I can't decode their encryption." My voice breaks, exhaustion and defeat making me feel utterly worthless. This is what I'm good at. It's the *only* thing I can do to help. "If I can't get in, then we—"

Hawk claps his hand on my shoulder, cutting me off. "You'll get it."

I lift my head and look into his eyes, seeing the swirling storm of emotions in his gray depths. We're all a complete fucking mess without Hadley—even Hawk. He might have been the last to come around to having her here, but now he's as invested as the rest of us, if not more so.

"I know you will." He takes the mug from my hands. "Now go get some sleep. You're no good to anyone when you can't think straight."

I open my mouth to protest, before sighing and closing it. Maybe he's right. A power nap wouldn't hurt. It's not like I can do anything while the program runs the new code.

"Yeah, maybe you're right," I reluctantly agree, moving past him back to my room. Glancing at the computer, I don't see any updates, so I take Hawk's advice and grab a quick nap. I don't even bother to get undressed, collapsing onto the bed. I'm out before my head even hits the pillow.

A loud beeping noise interrupts my dead sleep, making me groan. My eyes are so heavy, I don't think I could open them if I tried. The noise infiltrates my foggy brain again, making me jolt upright.

I squint at the computer screen, unable to make out the blurry text as I fumble around on the mattress for my glasses. Finding them, I hurriedly slide them up my nose and fix my gaze once again on the screen as I rush across the room.

Taking a seat, I get to work, my eyes bouncing across the screen, unable to believe what I'm seeing. I did it. *I motherfucking did it.* A disbelieving laugh escapes me as my fingers fly across the keys.

"Guys!" I call out, unable to rip my eyes away from the lines of code in front of me long enough to share my good news with everyone else.

I hear footsteps as the guys come running.

"You're in?" Excitement threads Hawk's voice as he rushes into the room, and I hear the others close behind him.

"I am." I've managed to find a backdoor access into the compound's central system, meaning I can access their door codes and control the gates.

I feel everyone crowd around me as I remain focused on the screen, working my way through the system. My brows furrow the more I search. "We might have a problem, though." I huff out a breath, becoming frustrated when I can't find what I'm looking for.

"What is it?" Cam asks, leaning in for a closer look, as if that will help him understand what he's seeing on the screen. Based on the way his face wrinkles in confusion, it doesn't.

I groan in frustration, having gone through every nook and cranny I've gained access to. "I can change the door codes and lock down the facility, and I'll be able to open the gates to get us in and out."

"That all sounds like good news," Mason says warily.

"Yeah, but I don't have access to the cameras."

"Why not?" Hawk's voice is all business, ready to deal with this new setback.

I shake my head. "They're not on here. They must not be connected to the internal system." I run my hand through my hair in exasperation. "They must have the cameras hooked up to a remote network."

"And you can't just hack into that too?" Hawk asks.

"No." I sigh. "Not without knowing what network it's connected to."

"The compound's not connected to the same network as our parents' houses?"

"I don't think so. I'm still trying to work through some highly encrypted pathways, but I haven't found anything yet."

"You'll get there." Hawk squeezes my shoulder. "This is great, West. Now we'll be able to get into the compound and move around unobstructed."

I give him a small smile, but I'm frustrated about the cameras. I'm desperate to get eyes on Hadley and reassure myself that she's okay. Plus, seeing inside the compound would enable us to pinpoint exactly where they're holding her and allow us to keep tabs on each other once we're inside. I have a bit more time to work on it, in any case. Beck won't be back from Black Creek until later tonight, and it will take us a day or two to put a plan in place.

***

It's been two days since Beck came back from Black Creek. Fourteen days since Firefly disappeared and nearly three weeks since I laid eyes on her. But tonight, all of that changes.

We've been chatting to Cain ever since, formulating a plan, and tonight's the night we finally make our move. I've been through the company's mainframe, and I know how to change the access codes and lockdown the whole compound. The entire place is set up similarly to a prison so that if there are any issues in one part of it, that area can be locked down until an override code is entered. Once we're outside the gates, I'll change the override code and lock down the entire compound so we can get to Hadley without interference—assuming they are still holding her in the interrogation block. When we got back from the open day and told Beck where she was, he was surprised, claiming he'd only ever seen new recruits being held there, so she may have been moved somewhere else since the open day, but we won't know for sure until we get in there.

Unfortunately, I haven't managed to gain access to the security cameras, so we're going in blind. I'll need to find the control room as soon as possible to deactivate the cameras so no one can track us or sound the alarm.

Pulling up the map I drew of the compound—based on what we saw on the open day and Beck's limited knowledge—on my tablet, I trail the route to the control room and from there to the interrogation block.

"You've got the security side of things sorted?" Hawk asks. All four of us are in the living room, anxiously waiting for Beck so we can head out. He's not questioning my ability; he just needs the reassurance that everything is ready.

"Yup, we're all good." Despite the nerves taking over me, my voice is confident. I won't be much good if we run into any guards or, god forbid, an actual mercenary—although, at least, I've got my contacts in this time—but *this* I can do. I have the same confidence in my computer skills as Mason or Hawk do when they take on an opponent in the ring, or Cam when he obliterates his competitor in the pool.

With a sharp nod of his head, not needing to hear anymore for him to be convinced that the job is handled, he focuses back on his stretches, limbering himself up for the inevitable fight to come.

There's a knock at the door, which must be Beck, and Cam goes to answer.

"What the—"

Wilder shoves his way past him into the apartment.

"What are you doing here?" Hawk growls angrily as he glares at Wilder, pissed-off with his intrusion, now of all times, when we're all on edge.

"You didn't think I was going to let you go without me." He scoffs, uncaring that he's angering an already temperamental Hawk.

The idiot is wearing all black, but in white, across the front of his top, is written #darkknighttotherescue. I can see Mason staring daggers at it, as I ask, "How did you even know we were going tonight?"

He just shrugs, and before any of us can argue with him any further, there's another knock at the door. Fuck, that better not be Emilia trying to tag along too. We don't need even more people to worry about tonight.

"Shall I get that?" Wilder doesn't wait for a response before pulling the door open, a completely out-of-place grin on his face.

"What the fuck is he doing here?" Beck retorts, storming past him with a small bag slung over his shoulder. Just like the rest of us, he's dressed in all black, the long sleeves covering up his tattoos. There's a determined set to his jaw, and his shoulders are pushed back, his chin held high.

"He says he's coming," I answer him, as he drops his bag on the island in the kitchen. Turning, he gives Wilder a cursory once-over before dismissing him, pulling open the zipper on his duffle.

"Fine, but it's at your own risk. We're not going to carry your damn ass if you end up with a bullet in you."

Beck's too busy rifling through his backpack, so he misses Wilder's crazy grin. It's as if the thought of getting shot excites the fucking psycho. I don't know what the fuck happened to him to make him think taking a bullet is something he wants to experience, and I'm relatively sure I don't want to know.

"What?" Hawk snaps, turning his glare on Beck and gesturing to Wilder. "He can't come with us."

"Why not? He's another body. We have no idea what we're going to be up against. If he wants to come, let him." Beck lifts a handgun—a fucking handgun—out of his bag, and suddenly any argument about Wilder is forgotten as all eyes fall on the sleek, black, metal contraption in his hands.

"What the fuck is that?" I exclaim.

He quirks an eyebrow. "A gun." *Asshole.*

I narrow my eyes on him, and he explains before I have to ask him more asinine questions.

"Cain gave me one for each of us, in case we need it."

Cam moves closer, looking at the gun with wary interest, and Beck holds it out for him to take.

"I've never shot one before," Cam murmurs, reaching out to take the gun and weighing it in his hand.

"None of us have." Hawk's glaring at the gun, looking equally unsure as he debates what to do.

"It's easy." Beck takes the gun back from Cam. Pointing to a small lever on the grip, he flips it down. "Safety off"—he flicks the switch back up—"safety on." He tightens his hold on the grip and lifts it until his arm is stretched straight out in front of him. "Point, aim, and shoot." He drops the gun back to his side, looking at each of us. "Easy as that."

I scoff, not buying that bullshit for a second while squashing the questions I have about how he knows how to do that shit. Wasn't he like thirteen when he left Black Creek?

Lifting another gun out of his bag, he hands it to Mason. Well, he tries to. Mason sneers at the thing and waves it away. "No thanks. I prefer to rely on my fists."

Beck shrugs, moving to hand Mason's gun to Hawk. Still scowling at the metal contraption, he takes it, glancing at the safety before shoving it down the back of his pants. Cam follows his lead while Beck hands yet another one to me. Without giving it much thought, knowing I can't rely on my fists or athletic ability like the others can, I take it from him, placing it in the small bag along with my tablet. Despite the fact I haven't a clue how to shoot the damn thing, I know I might need it. I'd be a fool not to at least have it on me. If worse comes to worst, I can at least bash someone over the head with it.

He hands the last gun to Wilder, but he waves him off. "Nah, I'm good too." He pulls a savage-looking knife—like nothing I've ever seen before—out of a holster strapped to his waist, which I hadn't initially noticed.

"What the fuck is that?" Cam gapes at the dagger Wilder is wielding with a proud smirk. The blade is about six inches long, with a sharp tip intended to puncture through flesh and muscle easily. One edge is serrated, while the other is a violent-looking sawback designed to tear a person's skin apart as it's yanked out. It's clear the weapon is intended for maximum damage.

"This," Wilder begins, with all the theatrics of a showman, "is a Marine Recon Bowie Knife, or as I've decided to call her, Marie." He flips the handle in his hand while Hawk scoffs.

"You're going to end up stabbing yourself with that thing."

Wilder narrows his eyes on him. "I'll have you know I'm professionally trained by Sunshine herself."

"Good to hear she's encouraging this insanity," Hawk retorts. "I'll be having words with her when we get her back."

"Well, what are we waiting for then?" An unusual seriousness takes over Wilder's features, and a maliciousness I've never seen before darkens his eyes.

I grab my bag with my tablet and newly acquired gun in it, and the six of us hastily leave the apartment. I glance at the others as we walk in silence to the car, taking in their tense postures and the determined glint in their eyes. All of us are more than fucking ready for tonight. Beck catches my eye, his brows lifting in a silent question. I give him a sharp nod, letting him know I'm good, and focus my gaze straight ahead, mentally running over the plan again.

When we reach the parking lot, we split up, taking two cars. I go with Hawk and Cam in Hawk's SUV, while Mason, Beck, and Wilder take Mason's four-wheel drive.

The drive passes mostly in silence, and when we're half an hour away, Hawk dials Mason's number, the sound of the call ringing over the car's Bluetooth before he answers.

"Let's go over the plan one more time," Hawk says tersely, before Mason can say anything.

"When we arrive," I respond immediately, diving into the plan. I have gone over it in my head multiple times today, as I'm sure Hawk has. However, ensuring everyone knows exactly what we're doing, especially with Wilder's last-minute addition, makes me feel better about our chances of success tonight. "I'll change all access codes remotely and lock the guards out of the system. I'll put the compound on lockdown so no one will be able to freely move around, unless they know the new code. I've sent the code to your phones. Beck, can you send it on to Cain?"

There's a pause where everyone checks their phones before murmurs of confirmation are heard.

"Will do," Beck responds before filling us in on Cain's role. "We're meeting Cain at the back entrance. West, you'll be able to get us in okay?"

"Won't be a problem. Once I lock them out of their system, I'll be able to activate the gate. They'll see that it has been opened. Still, they won't be able to do anything about it, and with the signal jammer Cain recommended, none of the guards will be able to communicate with one another or send for help to anyone outside the compound."

"Good." Beck's voice comes across gruff over the Bluetooth. "Cain and his men will get the kids out and any willing recruits, so we just need to focus on finding Hadley."

Even though he can't see me, I nod and direct everyone on how we'll achieve our part of the plan. I don't know how Cain plans on rescuing the kids, and honestly, I don't care. All of my energy is on Hadley.

Not long later, we turn off the main road onto an overgrown track leading to the compound's back entrance, and Hawk switches off the headlights. Following behind us, Mason does the same, and we drive in darkness for another few minutes, the car bumping over the uneven ground until we come to a stop. Squinting through the dark of night, there's no sign of anyone else around. We must be the first to arrive.

Grabbing my backpack, we get out of the car, and the others meet us at the hood. Unzipping the bag, I pull out the tablet and open the necessary program, getting ready to send the compound into lockdown once Cain and his men arrive. Once I'm sure everything's in order, I pull up the map for the building, and the others huddle around me so they can look as well. With the exception of Wilder, we've all been inside and spent all week constructing the layout as best we can. There are plenty of blank areas on the map —areas that weren't pointed out to us on our tour or that Beck hasn't been privy to, but it's the best we've got. We know enough to get to where they're hopefully holding Hadley, and that's all that matters.

"Currently, we're here." I point my finger to the back entrance to the compound, mainly for Wilder's benefit, but it can't hurt for all of us to go over the route one last time. "The last time we saw Hadley, she was here." I move my finger to the interrogation sector where we're hoping Hadley is still being held and quickly walk us through the plan one final time. I've been over it so many times now that I could navigate my way to Hadley's cell blindfolded and drunk. As I'm finishing up, the beam of headlights washes over us and the overgrown field we're parked in, before they're switched off, and several large vehicles pull up behind our own cars.

All of us watch tensely as a tall, broad man, covered in tattoos and looking like the last person you want to meet up with in the dark, climbs out of the nearest vehicle. I'm guessing this must be Cain. Beck moves to greet him and, despite his thuggish appearance and tight set jaw, he embraces Beck in a quick bro hug before coming to join the rest of us.

Casting my eyes behind him, I notice who I'm assuming are

Cain's men climbing out of the vehicles and hovering nearby, eyeing us warily as they wait for further instructions.

"Guys, this is Cain," Beck introduces as the two of them move to join us.

Cain gives a sharp nod of his head, running his eyes in an assessing manner over each of us. His gaze lingers on me for a second longer. "This one's your brother?"

My eyebrows lift in surprise, not having expected him to know who I am, let alone be able to figure out in the darkness that I'm *the brother*. His voice is gruff and unfriendly, and combined with his hard, penetrating stare, I'm pretty sure he doesn't like me.

"Yeah," Beck confirms. "This is West."

His eyes sweep over me again, and I swear I see the corner of his lip lift in a small smile, but it's gone in a second, and I'm left wondering if it was just the darkness playing tricks on me. In a surprising gesture, he holds his hand out for me to shake, and I notice every inch of visible skin on his wrist and the back of his palm, right the way to his nail beds, is covered in ink.

Placing my palm in his, he gives it a quick shake before dropping his hand back down to his side. "Well, we can do proper introductions after we get your girl back." With a final look around the group, he asks, "Everyone ready?"

With my muscles tensed and my body coiled tight, ready for action, I nod along with the others.

"Alright then, let's do this."

Now that we're all here, I pull up the program to put the compound on lockdown and change the security codes. Checking that everyone has the new codes, I turn on the signal jammer, and before we all set out, I lift the gun out of my backpack and tuck it into the waistband of my pants, slinging the bag over my shoulders.

As a group, we move toward the back gate. When we're far enough away that we're still hidden amongst the tall grass of the field, out of sight of any guards, but close enough that we will be able to see when the gate is opened, Cain signals for everyone to stop, and I slip the tablet out of the bag and put in the code to open the gate.

The creak of the metal as it rolls back sounds like thunder in the otherwise quiet night, quickly followed by the yells of guards as they realize something is going on.

Once it's open enough for us to squeeze through, Cain and his men slip through the narrow gap, and a second later, we hear gunshots going off. Beck rushes through the narrow opening next, closely followed by Mason, Hawk, Wilder, and Cam, and I bring up the rear as another gunshot echoes in the still night air.

Standing on the other side of the compound wall, I watch as a guard crumples in a heap on the ground. Following his body to the ground, I stare transfixed at the two dead bodies in front of me. I knew there would be bloodshed tonight, but it's one thing to think it and another to see it unfolding before your eyes.

"Go," Cain insists in a whispered order. "Others will have heard the commotion. We'll distract as many of them as we can."

Giving him a sharp nod, Beck jerks his head for the rest of us to follow, and the six of us take off across the compound toward the main building. We stick to the shadows, crouching low and moving as silently as we can. We're about halfway across the open space when a large explosion goes off, and the sky lights up.

"What the hell?!" Cam whisper-yells as we all turn to look toward the source of the blast. All we can see are the tips of flames as they climb toward the night sky.

"Cain's distraction," Beck explains, quickly turning his back on the fire and moving on. The rest of us quickly chase after him, not about to waste the opportunity. Now that we no longer need to worry about avoiding the guards, we take greater risks, running across the open space instead of moving from building to building, relying on them for cover.

When we reach the main building, where the open day was held and where we last saw Hadley, I put in the new cipher, releasing a silent breath of relief when the keypad flashes green, and I tug the door open. Once inside, we keep our eyes peeled as we move stealthily toward the control room. It wasn't pointed out on the tour we received on the open day, but a guard had opened the door as we walked past, and I caught a glimpse of the room, with wall-to-wall computer monitors showing various camera angles, covering what looked to be most of the compound.

As we approach an intersection, with one corridor leading into the center of the building and the other running around the perimeter, a guard appears in the hallway in front of us, and we all slam to a stop. *Fuck.*

"Hey!" he yells. "What are you doing here?"

His hand goes to the holster on his hip, but before he can get his gun out, Beck fires off a shot, hitting the guy in the shoulder and propelling him backward. The sound of the gunshot seems to ricochet off the walls, alerting anyone who might be nearby to our presence. Although, given the distance between the guard and us, there was no way Mason or Hawk would have been able to tackle him before he reached his gun.

Another shot and the guard drops to the floor, lifeless. We all stand and stare at his unmoving form for a second, before I turn to look at Beck. His face is pale, his features drawn tight, but there's no regret there, only acceptance of what had to be done.

We hear them before they round the corner, the sound of boots thumping against the floor as what sounds like two more guards rush our way. Mason, Hawk, Cam, Beck, and Wilder all charge toward the far end of the corridor, wanting to take the newcomers by surprise when they come around the corner.

Hanging back, I let them do their thing, tag-teaming the guards while I move down the corridor to our left toward the steel door that marks the control room. No one has come out to respond to our commotion, but if there's anyone watching the security tapes, they'll know we're here and are likely frantically trying to get in contact with someone to raise the alarm.

I glance back at the guys over my shoulder, finding them still battling the guards. I can't wait around for them. *We can't waste any more time.* Pushing back my shoulders, I lift my gun out of the waistband of my black pants. I flick off the safety and hold it as steadily as possible in my trembling hand as I enter the security override code. Hearing the door unlock, I take a deep breath, whip open the door, and step into the room.

With my gun raised, I stare wide-eyed at the guard in front of me, who is leaning back in his chair, his legs spread wide, with his head tilted back and his mouth open and eyes closed.

A flashing light on the far wall snags my attention, and looking at it, I notice a list of various gates and buildings, with a lamp beside each one. All of them are turned off, except the one beside *the back gate*, which is flashing, mostly likely to indicate that it's open.

"Fuck, yeah, just like that," the guard groans, as I steer my attention back to him. Glancing down, my nose scrunches in disgust as the guard pushes some girl further down his disgusting dick. I hear her gag, and tears stream down her face as she stares wide-eyed at me.

I'm not even sure if she can see me clearly, but I lift my finger to my lips in a *stay-silent* gesture and return my focus to the guard. Confused about how he hasn't heard the commotion outside, I realize he's got wireless earbuds in. Then, as I look at the desk in front of him, I see he's got his laptop set up, covering one of the monitors. On the screen, some woman is trussed up in a way that looks like it can't be anything but painful as three men fuck her.

My scowl deepens, and I focus instead on the monitors that show Cain and his men fighting several guards out in the yard, and Mason taking down another guard right outside the door. This fucking waste of space is too busy getting himself off to notice the compound is being broken into and destroyed right before his eyes.

I almost can't believe our luck, but then I hear the girl gag again, and I remember that our luck is her misfortune. I tear my gaze away from the cameras and focus on the problem in front of me. Pursing my lips, I know what I have to do. I move on silent feet until I'm hovering over him, so close there's no way I can miss the shot. I raise my arm, ensuring the girl on her knees between his legs isn't going to get hit and, with my finger resting on the trigger, I point the gun straight at his head.

He doesn't deserve to live. He's involved in the fucked up shit going on here. Whether or not he actually touched a hair on her head, he hurt my Firefly. On that thought, my finger presses down on the trigger, and the next thing I know, blood is splattered all over me, the monitors, the floor, the girl, and the guard is slumped in his chair, with an undeniable hole in the side of his head.

My ears ring, and I think I lose track of time, or maybe the noise of the gunshot sent the guys rushing in here, as the next thing I know, Beck's face is taking up all of my vision. I can feel his hands on either side of my head and see his lips moving, but I can't hear what he's saying.

I blink a few times, focusing on him, and the noise around me rushes back in.

"West, West! Are you okay?"

I drop my gaze over my body. "Yeah. I'm fine, I think."

I'm faintly aware of the others talking to the girl, and a second later, she rushes out the door, hopefully to Cain and, eventually, safety.

Beck continues to stare at me for a second longer. Lines form around his eyes, and his lips press together, forming a thin line, before I feel his hand on mine, slowly pulling the gun from my grip and, glancing away, he flicks on the safety.

"You should have waited. You shouldn't have had to do that," he mutters under his breath, more to himself than anything else.

Now that the initial shock has passed, the fog in my brain is clearing. "I did what I had to do. If I hadn't killed him, one of you would have had to."

Returning his gaze to mine, his features are still tight. "It didn't have to be you."

He's wrong, though. I'm not about to let everyone else do all the dirty work. All these men deserve to die, but none of us are killers. Every life we claim tonight will haunt us, even Beck, despite the tough act he puts on. If the others are going to carry that burden for the rest of their lives, then I will carry it with them.

"It shouldn't be any of us, but here we are. We'll all do whatever it takes to get Hadley back."

After a moment, he reluctantly nods his head in agreement, knowing I'm right.

"Well, do what you need to do then, and let's go get her."

Turning away from Beck and the dead guard, I notice the others waiting nearby with worried and anxious glances, except for Wilder, who's palming his now bloody knife like he's about to shank someone. I'm not sure if it's terrifying or exactly what we need to survive tonight.

My hands are still trembling as I turn back to the wall of screens. I get to work and do my best to block out the dead guy dripping blood on the floor beside me. I scan my eyes over the various views of the compound, but when I don't immediately see Hadley, I focus on what I came here to do. I rewind back the security tapes to before we broke in and copy a strip of the recording, which I then set to play on a loop, so if anyone else in the compound, or remotely, looks at the cameras, they won't see anything amiss. I double-check that the communication systems are down, then nod my head at the guys so they know I'm done. Time to go get our girl.

As we rush out of the room, I notice a map of the compound on the wall beside the door. Lifting my tablet out of my bag, I snap a picture of it, just in case, and hurry after the others. All six of us run toward the interrogation sector, desperation pushing us faster with every step we take.

Hawk reaches the door first. His focus is single-minded as he hurriedly types in the access code and yanks open the door, rushing through it and over to the room Hadley was being kept in last time.

The rest of us are close on his heels. Like the last time I was here, it reeks of piss and hopelessness. It's a suffocating combination that activates my gag reflex and has me smothering a cough. My heart slams against my chest, worry for what state we're about to find her in, making me jumpy as Hawk once again enters the code at lightning speed. She sounded so broken when Hawk and I found her, and she's had to endure nearly another week here since then. The second the door unlocks, Hawk is tugging it open and storming into the small room, all of us hot on his trail.

My eyes dart around the drab room, and I feel the others pushing against me as we all try to squeeze into the small space.

"What the—" Hawk's words drift off as he turns in a circle, as if expecting to find her huddled in a dark corner. "Where the fuck is she?!"

CHAPTER 4

Hadley

I'M STARING AT THE DARK CEILING ABOVE ME, TRYING TO FIGURE OUT how many days have passed since I heard Hawk's voice through the door, but the days all blend together. Maybe a week? But it could be as little as a few days, or a lot longer.

Hearing the sound of the door being unlocked, I freeze for a second before quickly hiding my surprise, eyeing the unknown guard warily as he steps into my cell.

"Get up," he barks out. "I don't have all day."

Marcus is too new to be one of Bowen's trusted guards in charge of me, but he's been able to sneak in a couple of times. Each time he does, he brings me a pile of food that I've mostly devoured, but I have kept a few non-perishable items that I've hidden in the dark corners of the cell and rely on for sustenance on the days no one brings me anything to eat. None of the guards come in here unless it's to take me to see Bowen. They definitely don't expect me to have gotten anything past them, so they never bother searching the small, dank space I've been calling home for however long now.

He hasn't been able to do anything about the death metal music on the days they decide to sleep-deprive me, so I'm still functioning on next to no sleep, but with food in my belly and hope flaring in my chest, I'm feeling a million times better than I was. I'm not as disorientated or as out of it as I have been, but as I get to my feet, I make my movements seem weak and disjointed as I stumble toward the guard.

I force myself not to pull out of his grip as his meaty palm wraps itself around my bicep, squeezing so hard I can feel his fingers pressing painfully into the bone.

He hauls me out of the cell, and I let him drag me along the hallway. I expect him to take me to Bowen's special torture room, but instead, he leads me toward the showers and shoves me under the cold spray. The sudden drop in body temperature makes me gasp as my body tenses, and I begin to shiver, even as the guard throws a coarse rag and a bar of cheap soap at me.

"Shower," he snaps, crossing his arms over his chest as his eyes roam over my naked body. I have almost gotten used to the leering looks from the guards—almost. I do my best to block him out as I scrub the gritty soap over my skin. Sticking my face under the faucet, I tilt my head back and close my eyes, taking a second to just be; to just enjoy the feeling of being clean.

"Today!" the guard barks impatiently when I take too long. Sighing, I quickly finish up and turn the water off. He throws a threadbare towel at me, and I hastily wrap it around my anorexic-looking frame, thankful for the minimal coverage, even if the rough material scratches my skin.

Next, he tosses me a pair of black pants and a top similar to what I wore on the challenge night and open day. As I pull the clothes on, I try to work out why I'm suddenly being gifted them. There is no way it's time for another challenge night already.

I have barely pulled the top over my head when he again grabs my arm and pulls me out of the room. With his tight grip on my upper arm, he escorts me down several empty hallways. I assume we're heading toward the fight room, but when he directs me down a corridor I'm all too familiar with, one I've been down many times before, my blood turns to ice, and I trip over my feet as sweat trickles down my back.

No, no, no.

That spark of hope I have been feeling the last few days quickly extinguishes. I'm not even in his presence yet, and I can feel myself shutting down already. Fear wracks my body, making it nearly impossible to breathe, and I begin to hyperventilate.

If I end up back in that room with him, it won't matter when Hawk and the guys come for me. They'll be too late.

The guard's grip tightens—if that's even possible—as my steps falter, desperately trying to delay the inevitable while I wrack my brain for a way out of this. Before I can do anything more than internally freak the fuck out, we approach the door. It looks like every other door in this fucking place. It's unassuming, and as the guard types in a code, ensuring he covers the keypad with his large frame so I can't see—not that it matters, they constantly change the code as soon as I'm in there—the room beyond is just as unimposing. The room is furnished like some small, self-contained apartment with a small kitchenette, a sofa, a television, and a bed. I have no idea what its purpose is when Lawrence isn't occupying it. However, when he's here, it's always this room where we have our fucked up 'dates'. Where he dresses me up like I'm his personal Barbie doll and tells me all about the oppressive future I want no part of. Somehow, I doubt it's going to be the same song and dance tonight.

The guard shoves me into the room, and I struggle to remain upright. Steadying myself, I spin around as he closes the door behind him and locks me in the room. My breaths come in rapid pants, and my hands tremble. As far as I'm aware, Lawrence hasn't visited me since he dragged me back here, so if he's here now, it's because he thinks they've had enough time to break me. Whether he's here to claim me as his or discard me once and for all, it doesn't matter. Neither outcome is in my favor.

Turning in a circle, I struggle to think of an idea. I've been in this room enough times to know they never leave anything in it that I can use as a weapon, but desperation has me pulling the kitchen drawers open anyway.

Empty. Empty. Empty.

Growling, I slam the last drawer shut and turn back to face the room. I don't get the chance to do anything else before the telltale sound of the door unlocking momentarily freezes me in place. I must look like a deer caught in headlights as my worst living nightmare strides into the room. His every step is filled with arrogant confidence, and his unfaltering smirk as his gaze roams over me shows just how sure he is that Bowen has broken me.

I swallow around the lump in my throat, watching him while he takes me in. His gaze slowly lifts until he meets my eyes, and the dark smile on his face grows wider.

"I brought you a present." Lifting his arm, there's a small bag dangling from his index finger with the brand name of a designer clothing store; the same store he brings me dresses from every time he visits.

When I don't move to take it, he walks over and sets it on the small kitchen table. He pushes it toward me, quirking a brow. "Aren't you going to have a look inside?"

I hesitate for a second before slowly approaching the table. The hair on the back of my neck stands on end with every step I take closer to him, and I watch him intently, alert for any sudden movement.

Without removing my gaze from his, I lift out the dress and set it on the table.

"You should try it on."

It's not a request, but for the first time, I don't obey him. I think he might be right; I think the last few weeks here have broken me, just not in the way he wanted it to.

Even though sweat coats my palms and makes my top stick to me, I say, "You forgot the heels."

Instead of angering him, my snark makes his sleazy smile

deepen. "I've got a matching pair for you...when you're ready to come home."

Goosebumps pebble my skin, and I have to fight back a shiver at the thought of calling anywhere I'd have to live with him *home.*

In the next second, the smile drops off his face, and the way he looks at me—like I'm nothing more than a possession, someone to control and manipulate, is even more terrifying than his sleazy leer.

"Put. It. On." His words are sharper this time, leaving no room for argument. I clench my fist at my side as I try to stop the trembling in my hands. Licking my dry lips, I wrap my sweaty palm around the edge of my shirt, and with one final strengthening breath, I quickly whip it off over my head, ignoring the fact I'm exposing myself to this fucking asshole.

I quickly shrug off the pants, mourning their loss after only getting to wear them for such a short period of time, before I snatch up the dress and hastily pull it on. It falls to just above my knees, with a small slit up the back of the skirt. It hugs my chest, pushing up my tits in a disgustingly inviting way, and I swear, if I ever get out of here, I'm never wearing anything but pants ever again.

Stepping toward me, he reaches out a hand to fix my still-damp hair over my shoulder. I flinch, and a satisfied gleam ignites in his eyes.

Come on, Hadley. You don't need to be afraid of this asshole and his pathetic dick. I take a fortifying breath, telling myself, not for the first time, that I'm stronger than him. The words have never made a difference before, but it doesn't stop me from reciting them over and over in my head.

"Have you had fun the last few weeks?" he asks, knowing damn well what I have had to endure. At least he's confirmed my suspicions that I've been here for some time. I wonder how long it's been since the guys showed up. Surely, no more than a few days. They wouldn't have left me in here any longer than necessary. They have to be coming soon—any day now. But there's not going to be anything left of me if I let Lawrence have his way tonight.

"Wh—why me?" I ask, stuttering out the words as my palms sweat. I'm not even sure I care why he stole me. The why of it doesn't matter; it won't change anything, but I need to stall for time, because I see the ill intent in his eyes, and it terrifies me more than anything else I've had to face within these concrete walls.

His face pinches, and his hand that was playing with my hair freezes. He doesn't say anything, and I brace myself for the slap or sharp tug on my hair that I'm pretty sure is coming. As his brown eyes darken in anger, I regret saying anything at all, and my chest rises and falls rapidly as I wait for whatever punishment he decides to dole out.

He unwraps the curl of hair from around his finger, and I flinch as he raises his hand, but instead of hitting me, he runs his palm down the length of my blonde hair.

"Did you know your mother and I used to date?"

My eyes widen in surprise. Not at the fact I don't know something about my mother—I know next to nothing about her—but at the fact she would ever date someone like him. To me, he looks like a monster. Then again, as I've said before if you didn't know him as I do, didn't *hate* him as vehemently as I do, you'd probably think he was attractive. He's got Cam's good looks but none of his charisma or generous heart. He might look stunning on the outside, but his core is rotten.

"We were going to get married."

And the surprises just keep coming.

"Until your *father*"—he snarls out the word, spittle hitting my cheek as his face turns into the demonic thing I know all too well —"started taking an interest. One measly compliment from him and I was all but forgotten, kicked to the side so they could run off into the sunset together."

His fingers grab hold of my hair as his anger skyrockets, squeezing the strands in his fist and inadvertently tugging on the roots, making me wince—not that he seems to notice or care, too lost in his past to see me standing right in front of him.

"Then you and Hawk came along, and they had the picture-perfect family." His lip curls up as he sneers. "Meanwhile, the pathetic excuse of a woman I was forced to marry gave me an idiot son who only cares about chasing girls and swimming."

My own temper flares at his demeaning words. He's got no idea just how capable his son is. Cam is *the* top swimmer in the region, and he's got his national meet coming up soon, and I *know* he's going to ace that too. Beyond his swimming achievements, Cam is smart—when he applies himself—and more importantly, he's kind and loyal. He's got something his father will never understand—integrity.

As quickly as my anger ignites, it's washed out in fear as his hand wraps around my throat, and I stare into eyes overflowing with fury.

"What was it that made you spread your legs for him? Are you so stupid that you fell for his fake charm, like every other slut in that school?"

My eyes bulge as he squeezes my throat. I can feel my pulse hammering against the skin at the base of my neck, and my breaths come in short, frantic pants.

"You were supposed to be MINE," he roars. Color stains his cheeks red as his lip curls back, baring his teeth. He looks like a wild animal—unpredictable and dangerous.

His eyes are wide and manic as he stares back at me, disgust and revulsion clear to see. "I have no need for a slut," he sneers, "so which is it going to be—are you a whore, or are you mine?"

I must have a death wish, but then, death would be preferable to any sort of life with him. He resembles every one of my nightmares; it makes my limbs shake and my heart race at just the mention of his name. I have always hated how weak he makes me. In his presence, I'm nothing more than a trembling, terrified statue, barely able to speak, but I'm at my lowest point right now, so close to giving up that the thought of angering him doesn't affect me the way it should.

Lawrence was my own personal monster before I learned how to fight, before I was molded into the killer I am today. He makes me feel like the scared kid I used to be. But I'm not that kid anymore. He affects me in ways I don't fully understand, but regardless of the reaction he evokes in me or how his presence turns my body to lead, he will never, *ever* own all of me.

I tilt my chin and stare into the dark, bottomless pits that have become his eyes. "I will *never* be yours."

Violence flashes across his face, darkening his features, and my whole body shakes. I'm frozen in place, petrified, despite my inner bravado.

With his tight hold on my neck, he propels me backward toward the bed that occupies the far corner of the room.

"Maybe I should just start fresh with the next generation," he snarls. His face is inches from mine, but I can hardly focus on it as my vision blurs from lack of oxygen. Whether that's due to him cutting off my air supply, or my hyperventilating state, I'm not sure.

He loosens his grip on my throat as he shoves me onto the bed, and with the little bit of distance he's created, I'm able to gather my wits enough to calm myself somewhat and gulp down several lungfuls of air, relieved when the fog in my brain lifts somewhat, and I can think more clearly.

The meaning of his words finally registers with me, sickening me to the core. "You want to impregnate me and try your luck with my daughter when you're old enough to be her grandfather?" I bark out a caustic laugh that comes out more high-pitched and hysterical than I'd like. "Tough luck, you sick fuck." I've already pissed him off, so I might as well keep going. He's going to do whatever he wants with me anyway. The last couple of weeks here have undoubtedly robbed me of my sanity because I don't even care if I can't get my limbs to cooperate enough to fight him off. I'm so. Fucking. Done. Done with being at his mercy, with letting him dictate my every thought and control my every movement. Alive or dead, what does it matter, so long as I'm free of him.

So, I'm all in as I say my next words, knowing they're going to infuriate him beyond belief. "You think you have the men here under your thumb? You think they were okay with babysitting a pampered princess?" I laugh in his face, even as his fingers tighten around my throat, threatening to cut off my words. "If I wasn't a soldier, in their minds, I served no purpose...you must know what they do to their soldiers."

The blood drains out of his face, and his eyes flare in outrage. Quicker than I can blink, he's yanking up my dress, tearing it in his rush to confirm what I'm saying. With the fabric around my hips, he can plainly see the small white scars just above my pubic hairline or the one right below my belly button. If you didn't know to look for them, you'd hardly notice they were there.

"No," he gasps.

His fingers dig into my hip, and I know they'll leave bruises, but I don't even register the pain.

"Yup." I've never been so gleeful to have something so basic taken away from me. "They sterilized me. Wheeled me into the operating room like a fucking dog getting spayed."

His eyes are wide with shock as he moves his gaze to the other scar, and I notice when he spots the owl tattoo, with its wings spread out and a dagger driven down through its head, sitting just above it, entangled in the tail of the phoenix tattoo I had done as soon as I escaped last summer. It might have seemed like a waste of money, especially when I didn't have much. I had to forgo several nights in a motel just to afford it, but it was worth every penny. It reinforced everything I'd fought for, and everything I still had to achieve in order to claim my freedom. Since then, I've found something so much more meaningful than simply being free. I have found acceptance, love, family.

His eyes bounce between the mercenary symbol tattooed on my hip, and the small white scars, glaring daggers at them as if he can make it all disappear by sheer will. As fury builds within him, his gaze flicks up to mine and his grip on my neck tightens.

"You have been a complete waste of my time," he hisses scathingly. His face is scrunched in anger as he hovers over me, pushing against my neck and using his weight to drive me further into the mattress. The intent is clear. This time, he's not trying to scare me.

"She never gave a shit about you. She discarded you, wrote you off as dead. You were mine to do whatever I wanted with, but as you grew older and you looked so much like her, I thought I was getting a second chance." He laughs humorlessly, the harsh bark sounding unhinged in my ringing ears.

Unable to breathe, panic flares to life, and I claw at his hand, frantically trying to push him off me. Adrenaline courses through my body, clashing with the paralyzing fear I always experience in his presence. I feel like the two parts of myself are at war with one another.

Black spots obscure my vision as he leans in and presses his lips to my ear. "I know you've come to care about that brother of yours. Maybe once I'm done here, I'll send one of my men to torture and kill him. Tell him how you screamed for his help as I drained the life out of you."

Something in me snaps, and everything goes hazy. It's like I go into a rage blackout. Anger surges through my veins, burning away the all-consuming fear. It's one thing for this sick fuck to threaten and terrorize *me*, but not my brother. He's done everything he can to protect me, and I know he's fighting to get to me now. We only just found each other, and I'm sure as fuck not about to let anyone harm him.

I'm not sure what happens, but the next thing I know, Lawrence is lying on the floor on his back. His eyes are wide, his face pale, as I drive a knife into him, over and over again. I feel the warm flecks of blood hitting my face, and my hand slips on the blade as it sinks with sweat and blood. Yet I don't stop, even as the life drains out of his eyes and his body falls still beneath me.

I stab.

And stab.

And stab.

CHAPTER 5

Cam

My eyes dart frantically around the empty cell.

"Where the fuck is she?!" Hawk snarls, echoing my inner thoughts. He spins, pinning West with his intense stare. "Where else would they be holding her?"

West's tablet is already in his hand, and lines furrow his forehead as he pulls up an image on the screen. Leaning in so I can get a better look, I notice he's looking at a much more comprehensive layout of the compound than the half-complete one we drew up several days ago.

"There's a couple of places, but I don't know for sure." Beck leans in over his shoulder to study the blueprints too, and West spares him a glance before focusing back on the screen. "You don't know where they conduct punishments?"

"No," Beck murmurs, staring just as intently at the tablet. He reaches out to touch the screen, zooming in on a particular part of the map. "But if I had to guess, I'd say it's there."

THE REST OF US MOVE CLOSER TO SEE WHERE HE'S POINTING. "WHY?" I ask, trying to work out how he's narrowed it down to that corner of the compound. The area he's pointed out on the blueprint isn't labeled as any particular sector. It could be a storage room or anything.

He grimaces. "Because there's a small morgue beside it and a loading dock out back."

His words make my stomach revolt, and a desperate need to find Hadley claws at my insides. Tension fills the air as the guys shift uncomfortably, and I can feel the molten hot anger pouring off Hawk as he restrains himself from storming out of here until we've got a plan.

Still deep in thought as he stares at the screen, Beck ponders, "Hadley once mentioned being taken to a room when Lawrence visited her."

"You think my father is here?" I snarl, my own anger flaring.

He shakes his head. "I mean, Lawrence would have ensured that whatever room she was taken to for his visits was secure, so they might be holding her there, away from any other guards or recruits.

I grit my teeth in anger, itching to get a move on. "Okay, so she might be there or wherever they take recruits to punish them." My nose wrinkles just saying those words, and I try not to picture young children being dragged kicking and screaming to some hellish corner of this place where they can be tortured. It doesn't work, and vomit blocks my airway as I struggle to swallow it down.

West, whose gaze hasn't once left the tablet while the rest of us talk around him, points to another unlabeled blueprint area. "There are a few blanked-out areas; they could be keeping her in any of them."

"We need to split up." Hawk's words are sharp. He's just as keen as I am—as we all are—to get a move on. We can't afford to waste time just standing around.

West nods his head in agreement. "You guys check out the

blank areas on the map. I can go back to the control room and review the security footage to see if I can track her movements."

"You're not going there alone," Mason snaps. "I'll go with you."

"Wilder and I will check out the blank area beside the morgue," Hawk states before West can argue with Mason. "Cam, you and Beck go through the other unlabeled areas. We'll all meet back here in twenty minutes."

We all nod, and snapping a picture of the blueprint on West's tablet, Beck and I take off, heading for the closest area on the map.

Please be there, baby.

Reaching the first unmarked area, I share a glance with Beck, and with guns at the ready, we pull open the steel door. Nothing but an empty space lies beyond, with doors leading off of it. A pit forms in my stomach. *God, please let this just be a storage space.*

Each of us takes a side of the room, and I enter the code and pull open the first door, ready to shoot any fucker who lunges at me. I breathe out a sigh of relief when I find the room empty. My brows pull together in confusion as I glance around the small space. There's nothing but a bed in the room. Maybe it's sleeping quarters for guards on duty?

My gaze catches on chains dangling from the wall above the headboard, following them down to metal cuffs resting on the mattress, and any hopeful thoughts I had quickly dissipate.

"Beck." My voice sounds strained even to my own ears.

"I see it." The heaviness in his tone only makes me feel more ill, and I hurriedly shut the door, spinning around in the small space as I stare at each of the closed doors. One, two...five, six. *Six.* There are six rooms in here, and I'm guessing each one is laid out the same.

As my thoughts spiral, I stare wide-eyed at Beck, taking in the ticking of his jaw and the darkened color of his eyes. I'm too shocked to move, watching him as he clears the rest of the rooms. As soon as he enters the code for the last room, the door flies open, and a guard comes crashing through it, colliding with Beck.

The two go tumbling to the ground in a brawl, fists flying as Beck wrestles to gain the upper hand.

Frozen for a second, I stand and watch them, before raising my gun and aiming it, except I can't get a clear shot. Tucking it back in my pants, I'm about to dive in and help when I hear a frightened whimper coming from the darkened room behind me. Forgetting about the fight in front of me, I take a hesitant step, then another, toward the noise.

Stepping into the doorway, my jaw drops when I find a young boy, no older than ten or eleven, wearing only a pair of briefs and chained to the bed. His eyes widen in fear, giving him an owlish appearance as he stares at me. When his lower lip trembles, it releases my feet and I rush toward him.

"Hey, you're okay," I try to reassure him in a low, calm tone. My eyes roam over the chains and the cuffs fastened around his wrists. "I'm going to get these off you. Do you know where the key is?"

The kid looks at me for a long second, before he glances behind me. Turning, I notice the guard's uniform shirt and holster in a pile on the floor. Moving over to them, I find a key sitting on top of the pile. Grabbing it and the shirt, I hurry back to the bed and quickly undo the cuffs.

"Here, put this on." I hand the kid the guard's shirt so he can cover it up, and he doesn't hesitate before taking it from my outstretched hand.

As he's doing up the buttons, a shadow darkens the doorway, and the kid freezes.

"He okay?" Beck's deep voice seems to echo around the small room.

"Yeah, he's fine. You?" I notice he's got blood trickling from a cut to his brow, and his lip is split, but he nods his head.

The kid's eyes bounce between us, filled with wary suspicion.

"What are we going to do with him?" I whisper to Beck. "We can't just leave him here."

Beck nods his head as he thinks, before moving to the bed where the kid is sitting and crouching down in front of him.

"We're here to get D. Do you know who she is?" Biting on his lower lip, the kid slowly nods his head. "Do you know where they're keeping her?" This time, he shakes his head, and although not being any closer to finding Hadley must frustrate Beck as much as it annoys me, he doesn't let it show. "We have a friend who is going to get you out of here, but I need you to do something for me. Do you think you can do that?"

The boy hesitates before nodding his head again, and Beck smiles reassuringly. Who knew he was so good with kids? I wouldn't have a clue what to do if he wasn't here. "Good. I need you to stay here." The boy's eyes widen, but Beck continues, reassuring him, "Nobody will be able to get in here. The code didn't work for the guard who was in here with you, did it?"

When the kid shakes his head, Beck explains, "That's because we changed it. If you stay here, I will tell my friend where you are, and he will come get you. You'll know you can trust him, because only the good people will have the code to open the door, okay?"

The kid's gaze lifts to mine. I give him what I hope is an encouraging nod, and when he looks back at Beck, he silently nods.

"Good man. You're going to be alright, kid. My friend will be here soon to get you."

Beck gets to his feet, and with one final look at the wide-eyed kid, we return to our mission of finding Hadley.

My brain is still trying to process the fucked up shit we just saw as we make our way back to the main corridor.

"Hold up a sec," Beck says, throwing his arm out to stop me. "Let me see the blueprint again."

Pulling up the map on my phone, I hand it over to him, and his lips thin as he presses them together, analyzing the map.

"What is it?"

"I remembered something Hadley once said." He lifts his gaze to look at me. "Those rooms back there were too small. The way she described her visits with Lawrence…she told me he would get her to make drinks for him, and he liked when they ate together."

My lip curls back on a snarl. "Like a fucking date?!" What the hell is wrong with that sick fuck?

Ignoring my angry outburst, Beck continues on with his train of thought, "It sounded like she was in an apartment. Not a small room like the ones we just saw."

Catching on to what he's saying, I lean in to look at the map with him. Zooming in on one of the unlabeled areas hidden at the back of the building, it seems like one relatively large room away from everything else.

"There. That must be where Lawrence took her."

My blood boils with anger, renewing my determination, and I take off toward that part of the compound, ready to take down any fucker that gets in my way.

Blood rushes in my ears, and my thoughts are only on holding Hadley in my arms again as I run to the far end of the building. I can just about hear Beck's footfalls as he races beside me; my focus is so fixed on finding Hadley that I don't even realize we have company until I hear a gunshot, and a second later, a weight slams into me, knocking me off my feet. I go crashing to the floor, the impact forcing the air out of my lungs.

A fist crashes into my face, and the tangy taste of blood floods my mouth. Snarling, I slam my knuckles into the asshole's side. I shove him off me and roll over until I'm straddling him, delivering another blow to his head. My fists connect with his face, over and over, until he's nothing but a bleeding pulp beneath me. Lifting my gun out of the back of my pants, I flick off the safety and point it at his head. With my finger on the trigger, I take a deep breath and pull. The shot rings out, and blood splatters me, but I'm barely aware of it over the whooshing of my pulse in my ears.

Panting heavily and still in shock, I lift my gaze, finding Beck fighting off two more guards. Stumbling to my feet, I go to help him, but he sees me.

"Hadley," he shouts, delivering a round-house kick to one of the guards. I hesitate a second longer, and he spares me a glance. "I got this. Go get our girl."

I give him a curt nod and, swiping a dribble of blood from the corner of my lip, I race away from the fight to the steel door at the end of the corridor that should have our girl locked behind it.

Entering the code, I pull open the door and step into an empty corridor. There's nothing here except a single door at the far end of the hall, and I rush toward it. Holding my gun in my right hand, the keypad flashes green and the door unlocks. I quietly open it and steady the gun in front of me, freezing at the sight before me.

My eyes dart from the dead man to the deranged, blonde-haired, blood-soaked angel straddling him, as she drives a knife into him like someone possessed.

Stepping forward, my gaze falls back to the dead body on the floor, and this time, I see past the blood, taking in the lifeless eyes of my father.

"Baby Davenport." The words are barely more than a whisper, coming out on the end of a shocked gasp. Nevertheless, they break through whatever trance she is in, and with the knife held above her head, ready to plunge into my father again, she freezes.

She lifts her eyes to mine. "Cam?" Her voice breaks, and studying her closely, I notice how thin her face has gotten. Her eyes look dull, her cheeks sunken, and tears track down her face, mixing with the blood spatter. She should probably look night-marish, like some sort of born-again demon, but hovering over the dead body of her very own monster, knowing she conquered her fear—that she fucking saved herself—she looks like the fucking queen of hell.

The knife slips from her grip, clattering to the floor, and in the next second, I've closed the distance between us as I fall to my knees beside her. Her lips crash against mine, and her thin arms wind around my neck as my father's blood soaks into my pants.

"It's really you," she murmurs in wonder, her warm breath tickling my lips. My hands roam over her, unable to believe she's truly in my arms, relatively safe and sound. "You came for me."

Cupping her face in my palms, I drink her in. "It's really me, baby. It took too long for me to sort out my shit and let you in, I'm not about to lose you now."

She leans in, fusing her lips to mine once again. With every clash of our tongues, my fear and worry abate, replaced with an overwhelming need to hold her close and never let her go again. My arms wrap around her, and I mentally note how much thinner she is as I effortlessly drag her into my arms, not giving one single shit that she's drenched in blood.

"Cam," she moans, grinding against me. Her sultry tone goes straight to my crotch, and I pull back, highly aware of how fucking inappropriate all of this is.

Refusing to put any distance between us, she follows me, her lips chasing mine.

"Hadley—"

"Cam." Her voice is much more insistent this time, and as I look into her eyes, dilated with adrenaline, I notice how dull they look. They've always reminded me of the sky after a thunder-storm—electric and energized—but right now, they're hollow and listless. Like everything that made Hadley, Hadley, has been sucked right out of her.

Running my hands down her arms, I feel numerous lacera-tions. Tearing my gaze from hers, there are more cuts than I can count, littering her skin. Some are shallow and partially healed, while others look fresh from the last few days. Dropping my gaze to where her thighs straddle mine, I notice the same slashes across her legs. One particularly savage-looking gash running up the side of her thigh has me gritting my teeth as I struggle to contain my anger.

She places her hand under my chin and forces my gaze back to hers. Her small fist wraps around the front of my top, pulling me into her, and she kisses me deeply until I get lost in the feel of her. "Please," she murmurs. "I need to know this is real."

Those words threaten to break me, and her desperate, vacant look is my undoing. Even though I don't understand, I can tell she needs this now.

Beck's going to cut my fucking balls off if he comes in and catches me taking advantage of her in her vulnerable state, but fuck me if I'm going to let her down.

I surge forward, returning her kiss with a fierce passion. I let her taste every part of the panic and desperate longing I have felt since I discovered she was missing; let her see how much she's been missed, how much she's needed, wanted, and loved.

Holding her against me, I get to my feet, noting how light she feels in my arms as I set her on the small table. She never lets our kiss break, clinging to me like she's scared that if she lets go, I'll disappear, but she should know I'm not fucking going anywhere. I'm never letting her out of my sight again. I've been such a fucking idiot, wasting so much time being pissed at her and angry with myself when all along, I should have been doing this— showing her exactly what she means to me. She's had me captivated since I first saw her in the quad in her combat boots, with her hair whipping wildly around her face. In the last two weeks, I have realized that the way she makes me feel is so much stronger than lust, more powerful than like. I love her in an all-consuming, dark, possessive way, that means I'll always fight to get to her. I'll slay whoever I need to and conquer whatever obstacle is in my way. I don't want to control her the way my father did. I don't need to dictate every part of her life. I want to watch her fly free, to see her vanquish her enemies and become the formidable queen she was born to be.

Our teeth clash as my hands run down her sides. My skin tingles under her touch as she slips her hand under my top, and I groan at the contact. Kissing her passionately, I stroke along her inner thighs, hesitant to go further as her words echo in my mind.

My body tenses at the spark of anger. Questions swim in my head as I wonder, not for the first time, what she's had to endure the last two weeks. She must pick up on my distracted train of thought as she pulls me further into her, leaning back on the table until I'm hovering over her. Her legs wrap around my waist, causing the god-awful dress that asshole has dressed her in to slide up. Running my hand along her thigh, I push it higher and slip my hand between her legs, gritting my teeth at the absence of her underwear.

Breaking the kiss, her head falls back, and she moans as I circle her clit. I dip my head, kissing along her neck and uncaring of the blood coating her skin, as her needy moans spur me on. When I sink two fingers into her, her face falls slack, and her eyes become hooded. She tugs me up to kiss her as I push her closer to oblivion.

Gazing into her eyes while I give her what she needs, I murmur, "You deserve to feel nothing but pleasure."

Her eyes bore into mine, and her fingers dig into my skin as she comes apart. A single tear escapes and runs into her hairline before I can wipe it away, and she begins to tremble in my arms. Her hand shakes as she places it on my chest, over my rapidly beating heart.

"I didn't think I'd get to feel this again."

The sound of footsteps coming toward us has me spinning around, ensuring Hadley's hidden behind me. I move to grab my gun, but my fingers wrap around nothing but air, and I curse myself for being so stupid when I notice the gun lying uselessly on the floor beside my very dead dad.

Lowering into a crouch instead, I ready myself to fight my way out of here as the footsteps draw closer.

"Jesus, you scared the shit out of me," I huff out, sagging and dropping my arms as Beck stalks into the room. His shirt is torn, and he's got a nasty gash on his arm, but otherwise he looks relatively unscathed.

His eyes drift behind me, and they flare when he spots Hadley.

As he steps forward, I move to the side. His gaze roams over her, most likely noting the same physical changes I did.

Tears stream continuously down her face, and as she pushes herself off the table to get to Beck, her legs give way beneath her.

Beck and I dive for her at the same time, but he gets there first, wrapping her in his arms, and I hear her sob into his chest. Now that the adrenaline is wearing off, she's starting to crash—hard.

Giving them a moment, I move to the sink and wash the blood off my hands and face. Finding a worn-looking dishcloth beneath the sink, I wet it under the tap and turn to move back to Hadley, wanting to clean my father's disgusting blood off her. Only I pause when my gaze lands on his unmoving body. Stepping closer, I take in his blood-soaked shirt, the shocked look frozen on his face, and the numerous stab wounds that speak of all the pent-up aggression Hadley had toward him. The lack of emotion I feel, or rather the absence of the grief I should probably be feeling, is unnerving, yet it seems appropriate. He was my father in name only. We shared DNA, but that was it. I won't mourn his absence or wonder what could have been. Knowing Hadley will no longer have to fear him makes a sadistic grin brighten my face, and looking away from his rotting corpse, I focus on my girl, still held safely in Beck's comforting arms. I step over my father and, without a backward glance, I move to clean her up, wiping the damp cloth over her face, neck, chest, and arms. All the while, she leans against Beck's chest, watching me. The deadened look in her eyes worries me as she stares blankly back at me, and I stroke my hand over her hair.

"You ready to get out of here, baby?"

She sighs, and her eyes drift shut. "You have no idea."

"You need me to carry you?"

She gives a small shake of her head, burying her face in Beck's chest and inhaling a fortifying breath before pulling away. I'm relieved to see she looks stronger as she pulls her shoulders back and straightens her spine. She moves toward my father with a steeliness in her eyes that wasn't there before. I reach forward, intending to stop her from doing whatever she's going to do, but she sidesteps me, bending down to grab the knife she had. She stares at it for a second before running her gaze over my father, pausing when she notices the sheath on his hip.

There's no emotion on her face as she wipes the blade on his gray suit pants and gets to her feet. *Fuck me*, if I don't get a little hard at the sight of her covered in blood and wielding a deadly weapon. If the look of adoration in Beck's eyes and sudden tightness in his pants is anything to go by, he's feeling it too.

We leave the room without another word or a backward glimpse at my shitstain for a father. I make a mental promise to Hadley to destroy every piece-of-shit scumbag associated with this godforsaken place.

We move at a slower pace, making our way back to the interrogation room to meet the others. I'm sure our twenty minutes are well up by now, but despite Hadley's determined face, it quickly becomes apparent that she's struggling. I watch her closely, and it's clear from her stick-thin frame and the bags under her eyes that she's been starved and hasn't had much chance to rest while she's been here. Not to mention the cuts all over her body. The large one on her thigh seems to catch every time she over-extends her leg as she keeps wincing, and it's taking everything in me not to whip her off her feet and carry her the rest of the way.

Thankfully, we don't run into any issues, and it doesn't take long before we round the corner into the corridor with the interrogation room.

I've been walking behind Hadley, watching her obsessively, and I'm immediately on alert when she freezes. Looking past her, I discover the reason she's stopped.

"Hawk." The emotion is thick in her voice, and even though she doesn't say the word all that loudly, her brother, who's standing further down the hall in front of our designated meet-up spot, turns toward her. The permanent scowl falls off his face as his eyes widen, and he takes her in.

Hadley flies off like a bullet, running toward him at a speed I wouldn't have deemed possible in her weakened state, and Hawk rushes to meet her halfway. The two collide like something out of a movie, and *holy fuck*, if it doesn't make my insides go a little gooey. The two of them are a fucking twinmance for the ages. As the two of them embrace each other, clinging to one another like it's the end of times, this moment epitomizes just how far Hawk has come in the last few months. It's good to see the fucking asshole has a heart, after all.

After what feels like forever, the two of them break apart, and Hawk takes a step back, running his gaze over her. His brows pull together as he registers the red tinge to her skin and the very obvious blood stains covering her previously cream dress.

"Why are you covered in blood?" Without giving her a second to respond, he snaps his gaze to Beck and me. His eyes darken, and he barks out sharply, "Why the fuck is she covered in blood?"

"I'm fine," Hadley quickly assures him, reassuringly squeezing his arm. "It's not mine." She hesitates, glancing back at me with a mixture of emotions I can't place. Turning back to face her brother, she can't meet his steely gaze as she mutters, "I'll tell you later." I don't like how she seems almost embarrassed, or afraid to tell him. I don't give a fuck that my dad is dead, and I know Hawk and the others will be as proud as I am that she overcame her fears and did what needed to be done.

Losing his patience, Mason shoves Hawk to the side, wrapping his arms around Hadley, and West, needing his moment with her too, does the same. So our poor girl is squished between them.

As they pull away, Wilder pipes up, "Good to see you, Sunshine. I was worried you wouldn't get to see my incredible knife skills." He holds up his bloodied blade, and I quirk a brow at Hawk, but he just shakes his head. Guess that's a story for another time.

Despite Wilder's nonchalance, there's a softness in his eyes when he smiles at Hadley, and I can't decide if I like the way he looks at her, or fucking hate it.

She lifts her own still partially bloodied blade, and although it doesn't look as deadly as Wilder's, she grins wickedly.

Wilder's eyes light up. "Twinsies."

It's Hawk's turn to raise an eyebrow in question, and I simply murmur, "I'll fill you in later."

"Let's find Cain and get the fuck out of here," Hawk barks, wrapping his hand around Hadley's and tugging her toward the exit.

"Wait," Hadley calls out, digging her feet in and forcing Hawk to stop in his tracks unless he wants to drag her along behind him. "What about Michael? I was with him when…" Her brows scrunch together as she struggles to remember something before shaking off the thought. "He might be here."

"Michael?" I question. "No, he's fine. He's back at school."

"What do you mean you were with him?" Hawk growls angrily. "He said you'd parted ways before you disappeared."

Wrinkles form along Hadley's forehead as she struggles to think, before sighing and shaking her head. "I don't remember. I think I was drugged. It's all a blur. The last thing I remember was walking toward the lake with him."

"We can sort all of this out once we get the fuck out of here," Beck interjects, but his lips are pressed tightly together, and there's a hardness in his eyes that wasn't there a second ago. When he looks my way, I know he's thinking the same thing I am —Michael didn't say anything about going to the lake with our girl.

Sighing, Hawk nods his head in reluctant agreement and starts moving toward the exit again with Hadley by his side. The rest of us fall into formation around them, moving as a single unit toward the back entrance of the building.

Reaching the exit, we pull open the door and step out into the night. Hadley pauses to tilt her head up to the dark sky, sucking down a deep breath of the fresh air, and I once again curse my fucking father for everything she's had to endure.

Scanning our surroundings, the yard seems quiet. I'm hoping

that means Cain has managed to take out any guards that were lurking around out here.

We're making our way silently toward the compound's back exit when we hear footsteps—someone running in this direction. Falling still, I raise my gun while positioning myself in front of Hadley, noticing Hawk doing the same on her other side and the others closing in behind her. Regardless of our attempts to block her, Hadley crouches into a fighting position between us, wielding her knife with all the skill of a trained mercenary.

The second the asshole guard comes into view, I fire off a shot, but he's too far away and it's too dark out, so the shot goes wide.

Spotting Hadley, the fucker's eyes widen and he calls out, "D!"

"Wait!" Hadley shouts, surging forward and throwing out her arms in an attempt to stop us from shooting at him. "I know him."

"He's a guard," I growl, refusing to look away from the enemy, even though he's holding his arms in the air in surrender and no longer advancing toward us.

Hadley gives me a stern look. "He helped me." Turning back to the guard, she calls out, "Marcus, what are you doing here?"

"I heard gunshots. As soon as I realized what was happening, I figured it was your guys. I wanted to help but couldn't get into the building."

I tense as the guard approaches, and Hadley looks at me over her shoulder, doing the same with Hawk, pinning us both with a *behave yourselves* look, before her eyes move to Beck. "He's Meena's brother."

I don't know what that means, and neither does Hawk if his furrowed brow means anything. Although Beck obviously does, as his shoulders relax, even though his brows pull together in confusion. His gaze runs assessingly over the guard before he glances at Hadley. She gives a tight nod of her head, and he returns his focus to the guard once again. "If you want to help, there's a boy inside, in the far-right corner of the building."

"I'll get him." There's a promise in his tone that has me giving him another once-over, but I still don't trust him.

Beck must be hesitant too as he studies him for a second before responding, "The code is four-two-three-five-three-nine. Take him to the back entrance. I'll tell Cain to look out for you."

The guy nods, and with a final glance and a small smile directed at Hadley, he takes off into the building behind us.

The rest of us keep moving forward. The previously silent yard is now ripe with life. Sounds of children crying, along with smoke from burning buildings, filters the air. The place is frenzied, and as we approach the back entrance to the compound, children are running or being carried through the open gate.

We're most of the way across the yard when Hadley's leg gives out, and she falls to the ground, hissing in pain. Hawk is beside her in a flash, hauling her into his arms.

"Shit, are you okay?" I brush my fingers over the reddened skin on her knees, swiping away the dust and grit, relieved to find no fresh cuts from where her knees collided with the hard asphalt. Running my eyes over her as I inspect for any other damage, I notice the deep cut on her thigh has opened up. Blood trickles from the wound, and when I look back at her face, she looks paler than before. Honestly, she seems completely fucking wrecked.

"I'm fine." She waves me away, but there's a fine tremor in her hands which she tries to hide. "Just not used to such strenuous exercise." She tries to laugh it off with a small, tired smile, but none of us find it funny. Hawk's arms tighten around her and his face turns thunderous. My own jaw clenches and I have to look away for a second so she doesn't see just how much her words fucking infuriate me.

"Hawk," she grumbles, pushing against his chest, "I can walk."

He glowers, but none of the heat is directed at Hadley. "I don't give a shit if you think you can somersault the rest of the way. You're fucking exhausted." Huffing out a breath, he clenches his teeth and pleads with her with his eyes. "Just let me help you, okay?"

The two of them share a twin moment, where the rest of the

world doesn't exist, before Hadley relents and gives a quick nod of her head, relaxing into his embrace.

We set off again, quickly closing the distance to the back gate. Spotting us heading in his direction, Cain strides toward us.

"Go on. I'll catch up in a sec." Beck focuses on Hadley, before sparing the rest of us a glance. As we pass by, Cain nods his head at us, a gesture I return. Tonight wouldn't have been possible without him.

Leaving the chaos of the compound behind, we make it back to the car, and Hawk slides Hadley into the back seat. I climb in beside her, and Mason slips in on her other side as Hawk gets in behind the wheel.

"You go," Wilder insists, watching Hadley as she slumps against Mason, barely able to keep her eyes open. "I'll wait for Beck."

Hawk nods, starting the engine, while West slides into the front passenger seat. Not having to be told twice, he guns it down the lane, onto the main road, and away from the burning buildings behind us.

CHAPTER 6

Hadley

THE WORLD COMES BACK TO ME SLOWLY AS I GROGGILY WAKE FROM the land of the dead. Or maybe I'm actually dead. *Did Lawrence and Bowen finally get the better of me?* I'm struggling to think through the thick fog of sleep, to remember what happened or where I am, and I can't for the life of me manage to peel my eyes open. They may as well be glued shut.

I give up on trying to open my eyes and focus instead on what I can feel and hear. The room is silent, and if it wasn't for the smoothness of the soft sheets wrapped around me, I'd believe I was still in my dingy cell back in the compound.

Someone squeezes my hand, and on instinct, I squeeze back.

"Hadley? You awake?"

Hawk's soft murmur and his worried tone give me the energy to crack open an eyelid, and I groan as light floods in. Lifting my hand to block it, something tugs the skin and, looking down, there's a bandage stuck to the back of my hand, with a tube coming out of it that's attached to a bag of fluids.

"The doctors said you were extremely dehydrated when we brought you in," Hawk explains.

"Where am I?" My throat is so parched the words are barely more than a croak, and my lips are dry when I run my tongue along them.

Letting go of my hand, Hawk stands and fills a cup on my bedside table with water, bringing it to my lips. I down it in two gulps, feeling the cold liquid slosh around in my otherwise empty stomach.

"You're at a private hospital. You passed out on the way home, and we didn't know what else to do." He glances away, and I notice the muscle in his jaw tick. "Given the cuts all over you…" Gritting his teeth, anger overwhelms him. Unable to stand still, he paces back and forth across the end of the bed in my small private room.

Resting my head against the pillow, I sit and watch as he stomps to one side of the room, then turns around and strides toward the opposite wall. His eyes are molten fury, his face like thunder. There's nothing I can say or do that would calm the rage consuming him right now. I know, because, despite the sheer exhaustion threatening to pull me under, I feel it too. That boiling ball of rage and fury, of wrath and malice that grows in my stomach, demanding retribution.

Lawrence might be dead, but I need *everyone* connected with that cesspit of a compound to be punished. The guards, Bowen, our parents. I won't be able to move on with my life until they've *all* suffered.

Hawk stops pacing, spinning to face me from where he stands at the end of the bed. His angry eyes fall on mine, but behind them, I see the pain he's masking; the vulnerability that he doesn't know how to process.

"Hawk—"

He shakes his head, unwilling to hear my platitudes. His fists clench tightly around the footboard, turning his knuckles white and threatening to crack the flimsy plastic.

"Just tell me," he hisses between gritted teeth. Unable to look at me, his gaze is laser-focused on a random point on the plain white bedsheet. "I need to know what they did."

Tense silence fills the room, choking me as memories I'd rather not relive assault me. I endured my fair share of grueling workouts and terrifying punishments growing up in the compound. Still, I was never locked away and isolated for so long or subjected to Bowen's cruel form of torture so frequently. And having tasted true freedom, even if it had been for only a few months, made being back there so much harder to handle.

I can barely come to terms with what I've been through, never mind telling Hawk every grotesque detail.

When I don't answer him, he lifts his head, pinning me with his swirling gray eyes. "Did they…" Unable to finish his sentence, his words hang in the air, their meaning more than clear.

"No," I choke out, even as memories of Bowen's threats, and Lawrence's leer while he forced me to change naked in front of him. Of him shoving his unwanted fingers inside of me, battering against my mental walls.

Hawk's penetrating gaze holds me captive for another moment as he searches for the truth. After a moment, his shoulders drop slightly in relief, and he nods. His Adam's apple bobs as he swallows roughly. Despite the tension still pouring off him, he seems somewhat reassured that at least I wasn't violated in such a heinous way.

The door to the room opens, and expecting it to be the guys, I'm entirely fucking shocked when Barton Davenport, my fucking father, walks into the room.

His eyes land on me and widen in shock. Under his scrutinizing gaze, I can only think that this is the first time he's ever really *looked* at me.

"What the hell are you doing here?" Hawk growls dangerously. He moves to block Barton's view of me and, suddenly feeling self-conscious, I rush to tuck the bed sheet tighter around me and flatten my hair with my hand—not that it does any good.

"I needed to check on you. Someone attacked the compound... What happened?" Barton's eyes narrow, and he tries to side-step Hawk, but the brute follows, continuing to block any advance Barton can make in my direction.

Scoffing, Hawk sneers, "Like you give a shit."

For the first time since entering the room, Barton tears his gaze from me to focus on his son. His eyes narrow in annoyance, and damn, if the two of them don't look eerily alike. It's freaky, and I'm not entirely sure what to make of it.

"Watch it, son."

The two of them stand off against each other in some stupid silent duel, until I huff out my own breath of annoyance. I can feel a headache forming behind my eyes, and I'm way too tired to deal with this shit.

"What are you doing here?" I ask wearily, my voice nothing more than a dry rasp as I look at Barton.

His attention snaps from Hawk to me. His eyes are filled with anguish and sorrow, but I can't understand why. Maybe I'm reading him wrong. Only seeing what I want to see. After everything I've been through, any girl would want her dad in her hospital room with her, comforting her...but not me. Not when my father hasn't given a single shit about me my entire life. His presence here only means more problems to deal with. Problems I don't have the energy to face.

Hawk ensures he keeps Barton in his sights as he shifts on his feet, moving so he can also see me. "How did you even know she was here?"

"I tracked your car. Once I explained I was your father, the receptionist told me what room you were in."

His gaze runs over my bare arms, the only visible skin, taking in the numerous scratches and cuts covering them.

"Who did that to you?"

My eyebrows lift in surprise at his threatening tone, but before I can work out what to say, Hawk scoffs. "Like you don't know."

Barton rounds on him so quickly it's nothing but a blur. "What the hell does that mean?" he snarls. "*You* told me she was in bed with a stomach bug, but clearly, that was a lie."

Hawk's eyes darken, and in the next second, he's got his dad shoved up against the wall, his hands fisting his shirt. The two of them are of similar height as they face off. "Yeah, and you pretended not to have a daughter all these years. Clearly, *that* was a lie."

I huff out yet another breath—not that it seems to do any good—and, deciding if shit is going to go down in this too small of a room, then I'd rather have pants on when it does. I unhook the line attached to the back of my hand and push back the covers, sliding out of bed.

Hawk must see the movement out of the corner of his eye because as soon as my bare feet hit the cold tile floor, his head snaps in my direction.

"Hadley," he growls. "Back in bed."

I glare right back, unperturbed by his pissy attitude—I'm practically immune to it by now.

"No, asshole. If you're going to start shit, I want to be dressed. I can't kick anyone's ass in this stupid gown." I wave my hand over the flimsy gown with no back so my bare ass is exposed—who the fuck thought that was a good idea?! Would it really have been so difficult to add an extra tie to the back so I could maintain at least *some* of my dignity?!

His eyes narrow to slits. "You're in no state to be kicking *anyone's* ass. Get. Back. Into. Bed."

Barton's gaze jumps back and forth between us as he silently watches our argument, but we both ignore him. Glowering at Hawk, I make sure to keep out of his arm span as I stomp—okay, so it's more of a crippled shuffle—toward the attached bathroom.

There's a black duffel bag sitting in a vacant chair and, hoping it has spare clothes in it, I snatch it up on my way past and slam the bathroom door shut behind me.

Alone, I lean against the closed door, tilting my head back until I'm staring at the ceiling. Thankful for a moment's peace. My legs shake, and my hands tremble, that little bit of exertion too much for my fatigued body.

Dropping the bag on the counter beside the sink, I unzip it, breathing a sigh of relief when I find a pair of clean sweats and a top. Looking around, the bathroom is small but functional, with a narrow shower stall in the corner. I can't even remember the last time I showered—at least one that wasn't with cold water and some perv watching me. Even though my legs protest at the thought of holding me up for much longer, the clawing need to have a nice warm shower is all I can think about, and I hastily tear off the gown and turn the dial until steam billows out of the stall, fogging up the mirror. Stepping under the spray, my eyes drift shut as I let the warm water wash over me. It feels like fucking heaven against my skin.

I turn the dial until the water practically burns me, scorching my skin and turning it red. I don't know how long I just stand there, soaking in the moment, relishing the small privilege of a warm, private shower, before I finally grab the small hotel-like bottle of shower gel and scrub my skin raw. I do the same with my hair, emptying both bottles. I still don't feel completely clean by the time I turn the water off and step out, but then I'm not entirely sure I ever will.

Exhaustion hits me like a freight train, and I quickly dry and throw on the sweatpants, top, and hoodie, noting that each item belongs to one of my guys. Burying my nose in the neckline of the hoodie, I breathe in Beck's cedarwood and eucalyptus scent, letting it wash over me and soak into my skin, soothing me in a way that only Beck can.

Rifling through the bag, I find my toothbrush, toothpaste, and a hair tie. I smile gratefully, knowing West will have been the one to remember to pack them. Once I've brushed my teeth and scraped my hair back into a messy bun, I straighten my spine, and with a determination I don't feel, I pull open the door.

Barton has since taken one of the empty chairs beside the bed, while Hawk continues to stand over him. They both look my way as I step into the room and shuffle back toward the bed. My muscles feel looser after the warm shower, although my left thigh, where Bowen—that son of a bitch—drove his knife into it, tugs every time I put my weight on it.

Seeing me struggle, Barton jumps to his feet to come to my aid, but Hawk shoves him back in his chair with a growl before stepping toward me, intent on helping. I wave him away, though, needing to achieve this small thing on my own.

Once I'm settled in the bed again, I look between them before my gaze lands on Barton.

"Did you know?" There's no point in pretending anymore. Lawrence is dead, and all I want now are answers. "Did you know where I was all these years?"

Barton's brows draw together in confusion, and I have to give him some credit as he never breaks eye contact. "What? No. I had no idea where you were until Hawk showed up with you that night."

I can feel tears gathering behind my eyes. The last few weeks have worn me down and robbed me of the energy to keep my usual defense mechanisms erected around me.

"Why did you never look for me? I was your daughter." My voice breaks, and I swallow back the emotion in my throat as I shake my head. "How could you just move on like that?"

With a pained expression on his face, Barton leans forward as if to touch me, but I flinch away, shuffling to the far side of the bed as Hawk's arm snaps out, blocking Barton from coming anywhere near me.

"Don't touch her," he snarls, moving to sit beside me on the bed, acting as a barrier between Barton and me.

Barton's eyes widen and his lips thin, but he slowly sits back in his chair. Keeping his focus on me, he says, "I did search for you. I hired a private investigator, and all of his leads were dead ends. Eventually, he told me there was no point in continuing to look for you. I didn't want to believe him, but ultimately, I had to accept that I'd lost you." He seems pained as he adds, "I had to focus on the family I still had."

Unable to stand looking at him, I drop my head so he doesn't see the tears threatening to overflow.

"That was it? You just gave up?" Hawk's words are a harsh snap, and I can feel the anger radiating off him, the heat searing my skin. I lean into the warmth, reassured that my explosive volcano of a brother will always have my back. There's something to be said about knowing someone will always be in your corner, fighting for you. It empowers your own strength and makes you feel capable of pretty much anything.

Even now, when I'm at my weakest, Hawk's fierce need to protect me washes over me like a balm to my wounded soul, piecing me back together. Perhaps, with his help, I'll come back stronger than ever. "And now you're claiming ignorance of it all? I still don't believe you didn't just sell her off to be Lawrence's little plaything."

Barton looks completely confused as his gaze jumps between Hawk and I.

"What are you talking about? What does Lawrence have to do with any of this?"

"Lawrence is the one who's been hiding her all these years. He kept her locked up in that fucking compound you call a business. Had her tortured and threatened. He kept her fucking terrified every day of her life."

The words explode out of Hawk, his voice rising with each syllable until his chest is heaving, and he's glaring murderously at our father, uncaring of how the color has leached from Barton's face or the way his lower lip trembles.

"You're wrong." Barton shakes his head, and I can see the wheels churning frantically behind his eyes. "There's no way Lawrence is capable of something like that. We would have known if she had been there. *I* would have known."

"How?" My voice is monotonous, devoid of all emotion. "You only visited once or twice a year. And every time you did, I was locked away until you were gone. You and the others left the day-to-day running to Lawrence. He was the one in charge, the one who oversaw everything." My own temper starts to flare, and I feel Hawk slide his palm into mine, squeezing my hand in encouragement. "Do you even know what goes on in there? What the guards do to form the inhuman soldiers you utilize for your own gain?"

If Barton looked pale after Hawk's outburst, he seems like a fucking ghost now. His mouth opens and closes wordlessly as he struggles to process everything.

Leaning forward, I hiss, "They beat children, rape them, break them down using whatever means necessary, until they are nothing but a void. A shell that can be molded and rebuilt into something monstrous and destructive.

"I was tortured, beaten. I've had my skin torn open more times than I can count, and I've been starved for days. I've been so close to giving up that I prayed for death." Hawk's hand squeezes mine, and I can feel the telltale wetness of tears coating my cheeks. "My best friend was beaten to death because she refused to kill another child. She was only thirteen. Thirteen years old, and she had her life ripped away from her. *That* is the company that you run. *That* is the hell that you abandoned me to."

Barton looks like he's about to be sick, yet I have fuck all sympathy for him. He swipes his hand over his mouth, and I watch his eyes dart back and forth unseeingly as he tries to come to terms with what we are saying.

"That can't be true," he mumbles disbelievingly, staring at me like I'm a figment of his imagination come to torment him. I lean back and tug down the waistband of my sweats, exposing the tail of my phoenix tattoo and more importantly, the symbol of the mercenary company—*his* company—hidden amongst the tail.

Both he and Hawk look at the exposed skin for a second until they see it, and Barton gasps.

"They branded you?" Hawk snarls venomously.

I shrug. Really, it's the least intrusive thing they've done to me. "They do it to everyone."

Barton seems lost in his own thoughts for a long moment before he speaks up again, "It was you, wasn't it? You attacked the compound?" His gaze flicks over the multitude of injuries I have on display. "Is that how you got hurt?"

"LAWRENCE TOOK HER," Hawk yells, loud enough to make me jump. "*Again.* He's had her for *weeks. He's* the one that's done that to her."

"I don't understand," Barton murmurs in a quiet voice. "Why? Why would Lawrence take you at all? And hide you in the compound? It makes no sense."

"I think it started as some sort of payback for you stealing Maria from him, and grew into an obsession over time."

If it's possible, Barton just looks even more confused as he shakes his head. "What? The two of them had already broken up before we started dating."

I don't know what to tell him, so I just shrug, too tired to give a shit about why. I'm the innocent victim in whatever shit went down between the three of them before I was even fucking born. People do fucked up shit all the time without good reason. If I get caught up in why Lawrence chose me, or why not Hawk, or both of us, I'll drive myself mad. There's never going to be a good enough reason to justify what he did, and I just have to accept that.

Barton gets to his feet, stumbling before he rights himself. "I-I need to go talk to him."

He steps toward the door, looking dazed.

"Yeah, no can do, I'm afraid." I grimace. "He's dead."

Barton's eyes widen comically as he spins to face me. "He's what?" Hawk doesn't react at all though, so I'm guessing Cam or Beck already filled him in.

"He's dead. I killed him. And I'm coming for the rest of you next."

CHAPTER 7

Hadley

After Barton stumbles, wide-eyed and panicked, from my room, Hawk tugs me down beside him on the bed. I melt into his embrace, drained and exhausted. We lie there in silence for a while before he speaks up, "That girl, the one who died…"

"Her name was Meena. The guard last night, he was her brother."

Hawk mulls over my words before speaking again, "If he was her brother, why was he a guard there?"

"He's been searching for her all these years. They were put into separate foster homes when they were kids, before she was abducted and brought to the compound." I can feel the tears again welling up in my eyes, and my chest hurts for their lost relationship. I know how much it would have meant to Meena, knowing her brother never gave up on her; he'd been looking for her all this time. Hawk's arms tighten around me, and I bury my face into him. "It was because of her that I never lost myself in there. If it wasn't for Meena, I would have ended up like all the others."

WE LAPSE INTO SILENCE, ALTHOUGH I CAN FEEL THE ANGER emanating from him. Regardless, it's not much longer before exhaustion pulls me under, and I fall into a deep, dreamless sleep in the reassuring comfort of Hawk's arms.

When I next wake, I'm pressed against a strangely comfortable brick. Squinting, I gaze up at a sleeping Mason. *Huh, I wonder when the two of them switched out and how I didn't even notice.* Lifting my head, I gaze around the otherwise empty room before lying back down and snuggling in tighter against him.

"You alright, Little Warrior?" Mason's voice is low with the perfect amount of sleepy sex appeal, and his arms tighten around me even though he hasn't opened his eyes.

"Yeah. Where's Hawk?"

"We finally convinced him to go home and get some rest. You're being discharged in the morning, so he and the others will come pick us up when you're ready to go."

I nod against his hard chest and try to go back to sleep, but my mind whirls with thoughts of returning to school. I feel like a completely different person to when I was last on campus. How can I go back there and act as if nothing ever happened?

"Barton said Hawk told him I had a stomach bug."

Mason sighs, shifting in the bed so he's lying on his back, and I'm sprawled across him.

"Yeah. He phoned, wanting both of you to go over for a family dinner. We couldn't tell him the truth, so Hawk lied. We've told the school the same excuse for why you haven't been in class."

I swallow roughly. "What about Emilia?"

Cupping my cheek in his large palm, he tilts my head up so I have no choice but to look him in the face.

"She has been driving all of us crazy, wanting to know what's going on and demanding we bring you back."

"Does she..."

"No, but she knows something's up. We figured you'd wanna be the one to tell her the truth." I glance away, worrying my bottom lip, but Mason forces my gaze back to his. "You've got a true friend in Emilia. She was ready to take us all on, thinking we'd done something to you." A fond smile tugs at one side of his lip. "Hawk had no idea what to do with her when she wouldn't back off. He was in shock when she actually stood up to him."

I chuckle. "Damn, I bet the look on his face was priceless."

Kissing the top of my head, Mason fixes the covers around us. "Go back to sleep. We'll deal with everything else in the morning."

Sinking into his warm embrace, coaxed by the heady combination of his uniquely Mason scent, I drift back into a dreamless slumber. By the time I wake up again, I'm feeling a million times better, physically, at least. If only sleep and a bag of fluids were enough to fix me mentally too.

MASON AND I ARE SITTING ON A BENCH OUTSIDE THE HOSPITAL WITH a paper bag containing a bottle of painkillers they gave me upon discharge, waiting for the guys to pick us up. I can't stop looking at the blue sky, breathing in the crisp, fresh air, and relishing the sound of birds chirping and cars driving past. Just soaking in the everyday mundane that people take for granted. It feels like a fucking lifetime since I had the luxury to just sit and drink in the world around me.

We're not sitting there for long before Hawk's SUV pulls up, stopping in front of us. Hawk jumps out from behind the wheel, and rounding the car, his gaze immediately falls on me. He gives me a once-over as if he expected something to have happened in the last few hours we were apart. Seeming satisfied, he nods at Mason and comes over, reaching out to help me up.

"Hawk," I grumble, waving him off. "I can walk. I'm not a fucking invalid."

He scowls but backs off—a little. He's like a fucking shadow, sticking to me like glue as I shuffle toward the front passenger seat. I can hardly be annoyed, though. If anything, it's sweet to see how much he cares. He grabs the door handle before I can reach it and doesn't move away until I'm buckled into the seat, like I'm a goddamn child. I roll my eyes when he's not looking, even while a slight smirk lifts the corner of my lip.

He and Mason exchange a few words before they both climb in, and we head back to campus. With every passing mile, anxiety ratchets up within me. My leg bounces repeatedly, and my palms sweat. I'm not even sure why I'm so on edge. I've done this before —successfully integrated into normal society. Sure, it took a while. The first couple of weeks were the hardest. I kept expecting someone to come after me and drag me back there. I couldn't get used to no one hurting me on a daily basis, and the tiniest touch from a passing stranger would send me into a downward spiral.

So, I've been here and survived it before. I should be able to get through it again, yet my nerves are still frayed. Anxiety claws at my throat, threatening to suffocate me as we drive through the campus gates and up the drive.

"Hey, are you okay? You're looking a little pale," Mason remarks once we've parked and he's opened my door for me. He takes my hand and helps me out of the car as Hawk rounds the hood, eyeing me warily, like he's worried I'll pass out.

"I'm fine." The words come out more sharply than I intended, and I grimace. *God, I'm such a bitch. They're only trying to help.* I give him an apologetic smile. "It's just weird being back here... after everything."

He nods in understanding and steps back, giving me some space to breathe before the three of us start toward the dorms. The anxiety only gets worse with every step I take, however. I swear I feel eyes on me, and as I bury myself deeper in my hoodie, I glance discreetly around me. Every student we pass seems to stare openly at me and whisper with their friends, and I constantly glance down at my arms, wondering if they can see the cuts marring my skin. Everything is covered, though; the only give-away that I'm not my normal self is my thinner, paler face.

"What the fuck are you staring at, asshole?" I snap when yet another person gapes at me as we walk past. The jerk startles and scurries off.

"Hadley," Hawk chastises. "What the hell? He was barely looking at you."

"*Everyone's* looking at me."

He shares a look with Mason over my head before pulling me to a stop and focusing on me. "No more than usual. What's going on?"

My eyes dart back and forth between his. *But I swear they were looking and whispering.* It was almost like they were surprised to see me. My brows furrow, and I scrub my hand down my face. I'm becoming fucking paranoid.

"I need to go to the lake." Hawk's eyebrows scrunch in confusion, and I can see the protest forming on his lips, but I rush on before he can argue. "I need to know what happened. How Lawrence got to me." I lean in and lower my voice. "Someone must have helped him. I wouldn't have gone there willingly."

"Alright, let's go to the lake," Mason agrees, earning a warning glare from Hawk. "What, man? She's right. We've been thinking the same, and she needs answers before she drives herself crazy trying to psychoanalyze every kid in school."

Pursing his lips, Hawk returns his gaze to mine, staring at me for a long moment before huffing out a sigh. "Fine, but we're leaving the second you start to feel tired."

I smile at him and nod my head. "Deal."

"I'll message the others and tell them to meet us there."

I'm still jittery with nerves, but the thought of finally getting answers and working out what happened the day I was taken settles me somewhat. I've been wracking my brain to figure it out, but it's nothing more than a hazy blur. I'm hoping being back there will spark something.

It takes us longer than usual to slowly make our way through the campus and down to the lake.

"Baby Davenport," Cam calls out, bounding toward me with a

massive grin on his face that I can't help but return. He wraps his arms around me, lifting me off my feet as he spins me in the air.

"Watch it, asshole," Hawk barks. "She's hurt."

Cam drops me like I'm on fire, his eyes wide as his gaze darts over me, checking for any injury.

"I'm fine," I assure him in a soft voice, reaching out to touch him.

He analyses me for a second longer, until he's satisfied I'm telling the truth. "Ah, he's in protective big brother mode, isn't he?"

"More like annoying big brother mode." Cam barks out a laugh, and I return it with a grin while Hawk grumbles beside us and stomps off, only making Cam laugh harder.

I can't help but watch him, noting the lightness in his eyes that hasn't been there in months. He seems like his old self, the Cam I fell for when I first arrived, and I have no idea how he can be so at ease. It was only a few days ago that he found his father brutally murdered…at *my* hands. Yet, he seems utterly unaffected by it.

"What are we doing here?" Beck asks. His eyes are glued to me, and I gently squeeze Cam's hand before I move over to join him. He tugs me in against him, turning me so my back is flush against his chest and his warmth seeps into my body, even through the thickness of my hoodie, as he wraps his arms around me.

I glance at West and Cam before looking past them to the forest stretched out behind them. My forehead creases as I try to think through the fog that is my memories. "I wanted to see if I could remember what happened the day I disappeared."

"What's the last thing you remember?" Beck asks.

"I went to meet Michael. We'd had a fight just before Easter break, and he messaged saying he wanted to talk." I pause, trying my best to remember that day. "We grabbed a coffee in the dining hall and brought them down here."

"You're sure?" Something in West's voice has me looking away from our surroundings to focus on him. There's an unusual darkness coating his expression, and his muscles are tense. Pinching my lips, I shrug it off as jealousy. I thought he'd gotten over that shit, but maybe not.

"Yeah." Slipping out of Beck's arms, I move to the edge of the forest where I last remember standing. I turn on my heel, so I'm facing out over the still water of the lake, with the dark cover of the trees behind me. "We were standing right here."

Mason moves to stand beside me, looking at a point deeper in the forest behind me. "That makes sense. We found your phone back there." He lifts his chin, indicating a spot behind me, and I turn to look into the gloomy depths of the forest.

Something bangs against my consciousness and goosebumps rise along my arm as I move toward the treeline. Stepping into the shadows, I shiver as the heat of the sun is blocked out. I reach out, trailing my fingers over a tree to my right, and I'm assaulted by memories coming so quickly I can't initially process them.

"What is it? What happened?" someone asks, a hint of urgency and concern to their voice.

"I knew we shouldn't have fucking done this," Hawk snarls angrily, but I'm barely paying attention to any of them.

"Wh-where a-are we…goin'?" It takes more effort than it should to force out the words, and even when I do, I'm not sure how intelligible they are. What's wrong with me? My body feels weird, disconnected, and it takes all my energy just to put one foot in front of the other. Where are we going again?

I trip and stumble against a tree. Someone huffs out a frustrated breath beside me, pulling on my arm until I'm standing upright once again. "Just keep going. We're nearly there."

Nearly where? And why does Michael sound so angry?

"Don't…feel…good." My eyes droop, and my head falls against my chest. I lose all track of time; the next thing I know, pain rattles my bones as my body collides with the compacted dirt of the hard forest floor.

"No problems, I assume?"

I recognize that voice, but everything around me is a blur as I squint up at the two dark blobs standing over me.

"None. Eh, what are you planning on doing with her?"

One of the blobs laughs humorlessly. "It's too late to grow a conscience now, boy. Just take the money and get out of here."

There's silence for a second before one of the blobs shifts out of my view, and I hear footsteps getting quieter and quieter as whoever it is walking away. The other blob crouches down in front of me, and I have to blink several times before his face comes into focus. I wish I could say I was hallucinating the devil's face hovering in front of me, but I'm all too familiar with the grotesque features smiling cruelly at me.

"No," I croak out the word, making his grin widen.

"Oh, yes, Dove. You're all mine now."

I GASP, FEELING LIGHTHEADED AS I BLINK BACK TO REALITY, FINDING all my guys crowded around me with various looks of concern on their faces.

"Did you remember something?" Beck asks, and I lift my gaze until I'm staring into his moss-green eyes, finding none of my usual comfort in them.

My mouth is dry, but I manage to croak out, "Michael."

Hawk snarls, "I fucking knew it was that asshole! I'm going to fucking kill him." His lip curls back, and there's a determined set to his jaw. Murderous intent glows in his eyes, making him look more terrifying than I've ever seen him before—which is saying something.

Beck reaches out for my hand, placing it between his warm palms. "You're shaking. You need to rest." I hadn't noticed the tremor in my hands until he mentioned it, but now that I'm aware of it, my whole body is vibrating. He glances around at the others. "We can discuss this back at the dorm."

Everyone quickly agrees, and Beck practically carries me back to the dorm.

"My room," I protest as we bypass the girls' dorm, heading for the guys.

"Fuck that shit," Hawk snaps, but I know his anger isn't aimed at me. "You're staying with us. I've cleared out a room for you."

I raise my eyebrows at him. "When did you do that?"

He shrugs. "Last night."

"You mean, when *you* were meant to be getting some rest."

The asshole acts like I never spoke, ignoring me as we climb the stairwell to their apartment. I get a weird sense of coming home as I walk in, a small smile growing at finding the place the same as how it was the last time I was here.

"Come on, I'll show you the room, and you can sleep for a while." He must see me about to argue as his eyes narrow in a warning and he continues, "Everything else can wait. We'll discuss it all when you get up."

My lips thin, but I can see that arguing with him would be futile, and I am pretty tired after today. "Yeah, okay," I agree on a sigh.

He shows me to a spare room at the back of the apartment, and I'm speechless as I walk in, finding the walls painted a dark blue, with cream covers on a large California king bed. My meager belongings have been moved from my room in the girls' dorm, and a few potted plants have been placed around the space, making it feel more lived-in. I spot the boxing gloves Mason got me sitting on the dresser and my textbooks on a desk.

"You can, uh, decorate it however you want," Hawk mumbles. His eyes dart around the room, as if he's trying to see it through my eyes.

"You did all this for me?" I gasp, turning in a circle and taking it all in.

When he doesn't reply, I tear my gaze away from the room to look at him, and he shrugs a shoulder. Closing the distance between us, I wrap my arms around him as a tear leaks out of the corner of my eye. "Thank you," I murmur. "It's beautiful."

He pats my back, and I can feel the awkwardness in his movements. He coughs, clearing the emotion from his throat. "Um, yeah. It was no big deal."

I smile into his shirt before letting him go and spin around to take in the room again.

"Get some rest, I'll check on you in a bit."

Once he's gone, I take my time walking around the room, opening drawers and rifling through my tatty duffle bag before stripping down and sliding between the clean sheets. *Oh yeah, this is by far the comfiest bed I have ever slept in.* Despite the horrors of the last few weeks and today's revelation, I feel safe and content as I fall asleep.

I'm pretty sure I've got the best grumpy brother in the world.

CHAPTER 8

Hadley

A NOISE STARTLES ME AWAKE, AND I JUMP UPRIGHT IN THE BED, ALERT and on edge.

"It's okay," Cam rushes out in a whisper. "It's just me."

Even though the tension drops out of my shoulders, my heart keeps slamming against my ribs, and my breaths come in rapid pants.

"Hey, shhh," Cam soothes, sliding into the bed beside me and pulling me into his arms. He strokes his hand over my hair and just holds me until the adrenaline rush passes. "I'm sorry, I shouldn't have snuck in like that, I-I didn't think."

Lying back, I pull him down so his head rests on the pillow beside mine, the two of us facing one another.

"I couldn't sleep. Every time I close my eyes, I worry I'm going to wake up and this will all have been a dream." I can see the genuine fear in his eyes. "I thought, maybe if I just came in and saw with my own eyes that you were really here, I'd be able to sleep."

"I'm here." I lift my hand and run it through his short, blond strands, and he closes his eyes, leaning into my touch.

We lie there in silence for a while, until the burning need for answers and reassurance becomes too much.

"Your dad…"

"Don't worry about him," Cam murmurs, slowly opening his eyes.

How can I not worry, though? "Cam, I killed him."

He reaches out, tucking a stray strand of hair behind my ear. "I know, and he deserved every painful second of what you did to him."

My eyes widen and I stare at him in shock. "You're not the slightest bit bothered by what I did? He was your *dad*."

"He was a controlling, manipulative asshole, who dictated everything in my life, and made it perfectly clear I never met his expectations. I can't think of one fond memory with him—not one fatherly moment. He was nothing but the demon on my shoulder my whole life, telling me to try harder and do better. After discovering what he did to you all these years, I would have killed him myself."

He shuffles closer to me on the bed, until our bodies are flush against one another, his head resting on my pillow inches from mine. "You mean more to me than he ever did. I've never been more proud than I was when I walked in and saw you wielding that knife. You didn't just face your greatest fear, you conquered it and made sure he could never come after you again."

Even in the dark room, I can see the honesty shining in his hazel eyes, and for the first time since Cam stormed into that room and found me murdering his father, I feel like everything between us might be okay.

"It might have been completely inappropriate, but seeing you covered in his blood, knowing you hadn't been afraid to do what you had to do, made me so fucking hard." I snort out a laugh as one side of his mouth lifts in a grin, and a sense of accomplishment shines in his eyes. "Now roll over so I can be the big spoon."

Doing as he says, I shift onto my other side, and he drapes his arm over my hip, tucking me in against him. Just as my eyelids droop, he murmurs against my ear, his warm breath tickling the skin, "I'm pretty sure you're the love of my life."

Well, if I don't fall asleep with a smile on my face after that.

"WHERE IS SHE?!"

Emilia's shout wakes me from the land of the dead the next morning—damn, those pain meds knocked me out—and I can't help but chuckle as I hear Hawk grumble a response, his voice too low for me to make out the words.

The two argue back and forth, and I feel Cam's chest rumble as he laughs. "Sounds like she's giving him hell."

"I should probably go save him."

Cam groans in protest as I disentangle myself from him and climb out of bed. Grabbing a pair of shorts from my duffle bag, I slip them on and snatch Beck's hoodie from yesterday off the floor on my way to the door.

"She's resting," I hear Hawk snap at Emilia as I walk down the hall, following the sound of their voices as they argue.

"I want to see her. I need to know she's okay."

"She's fine."

Emilia scoffs. "Like I'm going to take your word for it."

The two are standing at the front door, facing off against one another as I enter the room. Hawk's back is to me, so Emilia sees me first, her gaze moving to mine as her eyes widen and her mouth drops open in shock.

"Oh my god," she gasps, and Hawk turns to see what's gained her attention.

She shoves her way past him and throws her arms around me. "I have been so worried about you," she cries, squeezing me so tightly it hurts. I momentarily stiffen at the sudden contact, but after a second, I relax and return her hug.

When she eventually pulls back, her eyes roam over me, widening as she spots the cuts on my legs and the large bandage wrapped around my thigh.

"What happened to you? Where have you been?"

I grimace, looking past her to Hawk. He purses his lips but gives me a nod of encouragement before slipping down the hall, giving me some privacy to explain everything to her.

Taking her hand, I pull her with me over to the sofa and sit so I'm facing her. I chew on my bottom lip while debating how to tell her everything. It's all pretty fucked up, and I can only imagine how it's all going to sound to her.

When I take too long to start explaining, she sighs in exasperation. "Just spit it out. How bad can it be?"

Ha, if only she knew.

Taking a steady breath, I blurt out, "I grew up in a mercenary compound that I recently found out is owned by my parents. I was kidnapped as a baby by Cam's dad, in some revenge plan to get back at my parents, but he developed some sort of fucked up attachment to me while holding me captive. I escaped, but Michael lured me into a trap with Cam's dad, and he kidnapped me *again*. But the guys rescued me. Oh, and I killed Cam's dad."

By the time I'm finished, Emilia's mouth is wide open, and I can see the whites of her eyes. She gapes at me, speechless for probably the first time in her life.

"Michael?!" she eventually screeches, making me huff out a laugh. *Of course, that's the part she focuses on.* Color works its way into her cheeks and tight lines form around her eyes as they narrow. Her lip curls back and she jumps to her feet, unable to sit still as she paces back and forth in front of the sofa. "That asshole! Do you know he's been walking around here like he doesn't have a care in the world?" She waves her arms around her in fast movements that match the rapid pace of her words. "Oh my god!" she exclaims. "All those times I told him how worried I was about you." She barks out a caustic laugh, upping her pacing as she wears a path on the hardwood floor. "He pretended to be fucking there for me—telling me not to worry about you. He fucking *hugged* me." She's snarling like a rabid dog by the time she's done, making me dizzy with her back and forth.

"You, uh, don't have anything to say about the other stuff I told you?"

"Huh?" She spins to face me. "Oh, uh…" She pauses, eyeing me critically before she moves back over to reclaim her seat on the sofa. Reaching out, she clasps my hands in hers. "You're going to be okay, right?"

Her eyes show genuine concern, and I swallow roughly before plastering on a watery smile. "Yeah." I smile coyly. "They might have bent me a little, but they'll have to do more than that to break me."

She smiles placatingly, but I can tell she doesn't believe the lies I'm feeding her. Squeezing my hand in reassurance, she says, "Your past doesn't change anything for me. I love you for you." Her eyes soften. "I'm so sorry for whatever you had to go through and for being robbed of a life you should have led, but don't think you're going to scare me off with all your baggage. You're not getting rid of me that easily."

One side of her mouth lifts in a rueful smile, and I can't help but smile back as I lean in to hug her. "Thank you."

"Please tell me you've got a plan to deal with Michael?"

"Oh, we do," Mason practically growls out the words as he comes striding into the room. Despite the anger on his face, his eyes soften when they land on me.

He comes toward us, kissing my temple before dropping onto the couch beside me and pulling me into his lap.

"We do?" I question. It's the first I'm hearing of any plan.

"We'll deal with him, and you just rest."

I scoff. *Yeah, right, like I'm going to miss out on the asshole who betrayed my friendship getting what he deserves.* "Not happening. If you're planning something, I want to be there."

"Me too," Emilia tacks on. Mason sighs, but before he can protest, Emilia speaks up to argue her case. "He betrayed us both. He pretended to be our friend, then stabbed Hadley in the back." I can see her getting worked up again as she clenches her fists and glares daggers into the couch cushion. A pained expression crosses her face. "I blamed you guys for doing something to her. When all along, it was *him*. Fucking duplicitous shitstain."

Mason is silent for a moment. "I don't blame you for thinking that. We were pretty horrible to Hadley when she first showed up, and no doubt we came across as suspicious when she disappeared. Hopefully, you can understand now why we couldn't tell you anything."

"Yeah," Emilia sighs heavily. "I get it."

"We're still not missing out on whatever you have planned for Michael, though." I cock a brow at Mason, silently daring him to stop us from coming. He returns my look with a hard stare of his own, which lasts all of a few seconds before he gives up and rolls his eyes.

"Fine."

"I want a go at Michael," I state after dinner that evening. The six of us are gathered around the island, and the second the words leave my mouth, all eyes focus on me.

"No," Hawk snaps, getting up to set his plate in the sink, as if somehow leaving the table ends the conversation.

"I wasn't asking for permission, asshole. I'm telling you. I don't want to just stand and watch you guys deal with him."

Hawk spins around to glare at me. "You're in no state to be beating the shit out of him."

I scoff, highly offended at his weak impression of me. I mean, he *might* be right—but that is totally beside the point.

"Have you forgotten who I really am? You have no idea what I am capable of."

Hawk's deadpan stare holds me in place. "I'm sure you could obliterate him in ten different ways, but just because you can, doesn't mean you should."

"Babe," Mason interjects softly. "That fucker isn't going to be walking away from tonight. Just let us handle him for you, and you can watch." He stares deep into my eyes before uttering the final words that leave me with no room to argue, "Please. All of us need to do this for you."

I sigh, dropping my shoulders in defeat. "Fine," I relent. "But I want to talk to him first."

"Why?" Hawk sounds exasperated as he throws his hands up in the air.

"Because I'm the one he wronged," I snap back, anger making me raise my voice. "I can count the number of friends I have ever had on one fucking hand, and he was supposed to be one of them. I—" My voice breaks as emotion clogs my throat. "I need to know why he did it."

The room falls silent for a second, before Hawk reluctantly relents.

"Well, now that the subject's been brought up, can we talk about the fact you're a real-life fucking assassin?" Excitement colors Cam's voice, and when I turn to look at him, the shock and horror I expected to see are nowhere to be found. In fact, he looks seriously impressed, like it's somehow cool to be a trained killer.

"Cam," Beck chastises.

I glance around at the others, confused. "You're seriously not put off by, uh, what I am?"

"Baby!" Cam exclaims. "Didn't you hear me? You're a fucking badass. I have never been more turned-on in my life than I am at the thought of you going all ninja on some douchebag's ass."

"Fucking hell, Cam. I don't need to hear that shit," Hawk snarls, looking thoroughly disgusted.

Cam ignores him as he leans in to kiss my cheek, whispering in my ear, "Maybe you can get all dressed up in some tight leather pants for me and go all assassin on my ass."

I gape speechlessly at him as he laughs and plants another quick kiss on my lips. *I'm not even sure what the fuck that means.*

Once I've gathered my wits again, I glance at Hawk, Mason, and West and hesitantly ask, "What about you guys?"

"I'm with Cam, I think it's hot." Mason shrugs, not noticing or deliberately ignoring the threatening look Hawk throws his way. He must see my unasked questions, as he explains. "I like knowing you can look out for yourself if one of us isn't around. It made me feel better when I knew you could fight, but this is on a whole other level."

"Same," West agrees. Leaning in, he places his warm palm on top of mine. "It doesn't matter to any of us. This wasn't something you chose for yourself, and we know you're nothing like those guards or the kids they successfully turned into soldiers. Somehow, you were able to hold on to your humanity. You've learned to trust and let people in—"

"Yeah." I scoff. "I let Michael slip right past me."

"That's not your fault," Hawk insists in a tone sharpened with anger. "That's all on him. He *pretended* to be your friend."

"Don't let one misjudgment undo all the hard work you've achieved," West implores. "And don't, for one second, think finding out about your past changes things for any of us."

I smile fondly at him before Cam speaks up again, looking slightly hesitant, "Can we, uh, ask questions about the sorts of jobs you did or what you can do?"

"Umm, yeah, sure," I agree hesitantly, not entirely sure how much of my life at the compound and what I was made to do I'm willing to share with all of them.

"Were they all jobs where you had to kill your mark?"

"For the most part, but sometimes we were sent to get information from people or scare them."

"How would you do that?" Hawk asks, his head slightly tilted to one side, seeming genuinely curious about my answer.

"There are lots of different ways. I'd usually start off with verbal threats and show them various tools I could use to hurt them. If that wasn't enough, I'd move to carving flesh wounds in their bodies or breaking their fingers. You just keep escalating until they eventually give in…or they die."

My words are met with a shocked silence before Cam asks, far too excitedly, "How many ways do you know how to kill a man?"

I begin to count them in my head, before realizing it's way too many. "At least one for every day of the year."

"Fuck, that's hot," he murmurs, shifting in his seat and reaching under the table to adjust himself in his pants.

"Fucking gross," Hawk snarls at him. "If you can't keep it in your pants, then this conversation is over."

I'm both confused and loving the fact that Cam finds the fucked up shit I can do such a turn-on. But I have to say, out of all of them, I'm surprised he's the one who seems so excited by it. Sure, there's a darkness in him, but it takes a lot to set him off and given everything he's been through this year, part of me expected him to be done with me when he discovered the truth. I genuinely thought it would be too much for him to handle. Of course, I should have known better. When Cam decides something is worth his time and energy, he gives it everything he's got, and for some reason, he's decided I'm worthy.

"How did they stop you from just running away when you were out on jobs?" West asks, moving the topic along.

"We weren't allowed out until we were older and had proven our loyalty to them. Even then, a guard was always assigned to watch over me, since I was Lawrence's little pet." I sneer in disgust, the guys' expressions matching my own.

"Fuck, if that asshole wasn't already dead, I'd kill him myself," Hawk bites out, and every single one of my guys murmurs their agreement.

"Hello, Michael," I greet with a bright smile, stepping out from behind a bush into his path as he leaves the library for the night, acting like we're still friends and I haven't been to hell and back in the last few weeks.

"H-Hadley?" His eyes dart nervously around us. "Wh-what are you doing here?"

"I just had a quick question for you."

His face is panicked, and his eyes never rest on me for more than a few seconds before they bounce away again. I'm not sure whether that's because he can't bear to look at me, knowing the part he played in Lawrence's plan, or because he's worried he's about to be jumped.

"Oh, uh, o-okay?"

"Why?"

His gaze jumps back to mine, wide-eyed and terrified, before he quickly glances away again. "W-why what?"

I step in closer to him, and he steps back, desperately trying to maintain the distance between us.

The friendly expression drops off my face, quickly replaced with hardened eyes as I channel Hawk, donning his resting bitch face—which is pretty fucking terrifying—and glower at Michael.

"*Why* did you do what you did?"

"I don't—"

I take another threatening step toward him, cutting off his words as he scrambles back a step away from me. "*Why* did you drug me? *Why* would you betray our friendship like that? *Why* would you do what Lawrence fucking Rutherford tells you to?"

He shakes his head frantically, mumbling something I can't make out. Before he can react, I jump forward, closing the distance between us and wrap my hand around his tie, yanking him toward me.

"What the fuck did I do to you that you thought it was okay to hand me over to that psychopath?" Spittle hits his cheeks as he stares petrified into my eyes.

"I-I didn't kn-know what he w-would do," he stutters pathetically. "He…he said he j-just wanted t-to talk."

"Please," I sneer. "You drugged my fucking coffee. If that's not malicious intent…"

His eyes narrow, and I catch a flash of something I've never seen in him before. A jealous darkness that he's managed to hide. His lip curls back in a snarl, and I'm momentarily stunned as his face seems to change before my eyes.

"You waltz in here and get everything handed to you. Then you string me along like I'm a fucking dog—flirting with me one second, then running off to fuck one of the Princes the next."

What the actual fuck is he talking about?

"You were supposed to be one of us, but just like every slut in here, you had to go and fall for the fucking Princes. Sucked in by money, like every other greedy whore."

My palm cracks him across the face. I have heard enough of that crap from Lawrence; I'm sure as fuck not about to take it from this sorry sack of shit.

"Jealousy is not a good look on you, Michael. Nor does it give you the right to have me handed over to a fucking psycho to be tortured and threatened."

Something flashes behind his eyes too quickly for me to register, yet the dark scowl on his face never lessens. I hear footsteps as the others close in around us, and I lean in with a malicious smirk and whisper, "I'm going to enjoy watching them tear you limb from limb."

His eyes widen, and the dark expression melts away as fear takes hold. "W-what?" he screeches, squirming in my grasp until Mason's large hand claps down hard on his shoulder.

"Good to see you again, Michael."

The pathetic shit begins to tremble, his eyes darting from face to face as he takes in the ring of muscle surrounding us.

"N-no. I didn't know," he cries.

No one pays him any attention as Hawk and Mason pin him between them and march him toward the forest. The rest of us form a tight circle around them, Emilia on one side and Wilder on my other.

I feel like a fucking god as Michael's screams for help are ignored by passing students, everyone looking away as we pass them, proceeding on our death march into the night.

CHAPTER 9

Mason

I CRACK MY KNUCKLES MENACINGLY AS THE EIGHT OF US FORM A circle around Michael. The worthless fuckhead is already on his knees, crying like a baby and begging for mercy, like the pitiful sap I always knew him to be.

Thanks to the cloudless sky above, there is enough light from the moon to light up the clearing, eliminating the need for flashlights tonight and adding a macabre feel to the whole ordeal. Fitting, considering this piece of human trash is about to wish he was never born. No one—and I mean fucking *no one*—crosses the Princes, and messing with Hadley is something none of us will stand for.

"Please," he blubbers. I roll my eyes, *fucking pathetic.*

"Jesus Christ," Hawk snarls. "Be a fucking man and stand up."

He doesn't even try to get to his feet, too busy looking between each of us, hoping he'll find a sympathetic face—he won't. Hawk, West, Cam, Beck, and I look like the harbingers of death as we tower over him with stone-cold expressions, while Wilder wears his usual psychotic fucking grin. The dude gets way too much enjoyment from watching others suffer. The rest of us do this shit because we have to, because it's necessary, but Wilder fucking revels in it.

Wilder huffs impatiently when Michael shows no signs of getting to his feet on his own. "Dude, you're killing my buzz. Get the fuck up." Not giving Michael a second to obey, he stomps into the circle, grabs Michael by the hair and all but drags him to his feet, screaming and crying. *Well, that's one way to go about it.*

"Please, Hadley," he pleads, turning imploring eyes on my girl. "I didn't mean to. I-I didn't know—"

"Don't fucking talk to her," I snap, my menacing tone making him jump. "Don't even fucking look at her."

My Little Warrior is so fucking strong, standing there with her back ramrod straight and her chin in the air, her signature *fuck off* expression on her face.

Emilia stands at her side, looking equally repulsed as she scowls at Michael.

"Emilia," he pleads, trying to gain her sympathy next. "Don't listen to them. They've got it all wrong. I didn't do anything."

He starts toward her, and as he reaches out a hand to grab her, Hawk intercepts and grabs him by the neck of his shirt and hauls him back into the center of the circle. "Don't fucking touch her, either. Emilia's one of us. She's not going to fall for your pathetic act." Standing over a head taller than Michael, he sneers down at him, "You know what you did, why you're here. Accept your punishment like a fucking man."

Without further delay, he swings his arm back and drives it into Michael's face. I hear the sweet sound of a bone snapping, quickly followed by a howl of pain. Fucking music to my ears.

I let Hawk get in another few blows before I step forward,

needing to sate my own anger before the fucker becomes unconscious. Seeing me, Hawk steps aside, and with a shit-eating grin on my face, I take up where he left off. I plow my fist into his nose, snapping the cartilage, and blood rushes over his face. My next hit is aimed at his stomach, following several more to his ribs. By the time Beck moves to take over, I'm sure he's got a few broken ribs to match his broken nose.

Blood is splattered over my top and dusts my knuckles, and as I stare down at my hands, I feel more satisfied than I ever remember feeling after a fight. There's something about fighting for vengeance that makes it all the more gratifying, and correcting any wrongdoing against Hadley makes it sweeter still.

Cam takes his turn after Beck, followed by West. He might not have the same power behind his punches as the rest of us, but he more than makes up for it with the palpable rage pouring off him.

By the time it's Wilder's turn, Michael is a curled-up ball on the ground. Usually, I'm not one to beat on a man when he's down, but in this case, that fuckface deserves every second of pain he's experiencing. He deserves to feel every moment of suffering Hadley endured over the last two weeks. We haven't gotten any details out of her yet, but the new scars marking her body tell enough of what she's had to survive.

Wilder starts kicking Michael, and just as he appears to be getting into the swing of it, Hadley shouts, "That's enough!"

Surprised, I glance over at her. There's a pained expression on her face, and she's squeezing Emilia's hand tightly, yet I don't think her reaction has anything to do with Michael.

"But—"

"Hadley's right," Hawk snaps, talking over the top of Wilder. "He's had enough."

Stomping over to Michael's bleeding, curled-up body, I crouch down in front of him. "Hey!"

He groans but doesn't open his eyes. "Hey! Don't pass out on us yet," I snap more harshly, smacking him on the cheek. The surprise sting spikes his adrenaline, and his eyes jump open. He blinks several times, struggling to focus on me, but I don't need him to see me; I just need him to hear what I have to say. I lean down, getting as close to his ear as possible. "If you tell anyone or show your face back here again, we'll tear your entire fucking life apart."

I take his responding groan as an agreement that he'll heed my warning. "Glad we understand each other." I give his cheek a condescending pat and stand up.

"Uh, what now?" Emilia asks, frowning at Michael's unmoving body.

We all look at one another, expecting someone else to have an answer to her question.

"Ugh, fuck me," Wilder groans, tilting his head back and rolling his eyes like the dramatic weirdo he is. "Put him in my backseat. I'll drop him off at the hospital and say I found him like that in town."

We all share a look, and I shrug my shoulders. "Sounds like as good a plan as any. I'll help him get Michael to the car, and then we can meet you back at the dorm."

Between the two of us, Wilder and I haul Michael off the ground, none too carefully, and drag him back through the forest. Parting ways with the others just before the forest meets the campus pathways, Wilder and I remain hidden in the trees until we're near the parking lot.

Once we reach his Mustang, he fishes his keys out of his pocket and unlocks the back passenger door, so we can maneuver the passed-out shithead into the back seat.

I *accidentally* knock his head against the top of the door as I shove him into the car. "Oops, my bad."

Wilder chortles ridiculously. "Don't get any blood over my seats, asshole."

"Dude, he's unconscious."

Wilder quirks a brow at me. "So? That's no excuse. Do you know how difficult it is to get blood out of that upholstery?"

I gape at him for a second before shaking my head. "I don't want to know."

He laughs and slams the back door shut.

"You good here?"

"Yeah, man. You go back to Sunshine. I'll make sure he doesn't die."

"Thanks, man." I tap my finger against the hood of his car as I pass and make my way back through campus to the dorms.

I feel like a weight has been lifted off my shoulders. I knew I never liked that fucking dweeb. The way he'd look at Hadley always got my hackles up, but Jesus, I never thought Lawrence would get his claws into him. It doesn't matter that he doesn't know what Lawrence is capable of, he had to have known what he was doing wasn't right. There's no excusing what he did. Hopefully, with him and Lawrence gone, this campus should be a safe place for Hadley. Now we just need to sort out the rest of our fucked up families then we might actually have a shot at a free life for all of us.

Walking back into the dorm, I find Hadley, Beck, and Cam on the sofa, with West sitting in a nearby chair. The four of them are chatting away like it's any other night, and a smile brightens my face as I stand and watch them. This is what I want to come home to every night—my best friends and the woman I love. I've never been able to picture a future for myself other than the unwanted one my parents set out for me. Still, everything's changing, and now that we've found Hadley, and Beck has joined our ranks, I'm starting to see a different future, one that I actually want.

"Hey, man," Cam greets, when the door closes behind me. "There's beer in the fridge."

Grabbing a bottle, I join them in the living room. "Where's Hawk?"

"He walked Emilia back to her dorm."

I quirk an eyebrow at West, who just shrugs. *That's strangely thoughtful of him.*

"Well, now that the violence of the evening is over, what are the plans for the rest of the night?" Beck whacks Cam around the back of the head, and the idiot just laughs.

"I think we're long overdue for a chill night on the sofa with popcorn and a movie," Beck responds instead.

"Mmm, that sounds good," Hadley agrees.

Lifting Hadley's legs off him, Cam gets up to sort out the popcorn and West flicks through the films. I take advantage of the open seat beside Hadley and slip into it, draping my arm over the back of the couch cushions.

Hadley watches me. "Can I try some of that?" she asks, pointing at my beer.

"Uh, you sure?"

"Yeah. I'm curious. I had a sip of champagne once with Emilia and—" She pauses, unwilling to say his name before changing direction. "Well, it was nice, so now I'm wondering what beer tastes like. Besides, I think I deserve a drink after the last few weeks." She laughs, but there's no humor behind it, and it quickly falls flat.

"What about the pain meds you got at the hospital?" I question, knowing it's not wise to mix the two.

"I only got a couple of days' worth. They're all gone now."

I hand over the beer, and she sniffs the bottle before bringing it to her lips and downing a large gulp. "Huh, not bad." She takes another long swig before passing it back. I'm barely paying attention as she pushes the bottle into my hands, too busy watching her. I take in the bags under her eyes, the dampened color of her irises, and the hard edge to her that I haven't seen in quite a while.

"You know, you don't have to be so strong all the time. It's okay to not be okay. You've been through more than most people experience in a lifetime. It's alright to take some time and just process it all."

"I'm fine. I'll *be* fine."

There's a determined set to her jaw, that newfound hardness solidifying further. I'm not sure if she's trying to fool herself or me, but I don't push her. If that's what she needs to tell herself, then so be it. I—*we*—will be here when the words are no longer enough to hold her together. For now, I pull her in against me, kiss her forehead, and hope I'm not losing the one thing that makes me feel alive.

***

PRYING MY EYES OPEN THE NEXT MORNING, I GROAN WHEN THEY LAND on Cam's sleeping face, lying on my goddamn pillow. So fucking close I can smell his god-awful morning breath. *Fucking gross.*

Sitting up, I'm surrounded by half-naked men. *Jesus, fuck, what has my life become?* Hadley's gone, and when I check my phone, it's not even five a.m. yet.

Climbing out between the sleeping bodies, I pull on a pair of sweats and saunter through the apartment, quickly realizing she's not here. When I check her bedroom, I notice her gym bag is gone. *Damn woman doesn't know the meaning of rest.* Huffing out a sigh, I grab my own bag and head out the door after her.

As I walk into the gym, I pause in the doorway and watch as she beats relentlessly on a bag. Sweat coats her skin, and it's obvious she's been at it for a while. Regardless, she delivers blow after blow like she's not the slightest bit tired. The way she attacks the bag, she's like a woman possessed, and I'm pretty sure I know what demons are chasing her. I just wish I knew how to help her.

"Are you here to work out or watch me?" she pants breathlessly. I don't know how the hell she knows I'm here, with her back to me and all of her concentration on the bag.

"Can't I do both?"

She puffs out a laugh, dropping her arms and taking a step away from the bag to grab her water bottle. She watches me over the lip as I move to the weights bench and get set up. Seeming satisfied that I'm not here to keep a close eye on her, like I imagine Hawk would do if he knew where she was right now, she gets back to work.

Stepping up to the bag, she rolls her shoulders back and

swings her arms. She moves into a wide stance, centering her weight before starting another punishing round of punches. I notice she's favoring her right leg, though, and despite the determined look on her face, she's sweating more than usual.

I watch her as I go through my usual morning routine, and when she shows no signs of letting up, I decide I need to interfere before she hurts herself.

Swiping a towel over my face, I move over to the mats.

"Little Warrior," I call out, "come spar with me." She stops and turns to look at me but doesn't move or respond as she debates what to do. "Come on. This is probably the only shot I have of beating you."

She scoffs. "Even with my injuries, you have no chance of beating me."

She still doesn't move, and I soften my features, pleading with her. "Just get over here. Trust me, hitting a bag isn't going to rid you of that anger. You need a human outlet. To hit flesh and bone and feel the damage you inflict beneath your own hands."

My words break through that hard exterior she's erected around herself since she got back, and for a second, I see the real Hadley hiding beneath it all. She's putting on a brave face, acting like everything is okay, but that can only last so long. She has to work through everything she's feeling and struggling to process.

The only thing that worked for me was fighting. I *had* to find a physical outlet for my anger, or it would have eaten me alive. Every time I felt an opponent's skin break beneath my own, their blood coating my hands, it was like I could breathe again. That insurmountable rage abated, at least for a while, and so long as I pretended every blow I delivered was directed at my father, I could find some sort of inner peace. I couldn't attack the source of my problems, so I used surrogates.

Hadley and I are alike in that way. I can see the flames of anger in her eyes, and if she's not careful, all that animosity will burn her alive. It'll consume her, until it becomes all she can think about. Dream of. Live for.

She moves toward me, until she's standing opposite me on the mat. "You better fight back this time, Hayes."

I smirk back at her. "Don't you worry about me, Little Warrior. Just focus on not letting me kick your ass."

She barks out a laugh and lunges toward me. Going straight in for a jab, she jumps back out of my arm span before I can retaliate.

We go round after round, neither one of us going easy on the other—okay, I definitely hold back a little, but I'm not about to tell Hadley that. Every punch she delivers is precise and well-balanced, delivering maximum damage but with the least amount of impact to her hands and wrists. She grits her teeth, and there is a determined set to her jaw. I can feel the fury burning off of her with every hit she lands, and see the flare of triumph every time she one-ups me. I've never been up against such an experienced opponent, and damn, if I'm not seriously turned on right now.

I'm blaming it on the fact that all the blood in my body has rushed south as to why I get distracted and give her the in she's been waiting for. She slips past my defenses, swooping my legs out from beneath me, and before I can comprehend what happened, I'm flat on my back on the mat. She stands over me with a smug smirk on her face, even as she pants heavily.

"What was it you were saying, Hayes? Something about kicking my ass?"

"No need to rub it in," I grumble, holding out my hand for her to help me. When she slaps her hand in mine, instead of letting her pull me to my feet, I tug her down on top of me and roll us over so she's pinned beneath me.

As I look down at her, I'm pleased to see a lightness in her eyes, and she appears more herself than when I first walked in. I don't know how long it will last, but if I've been able to bring her peace for at least a little while, then that's something.

Her hands slide up over my chest before she winds her arms around my neck and pulls me down until my lips brush hers. *Fuck.* It's been way too long since I tasted her lips on mine or felt her soft curves beneath me. I'm wholly lost in her touch. The second her tongue sweeps into my mouth, it's as if nothing else exists. My hands slide into her hair as I return her kiss, my tongue tangling with hers until we're both breathless.

Everything in my body is encouraging me to keep on, but I force myself to slow down—which is seriously fucking difficult, especially when she starts grinding against me.

"Hadley." The word is a half pant, half groan.

Ignoring me, Hadley hitches her leg over mine, using the momentum to turn us until she's hovering over me. She presses her finger against my lips. "Shh, don't talk." Leaning down, she kisses me again while she slips her hands under my muscle shirt and pushes it up my body until she can tug it off over my head.

My hands land on her hips as I look up at her reverently. I still can't believe she's here, that she survived. That I got so lucky as to find this amazing spitfire of a girl in this crazy, fucked-up world. I slide my hand into her hair, holding her still as I pillage her mouth, and roll us again so I'm settled between her spread thighs.

I grab her thigh and hitch it over my hip, opening her more as I grind against her, making her head fall back as her eyelids close and she moans.

"Mason," she pleads in a breathless pant.

I kiss my way down her neck and over the swell of her breasts, pushed up by her sports bra, then along her toned stomach until I reach the high waistband of her lycra shorts. I tug them and her panties down her legs until she's left bare before me, pausing for a moment to just appreciate all of her. My eyes roam over her fresh wounds that will leave new scars, noting how prominent her ribs have gotten, and by the time I lift my head to meet her gaze, I imagine the fire in my eyes matches hers.

Crawling up her until I'm once again situated between her thighs, I slide my hand into her hair and kiss her deeply. "You're fiercely beautiful. I'm in awe of your strength."

She looks up at me with a rawness I've never seen before, and I realize, for the first time, she has stripped herself bare, and what I'm seeing is all the vulnerability she works so hard to hide.

"It's tiring, being strong all the time."

"Then don't be. Fall apart, baby. I'll be here to put you back together." I rest my forehead against hers so all I can see is the turbulent thunderstorm whirling in her eyes. Nothing else exists but her. "It's you and me."

She tilts her head so her lips meet mine. In that kiss, I can taste everything she's not ready to say yet. I can taste how lost she is, the hopeless void she's on the cusp of falling into, and I return her kiss with all the ferocity of someone begging her to hold on, to keep fighting, to stay with me.

"I love you." Her words are a quiet whisper against my lips before she captures them in yet another kiss. She wraps her legs around my waist, crossing them at the ankles and using her heel to push my shorts over my ass. Lifting, I tug them down and check she's ready, then I line my dick up with her entrance and slide into her. My eyes roll back in my head, and I let out a blissful sigh. This, right here, is the best feeling in the world. It's like coming home after being away at war. When we're one like this, everything I've had to endure to get here suddenly feels worth it.

She moans and her legs tighten around me, encouraging me further until I'm so deep inside her I won't ever want to leave. I can't tear my eyes away from her face as I pump lazily into her, and she watches me back with that same open and awed-expression, like she feels the same things I do when we're together. The air seems to crackle around us, filled with sexual tension and something so much more meaningful. Something everlasting.

I drink in the flush that rises on her cheeks, commit every breathless moan to memory, until she's falling apart beneath me, and I follow her over the edge, reiterating my promise to her: *I'll be here to put her back together.*

CHAPTER 10

Hadley

"What exactly do you think you're doing?" Hawk demands when I step into the kitchen later that morning, dressed in my school uniform.

"Eh, going to class? It is a weekday, after all."

"No, you're not. I've told your teachers you need another week off."

"No need, I'm all good."

"Firefly, you just got back. Why don't you take a couple of days to just relax? Chill on the sofa and watch some daytime television," West suggests, his tone more soft and coaxing than Hawk's sharp bark.

"Honestly, I'm fine. I have missed so much work, and I don't want to fall even further behind."

Hawk scowls at me for another moment before finally relenting. "Fine," he huffs out. "But don't overdo it, and stay with one of us."

"I don't need a babysitter," I seethe.

"Tough shit," he barks, sounding just as annoyed. "That's the only way I'm letting you out of this apartment."

"*Letting* me?"

West steps forward to stand between us, glowering at Hawk before turning to me, his eyes softening around the edges. "Please," he pleads. "We're all going to be stomping about like angry bears all day if we can't keep an eye on you."

My posture relaxes as I smile at him. "Of course. It's not like I'd want to spend the day with anyone else." His smirk grows, and we both ignore Hawk in the background as he throws his hands up in the air in exasperation and grumbles under his breath before stalking off like the grown man-child he is.

West moves to make me a cup of coffee, setting it down in front of me as I slide into a seat at the island.

"So, what have I missed?" I question, looking up at him over the lip of my mug. "I bet this month's girls are brewing up a storm over the fact that none of you have been around much the last couple of weeks."

West chuckles. "I bet they're more upset that we once again put a stop to the whole tradition."

My eyebrows climb up my forehead as my eyes widen. "You, what? When?"

"As soon as we got you back. We couldn't risk saying anything before then, and bringing any more trouble to our door, but we're fucking done with all of it now."

"But, what about our parents?"

West shrugs. "They're going to be too busy scrambling to rebuild the compound while freaking out over Lawrence's death and the company's future, to worry about what we're up to at school."

I gape at him for a moment before finding my words. "So it's done? For real this time?"

He leans across the island toward me, until he's so close I could just lean forward and kiss him. "Yeah, Firefly, it's done.

We're sick of hiding our relationship with you. I want the whole school to know you're ours."

I quirk an eyebrow and smirk. "You mean that you're all mine."

He grins and murmurs against my lips, "That too," before stealing my breath with a dirty kiss.

Half an hour later, we're making our way to the dining hall. My palms are slick with sweat, and my body tense as my eyes dart around our surroundings. I'm not even sure why I'm nervous. My uniform covers all my healing cuts and new scars, and other than being the only girl wearing tights in May, I look like everyone else. Yet, my pulse is pounding so hard I can barely hear over the rushing of blood in my ears, and I feel like I can hardly breathe.

We pause outside the door to the dining hall, and I squeeze my eyes shut and take a few deep breaths to try and shake off the clawing anxiety threatening to overcome me.

The guys decided to send out a mass text telling everyone about the end of the tradition, so of course, since today is the first day they've all faced the school since then, it's guaranteed to be an epic shitshow. I can just imagine the carnage waiting to erupt behind these doors.

"Hey, guys, Sunshine," Wilder greets far too enthusiastically as he shoves his way between Mason and me, throwing his arm over my shoulder. "What are we all waiting for?"

"Get off her, asshole," Mason snarks, jamming his elbow into Wilder's ribs and shoving him backward before reclaiming his position beside me.

"Alright, man," Wilder wheezes from where he's hunched over, struggling to take in a breath. "No need to get violent."

He takes a minute to recover before standing upright, an obnoxiously bright smile lighting up his face as he stares at me. "Sunshine, good to see you back in your uniform again. Shame about the fake dating, though. I thought I made an excellent faux boyfriend."

"Dude, what the fuck is your problem?" Mason snaps. "You're just asking to get the shit beat out of you."

Wilder rolls his eyes, unbothered by Mason's growly tone or furious expression. "Calm your tits, big guy."

I fail miserably at holding back my laugh, as Mason's eyes narrow to slits.

"Hadley knows it's all in good fun."

I'm not sure that I do. I have no idea what Wilder really wants, but I find his honesty and the way he just blurts out whatever he's thinking without giving a shit what people have to say, refreshing.

"Come on, let's get on with this. It's been too long since I had pancakes, and I'm going to be a bitch all day if I don't get some before class starts."

"Sure you don't want a grapefruit instead? Much healthier start to your day." Hawk laughs at his own joke as I scowl at him.

"If you ever force a slice of grapefruit on me again, I'm going to ram it down your throat."

My threat only makes him laugh harder as he opens the door, and surrounded by my guys, the five of us walk into the dining hall. The whole room goes silent as everyone's eyes land on us.

Out of the corner of my eye, I notice Wilder slip in behind us and head over to Emilia before I turn to focus on the top table. I nearly stumble over my own feet when I find the most recent girls of the month sitting there, waiting.

"What the fuck?" I hiss under my breath to Mason. He doesn't say anything, and when I look up at him, his face is set in its usual stony expression, but I don't miss the tight set to his jaw or the anger burning in his eyes. He's just as pissed off about this as I am.

"What the fuck are you four doing here?" Hawk barks, not even trying to lower his voice. He doesn't give a shit if the whole school bears witness to him humiliating these pathetic girls.

"What are you talking about?" the one he's been "dating" asks, batting her eyelashes at him. "This is where we always sit for breakfast."

"Didn't you get our text?" Cam snaps irritably.

"Oh, that?" One of the other idiots giggles. "Wasn't that just some silly hoax?"

"No," Mason growls. "It wasn't."

The smile falters on the girls' faces for a second before they fix it back in place, but this time there's a sharp edge to them.

"You're joking, right?" Hawk's girl snaps. "There's no way you're doing this to us—*again*."

Hawk's jaw ticks, the only warning sign before he stomps the last few feet to the table. He grabs the back of the chair the girl closest to us is sitting in and drags it away from the table.

She screeches, but we all ignore her.

"Get. The. Fuck. Off. Our. Table," Hawk shouts, stomping to the next girl and doing the same thing. The last two catch on and scramble out of their seats before Hawk can reach them, the four of them scurrying off to sit elsewhere. His nostrils flare as he looks out over the rest of the hall, his turbulent gray eyes searing each and every person. "At the risk of repeating myself, this stupid, fucking tradition is over. For good. None of us are interested in dating you, fucking you, or doing anything else with you."

All three of my guys move to surround me—West on one side, Cam on the other, and Mason behind me, with his hand resting possessively on my hip. I feel his chest vibrating against my back as he speaks, his voice booming around the room in a declaration for all to hear, "We're dating Hadley. She's ours, and we're hers." Whispers immediately break out around the room. "Anyone who gives her any flack will answer to us."

I grumble under my breath about being able to take care of myself, and Cam nudges me in the ribs, smirking when I catch his eye.

"Ewww, like *all* of yours?" Bianca speaks up, wrinkling her nose in disgust as she glances toward Hawk, making her insinuation crystal fucking clear.

"What the fuck is wrong with you, Bianca?" Hawk snarls.

"Wait, hold on," Deke calls out, getting to his feet. "Her name's Hadley again? I thought it was Elizabeth."

"It's Hadley," I confirm forcefully, running my eyes over everyone else in the hall to ensure they understand me. I won't answer to Elizabeth, or any other name. If we're done with the pretense, I want to be done with it all. Fuck following the rules and doing what our parents want. I'm done hiding; done giving a shit.

Quirking a brow, Deke just looks baffled as he shakes his head, as if that will help him make sense of it all. "Jesus, your drama belongs on a shitty daytime TV show. I can't keep up with it all. One minute you're doing this or called that, and the next, it's something else. Who gives a fuck?"

I think that's the most insightful thing he's said all year.

"We give a fuck," Bianca snaps, the girls around her murmuring their agreements. "You've been messing us around all year. One scholarship girl can't just come in here and upend the whole system."

"Watch it, B," Cam growls in warning. "Hadley's a Davenport."

Hawk pins her with a ferocious look that brokers no argument. "Regardless, it's done. Get over it."

"What about you?" a girl asks. I vaguely recognize her as one of the girls Hawk chose back at the beginning of the school year, but I don't remember her name for the life of me. "If you're not dating *her*, then why are you not continuing the tradition?"

There's an underlying current of hope in her voice, and I can't decide if it's sad or just fucking desperate.

"Can't you all see how fucked up this tradition is? You offer yourselves up for us to fuck and throw away, and for what? We would never pick any of you to be anything more than an easy lay. Your ability to fuck our brains out has no bearing on any business decisions made by our parents. None of us are interested in any sort of relationship with shallow, vapid, social climbing brats."

Oh, wow. Hawk has gone full asshole. Even my eyes are rounded in shock as I stare at him. His nostrils flare as he glowers around the otherwise silent room before storming off.

Cam sighs beside me. "We should probably follow him."

"But pancakes..." I pout as my stomach grumbles in protest.

"Go check on him," Mason encourages. "I'll grab breakfast for us all." He winks at me, and I return it with a bright grin before he moves over to the kiosks to order food to go, and the rest of us make a hasty exit. As the door closes behind us, I hear the hall erupt into chatter.

Glancing around, I spot Hawk storming back toward his dorm. "Why don't you two help Mason with the food, and I'll go talk to Hawk."

"Sure." West gives me a quick kiss, and Cam wishes me good luck before I take off after Hawk.

"Hey!" I call out, but he doesn't turn around. "Asshole, don't make me chase after you."

That gets him to slow his pace, allowing me to catch up.

"Do you need a tampon?"

He stops in his tracks to stare at me in a mixture of confusion and disgust. "What?"

I point over my shoulder toward the dining hall behind me. "I figured that was a PMS bitch-fit you had back there."

"Ha ha," he snarks, rolling his eyes.

I grin. "I've discovered ice cream is the best thing in the world when I feel crabby. My personal favorite at the minute is peanut butter, but it changes like every week."

"I'm not PMSing!" he snaps.

I quirk a brow, unfazed by his outburst, and pull my tablet out of my bag, firing off a quick message while I wait him out. Eventually, he sighs, scraping his hand through his hair in frustration. "I'm just so sick of all this shit." He waves his hand around, indicating the campus. "I'd reluctantly resigned myself to the life our parents wanted for me, but with everything that's happened recently..." He trails off, shaking his head and huffing out another frustrated sigh. "Life's too short for me to be so fucking miserable all the time."

I shrug. "So, what will make you happy?"

At my question, he chuckles humorlessly. "That's the kicker. I have no fucking idea."

I knock my shoulder against his and lift one side of my lip in a soft smile. "I have no idea what makes me happy either. I don't even know where to start to figure it out." I notice the others coming toward us out of the corner of my eye, but I keep my focus on Hawk. "We could work it out together?"

He stares back at me for a long moment, and the guys have nearly reached us by the time he responds. "I'd like that."

"Like what?" Cam asks.

"I'd like to get some breakfast before my stomach eats itself," Hawk retorts, making Cam laugh.

"Why don't we eat on the grass?" Mason suggests, and we move to a grassy area just off the path. It's a gorgeous sunny morning, albeit it's spring, so the mornings are still on the chilly side, but it's nothing a warm breakfast and a cup of coffee can't fix.

Mason passes around the containers with each of our break-fasts in them. "Here's your ice cream," he says, handing me a tub and spoon. I thank him with a smile and pull off the lid, inhaling the nutty goodness before digging my spoon in. It tastes like fucking heaven in my mouth, and I struggle to hold back an obscene moan—pretty sure Hawk won't appreciate that.

Licking my lips, I pass the tub to Hawk beside me. He looks at it for a second, not immediately taking it from me. "I promise it helps." Leaning in, I add, "And where's a better place to start figuring yourself out than deciding your favorite flavor of ice cream?"

He still looks hesitant as he takes the tub and tries a small spoonful, before he smiles. "Mmm, that *is* pretty damn good."

Emilia and Wilder join us, and, even though I can't seem to relax, and my eyes dart anxiously around our surroundings, as if

I'm expecting an ambush at any moment, I feast on my pancakes like nothing's wrong and listen to everyone around me laugh and chit-chat. I wasn't lying when I told Hawk I don't know what makes me happy. I have no idea who I am, or what I want to achieve with my life, but I didn't tell him that I don't even know how to be happy or even think about a future when I'm struggling just to get through the day.

West nudges my shoulder. "You okay?"

I plaster on a fake smile. "I'm all good."

———

By the time math rolls around that afternoon, my head is pounding, and I'm exhausted from being on edge all day. I nearly jump out of my chair when Emilia drops her backpack on the table beside me.

"Jesus, do you have to be so fucking loud," I snap irritably, and immediately regret it when her eyebrows jump up to meet her hairline and her jaw drops open.

I blow out a breath and close my eyes for a second, trying to rein in my anger. "I'm sorry. It's just been a long day."

She casts her eyes over my face before slowly sitting beside me. "Sure. It can't be easy to be back here...after everything." She chews on the inside of her cheek as she internally debates something before she glances warily around and leans in to whisper in my ear. "I can't pretend to understand what you've been through, but you know if you ever need to talk, I'm here."

I smile softly. "I know. I'm good. I-I'd rather not relive any of it, however. It's in the past."

She nods in understanding, and the teacher starts the class, thankfully ending our conversation. I barely take anything in for the next hour. If I'm being honest, I haven't heard a word anyone has said all day. I'm struggling to focus. Every time I let myself relax into a lesson, my palms start to sweat, my heart rate picks up, and the little voice in my head questions whether or not any of this is real. Maybe I'm still locked in that cell or strapped to the wall in Bowen's torture room, and this is all just a hallucination.

I feel along the side of my thigh, identifying the stitches holding the two sides of the wound on my leg together, and press my fingers into them. My face scrunches in pain. *Real. All of this is real. I'm not dreaming.*

Now, if only I didn't have to keep telling myself that just to make it through the day.

CHAPTER 11

Hadley

Do you miss me, Dove?

I awake with a gasp, quickly sitting upright in the bed as I clasp my chest. With trembling hands, I reach out and flick on the bedside lamp. I can feel the pulse hammering at the base of my neck, as I work to calm my breathing. *You're safe. You're in your room on campus. You're not back there.*

I toss back my covers, noticing how my top sticks to my clammy skin as I get out of bed and throw on my gym gear, not bothering to check the time. I can tell by the lack of light coming through the window that it's not even dawn yet, but there's no way I can get back to sleep now. My mind is racing in tune with my pulse, and the only way I know to stop the thoughts is to exhaust myself at the gym. These few hours each morning have become my only moments of peace all day.

I don't know what's wrong with me, but when I'm not beating on a bag, or Mason, or pushing myself on the treadmill, I can't seem to focus. I've been snapping at everyone all week over the stupidest of things, and it's only getting worse, no matter how hard I try to hide it.

I push open the door to the gym and pull on the fingerless gloves Mason bought me. I drop my bag on the floor and quickly go through my warm-up routine, jumping up and down on the balls of my feet and windmilling my arms to loosen them up.

Once I'm ready, I fixate on the bag in front of me until I can clearly picture Lawrence's grotesque face—his too-bushy eyebrows, the way his nose curved slightly, the dimple in his chin—then I beat and beat and beat on that bag. The whole world fades around me. Nothing exists but Lawrence and me. This is the only time I feel in control, when I feel like *I* have all the power. The rest of the day, his ghost chases me around, whispering in my ear and taunting me from afar until I'm a strung-out mess. I can tell the guys are starting to worry. They keep asking if I'm okay, and the words *I'm fine* are beginning to lose all meaning.

I sense when he enters the room, the same way I get an inkling whenever he's nearby. It's like the air around him reacts to his presence, sparking to life. I respond to the change in the air like it's an extension of my own skin, yet I don't stop pummeling the bag. It's been the same all week. He stands and watches me for a while, before moving to the weight bench and going through his usual routine. When he's done with that, we duke it out on the mat, and I don't know what it is about us tackling one another, but when I'm facing off against him, drinking in his ripped abs and broad shoulders, I feel more like my old self. It's not the same feeling of control I get when punching the bag, but it's a different kind of contentedness. I can *almost* forget all the shit that happened to me. It's the same when I'm around any of the guys. The adrenaline that courses through my veins, creating a constant buzz just under the surface of my skin, seems to die down for a while, and I feel like I can breathe again.

But it never lasts long. Eventually, the fear seeps in, and I become consumed by runaway irrational thoughts. It's like an electrical typhoon in my brain that messes with the synapses and prevents them from firing properly.

By the time we're done with our workout, showered and ready for class, Cam is entering the apartment with breakfast for everyone. Since our showdown in the dining hall on Monday, we've avoided going back. Instead, Beck, Emilia, and Wilder join us every morning, and the eight of us enjoy a nice, peaceful breakfast before we have to leave and mingle amongst the prying eyes of the rest of the school.

Since Mason announced I was dating the three of them, the whispering and staring have gotten ridiculous. I can only imagine how bad it would be if they found out I was also dating the school counselor. I don't miss the whispered 'slut' when girls walk past me or the filthy looks guys throw my way. I don't even want to know what disgustingly dirty things they're picturing. Thankfully, none are brave enough to do anything more than whisper or leer.

A pounding I'm becoming far too familiar with has started up behind my eyes by the time lunch rolls around. I meet the guys at the dining hall to grab our food, and we take it to eat back in the dorm.

As I'm walking out of the hall, the guys behind me, Bianca stomps past and scowls at me. "If it isn't the Slut of Pacific Prep," she sneers.

I spin to face her, my fists clenching at my side.

"What the fuck did you just call me?"

"You heard me. Anyone's vagina that's loose enough to take three dicks at once is obviously a whore."

Cam snorts behind me, and I think I hear him mumble, "That's not how it works," before someone whacks him around the back of the head.

"What the hell is your problem, bitch? What the actual fuck did I ever do to you?"

"You ruined everything when you showed up here!" Bianca cries.

I roll my eyes. "Grow up, Bianca, and take responsibility for your actions. I didn't do shit."

"HE LOVED ME!" she yells, before breaking down in tears. "We were going to get married. Then *you* showed up, and he changed."

I quirk a brow at Cam, who rolls his eyes at her dramatics. "That was *never* going to happen, B."

"Not you!" she sneers. "Lawrence."

We all freeze. "Lawrence?" Cam repeats. "As in my *dad*, Lawrence?"

"Yes," she snaps. "We were in love."

Damn, I kinda feel bad for the girl. He was most definitely *not* in love with her. I'm pretty sure he was incapable of giving a shit about anyone other than himself.

"Then *she* showed up here, and he became as fucking infatuated with her as you idiots." She glares thunderously at me. *And my moment of feeling sorry for her disappears just like that.* "He'd make me style my hair like yours." Her lip curls back in disgust. "And call him Sir." She steps toward me menacingly, unaware of the precarious churning of my stomach. "It was *your* name he'd call out when he was balls deep inside me. You and that fucking magical pussy you have that makes men drool all over you like fools. You're like the Pied Piper of dicks."

Bianca looks like she's about to launch herself at me and claw my eyes out. Hawk must see the unadulterated hatred in her eyes as he pulls me back a step. "Is Lawrence your baby's father?"

Bianca's gaze jumps to Hawk, her menacing expression melting away as a fresh set of tears well up in her eyes. Her lower lip quivers. "He told me to get an abortion, but I couldn't. He was just worried because I was still in school. It wasn't part of the plan, but I knew that he would see it differently once I graduated and we were married, and he'd regret making me get rid of it."

"I have a brother or sister?" Cam gapes.

"Half," Bianca snaps, her hostility making Cam scowl.

"If you've been with my father this whole time, then why have you been chasing my ass all over campus, demanding I pick you every month?"

Bianca's tears quickly dry up and her snooty attitude re-emerges, making me question just how much of this whole act is genuine.

"Lawrence has been weird all year. While I was certain I could bring him back to me, I couldn't put all my eggs in one basket. Not when I have a child to take care of now. I figured if something happened and Lawrence left me, I could convince you to marry me instead." A conniving smirk lifts one side of her lips. "That would teach Lawrence not to mess with me."

Dear god, this psycho bitch is as duplicitous as Lawrence. Perhaps the two of them would have been perfect together.

Cam gawks at her, likely seeing for the first time just how crazy she truly is.

Bianca dismisses him, once again searing me with a look of disgust. "But you just had to dig your claws into him too. You're such a whore."

I shrug my shoulders. "What can I say? I love me some good quality dick."

I bite my lower lip, holding back my laughter when I hear Hawk mumble, "Gross," under his breath.

Bianca snarls, stomping her feet like the entitled brat she is. "Just give me Lawrence. You can keep these idiots, but Lawrence is mine!"

Cam hedges forward, as if he's trying to get closer to a feral cat, but is unsure if it will scratch him. "Bianca," he starts hesitantly, grimacing as he blurts out, "my dad is dead."

Bianca spins toward him with wide eyes. "Wh-what? N-no. That can't be right. He's just been angry with me the last couple of weeks, because I couldn't do what he wanted. But he'll get over it. He always does."

Cam glances at each of us with a pleading look, not knowing

what to say or do next. He needn't bother though, as Bianca, who's muttering to herself, pulls out her phone and dials a number that I'm assuming is Lawrence's. When he doesn't answer, she dials again, glowering at each of us with deadly eyes.

"You're lying," she snaps when he doesn't answer for the second time, dialing his number yet again as she shoves past us and away from the dining hall.

On Thursday, I'm on my way to my session with Beck when someone calls out my name. I turn to look over my shoulder, and I swear the world stops spinning for a second.

"L-Lawrence?" I squeak.

No. It can't be. I killed him.

I blink, and instead of Lawrence, I see Barton striding toward me. My breaths come in short pants and I swallow roughly as I glance around me, as if expecting Lawrence to jump out from behind a door or something.

What the fuck is happening to me?

"I've been searching for you everywhere."

I'm still looking nervously around me, but when he speaks, I try to shake off whatever the fuck that was and focus on him.

"I don't...What are you doing here?"

"Hawk hasn't been returning my calls, and I needed to talk to you."

I don't trust him, and his showing up here like this is just weird. It doesn't help that he looks nervous as he shifts awkwardly from foot to foot.

"I, uh...how have you been doing?" he asks.

"Fine."

An awkward silence passes between us for a second, and when he realizes I'm not going to divulge any more of my life to him, he jerks his head in some sort of a nod. "Good. Good. I'm glad. I, eh, wanted to give you this."

He holds out an inconspicuous white envelope, and I hesitate, reluctant to take it—or anything—from him. Seeing that I'm not going to accept whatever it is without more explanation, he says, "It's, uh, a bank card. I've set you up with an account and transferred funds over, so you've got the same as Hawk."

Frowning, and even less sure if I should accept it, I simply continue to stare at the envelope. "I don't want your money."

"It's your money. It's everything you would have had access to if you'd...you know." He looks away, unable to meet my eye as he cringes, leaving the rest of his words unspoken.

If I'd grown up under the Davenport roof, with my brother.

I'm still debating my response when I hear a door open behind me, and Beck's voice as he calls out. "Hadley?"

I turn to find Beck poking his head out of his office, his eyes darting between Barton and me. Straightening, he steps out and closes the door behind him, never taking his eyes off my father as he strides toward us. "What is going on here?"

Still clutching the envelope, Barton's hand falls to his side. "Ah, Beck. I just wanted to have a word with my daughter, in private."

Standing at my side, with his arms crossed over his chest, the edge of his tattoo sleeve creeping out from under his crisp white shirt, Beck stares deadpan at my father. "I'm afraid I can't let you do that."

Most likely shocked that someone has the audacity to say no to him, Barton stares surprised at Beck for a moment, before his brows pull together and his eyes darken somewhat. "I don't believe my family's business is any of your concern."

Beck takes a threatening step forward, and I can see him gearing up to tear Barton's head off. Before he can do any such thing, I place a hand on his arm and stop him, then look at Barton when I say, "Actually, it is his business. He knows everything." I can practically see the questions running rampant in Barton's head. "Besides, I'm not going anywhere alone with you. The last time I ended up alone with Lawrence, I was drugged and dragged back to Hell. God only knows what you'd try to do to me."

Barton's eyes bulge in shock, and the color seems to drain from his face. "What…I…No," he splutters, shaking his head as if the thought of him doing anything to me is outrageous. However, he's more than shown he doesn't give a shit about me.

I notice Beck glancing nervously around us, checking that no one else is around before he murmurs, "Why don't we discuss this in my office?"

I'm not fussed about being stuck in a small room with Barton, but he's here, and he's probably not going to leave until he's said whatever he has to say, so I guess I may as well get it over with. "Sure."

He holds his arm out, gesturing for Barton to go into his office, and we follow closely behind him. I haven't heard anything from him since he showed up in my hospital room. No doubt, he left and went straight to his buddies, to tell them all about what happened in the compound and of my little threat. So, the question is, what is he doing here now?

Hawk and I filled everyone in on Barton's little visit, so Beck is probably just as baffled by him showing up here unannounced as I am.

"What do you think he wants?" I whisper conspiratorially to Beck while keeping my eye on Barton as he moves to sit in one of the chairs in front of Beck's desk.

"No idea." He shrugs. "Guess we should find out."

Stepping into the office, I lean against the wall beside the door, refusing to move any further into the room when a threat lurks nearby.

Beck closes the door after himself and sits behind his desk, resting his arms on the table and pinning Barton with an assessing look. "What is this all about, Mr. Davenport?"

My father shifts in his chair to focus on me. "After, uh, what you said in the hospital, it got me thinking…about the night you disappeared."

The thought of finding out more about what happened to me perks my interest, and I straighten slightly against the wall, darting my gaze to Beck before focusing back on my father.

"Your mother and I were celebrating our wedding anniversary. We had a big party like we do every year." He sighs and shakes his head. "I honestly don't remember anything in particular about that night. It was just like every other party...until the next day, when I went into your room to check on you and Hawk...you were gone." There's a genuine look of sadness in his eyes and a heavy ring to his voice, but I refuse to let his show of grief bother me. "I looked everywhere and interrogated all house staff, but no one had seen you. Then I called a meeting of all four families.

"That morning, I couldn't get a hold of Lawrence, which isn't all that unusual. Nonetheless, he was the one who gave me the number for the private investigator."

"Why didn't you just go to the police?" Beck interrupts, frowning.

My father sighs, and I swear he looks years older than he did when he walked in here. "I wanted to. I argued with the others about it, but ultimately, we couldn't risk bringing the police in and having them dig too far into the company."

"Right, so you chose the company over your daughter. Real nice, *Dad*." He grimaces at my snarky attitude.

"Lawrence promised this PI was the best in the country. He said he'd do a much better job than the police—that this guy was my only hope of finding you." The last sentence is exhaled on a forlorn sigh, and despite my mental chant to not let him sucker me in, my heart clenches in my chest. Not so much for Barton, but for Elizabeth. Perhaps she could have been saved if he hadn't listened to Lawrence or done what the others wanted. I can see the same thoughts in Beck's regretful gaze.

"So I'm guessing Lawrence paid off the PI or something?" I ask the question in the same tone I'd use to ask about the weather, using it to mask my inner turmoil.

"I'm guessing so. At first, he'd update me on leads he had and show me pictures of girls who could be you, but nothing panned out. After a few years, he tried to convince me to stop. I wasn't ready to hear any of it, and I just kept throwing more money at him, but eventually, your mother gave me an ultimatum. She had managed to move on with her life—her own way of coping, I imagine—and I ultimately had to do the same. I still had Hawk, and I needed to focus on him."

"Except you didn't," I bite out angrily. "By the sounds of it, you were never around."

He grimaces, knowing he's been caught out. "It wasn't easy. Every time I looked at him, I saw you. It became easier to keep an eye on him from afar, but just because I wasn't always around doesn't mean he was ever far from my thoughts."

"He deserved better." I sigh, broken-hearted for the lives both Hawk and I lost out on.

Barton lifts his head, looking me in the eye for the first time since he walked in here. "You both did."

The office door bursts open, making me jump as Hawk stomps in, bringing with him a hurricane of emotions. He strides right over to his father, towering above him. "What the hell are you doing here?"

He doesn't wait for an answer, his gaze roaming around the room until he spots me leaning against the wall behind him. His eyes critically run over me before he meets my gaze, asking a silent question—*are you okay?* I nod, letting him know I'm fine, and he returns his intense stare to Barton, cocking a brow as his impatience wears out.

"You weren't answering my calls," Barton barks, "and I wanted to check on Elizabeth."

"Hadley," I interrupt, my sharp tone cutting across whatever Hawk was going to say next. Barton's gaze snaps in my direction, his brows pulling together in confusion. "My name is Hadley."

"No, it's—"

"Elizabeth died," I seethe. "It doesn't matter what happened, or why. The daughter you knew died a long time ago. I'm not her, and I'm never going to be."

Barton looks like someone tore into his chest and ripped his heart out. His face crumples, utterly grief-stricken, and he seems to sag into the chair, boneless.

I hear footsteps racing down the hall, and a second later, the others come running in, breathless as their eyes dart around the room to assess the situation.

Cam's wide eyes land on me, and he comes over, brushing a thumb over my cheek. I'm not sure what I look like to him, but it must be worse than usual, given the concern etched into his features. "He didn't hurt you, did he?"

I give him a soft, reassuring smile. "No," I assure him. "Not in the way you're thinking." He looks at me, bewildered, and I can see the unasked questions in his eyes. Thankfully he knows not to ask them, not here, and instead slips his hand into mine, leaning against the wall beside me as we survey the room.

I notice Barton looking at where our hands are joined, before Hawk's pissed-off growl garners his attention. "Why are you suddenly giving a shit?"

"Watch your tone, son! I have *always* given a shit."

"Right." Hawk scoffs. "Like when you didn't look for her for fifteen years, or when you signed a business contract that involved marrying her off to some guy she doesn't know. Were you giving a shit when you—"

"Alright," Barton snaps, a mixture of regret and anger flashing across his face. "I get it. I've failed as a father, but I have only been trying to do what I thought was right."

I've got no idea how the fuck he thinks that, and apparently neither does anyone else, based on the various *what the fuck* expressions the others are sporting.

"It's fine, Hawk," I mumble, but the words only seem to stoke the fire of his anger.

"It is not fucking *fine*, Hadley!"

I turn to face him, my lips pinched. "No, it's not, but it is what it is. Nothing's going to change what happened."

Hawk and I share a moment, thick with all the memories we should have shared, but underneath all that pain is our newfound solidarity and a strengthening of the promise to always be there for each other from here on out.

When he looks away, Hawk straightens his shoulders and fixes Barton with a hard stare. "Alright, well, while you're here, we need to talk about what you know…and what you've told the others."

Unbothered by the sudden tension that has leaked into the air and the menacing glowers he's receiving from each of us, Barton returns his son's arduous stare. "I haven't told the others anything about your involvement in what happened at the compound, or Lawrence's death." His gaze flicks briefly to mine.

"Why would you do that?" I question. I half expected him to go back to his wife and West's dad and tell them everything.

He looks incredulous, like he can't believe I even have to ask the question.

"You're my children, and as hard as it is to believe that Lawrence would do such a thing, if I'd known where you were, I'd have done *anything* to get to you."

Pretty words, but that's all they are.

"Even at the expense of your precious company?" Hawk sneers.

Barton sighs, sinking deeper into his chair. "I know you'll find this hard to believe, son, but I never wanted any of this. I argued against recruiting children for years, but they outnumbered me in the vote, and after El—uh—Hadley disappeared, I just gave up caring." He shrugs. "I let them do whatever they wanted."

Sounds like a great excuse to me—blaming everyone else and shouldering none of the responsibility yourself.

I share a look with Beck, and I can see he doesn't quite believe Barton either. "What is it you do want, then?" he asks, watching him closely.

Barton glances at Hawk, then at me before he responds, "I just want my family back together."

Yeah, I can't see that happening anytime soon.

Hawk and I share a look, and I can see he's trying to figure out if we can trust him.

When he focuses back on his father, he's got a serious, no-nonsense expression on his face. "As far as we're concerned, Lawrence is dead, and the compound has been destroyed. Do we have anything we have to worry about?"

"I'm not going to tell your mother, or Wilbert, any of this. If they ever found out..." He shakes his head, not finishing his sentence, but he doesn't need to. We might have burned their compound to the ground, but they still have plenty of mercenaries working for them that are away on jobs and live elsewhere. If they had any reason to suspect it was us, we'd be dead.

"Why wouldn't you tell your wife?" I question suspiciously.

"She's as invested in the company's future as much as the others. She's been making the decisions for our family and running things for a long time now. I'm essentially just the figurehead."

Looking at the others, I'm not the only one surprised by that statement.

"She and Wilbert are planning to rebuild. They think a rival company attacked the compound."

"A rival company?"

Barton quirks a brow at me. "The mercenary business is extremely cutthroat. You didn't think we were the only ones out there, did you? The high level of security was intended for more than keeping people in. We've had issues in the past with competitors taking out our people, so the working theory is that this was an escalation in their attempts to wipe us off the map."

"At least that works in our favor." West chews on his bottom lip as he thinks. "They won't have any reason to suspect us."

"As long as no one gives them a reason," Beck sneers, glowering at Barton in warning.

"I've already told you I'm not going to tell them anything," Barton seethes, getting angry.

"I'm sure you'll understand if we can't trust you," Hawk states bluntly, not sounding as though he gives a shit about whether or not his dad understands.

Barton presses his lips together, and I don't miss the hurt look that flashes across his face. "I get that. I never wanted you this involved, not in this side of things. Unfortunately, you'll have to continue to play along for now."

"For how long?" I snap. "They've been playing by *your* rules their whole lives. When do they—any of us—get to start living our lives, *our* way?"

I can't place the look in Barton's eye, but I'm surprised at the strength of the promise in his words. "I know you don't trust me, and I don't blame you. Play along a bit longer, and I *promise* I'll help you shut the whole thing down. Then you can do whatever you want with the rest of your lives."

CHAPTER 12

Beck

I don't trust Barton Davenport, and thankfully it doesn't look like anyone else does either, as each of us share distrustful looks after his little *promise*. He's just as likely to toss us under the bus to save his own ass.

Unfortunately, if what he's saying is true, that they're talking about rebuilding the compound, then we might have no choice but to rely on him. We thought that with the building destroyed, and both Lawrence and Frank out of the picture, we'd be fucking done with this bullshit. But of course, you have to chop the head off a snake to kill it. Unfortunately, this snake still has three heads left.

"Fine," Hawk eventually spits out. "But we do things *our* way." Barton doesn't seem pleased, yet he doesn't argue. "Oh, and just so you know, we're done with the tradition."

"But—"

"And I'm not marrying Wilder," Hadley throws in, ignoring Barton's protest.

"She's not marrying *anyone*," I growl out before he can get any ideas about setting her up with someone else. He looks at me in confusion before he tries to argue again.

"I don't—"

"It's non-negotiable," Mason interrupts this time, stepping closer to Hadley so his arm brushes hers. Her other hand is still clasped tightly in Cam's, and I can see Barton getting more confused by the second. It's almost comical.

Seeing that there is no point in disagreeing, he stops trying. "Alright." His gaze keeps bouncing between each of us, questions swirling around in his head, but wisely he doesn't ask any of them. Not long later, after placing an envelope with Hadley's name scrawled across it on my desk, he leaves.

It takes longer for me to kick the rest of the guys out, so Hadley and I can salvage what remains of her session—ah, who am I kidding, our hour is long since over. I just wanted time alone with my girl. I've hardly gotten any since we got her back, and I've heard from the others that she's not sleeping well, and she's been jumpy and on edge. All perfectly normal considering everything she has been through, but it just makes it harder for me to keep my distance from her and maintain this pretense. Especially now that the guys are being open about their relationship with her. I'm mature enough to admit I'm jealous. A few times I have spotted her with them on campus, with their arms wrapped around her, kissing her, and *goddammit*, if I don't want to claim her as mine too.

The second the door clicks closed behind the others, I drag her into my arms and kiss her like she's the oxygen I need to breathe. "I think we need to look at upping the number of weekly sessions you're getting."

She laughs, her warm breath brushing over my lips before she kisses me again. "I won't say no to that."

Before I can let my dick start calling the shots, I drag her over to the sofa and bundle her into my arms. For a long moment, the two of us just lie there. It feels surreal to have her back in my arms again. I tried not to think about the worst possible outcome while Lawrence had her, but it was impossible to stop the dark thoughts from creeping in. The possibility of never seeing her again, of never having another quiet moment together, or watching her face light up when she tries a new flavor of ice cream. There are so many firsts she has yet to experience, and I want to capture every single one of them. This spitfire of a girl hasn't had the chance to live yet, and I can't imagine what sort of person I would have devolved into if Lawrence had robbed her of the opportunity to find out.

"What's in the envelope?" I ask, pointing at where it's still sitting, untouched, on the desk.

Hadley sighs and turns her head toward the desk, a frown tugging down the corners of her lips. "Barton set me up with a bank account."

"Is that a bad thing?"

"I don't know. I don't want his money or to be tied to him in any way, and I definitely don't want to feel indebted to him."

"I wouldn't necessarily consider it *indebted* to him, but more as acknowledging what is rightfully yours."

She turns to look at me. "That's what Hawk says too."

"Well, you don't have to decide what to do about the money right now. Let's just focus on getting to the end of the school year."

We lapse into silence for a bit before I dare to ask, "How have you been coping?"

She lets out a long exhale at my question and focuses on her finger as it trails a pattern across my shirt for several minutes before responding.

"It's weird being back here. Everything feels so...normal. I'm not sure how to go back to the way things were before."

"No one is expecting you to just dive back in like nothing happened. You went through a trauma, it's natural for you to have trouble adjusting."

She just sighs and snuggles deeper into me. She's got such

solid protection barriers erected around herself that if you didn't know her as well as I do—as we all do—or be on the lookout for small tells, you'd think she had assimilated back into her regular routine without any issues. She's more standoffish than she used to be, and the defenses she had in place when she first showed up here have been reconstructed and reinforced with steel. It's like she's here, with us, but she isn't. A part of her is still trapped back in the compound, and I have no idea how to bring her back to us. I'm a school counselor, not a goddamn psychiatrist. I'm not equipped to deal with post-traumatic stress. I know enough to know that's what this is, and that I don't have the necessary training in cognitive therapy to help her. I'm afraid of pushing her too hard and making things worse, but equally, letting her struggle alone isn't going to help her either. So instead, I'm settling for some middle ground where *hopefully* she knows we are here for her, except I'm not pushing her to talk about anything before she's ready.

I roll us over so we're lying side by side on the narrow sofa and I can look into her eyes. "Whatever you're feeling right now is perfectly okay. It doesn't make you weak or less of a person. Taking another person's life can take a huge toll on you, mentally."

Hadley scoffs softly. "I've killed people before, Beck."

"This is different, and you know it. Lawrence wasn't just some nameless, faceless hit." I tuck a strand of hair behind her ear. "It's okay if you're happy he's dead or if you have mixed feelings. It's even okay to not know how you're feeling about it."

She lowers her eyes, but I see the sheen of tears before she blocks them from my view, and I pull her in against my chest, stroking her hair reverently.

"It feels so surreal," she murmurs. "I see him sometimes or hear his voice…it's like—I feel like I'm going crazy." Her words are a barely heard whisper, but they break my heart all the same, and I wrap my arms more tightly around her, kissing the top of her head.

"WE NEED TO TALK ABOUT HADLEY," I TELL THE GUYS ON SUNDAY night. Hadley is at her movie evening with Wilder and Emilia, and it's the first time since she's been back that I've had a chance to sit down with the guys and actually talk. I hate talking about her behind her back like this, but I don't see that there is anything else for it.

"We do," Mason agrees. "I'm worried about her. She's running herself ragged. She's at the gym for hours every morning, and last night I caught her sneaking out for a run after we all went to bed. I don't think she's sleeping, not that she will let any of us in to sleep with her."

"I snuck into her room the first night we got her back, but she's started locking the door." I can see the hurt in Cam's face and the worry in his eyes.

"She seemed okay the first couple of nights, but since then, she's been distant," Mason explains.

I mull over his words for a second before saying, "I think she's having nightmares, and she doesn't want us to know about them. The painkillers she was on when she first came home probably knocked her out at night, and now that she's no longer taking them, she's not able to sleep as well."

"It's not just nightmares, though," West mentions. "She's not herself. Someone's phone went off in computer class the other day, and she nearly jumped out of her skin. I could see it in her eyes, she wasn't there anymore. It was as if the noise triggered something, and she disappeared somewhere else for a few minutes. She shrugged it off but was distant for the rest of the day after that."

I chew on my bottom lip before deciding to tell the others what she confessed to me the other day. "She's seeing and hearing Lawrence." I feel like I'm betraying Hadley's trust by telling them, but honestly, I don't know what to do. I know they're just as worried about her as I am. If we have any hope of helping her, we need to work together, and to do that, we all need to know what's going on with her.

"What?" Cam looks paler than he did a moment ago. "But he's—"

"Dead," I finish for him. "Yeah, you and I both saw him. There was no surviving that."

"That bad?" West's nose scrunches.

"I'm pretty sure I could see his intestines."

"She was in some sort of trance when I arrived. It was as if she couldn't stop herself, and she just kept stabbing him."

I sigh. "I think she has PTSD from it all."

Cam nods thoughtfully. "Who could blame her? Anyone else would be a curled-up ball, rocking back and forth on the floor, muttering nonsense to themselves."

"What can we do to help her?" Hawk asks. There's a serious set to his jaw, and it would be impossible to miss the underlying anger. "I have tried getting her to talk to me, but all she ever says is that she's *fine*." He spits out the word like it's acid on his tongue.

"Same," Mason agrees, and West and Cam nod their heads as well.

I wipe my hand down my face, feeling exhausted and unsure. "I don't know. I'm afraid of us pushing her too far, and she snaps or has a mental break or something, but it's becoming pretty fucking clear that she's not coping."

Our conversation halts when the door opens and Hadley walks in. She pauses, seeing us all gathered in the living room, probably looking suspicious as fuck.

Her eyes narrow, and she tilts her head slightly. "What are you guys up to?"

"We're just trying to decide what to do about our parents, if they're going to rebuild the compound," Hawk explains, his lie coming out flawless.

"Oh." She walks over to us, and West moves over to allow her to squish in between us on the sofa. "What are you thinking?"

"I say we tell them to go fuck themselves," Cam states, crossing his arms over his chest and leaning back in his seat, like that solves the problem.

"Yeah, that will go over really well." I roll my eyes.

"Any chance they'll just leave us all out of it?" Hadley asks optimistically, but the look on her face says she already knows the answer.

"No chance. We know too much, and it's only our parents and Wilbert left."

West scoffs. "Yeah, and my dad's going to be fuck all help. All he gives a shit about is drinking and fucking."

"We need to stand up to them and tell them we're not taking their shit anymore," Hawk snarls angrily. "Without the compound, what can they really do?"

"They still have the adult mercenaries," Hadley wisely states. "They don't live in the compound."

"Lawrence was the one who dealt with them, though, right?" Hawk asks her.

"I think so."

"And you said the rest of our parents never really bothered with the compound or getting to know the mercenaries. So they are unlikely to have any of them in their pockets. It's not going to be as easy to just phone them up and ask for their help."

"True." Hadley chews on her lower lip as she thinks through what Hawk is saying. "It's still a risk, though."

"I don't care. I'm fucking sick of them ruling over me." Hawk shifts so he can lean forward in his seat, placing his arms on his knees and looking intently at Hadley. "The compound is gone. Lawrence is dead. I'm not going to let them be the next ones to dictate your life for you." He looks at each of us. "I say it's about time we *all* claim our lives back."

Glancing at the others, everyone has an equally determined look in their eyes as they nod in agreement. When my gaze fixes on West, he catches my eye, and with a steely resolve, he silently tells me he's ready to get out from underneath our father and start his own life.

"Alright," I agree. "I guess we're telling them all to go fuck themselves."

Cam whoops-whoops. "Told you that was an excellent plan."

TWO DAYS LATER, WE PULL UP OUTSIDE THE HIGH-RISE OUR PARENTS' legitimate business operates out of. It's my first time here, and I optimistically hope it will be my last. I have no issues with the legitimate side of their business, but I want no part in any of it— legal or otherwise. This corporate world is not for me, and I'm more than ready to wash my hands of it.

We climb out of the car, and I follow the others through the glass door and across the lobby, into an elevator, and up to the thirty-seventh floor.

"Boys," a young receptionist purrs, her eyes bouncing over us like she can't choose which one of us she wants to focus on. The only one who doesn't get a mental undressing is Hadley. "I didn't know all of you would be stopping by today."

"We're here to talk to our parents," Hawk says sharply, barely paying the girl any attention.

"Oh, well, they're busy right now."

"We don't mind waiting."

The girl pauses for a moment before she gathers herself. "Of course, follow me." This time her smile is tighter and less flirta- tious, as she leads the way down a hall.

We follow her into a large board room with an impressive view over the city.

"Can I get you anything to drink?"

We all murmur, "No thanks," but rather than leaving us to it, she walks over to Cam, placing her hand on his forearm. "I'm so sorry to hear about your father. If you need *anything*, just let me know." She trails her long fingernails down his arm, making it clear precisely what she means by that, before giving him one last lascivious look and leaving the room.

Cam's lip curls up in a sneer, and my gaze darts to Hadley, who is glaring daggers into the door where the girl disappeared. "Bitch," she mumbles under her breath, making me chuckle.

The others move to take their seats along one side of the large boardroom table, but Hadley and I hesitate a second before taking a seat each on either end of the row. Despite being told they were busy, we aren't left waiting long before the door is pushed open and all three parents stride in, wearing various expressions ranging from confusion, to anger, to curiosity.

"What's this all about?" Maria snaps. The three of them move to sit opposite us, and I don't miss how Maria nudges her husband out of the way so she can sit in the middle of the table. *Interesting.*

Her eyes assess each of us, lingering longer on Hadley before focusing on her son. Hawk takes the lead. Leaning forward, he rests his arms on the table and steeples his fingers as he eyes each of our parents.

"We understand you're planning on rebuilding the compound—"

"That's right," Maria cuts across, sounding more enthusiastic than she did a second ago as she misunderstands where Hawk was going with his little speech. "We'll be soon calling on all of you to help us get back on our feet. We will need to rebuild as quickly as possible. It's great to see you all so ready to prove—"

Hawk smiles tightly. "I'm afraid you've misunderstood why we're here, *Mom.*" Maria's eyebrows lift and her lips thin. "We're done with all of this. We don't want a part in any of it. Taking over this company was never something any of us wanted, and we certainly never wanted to run some fucked up organization that snatches children off the street and forces them to become trained killers."

Maria's gaze roams over Hawk's face. She never once looks away from him. Instead, she leans in, matching his pose. "Is that so, son? And what makes you think you can just walk away from your legacy? You have no money, prospects, and apparently no common sense." Now she turns her steel-cold gaze on each of us. "Have you all forgotten what we said would happen to West if any of you stepped out of line? Maybe you need another demonstration?"

My hands form tight fists beneath the table, and *god*, do I want to dive across it and slap that fucking smirk off her face.

I notice the annoyed tick in Hawk's jaw, but it's the only tell of how angry he is. "It appears you've forgotten you have no mercenaries, no compound, and"—he glances at the two empty seats on their side of the table—"you're missing two board members. Would be a shame if that number became three."

"Are you threatening us, boy?" my father snarls, his double chin wobbling. Hawk barely spares him a glance, dismissing him as the non-threat he is.

Maria throws her head back and laughs, this high-pitched tinkling sound that lacks any humor. When she fixes her steely gaze on Hawk again, the corner of her lip curls up in a cruel smirk. "You think you can threaten us?" Her smirk morphs into a sneer, and the look she spears each of us with is one of pure disgust. "You're nothing but spoiled little children. You have *no* idea what it takes to thrive in this world. All of you should go back to school, and we'll pretend this little…visit never happened. We'll call you when we need you."

She goes to stand, but Barton speaks up, surprising me, "If they don't want to be involved, we should just let them be. We don't need them anyway."

Maria freezes in place, and the look she gives her husband is pure malevolence. It's like nothing I have ever seen on her face before, making me reconsider every moment I've seen them together. They always looked so happy—was all of it for show? Surely not.

Her lips pinch and she pins him with a look that would slay weaker men. "I always knew you were fucking pathetic," she spits, and I'm pretty sure I'm not the only one gaping slack-jawed at her hostile tone. "You know as well as I do that's not possible." She glowers at each of us. "I have had enough of this nonsense. You'll return to school and await our call, or there *will* be consequences."

Having said her piece, she gracefully gets to her feet, quickly followed by my father and Barton, and strides out of the room. My dad is right behind her, but Barton hesitates, looking between his son and daughter. He looks like he's about to say something, but after a second, he closes his mouth and follows after his wife.

After they've all gone, all six of us share a look, no one willing to say anything in case we're overheard, before we get to our feet and quickly make our exit.

CHAPTER 13

Hadley

I'm still stunned by what went down in our parents' office by the time we make it back to the dorm.

"Dude, did you see the way your mom turned on your dad?" Cam exclaims as we all walk into the apartment.

"Have you ever heard her talk to him like that?" West questions.

"Never. Sure, they've argued over the years, but for the most part, they seem to get along—at least, I thought they did."

Hawk grabs a six-pack of beers while the rest of us spread out across the chairs, getting comfy.

"It's pretty clear your mom only cares about the company but is it possible your dad was telling the truth the other day?" I can see West mulling over all the possibilities.

"That he gives a shit about us?" Hawk scoffs, running his hand through his hair. He drops into an empty chair, tilting his head back to stare at the ceiling. "Fuck if I know."

Silence settles over us as we each process this afternoon's events. My mother couldn't have looked more indifferent when she looked at Hawk and me. She may as well not have been looking at her own children at all. And the casual way she threatened West. Anger flares, and I feel the sting as my nails dig into my palm.

"What are we going to do now?" I snarl angrily. "We can't allow them to keep threatening West."

"We won't," Hawk promises, and the sharp edge to his tone, giving away how furious he is, has me looking his way.

"My dad cares more about his cushy life than the company," West pipes up, and I can see the wheels churning in his head as he thinks.

"We could scare him into disappearing," I say, thinking aloud. "Show Maria that we're making good on our threat." A wicked grin lifts one side of my lips. "I've found a knife to the hand or thigh is an excellent way to get people to listen to you."

"You're going nowhere near him!" Hawk growls aggressively, making me roll my eyes.

"What if Maria then makes good on her threat to send a mercenary after us?" West interjects before I can snark back.

"Once we've scared Dad off, we go back and spell it out for her," Beck says thoughtfully. "Make it clear to her that *we* are the ones who got Frank arrested and killed Lawrence, and tell her if she doesn't let us go, we'll come for her next."

There's a moment of silence as everyone thinks it over.

"That could work," West muses. "We'd have to watch our backs, in any case. I don't trust her not to send someone after us, even if she agrees to let us walk away."

"Let's sleep on it," Hawk suggests. "It's getting late."

Murmured agreements go up from everyone, and we all get up to call it a night. Beck says goodnight to the guys and kisses me before he leaves, and as I'm heading to my room, Cam wraps his arms around me, burying his nose in my hair.

"I could keep you company tonight," he murmurs against my skin. Damn, does that sound good, but I shake my head.

"Not tonight. I still have a bunch of schoolwork to do before I can get some sleep. I don't want to keep you awake."

"I don't mind."

"Raincheck?"

Something I can't decipher flashes across his face before it disappears as quickly as it came, and he plasters on a smile. "Sure." He gives me a quick peck on the lips before slipping away from me and into his room.

Mason and West have already entered their rooms, not even trying their luck. I've been turning them away all week, and I know they're starting to worry.

Sighing heavily, I let myself into my room and lock the door behind me. I strip out of my clothes and begin my new nightly routine. A set of press-ups, followed by sit-ups, finishing with a round of lunges, then I repeat the three moves until I'm drenched in sweat and feel like I might finally be able to sleep.

Wiping the sweat off me, I pull on a pair of sleep shorts and a top and climb between the sheets, but the second my head hits the pillow, sleep evades me as unwanted memories creep in. I can practically smell the dampness in the air, feel the cold breeze as it blows over my bare skin.

My eyes snap open and my breaths come in rapid pants. I throw back the covers and climb out of bed. Stuffing my feet into my trainers, I flick the lock and slowly open the door, peering out into the hall. All the lights are off, but I can see the light shining under Mason's door, letting me know he's still awake.

On silent feet, I stealthily move down the hall and out the front door. The campus is quiet, not a soul in sight as I set a fast pace, running along one of the longer trails that winds through the forest. I don't care that it's pitch-black and I can hardly see a foot in front of me. Nothing matters except exorcising me of these thoughts. I can't think straight when I feel like this.

My senses are on overdrive as I race through the dark forest, preventing me from thinking about anything except my next step, and for a short time, I feel free. Free from the nightmares, free from the fear.

By the time I make it back to the front door of the dorms, I can hardly put one foot in front of the other, and I have a stitch in my side, but for the first time all night, my mind is quiet.

I pause when I spot a dark shadow on the steps.

"Nice run?" Mason asks, and I release a sigh of relief.

I move to sit beside him, practically collapsing onto the step.

"You know you can talk to us, right?"

"I know."

"We aren't going to judge or think any less of you."

I don't respond—what can I really say?—and he sighs in frustration. "All we wanna do is help, but you have to be willing to lean on us. I know you don't know how to do that. I know you're scared, but it doesn't make you weak to ask for help. Knowing your limitations and realizing when you can't go on alone makes you more powerful. Then, when you're unable to fight your battles, you have others who will stand up and fight them with you." I swallow around the lump of emotion in my throat, blinking away the tears I can feel welling. He moves to crouch in front of me, so I have no choice but to look him in the face. Reaching out, he tucks a flyaway strand of hair behind my ear. "You're not alone anymore. You've got five guys, all of whom would wage war for you, but right now, none of us know what to do. Hawk's on the verge of losing his shit if you don't let him in, and the rest of us aren't far behind him.

"You don't need to talk about what happened or tell us anything you don't want to. Just tell us if you're struggling or if you're having a bad day. Tell me when you need a hug, or if you need to go for a run, or if you just want to be left alone. If you want to spend the day in bed with movies and ice cream, or you need to beat the shit out of someone. Just tell me what you need, baby, and I'll get it for you—whatever it is."

The tears spill over and run down my cheek, and Mason

quickly swipes them away before holding out his hand and helping me to my feet. He doesn't say anything else. He just walks me back to my room and makes sure I'm settled in bed before saying goodnight.

***

"Dad's been blowing up my phone all day," Hawk grumbles the next evening at dinner, when his phone goes off for the third time.

Shoveling a fork full of food into my mouth, I mumble, "Why?"

He just shakes his head in frustration. "He wants us to go over for dinner, probably so he can chew us out for showing up at their offices unannounced."

"Maybe you should go see what he has to say," West suggests. "If there really is conflict between him and Maria, and what he said in Beck's office is true, he might be able to help us."

I'm not sure if we can trust Barton, but he knows a lot more about Maria and the inner workings of Nocturnal Mercenaries than we do. For that reason alone, his help could be instrumental in taking down the company.

"Maybe we should give him a chance? At least go and hear what he has to say?" I suggest, looking at Hawk.

"Couldn't do any harm, right?" Cam questions.

"What if he's actually working with Mom," Hawk counters. "He could be trying to lure us into going along with their insane plan."

"Maybe, but there's only one way to find out." I cock a brow at Hawk and wait him out. Eventually, he groans.

"Fine, I'll text him back and set up a dinner."

Barton replies to Hawk's text almost immediately, confirming dinner the next night.

***

"Where's your mom?" I whisper as Hawk and I ascend the steps.

"You mean *our* mom, and I have no idea. This is why I don't trust him. How can he live under the same roof as her if he never wanted to be a part of all of this? He makes it sound like he just went along with whatever she wanted, yet he's not a prisoner here. He could have left at any time."

I shrug, not knowing what to say. I understand what he's saying, but I also know you don't need to be locked behind bars or steel doors to feel trapped.

He pushes down the handle of the front door, and we step in, the smell of food hitting us immediately and making my stomach grumble. *Damn, if nothing else, I'll have gotten a tasty meal out of tonight.*

"Hawk, uh, Hadley." Barton's smile falters for a second over my name before he rights it, greeting us, and the three of us stand there awkwardly for a second, no one sure what to do. "Eh, come in. Dinner will be ready shortly. Can I get you anything to drink?"

Hawk and I share similar *what the fuck* looks. I feel like I've entered the Twilight zone. Barton is more casually dressed than I have ever seen him, in a pair of jeans and a polo shirt, with brown loafers on. And, contrary to previous visits where he has been standoffish and unapproachable, never able to meet my eye, he appears relaxed and at ease this evening. Something is definitely up.

"Uh, no thanks," I respond, smiling tightly.

"I'm good," Hawk says when Barton looks his way.

"Ok, yeah, no problem. Please, have a seat."

He gestures toward the same sofa set we sat on when Hawk and I spilled the beans on my identity. *Oh, great, now the three of us can sit awkwardly instead of standing. That's so much better.*

"Where's Mom?" Hawk asks, looking around as if he's expecting her to suddenly appear.

"She's been staying at our apartment in the city since, uh, you showed up at the office."

This small tidbit of information gets both of our attention as we look at him in surprise.

"Why?"

Barton sighs and seems to almost collapse into his seat, the ice in his whiskey knocking against the side of his glass. There's an apology in his eyes as he looks at me. "I've already explained that I struggled to focus on work after you, uh, disappeared. Well, your mother's way of coping was to keep herself busy. Which worked well at the time, but she's become so invested in it now."

"You're saying she wasn't a cold-hearted, emotionless bitch before I was kidnapped?" Somehow, I find that hard to believe. What mother treats their children so indifferently? She couldn't have cared less that I was alive.

Barton flinches, confirming my suspicions. "She's not the most maternal of people."

I hear Hawk scoff quietly beside me. "Neither of you has ever acted like parents. You put in the bare minimum of effort when I was growing up. You did just enough to make me believe you gave somewhat of a shit but nothing more."

The last of Barton's energy seems to drop right out of him, and he hangs his head. "You're right, son. You deserved so much better. I have no excuse for my behavior, and I can't speak for your mother, but she loves you in her own way."

She's got a funny way of showing it, but then what do I know? Just because she's been a complete bitch to me, doesn't mean she's always been that way to Hawk. She's always seemed distant, yet somewhat fond of him. It's possible Barton is right; she may just have difficulty expressing how she feels. She and Hawk have had nearly twenty years together, developing whatever sort of mother-son relationship they can, whereas I have absolutely no relationship with her at all.

I catch Hawk's eye, and I can tell he's not sure what to think. "So why is Mom staying in the city when you're staying here?" he asks, moving the conversation along.

"Your mother and I haven't seen eye to eye in a long time."

Barton looks at me with a hopeful expression. "Now that you are back, I want to work on restoring our family…" He trails off, and it's clear he doesn't want to continue.

"But Mom doesn't, right?" Hawk finishes for him.

Barton grimaces. "No. All of her focus is on the company, especially now, after the attack on the compound. We've never agreed on the direction of the company, and I was hoping now that Frank and Lawrence were gone, and with the compound destroyed, I would be able to talk her into abandoning the whole idea. Between the legitimate side and the adult mercenaries we inducted, we were doing more than well enough for ourselves. We never needed to bring children into any of this."

"So why did you? How did all of this even start?" He's piqued my curiosity, although I'm probably better off not knowing. Just picturing these assholes sitting down over cognac and cigars, casually discussing the destruction of children's lives for their own gain, makes my blood boil.

He runs his hand through his hair, unable to meet my eyes. "We'd been losing clients for some time to Onyx, our primary competitor. They claimed they had the most highly trained, ruthless assassins in the business. We were just spitballing ideas when Frank mentioned using kids. At first, I didn't take him seriously, but the others were intrigued by the idea."

A cough interrupts our conversation, and I look over to find a butler standing at the room's entrance. "Mr. Davenport, dinner is ready, if you and your guests would like to make their way to the dining room."

"Ah, yes, thanks, Geoffrey." Barton gets to his feet, gesturing for us to follow. "The chef's pot roast is delicious."

We move the awkward conversation over to the dinner table, and Barton changes the subject as the food is set down in front of us.

"So, uh, how are you liking Pacific Prep?" He's staring right at me, and I have officially decided that having his attention is way more unnerving than having him ignore me.

"Umm, yeah, it's good."

I side-eye Hawk, not entirely sure what to make of this change of conversation. I'd almost prefer we went back to talking about assassins and mercenary companies than have him prying into my life.

"You've made friends okay?"

I slowly nod my head, saying, "I have," which earns a beaming smile from Barton.

"That's great! Hawk and the guys have been doing well there. They have bright futures ahead of them. I'm sure you're the same...Do you have any plans for next year?"

What the actual fuck? He's acting as though everything is normal, like he and his scumbag associates haven't been forcing the guys down a future they don't want, and he didn't try to marry me off like I'm a fucking possession.

"Uh, no. I've been a little busy, what with Lawrence trying to kidnap me again and helping the guys escape the clutches of *your* company. Simply making it to graduation alive is about as far in the future as I've gotten."

My snarky words seem to bowl right through Barton, knocking the wind out of him, and the congenial expression he was wearing crumbles, devastation marring his face.

No one seems to know what to say, as it looks like Barton mentally falls apart in front of us. Eventually, Hawk sets down his cutlery and I notice a flash of regret cross his face before he asks, "Why did you invite us over tonight, Dad?"

Barton blinks a few times, struggling to reorient himself. He clears his throat and reaches out a shaking hand to lift his tumbler of whiskey, taking a large gulp.

"Uh, right. I wanted to ensure you didn't have any other hair-brained ideas like the one you had the other day."

I scoff. *Is he for real?* "At least we're *trying*," I sneer. "Unlike you. You claim you had nothing to do with any of this, that you were just going along with everyone else, but what have *you* done to try and stop any of it from happening? To try and get yourself, or Hawk, or any of the other guys out of it?"

He has the good grace to look thoroughly chastised, even as it means nothing.

"You're right. I haven't done nearly enough. However, threatening Maria and Wilbert isn't the way to go, either."

I share a look with Hawk, but neither of us is willing to share anything with him regarding our plans. If he doesn't approve of our unexpected visit to their office, he undoubtedly won't approve of the next step in our plan.

We don't respond, and with the remnants of the shitstorm that is our current situation sucking all the oxygen out of the room, none of us seem to know what to say and an awkward silence falls over the table. In fairness, Barton appears wholly lost in his thoughts. I'm not even sure if he's aware we're still here.

After what feels like fucking ages, but is probably only five or ten minutes, Hawk jerks his head in a *let's get out of here* gesture. More than happy to comply, I jump to my feet, and the scraping of the chair legs on the wooden floor jolts Barton out of his trance as he looks up at us.

"We've gotta go," Hawk explains.

"Oh, right. Of course." Still looking dazed, Barton gets to his feet, showing much more grace than I did. I make a move to head toward the door, but Barton stops me. "Before you go, I just…" He holds up his index finger, indicating that we give him a second, and he quickly darts out of the room.

I quirk an eyebrow at Hawk, silently asking where the fuck he's going, but Hawk just shrugs. A minute later, Barton returns, holding a wooden box in his hand. The way his palm is placed flat on the bottom, his other one wrapped around it, he carries the box like it's important to him, a priceless possession.

He approaches me, chewing on his bottom lip before holding it out for me to take. Still, I don't immediately move to accept whatever it is, instead eyeing him and the box critically as though he's trying to hand over some sort of explosive device—I mean, he could be.

He licks his lips nervously. "I-I know I've let you down, and you have every reason to not trust me, but hopefully this box will help you understand. Just because you weren't around, didn't mean I didn't think about you every day."

I still hesitate, even as he pushes the unassuming box closer to me, and with unsure hands, I take it from him, seeing the relief in his features when I do. I just stand and stare at the box, not wanting to open it, but my mind whirs with the possibilities of what's inside. Whatever it contains though, isn't enough to offset everything that's happened. Pretty words and a box don't make up for the fact Barton didn't try harder to find me; for the fact that he gave up on me.

I feel the heat of Hawk's palm on my lower back, grounding me and, with a tight smile, I turn my back on Barton and walk out of the house.

My eyes are glued to the box as I settle myself in the car and Hawk climbs into the driver's seat. He doesn't start the engine, and after a while, I glance up at him, finding him looking at the box as well, with a slight frown and lines furrowing his forehead.

I sigh and shake my head, trying to clear it of my jumbled thoughts. "It doesn't matter what's in here," I say aloud, more for my own benefit than anything else. "It doesn't change anything."

Hawk nods his head slowly, but his face still has a thoughtful expression. "I remember seeing that box before…"

"You know what's inside it?"

He shakes his head. "No, he would snap it shut as soon as I entered the room. When I asked him about it, he told me it was a special box where he kept his happiest memories."

My gaze falls back down to the box perched on my knee, and an overwhelming need to know what it contains overtakes me. With sweaty fingers, I flick up the latch and slowly open the lid, peering cautiously inside. I feel Hawk lean over the center console to get a better look, and as the top drops back, we both take in the various items inside.

There's a small pair of pink baby shoes, no bigger than the length of my finger, and I can feel a lump forming in my throat as my eyes burn at staring at them. Blinking away the building tears, I look over the other items, noticing a collection of photos, a small, yellow baby blanket, and two knitted hats—one pink and one blue—that are so small, they must have been made for newborns. Noticing something wedged at the back of the box, I lift out a small book.

My eyes skim over the front cover. *Baby's Firsts*. Opening it up to a random page, I read, *Baby's first steps*. Scrawled underneath, in barely legible handwriting that can only belong to a man, is the date I took my first steps. Flipping to another page, the date I got my first tooth is recorded, and the same is on the page for my first word. I flip through the pages until I get near the end, noticing the last few pages have been left blank. I'm guessing I hadn't achieved those milestones before I was kidnapped.

Unsure what to make of all of this, I glance at Hawk, only his face is expressionless as his eyes roam over the box's contents. He leans in and lifts out the stack of photos, slowly flicking through each of them. There are some of just me and others of the two of us together, but there are also photos of Barton, Hawk, and I, out on day trips to the beach, or at a fair, or even just playing in the back garden.

"What do you make of all of this?" I ask, my voice a soft whisper.

"I don't know." There's an unusual gruffness to Hawk's voice, giving away the maelstrom of emotions affecting him, the same way they're affecting me. Careful to put all of the items back in their rightful places, I close the lid, and we start down the drive, making the journey back to campus in silence.

CHAPTER 14

Hadley

My mind whirs all night when we return to campus, and I'm second-guessing our plan to threaten Maria. The problem is, my brain is too sluggish to think straight. I'm just about getting through the day—with the lack of sleep I'm running on—never mind adding all this extra stress with our parents.

With all this talk of Nocturnal Mercenaries and rebuilding of the compound, I'm waking up even more frequently during the night. I don't know what else I can do to try and abate the demons nipping at my heels. I already run myself ragged every night and beat the shit out of the bag in the gym every morning, and *still* Lawrence's voice haunts me from the grave, and nightmares of the compound wake me at night.

The next morning, I'm attempting to kickstart my brain into action with my third cup of coffee when Hawk stomps in, looking barely alive and having just woken up, already pissed off at the world.

He bangs around in the kitchen, making himself a cup of tea with absolutely zero fucking grace.

"What now?" I moan, not ready to deal with any more shit, but evidently something has him in a pissy mood.

He frowns at me over the rim of his now full coffee mug. "We've been called to a meeting with our parents tonight."

Fucking. Great.

That text was the first indicator of what a shitty day it was going to be. I should have realized it then, called it quits, and gone back to bed. Foolishly, I didn't. So, when things go from bad to worse at lunch, I lose absolutely all fucking patience.

I'm spending some quality time with Emilia and Wilder, listening to her talk us through her *very* intense study schedule for the upcoming end-of-year exams that, honestly, has me freaking the fuck out on the inside. Every minute of her day is planned out, with ninety-nine percent dedicated to classes or studying.

On the other hand, I haven't given a single thought to our exams or the importance of passing them.

"I'm hoping that with four hours sleep a night and only fifteen-minute breaks for meals, I'll be able to fit everything in that I need to," she says, sounding panicked as she chews on her bottom lip, frowning at the little laminate cut-out of her study schedule. "Maybe I should—"

Wilder plucks the schedule out of her hand and looks it over. "I don't see any time to have fun," he remarks, looking more and more appalled the longer he looks at it.

Scowling at him, Emilia snatches it back. "Not every minute of the day is about enjoying yourself," she snaps. "Just because you like to flit from minute to minute with no plan or purpose doesn't mean that's how the rest of us like to live."

Wilder's brows climb up his head and he lifts his hands in surrender. "I just think you need to reward yourself every now and again to help keep you motivated."

Emilia stares at him for a second, before frowning and looking at her schedule thoughtfully. "I guess I could—"

"Hey, babe." Deke steps up to our table, his gaze running over Emilia in a disgustingly sleazy way that immediately has my hackles up.

"What the fuck do you want?" I snap, noticing Wilder watching him intently.

The asshole doesn't look at me, keeping his eyes on Emilia as he leans in toward her, planting his hands on the table right beside her plate.

He bites his bottom lip in a pathetically clichéd manner, giving her yet another once-over. *We get it, you're interested. Get to the fucking point already.*

"I don't know how I didn't see it before."

"See what?" Lines form on Emilia's brow as she looks up at him in confusion.

"How fucking hot you are."

Emilia turns beetroot red, and I want to deck the guy just for making her uncomfortable.

"I'm willing to overlook the whole scholarship thing if you'll come to this week's party with me."

"You fu—" I snarl, before Emilia can formulate a response, but Wilder jumps to his feet, looking ready to tear Deke to shreds.

"Get. The. Fuck. Away. From. Her." He bites out the words with more venom than I have ever heard from him, and I don't miss the way Emilia gapes at him in shock.

Deke sneers at him, and I can see the comeback forming on his lips. Wilder isn't a Prince, so he doesn't command the same respect from Deke, but that doesn't mean he should be any less feared. If anything, Deke should be even more afraid. My guys at least have lines they won't cross, things they won't do. I wouldn't have the same confidence that Wilder won't chop your body into tiny pieces and feed them to the pigs if you looked sideways at him.

"You heard him," I snap. "Get the fuck out of here."

He glowers at me, and I return it with a cocked eyebrow and

an unfazed expression—does he honestly think he's that intimidating? He looks like a pissed-off kitten.

Returning his gaze to Emilia, he winks at her. "I'll catch you another time...when your guard dogs aren't around."

He saunters off, swaggering like the fucking dipshit he is, completely unaware that I'm mentally picking out what tools I'll use to castrate him.

"Where the fuck does he get off?" Wilder snarls, collapsing back into his seat with a dark expression.

Emilia's eyes bounce from Deke's retreating form to Wilder, finally landing on me. "What the hell just happened?"

That dickwad just signed his own death warrant, that's what.

THAT EVENING, ALL SIX OF US ARE LINED UP IN OUR SEATS IN THE boardroom, overlooking the city spread out before us. Instead of focusing on schoolwork and our upcoming end-of-year exams like normal teenagers, we've spent all day speculating what this meeting could be about. Still, every possibility was worse than the last and we eventually gave up.

The swoosh of the door opening has me looking over my shoulder as Maria strides into the room, perfectly presented in a professional, yet attractive gray dress and matching sky-high heels that I could never pull off. She doesn't once look at any of us, keeping her head held high and a slight frown on her face as she strides into the room.

Barton is behind her, and his gaze goes straight to mine. I can see the questions in his eyes—Did you open the box? What did you think? Does it change anything? It's too much, so I quickly look away, focusing back on Maria as she takes her seat opposite Hawk. Barton sits on one side of her and Wilbert on the other, clearly placing Maria in the middle and silently portraying her as the one in charge.

"What's this all about?" Hawk snaps, the second their asses all hit the seats.

Maria quirks a brow, looking irritated at Hawk's pissy attitude, but it's Barton who speaks first.

"I have offered Maria my shares in the company." My eyebrows raise in surprise, and I hear Cam's intake of breath beside me. "In exchange, she has agreed not to involve you in any further business with the company."

I glance at Hawk from the corner of my eye, finding him watching his father closely, suspicion and a subtle flash of hope in his eyes. After a long moment, he focuses back on Maria.

"That's true? You'll leave *all* of us alone in exchange for his shares?"

Maria smiles cruelly. "While Barton's gesture is *touching*"—she spits the word out like it tastes disgusting—"unfortunately, his shares aren't enough."

"What, but you agreed," Barton stutters. Color coats his cheeks, and his eyes narrow in anger.

Maria smiles placatingly at him, and for a moment, I can almost see how she managed to manipulate him all these years, and yet, it's not enough for me to believe he just blindly agreed to whatever plans she and the others devised.

"Yes, I know, but I've changed my mind. I want the majority share of the company."

"I'll give you mine, too," Cam pipes up. I don't pretend to understand anything about this corporate world or the importance of company shares, but I trust Cam and the others to know what they're doing. "With Lawrence dead, his quarter of the company goes to me. I don't want it, but in exchange, you *have* to agree not to come after any of us. I don't know about the others, but I don't want to hear anything about Nocturnal Mercenaries ever again. I don't want to see your face or come back to this office."

We all murmur our agreements, and there's another moment of tense silence as Maria thinks it over before her gaze moves to

Mason, and he tenses beside me in the chair. She tilts her head, scrutinizing him. "I want Frank's shares too."

"I don't have them. They're still in my father's name."

Mason's words spark a flash of anger in Maria's gaze, and her nostrils flare. "Then get them for me."

Jesus, demanding bitch. I grit my teeth, holding back my retort, and thankfully Hawk speaks up before I say something scathing that will only further piss her off.

"We'll get them for you. Then you'll leave us alone?"

She waves her hand dismissively. "Yes, yes. Get me the shares, and you can go live your pathetic little lives. I won't have any need for pampered children."

It takes everything in me not to snarl at her like a rabid dog, and I feel Mason's hand squeeze my leg gently. He can probably see me practically vibrating with anger and the clenched fists I'm hiding beneath the large boardroom table.

Maria doesn't hang around, having delivered her orders, and like the pathetic sap he is, Wilbert follows her out of the boardroom. On the other hand, Barton hesitates, glancing at Hawk and me with a pained expression on his face.

"I'm sorry. I couldn't let you do something rash that would only escalate the situation. I thought, with both of your dads out of the picture"—he gestures to Cam and Mason on either side of me—"that owning the full Davenport quarter of the company would be enough for her."

"It's not going to be enough until she owns the entire thing," I tell him. What I don't say aloud, because I still don't trust him, despite this 'gesture,' is that her owning the entire company is unacceptable. Handing everything over to her might buy us our freedoms, but it won't solve the problem that is Nocturnal Mercenaries. Without anyone standing in her way, she will simply rebuild and go back to destroying children's futures. I *won't* allow that to happen.

His lips flatten, his only response to what I've said, and he glances at each of the others before his gaze comes back to meet mine. I can tell he wants to say more but won't with everyone else here. Eventually, he gives a sharp jerk of his head and strides out of the boardroom without another word.

"How the hell are we going to get Frank's shares transferred over to Maria?" Cam asks that night, once we're all back at school.

His question is met with thoughtful silence, none of us having a good answer for him.

Eventually, Mason sighs, running his hand through his short strands before he drops his head back to lean against the couch cushion to stare up at the ceiling. "I'm going to have to go see my father."

"What?" I argue. "No. You can't go see that shitstain!"

Lifting his head, he pierces me with a resigned look. "I have to."

"Should we even be handing them over to *her*?" I continue to argue. "What's going to happen when she has the majority? We might be free and clear, but if she rebuilds the compound, she can pick right up where they left off and go back to stealing kids. I"—I shake my head and sigh—"I can't stand back and let that happen."

Beck pulls me into his arms. "We aren't going to let that happen," he promises, but I've got no idea how they plan on preventing it, especially if we hand over control of the company to her.

"Even with majority control, it will take time for her to forge the necessary relationships and rebuild the compound," Hawk states.

"Could we get your dad to sign over his shares instead?" I ask West, desperate to avoid Mason having to go see his father. I saw how he acted when he was forced to be around his father at parties, and I *refuse* to put him in that situation again.

"We probably could, but she'll know they aren't Frank's. She probably thinks she has our father wrapped around her finger, which is why she's demanding Frank's shares instead. Our father will do whatever she wants, giving her full control of the company."

"No." I shake my head adamantly. "We can't allow that to happen!"

I see West thinking something over before he finally speaks, "But we *could* get my father's shares and keep them for ourselves."

"What would the benefit of that be?"

My question garners West's attention as he looks my way. "I've been through the company bylaws enough times while trying to find a loophole to get us out, to know that even if she has the majority shares, she can't make huge decisions like deciding to rebuild the compound without a unanimous vote from the board, i.e., us."

"So, what, we just keep blocking her by voting no?" I question. "That's not a long-term solution. It's a bandage on a gaping wound at best."

"It would be *something* for now," Hawk says, although his expression is tight, so I know he agrees with me. He focuses on West and Beck before speaking again, "You think you could get Wilbert to hand them over?"

The two brothers exchange a look before both of them nod. "Yeah," West confidently states. "I think he could be persuaded."

"Okay, so we just need to sort out how to get Frank's shares." Hawk sighs, looking grimly at Mason.

"Yeah, and to do that, I need to go see my dad," Mason states with a finality that lets me know he's not going to change his mind.

The rest of the week goes by in a blur. Between the stress from our parents, the pressure of upcoming exams, and how far behind in my schoolwork I am, not to mention the lack of sleep and constantly feeling like I'm barely keeping my head above water, I'm honestly beginning to struggle.

After Mason's chat with me last week, none of the guys have asked how I'm doing, and I appreciate them backing off a bit. I know they're worried, but how the hell can I even begin to explain to them how I'm feeling? I feel eyes on me all the time; I'm hearing a dead man's voice; every morning when I wake up, for those first few seconds, I'm convinced all of this is a dream and I'm still locked in my cell in the compound.

They've shouldered more than any sane boyfriend, or boyfriends, would when it comes to me. Finding out that my brain might finally have snapped and I'm probably losing my mind would push them over the edge.

It took me weeks to assimilate into 'normal' life when I first escaped from the compound and, while this is different, I'm confident it's just going to take some time. All this extra stress isn't helping, either. Once we get shit sorted with our parents, the company, and finals are out of the way, I'm sure I'll start to feel better. At least, that's what I keep telling myself.

"Shall we agree to meet in the library after dinner?" Emilia asks as we exit the main school building. Class has just finished for the day, and while all I want to do is just go back to the dorm, curl up on the sofa and ignore everything for the rest of the day, I know I really, *really* need to study.

"Yeah, sounds like a plan," I agree.

"Super, I'll see you then." Beaming like we're going on a trip into town or doing something fun, she takes off toward the music department for choir practice.

Continuing along the path toward the dorm, I'm not far from the dining hall when my tablet buzzes in my bag. As I go to grab it, a passing student knocks into me. In the blink of an eye, the campus grounds around me fade away, replaced with dark walls, as someone grabs my arm roughly and tugs me down a familiar hallway. The one that leads to Bowen's torture room.

Panic flares to life within me and I tug, trying to get out of the guard's grip. I wriggle and writhe until he loses his hold on my arm, and I spin to face him. Despite my petite stature and weakened state, I tackle him with all the pent-up rage I've been harboring all these years. Catching him by surprise, I quickly take him to the ground, and with him pinned beneath me, I pummel my fists into him over and over until he's bloody and beaten.

"Hadley!" The shout comes to me as though in a dream, and I pause with my fist drawn back, glancing up. The voice comes again. "Hadley!" And I blink. "What the hell are you doing?" Hawk barks.

Everything swarms back into view—the school, the trees, Hawk, and Mason running toward me. I'm aware of the grit from the path digging into my knees, and I look down. *What the fuck?* Some kid I don't even recognize is trapped beneath me, his face bloody and his eyes wide in terror as he scrambles to get free.

I hardly feel Hawk as he grabs my upper arm and pulls me off him. Mason helps the guy to his feet and whispers something to him before he scurries off without a backward glance.

"What the hell were you thinking?" Hawk snaps, stepping in front of me so he's all I can see. Not answering him, I blink down at my bloodied knuckles, trying to work out what happened. "Hadley! Answer me!"

"I-I don't know," I mumble, glancing up at his worried, furious face.

Mason comes to stand beside him, looking equally as worried as he checks me over. "Let's get back to the dorm. We can discuss this there."

I look past him to where the student has long since disappeared. "What about him?"

"He won't say anything." The sharp edge to Mason's voice has me wondering what he said to the kid to get him to keep his mouth shut. I don't have the wherewithal to ask, though.

Hawk tugs on my arm, maintaining his tight grip as he drags me to the dorms. I follow him, dazed, unable to stop looking at the dried, crusting blood on my hands and picturing the guard I could have sworn was trying to take me somewhere.

When we reach the apartment, Hawk throws open the door and storms in, making West, Beck, and Cam jump.

"What the hell's going on?" Beck demands, scowling at where Hawk is still holding my arm in a firm grip.

"Hadley here thought it would be a great idea to beat up another student," Hawk seethes, using his tight hold to turn me to face him. "Wanna fill us in on why you did that?"

My mouth opens and closes several times soundlessly before I snap it shut, refusing to say anything until I've worked out myself what happened back there. I've had moments where I forget myself for a second and forget I'm not in the compound again, but I have never lashed out at anyone like that before.

Hawk's lips flatten as he presses them together and his nostrils flare. I can see the effort it takes him not to snap or say something that he knows will only make this worse. Eventually, he closes his eyes and sighs.

"Hadley," he begins, opening his eyes and capturing me in his churning gray-blue gaze. "What's going on? We know something's wrong. Just talk to us."

"I'm fine, Hawk," I grit irritably.

The asshole scoffs. "Come on, Hadley. Everyone knows when a woman tells you she's fine, she's far from fucking *fine*."

I look at him like he's crazy. "What? Don't talk shit. That is *not* a thing."

"That is absolutely a thing," Cam pipes up, earning a dark glare from me before I focus my glower back on Hawk.

"I'm so fucking sick of hearing that word from you when it's obvious you're not *fine*," Hawk continues to press.

"Why are you pushing me? Just back off and leave me alone."

Hawk shakes his head like he can't believe I'm not getting whatever he's trying to do, and steps forward so he's crowding me. "Because I'm the asshole brother who lives to piss you off, and I'm not going to stop until you're honest with me."

My lip curls as I scowl up at him. "You wanna know what's wrong," I snarl, shoving him hard in the chest. The fucking asshole doesn't back up though, which only infuriates me further. "I can't sleep because every time I close my eyes, I'm back in that room with Lawrence, trapped and terrified. Every time I stop to just breathe, or take a moment, I hear Bowen's voice in my head, telling me all the fucked-up shit he wants to do to me. If someone plays loud music, I have a panic attack 'cause the guards would pump it through the speakers for days, so loud I hoped it would burst my eardrums, so that I could get five minutes of sleep. The slightest noise makes me jump. I can't get my mind to shut off, and today…I have no idea what the fuck happened back there. So you wanna know if I'm okay? No, Hawk, I'm so fucking far from being okay, I don't even know what direction to go in. I feel like I'm fucking drowning, and I don't know how to swim, so I'm treading water, just trying to stay above the surface. But I'm tired, Hawk. I'm so. Fucking. Tired."

A tear spills over and runs down my cheek as the wind goes out of my sails, and I collapse in on myself. In the next second, I'm wrapped up in a crushing hug and as soon as Hawk's arms encase me, something inside me breaks. The dam I've been trapping all my emotions behind cracks and comes tumbling down, and I fall apart in his arms.

I'm faintly aware of the others joining us, of bodies pressing in all around me, Although, instead of feeling suffocated, it's like all of them are holding me together, and Mason's words flitter across my mind—*When you're unable to fight your battles, you've others who will stand up and fight them for you.*

I'm not alone. I never was.

CHAPTER 15

West

The moment Hadley fell apart in Hawk's arms, we all felt it
—the change in the air—and we moved as one, crowding around them and embracing them in a group hug. I don't know what happened that she ended up beating up some kid, but I think it was the catalyst she needed in order to realize she's not okay. She's not coping, and she's unable to get herself through it alone. I think we've all been waiting for this moment. It was only a matter of time before it all became too much for her.

She cried herself to the point of exhaustion before Hawk carried her to her room.

"Is she okay?" I ask when he enters the room again.

Sighing, he collapses into a seat and shakes his head. "Far from it, but I think she will be." He pins Beck with a look. "This is a good thing, right?"

Beck nods. "Yeah. She's been living in denial, trying to shove everything she's feeling in a box and avoid dealing with it."

"What happens now?"

"I'm not sure. Let her dictate that, and we can go from there."

"I take it we all heard what she said?" Mason states, looking at each of us with an expression I can't quite place.

"About Bowen?" Hawk sneers.

"Do you think he's the one that cut her up?" I question, feeling both furious and devastated for Hadley all at once.

"Probably," Hawk spits out the word, and I can see he's struggling to hold his anger in check.

Beck nods his head in agreement. "He was the one in charge when Lawrence wasn't around."

Tension is thick in the air. "Did anyone see him when we were at the compound that night?" I look around at the others, everyone shaking their heads. *Great, so we've no idea if he's alive or dead.*

I sigh, running my hand through my already messy hair. There's nothing we can do about him right now. But there *is* something we can do. "This extra stress with our parents can't be helping her," I state. "We need to deal with them as soon as possible. She deserves to leave school and start fresh, with none of this shit following her."

Beck nods his head in agreement. "I say we go after our father tonight."

"Tonight?" Hawk questions.

Beck shrugs. "Why not? What's the point in waiting? Graduation is only a few weeks away. Don't you want to be free of all of this by then?"

Hawk thinks on it for a moment. "Alright, what are you thinking for tonight then?"

"Leave it to me. I'll make sure we get his portion of the shares."

"No." I pin Beck with a look. "I need to be the one to do this." He opens his mouth to speak, but I cut him off. "*I'm* the one he's been using to threaten all of you. *I'm* the one that was belittled by him. Told I was never man enough, never tough enough, but I'm not the weak kid he thinks I am."

He must be able to see the adamant look in my eyes as, after a moment, he reluctantly nods his head in agreement. "Alright, fine, but I'm coming with you." He holds his hands up before I can protest. "Just as backup, in case you need it."

"Alright, fine, but only if I need you."

<hr>

It's late by the time the two of us leave to make the journey to our father's house.

"You don't have to do this, you know."

I glance away from the road to look briefly at Beck. "I do. You have no idea what it was like growing up in that house, always hearing you're never enough. He always signed me up for sports teams, then gave me a hard time when I sat on the bench for the whole game. He constantly compared me to the other guys, wanting to know why I wasn't stronger, tougher, more outgoing. In his mind, that's the definition of a man—which is fucking ironic, given what a fat fuck he is."

I can feel Beck's gaze on me, but I don't look away from the road, not needing to see the pity in his eyes. My childhood might have been shitty, but compared to his, Mason's, or Hadley's, it was nothing I couldn't handle.

"What about your mom?"

"She couldn't handle having a cheating manwhore for a husband." I glance at him out of the corner of my eye, hesitating before continuing, "Finding out he had another son was the final straw for her. She fucked off to Europe when I was six, and I haven't seen her since. There's the obligatory *Merry Christmas* email, but that's all I hear from her."

"I'm sorry, you didn't deserve that."

I shrug, not sure what to say to that.

"You have a good family with the guys, though."

"Yeah. We've only ever been able to count on each other. Our parents were too self-centered to provide us with the families we needed, so we made a family for ourselves—one we wanted." I pull my gaze from the road once again to look at him. "They're your family now too…if you want them. I have no idea what your plans are after all of this is over."

"My plans are wherever you, Hadley, and the others are. I already lost one family, I'm not about to lose another."

Our conversation is put on hold as I pull up to the gate of our father's residential estate and type in the code. Once it's opened, I drive through and pull into the driveway, parking the car and turning off the lights.

Moving quietly and carefully, the two of us slip out of the car and silently close the doors before we sneak up to the house. It's the early hours of the morning, and my father should have long since passed out. The dark windows peering out at us confirms that assumption.

Inserting the key in the door, we let ourselves in, and I quickly turn off the alarm and jerk my head toward the stairs, indicating for Beck to follow me.

Keeping our steps soft and light, we climb up the stairs and along the hall to my father's suite. I can hear the snoring coming from his room before I've even opened the door, and Beck snorts softly behind me when I open it, and the snores become deafening. The sound of them is followed by the whirring noise of a machine on his bedside table that has a tube running from it, attached to a mask covering Wilbert's face.

"What the fuck?" Beck whispers.

"Sleep apnea."

"He looks like he's on a ventilator."

The two of us share a look, not entirely sure what to do next. However, true to his word, Beck lets me take the reins and gestures for me to go ahead. I hadn't exactly thought about what I'd do or say once I was here. I just knew I had to be the one to confront him. Taking a moment, I think about Hawk's deadly anger, Mason's stoicism, Cam's flippancy, Beck's steeliness, and Hadley's strength and channel each of them.

Stepping up to the side of his bed, I stare apathetically down at him before reaching out and poking his arm. He doesn't stir, so I poke him harder. When that still doesn't get his attention, I slap my hand down on his large, protruding belly, and the idiot jolts awake, staring up at me with wide eyes.

"Ah, you're awake." I smile spitefully down at him. "Good, we need to have a chat."

It takes him a few minutes to prop himself upright and remove the mask from his face, turning off the machine so we can all hear one another without yelling.

"What is the meaning of this?" he eventually splutters, breathless just from trying to sit upright. His gaze focuses behind me, and I know he's finally spotted Beck.

"I just wanted to stop by and have a quick chat," I tell him, garnering his attention once again.

"A—what? It's the middle of the night, West. Go back to school."

"Yeah, I can't do that. See, you have something we need."

I watch as my father's cheeks redden in anger. "What are you talking about?"

"We want your shares," I state bluntly, getting straight to it— no point in beating around the bush, after all.

My father stares at me incredulously, before huffing out a laugh. "Are you high? I'm not giving you my shares."

I sigh and shake my head as though I'm disappointed in him, although it's not like I expected him just to hand them over anyway. I tilt my head, feigning a thoughtful expression. "Did you ever wonder what happened to Frank?"

His brows tug together in confusion. "The idiot got caught murdering his mistress. What does that have to do with anything?"

"How did he get caught, though? Don't you have private security in your houses? No one should have had access to that… unless someone hacked into your system."

His mouth opens and closes wordlessly before he finds his speech again. "Th-that was you?"

"What about Lawrence?" I question, neither confirming nor denying my involvement in Frank's demise.

My father has the audacity to scoff. "Now I know you had nothing to do with that. Hiding behind your computers and hacking into cameras is one thing, but outright killing someone is something you're not capable of."

He says it like murder is the making of a man. He's got no idea what I'm capable of, though; what I'm willing to do for the people I love. I certainly don't feel like more of a man for killing that guard. I did what was necessary, and that's it.

I don't let him see any of my inner thoughts or feelings. Instead, I fix a sick sort of macabre mask on my face and do my best to mimic Wilder's insane grin. "Is it? Then how come I know he was stabbed—brutally. Attacked with such savagery that only someone who truly despised him could have torn him apart like that?"

My father's eyes widen to saucers, and he splutters incoherently before finally managing to string together enough words to form a sentence.

"What do you want?"

"I told you what we want."

Sweat beads along his forehead. "I can't get you out of the company. Maria is in control now. She's not going to let you just walk away."

"We can deal with Maria. We *want* your shares and for you to report back to us with what Maria is doing. Once we've made this deal, we don't trust her to stick to her agreement. I want *you* to spy on her."

"I—what? I can't do that!"

"You're also going to transfer the deed to the house into West's name and empty half your bank account into his," Beck speaks up for the first time. I quirk a brow at him but quickly return my focus to my father as his shock is replaced with anger, and his nostrils flare.

"I'm not doing that," my father snaps. "And I'm sure as fuck not about to hand over half of my wealth to you ungrateful bastards." He sears Beck with a hateful glare. "I should have known you would be a bad influence. I should never have pulled your sorry ass out of Black Creek. You and your mother —AHHH!"

The knife I stole from Hadley and had concealed under my oversized hoodie is sticking out of the mattress, between his thighs, inches from where I imagine his limp dick is.

"Do you want to end up like Frank or Lawrence?" I question in a dark, sinister voice that sounds nothing like me.

His lower lip trembles, and he frantically shakes his head.

"Then you'll do what we've told you." I wrap my hand around the handle and yank it out of the mattress. Without sparing my father a glance, I turn my back on him and head toward the door, Beck following close behind with a proud little smirk on his face.

"Holy shit." Beck laughs as we climb back into the car. There's a fine tremor in my hands, but ultimately I feel fucking great for having finally stood up to my old man after all these years. "Where the hell did you learn that fancy little trick with the knife?"

I chuckle. "I might have asked Wilder to show me some tricks Firefly taught him."

"Damn, well, he looked totally terrified. I wouldn't be surprised if he pissed himself a little."

I snicker, starting the engine and driving us back to school, feeling lighter than I have in a long time.

The guys are still awake when we let ourselves into the apartment, and I'm surprised to find Hadley wedged between Cam and Mason on the sofa. She jumps to her feet as soon as we step into the room, rushing toward us until she's got one arm wrapped around each of our necks.

"I was so worried about you both." I hug her back, enjoying the feel of her in my arms. When she pulls back, there's a stern look on her face, but I'm too busy noticing she looks so much better than she did earlier. The few hours of rest must have done her good. It's probably more sleep than she's gotten in weeks. "I can't believe you'd go without telling me," she argues, but her words have no heat.

"You needed to rest," I say soothingly. "How are you feeling?"

"A little better," she answers in a shy voice. "I, uh, owe you an apology." She turns to look at everyone else. "I owe you all an apology for how I've been acting recently."

"You don't owe us anything, sweetheart," Beck assures her, sliding his arm around her waist and pulling her in against him.

She smiles softly, looking at Hawk. "Still. You were right earlier. I'll try to be better." She fidgets with her fingers, giving away how nervous she feels. "I can't promise to be very good at it. I have no idea what's going on with me, but I don't want to lose any of you."

"You're not going to lose any of us," Beck promises her. "We'll figure it out together."

We all murmur our agreement, and Hadley ducks her head with a rosy tint to her cheeks and mumbles a thank you.

"Well, it's late. I'm off to bed," Hawk says, waving goodnight before disappearing down the hall.

"You should get some more sleep, too, sweetheart," Beck encourages. Hadley nods, chewing on her bottom lip.

"I don't want to be alone anymore."

I step in front of her, holding her chin in a firm yet soft grip. "You were never alone, Firefly. We've always been here, waiting for you to accept our help. Now, tell us what you need?"

She stares into my eyes, and I swear I lose myself in the swirling depths of her gaze.

"I need you," she murmurs, before her gaze bounces over the

others. "All of you." She tilts her head back to look up at Beck. "Will you all stay with me tonight?"

"Of course, we will." He leans down, brushing a kiss over her lips before we all head to her bedroom, everyone going through their nightly routine before climbing into bed. It's a tight fit with all five of us, but no one seems to mind. We're all just relieved to be in the same room as Hadley. Nestled against her back, I bury my nose in her hair and knowing she's safe in my arms, tiredness tows me down into its dark depths.

I jolt awake as Hadley jumps, another nightmare having woken her. It happened several times during the night, and each time one of us soothed her back to sleep. My heart ached for her every time, and I hate that she's been struggling alone with this.

Cam must have woken too, and I hear him murmuring to her, soothing her. I pull her in tighter against me and bury my face in her hair, breathing her in while I listen to Cam whispering to her. I'm nearly asleep again when I realize he's not trying to soothe her back to sleep. *Horny bastard.*

Unperturbed by my arm around her waist, he presses himself against her, and her breathy moan goes straight to my dick and *fuck me*. I try to talk him down, because, unlike Cam, I do not let my dick rule my life.

"Do you remember what I said to you in the compound?" Cam whispers, and I feel Hadley tense against me. I'm about to chew the asshole out, when she relaxes again.

"That I deserve nothing but pleasure."

Another breathless moan follows her words, and I can only imagine what he's doing to her to make her sound so fucking divine. My dick is rock-hard now, and suddenly, all I can think about is watching her fall apart. It's been so long since I have seen anything other than frown lines and tight smiles on her face.

I rock my hips, grinding my erection between her asscheeks, and she groans again, arching so her ass is pressed firmly against my hard length. Cam shifts, forcing Hadley onto her back, and settles between her thighs, kissing his way down her chest and abdomen as he pulls her top up.

He works his way to the waistband of her sleep shorts and pulls them down as I slide my hand up her stomach and cup her tit, squeezing it gently before tweaking the nipple. Her head falls back against the pillow and her eyes drift shut.

"Keep your eyes open," I say softly. It's not one of my usual harsh demands, but she obeys me anyway, snapping them open and looking up at me like I'm her entire world. "I want to capture every minute."

"Of what?" she asks in a breathless voice.

"Every minute you feel alive."

She reaches up and slides her hand around the back of my neck, tugging me down until my lips meet hers. Her lips part beneath me, and as I slide my tongue into her mouth, it's like my whole world rights itself. Everything that's been off-kilter the last few weeks suddenly slots back into place, and for a moment, everything is right again.

Fingers brush over mine as they slide along her body, and I know either Beck or Mason have joined in the fun. Hadley vocalizes her approval of another player with a dirty groan that turns into a gasp when Cam gets busy between her thighs, putting his tongue to good use, and I take advantage, claiming her mouth in another heated kiss that sends us both spiraling.

When we finally pull apart, Hadley is a writhing mess underneath our combined touches, and I find Beck sucking her tit into his mouth. I spot Mason watching the four of us, running his hand over the front of his boxers as he tries to soothe his hard-on.

Catching Hadley looking at him, he smirks and moves to join in. He shifts to the head of the bed, leaning in to kiss her as I shift my attention to her nipple, and under all of our touches, Hadley is crying out her release in no time.

Satisfied, we all collapse onto the bed, snuggling in against her. Her stomach grumbles, and I snicker. Laughing, Cam goes to get up. "I'll make us breakfast."

Hadley pouts. "But we're not done yet."

Cam gives her a dirty wink, leaning down to kiss her. "Far from it, baby. But you'll need your stamina for what I have in mind."

She laughs as he climbs out of bed, and the sound is like music to my ears.

Mason grabs his phone from the bedside table as Cam gets dressed, the rest of us unwilling to leave the bed just yet.

"Hawk's text. Says he's got stuff to do today and that the five of us should take the day to do something."

My brows lower. "What does Hawk need to do?"

Mason shrugs. "No idea."

"A day out sounds fun," Hadley says, looking at each of us.

"Oh, yeah, we could go to the beach," Cam says enthusiastically, jumping onto the bed and forgetting all about his breakfast plans.

Hadley laughs. "I don't have a swimsuit."

The look Cam gives her is positively evil. "Who said anything about needing swimsuits? Our parents own a private cove nearby. We could go there. No one else would be around."

Thrilled by the thought of us all spending the day together, away from school and all the other shit that constantly surrounds us, we all climb out of bed and get ready for the day.

CHAPTER 16

Hadley

"Wow," I gasp as we pull up on what is nothing more than a gravel area at the top of a cliff overlooking the ocean. Getting out of the car, the wind whips my hair around my face, and I can smell sea salt in the air and hear the distant noise of waves crashing against the rocks below.

"Over here," Cam calls out, leading the way toward the cliff face. As I approach, I notice steps carved into the side of the rock, and as we start to descend, a small strip of the beach comes into view, stretching out below us. It's well hidden, so no one passing by on the road would think to stop and come down here, although the outlook is absolutely spectacular.

"Who the hell owns their own private cove?" I gape when my feet hit the sand. I look around, completely mesmerized by the shimmering sand and glistening ocean.

"We do." Mason winks as he moves past me, carrying a large cooler filled with drinks and food. I catch Beck's eye, and I can tell he's just as amazed by all of this as I am.

We both let out a disbelieving chuckle and follow the others over to where Cam is laying towels on the sand.

"What do you think you're doing?" Cam asks, reaching out to grab a hold of me just as I go to sit on the towels. "We're going swimming."

I laugh. "Cam, I can't swim."

His eyes widen to saucers. "You, what?! Well, we will have to correct that as soon as we're back at school. For today, I guess you're just going to have to stay real close to me." He winks, and I shake my head, trying to wriggle out of his grip.

"Baby, you have five seconds to get your shorts and shoes off, or I'm carrying you in fully clothed."

"You wouldn't," I gasp.

The asshole just quirks an eyebrow. "Five."

I scowl at him, refusing to believe him.

"Four."

I still don't move.

"Three."

He steps toward me, and I can see the intent in his eyes. He's one hundred percent serious.

"Two."

His arms wrap around my waist, and I shift slightly out of his reach, frantically kicking off my shoes and unbuttoning my shorts. They're not even halfway down my legs when he wraps his toned arms around me and lifts me off the ground.

I scream, kicking my shorts the rest of the way off as he runs with me to the water, the other assholes laughing as they watch us. I give all of them the middle finger and scream again as the first drops of cold water hit my legs.

"Cam! It's freezing!" I yell as he runs deeper into the water, quickly submerging us. I move in his hold to wind my arms tightly around his neck, my legs doing the same around his waist. I'm clinging to him like a goddamn spider monkey, and he seems to find it fucking hilarious, based on the deep boom of laughter he emits.

"Baby, I've got you, but if you strangle me, someone will have to come in here and rescue us both."

"Shut up, asshole," I snarl, but I do loosen my hold around his neck—he is my human life vest, after all. "I can't swim."

"You're not going to drown. We're not far enough out. If you put your feet down, you'll be able to touch the ground."

I stare at him incredulously. "Put my feet down?" The water is already at the level of my nipples. There is absolutely no fucking way I am letting it go any higher.

"Trust me. I've got you, but I promise you're fine."

My nails dig painfully into the muscles on his shoulders as I slowly loosen my hold on his waist and lower my feet until I can feel the sand bed beneath my toes. His hands remain firm on my waist, even when I'm standing on both feet. The water is no higher than it was before, but it's still too close to my face for my liking.

Digging my toes into the sand, I take a bolstering breath.

"See?" He closes the tiny bit of distance between us, his bare chest brushing against mine as he looks into my eyes. "I won't let anything else happen to you."

He dips his head and presses his lips to mine in a passionate kiss until the sound of the others coming toward us has us pulling apart seconds before a splash of water washes over me, and I scream.

Cam grabs me, dragging me against his front and using me as a human shield as the others continue to splash us. His arm is like a steel band around my middle, making me feel safe as I get caught up in the water fight, laughing and splashing them back.

Lifting me, Cam places me on his shoulders. His hands are holding tight to my thighs as the five of us wage a water war against each other, until the need for food to replenish our energy calls a time-out to our antics, and we all traipse back up the beach to where we left our things.

I pull off my tank top, leaving me in just my bra and panties, and wring out the water so it will dry more quickly.

"Damn, forget food," Mason murmurs against my ear. "I wanna eat you out for lunch."

I laugh and lean back against his damp, sun-kissed chest, tilting my head up for a kiss. "I won't say no to that," I say against his lips, earning myself a warning growl and a spank to the ass that only has me wishing he would make good on his promise.

We spend the rest of the day talking and laughing, switching between messing around in the water and just chilling out on the beach, and as the sun starts to set on the horizon, I feel more at peace than I ever remember feeling before. I'm still a long way off from being okay, but today I wasn't haunted by my demons, so I'll take that as a win.

"Let's make a bonfire," Cam exclaims in excitement, not waiting for anyone to agree with him before rushing off to gather twigs. He's like a giant child, and it's hilarious to watch.

West sighs but gets to his feet, taking off to go help him, and Mason grumbles something but does the same.

Left alone, Beck drags me into his lap. "Wanna go for a walk?"

I smile up at him. "Sure."

He helps me to my feet, taking my hand in his, and we walk down the beach, away from where the guys are collecting sticks for the fire. The cove isn't big, but there's a bunch of rocks at the far end, and once we're hidden behind them, Beck tugs me against his hard chest.

My hands land on his warm skin, and I love how his muscles tense beneath my touch.

"I can't stop looking at you today," he murmurs in awe, drawing my attention to his face. "You look so happy."

I smile. "I am happy. I needed this."

He leans in to kiss me, and my hands slide up his chest, winding around his neck until my fingers are buried in his windswept hair. His fingers dig into my hips as he holds me against him, and between the thin fabric of his trunks and my panties, I can feel how turned-on he is.

He breaks our kiss, staring deep into my eyes. "Do you want this?"

How can he even question that.

I grind against him, making him groan. "So badly," I murmur, claiming him in a hungry kiss.

He pushes me back until I feel the cool surface of a rock at my back. His hands tug frantically at my bra strap before pushing my panties down, leaving me bare before him.

He groans, running his dilated gaze over me and heating my skin, before pressing his lips to mine in a desperate kiss.

I push my hand beneath the waistband of his trunks and wrap my fingers around his wide girth, stroking him until we're both panting heavily, and neither one of us can take it anymore.

Pulling his trunks down, he grabs a hold of my thigh, hitching my leg over his hip, and slams into me in one hard, long move. My head falls back against the rock, and he rests his forehead against my shoulder, stilling inside me. He kisses along my collarbone and up my neck, behind my ear. "Nothing could ever beat this feeling," he whispers. He starts to move, and *holy fuck*, the world feels like it's coming apart at the seams.

Nothing exists except the two of us here, in this moment, and as I get lost in his eyes, I can't picture being anywhere else. Beck is it for me. He and the others are all I'll ever need.

I feel him swell within me, and I plant my lips on his, kissing him with everything I have as the two of us fall over the edge, entangled in one another's arms.

By the time we walk back down the beach, the others have a fire lit, the embers blowing into the wind. It's the perfect view, watching the three of them goof around, with the sun setting into the ocean in the background.

I lean my head against Beck's chest. "I could get used to days like this."

He kisses the top of my head. "Me too."

"Hey," Cam calls out as we approach. "Where did you two

disappear off to?" He waggles his eyebrows suggestively, and Beck reaches out and slaps him across the back of the head, making the other guys laugh.

It makes me smile seeing how easily they have come to accept him as part of the group. He and West are still getting to know one another, but West's attitude toward him has completely changed now that he's realized Beck isn't here for money or status. I think finding out Beck only ever wanted to get to know him has resonated with him. Sure, the guys have always had each other, but they've never had anyone else really give a shit about them, and I think it just took West some time to believe Beck was genuinely here for him.

I slip away from Beck to join West on a log one of the guys has dragged over in front of the fire. I rest my head on his shoulder and just stare into the flames, feeling so at ease, as his arm wraps around my waist, his heat enveloping me. I wish we could just stay here forever.

"Are you having a good day?" he murmurs softly.

"The best."

"It's not over yet," Mason chimes in, handing out beers to everyone as the others join us around the fire. He holds one out to me, but I shake my head. I tried some a couple of times when they were drinking, and I liked that it helped me forget about my problems for a while, not to mention the deep sleep. They were the only nights I'd wake up without nightmares. Nevertheless, I don't like that feeling of losing control when I drink more than a little bit. "We've still got marshmallows to melt and starlight skinny dipping to do."

I bark out a laugh and cock a brow as he sits down on my other side. "Really? The four of you are going to strip naked and go swimming in the ocean?"

"Hey, I don't care if my sword crosses one of theirs, so long as you're naked and wet and writhing between us."

Well, damn, now I really want to go skinny dipping.

Cam groans and adjusts himself in his trunks.

"So," I start nervously, picking at my fingernails, "now that you won't have to go work for your parents, what are everyone's plans after graduation?"

My question is met by silence which only makes my stomach twist tighter.

"Well, I'll need to find a job," Beck pipes up.

"You're not going to stay at Pac?" Cam questions.

He shakes his head. "Nope. It's not for me. I only agreed to work there for West. I always wanted to help kids that grew up like I did." He shrugs his shoulders. "Maybe I could get a job as a counselor in an underfunded school, somewhere where I could make a real difference."

I smile warmly at him. "You would be great at that."

"I agree, but you don't need the money, man." West tells him. "You're entitled to half of everything I have."

"Nah, that's yours. I told you, I was never here for the money. I've never had money, and I'll never need it."

"It's still yours," West insists. I can see how much that means to Beck. I know he doesn't need or want the money, but West offering it to him, especially after spending months believing that's the main reason Beck was here, is a huge deal. It shows just how far the two of them have come, and it warms my heart.

"Okay, so we're going somewhere with some underfunded rundown school where Beck can go be some child's hero. What else do we need?"

I'm momentarily shocked at Cam's easy-going attitude. Just like that, he's on board to go wherever Beck is, assuming that we will all stay together after school ends. It brings a bright smile to my face, one that he notices and returns as I cuddle deeper into West.

"We obviously need to be near a college with a good swimming program," I state, watching Cam's brows climb up his forehead.

"We don't need that—" he begins.

"I could do college," Mason muses.

"Same. I'd definitely be interested in doing a tech course or something."

Cam gapes open-mouthed at West and Mason. "Guys, you don't need to go to college just for me."

"We're not," Mason assures. "None of us have ever had a chance to think about a future for ourselves that wasn't being chained to our parents' company. You've got swimming, and that's great, but I have no idea what I want to do with my life. Besides, they say college is where you figure out who you are."

Well, if that's the case, I need to go to college.

"What about you, Firefly? What do you want to do?"

"I'm with Mason—I'm all for going to college and spending the next four years working out who I am and what I want to spend my life doing."

The four of us look around at each other with slow grins forming.

"To college," Mason toasts, lifting his beer into the middle of our little group.

"To college," we all cheer.

"And saving disadvantaged children," Cam tacks on, making us all laugh.

The sun has long since set by the time we put out the fire and pack our things to head back to the car. It takes us much longer to climb up the steps in the dark, with only our phone lights guiding the way.

"Shotgun," Cam calls out as we reach the car, and Beck climbs in behind the wheel.

"Fine, idiot, that means West and I can have Hadley all to ourselves in the back." Mason smirks smugly as he pulls open the back passenger door.

Cam's face is comical as he realizes his error, and he curses himself out under his breath as he gets into the front seat, with

West and Mason both laughing at him. I'm overcome with sadness as we pull onto the main road and leave our day in the sun behind us.

"Promise me we can do that again soon," I pout to Mason, who chuckles.

"I promise."

He drapes his arm over my shoulder, and I shuffle in closer to him. My eyelids start to droop, tiredness hitting me.

"You're not tired, are you, Little Warrior?" he whispers in my ear, and the seductive ring to his voice has my eyes popping open as my tiredness recedes.

"It depends. What did you have in mind?"

His dirty smirk has my panties all but disintegrating, and my skin flares hot beneath his touch as he achingly slowly glides his hand up my bare thigh. His fingers dip beneath the cut-off edges of my denim shorts, inches from my apex.

"But I mean, if you're too tired…"

He moves to pull his hand back, but I latch onto it, not letting him get too far.

"I'm not."

His smirk only deepens. "Are you sure? You look pretty tired."

"I'm not."

He cocks a brow. "I wouldn't want you to fall asleep on me now."

I return his cocky smirk with one of my own. "Then you better make it good."

His dreamy blue eyes flare at the challenge, and his fingers move to rub me through my shorts. I'm faintly aware of Cam and Beck having some sort of discussion in the front of the car, and without turning to look at him, I can feel West's heated gaze burning into me, serving only to heighten my desire.

My head falls back against the headrest and my legs fall open. Mason deftly undoes the button on my shorts, lowering the zipper so he can reach his hand inside my panties, and the second his fingers connect with my clit, I jump and have to bite down on my lower lip to suppress a moan.

"Shh," West says, leaning in to bite my earlobe. "You don't want to distract Beck."

Right, no, that would probably be bad.

He pulls the strap of my vest top down my arm, low enough to expose my breast. My bra was still damp when it started to get chilly, so I took it off when I put my top on earlier and never bothered to put it back on again, so I have just granted West effortless access to my aching nipples.

He dips his head, flicking his tongue out before sucking my nipple into his mouth just as Mason's fingers slide inside me. The combination of their touch is too much, and a small moan escapes me.

"What the—Ooh."

I pry open an eye to see Cam staring transfixed at my bare chest while licking his lips. "Goddammit," he mumbles to himself, "I'm never claiming 'shotgun' again."

My gaze lifts to the rearview mirror where Beck is watching me with equally heated eyes, before he tears them away to look out the windshield, grumbling something about trying to get all of us killed. I'd laugh, if Mason and West weren't playing my body like it was their favorite instrument.

"Climb onto Mason's lap, baby," West instructs, and he helps maneuver me, so my back is pressed against Mason's chest, enabling West to pull down my shorts and panties while Mason pushes down his boxers. As I settle on his lap, I feel his long dick slide through my folds, my pussy clenching around nothing but air as it screams at me for what it really wants—as if I don't want Mason buried balls-deep inside of me too.

Reaching between my parted thighs, I wrap my hand around his length and give it a pump before lining it up with my pussy and feeding it into my dripping core.

"Oh, fuck," Mason groans, thrusting shallowly and driving himself deeper. "Fucking incredible."

I moan as he slides all the way into me, my head falling back against his shoulder.

"Spread her legs so we can have our fill." The desire dripping from Cam's voice has me clenching around Mason, and he buries his face in the crook of my neck, softly biting the sensitive skin.

West helps me kick off my panties and shorts, and Mason hooks my legs over his, spreading me wide for Cam and West to see. I don't even realize we've stopped moving, but I sense another pair of eyes on me as Mason slowly rocks in and out of me, and I look up into the rearview mirror, spotting Beck watching me intently. It's only then that I realize he must have pulled over to watch.

His eyes are hooded, and glancing down, I can see his arm moving as it tugs on his dick. Looking at Cam, I notice he has undone his seatbelt and turned around in his seat, leaning back against the dash with his hand down his shorts too.

With all of their eyes on me, and Mason's deft fingers rubbing my clit in time to his slow thrusts, it doesn't take long to reach that ultimate high. I cry out as I spasm around Mason, feeling his seed hit my inner walls as he grunts into my neck.

I turn my head to kiss him, even as I feel hands lifting me off his lap, and the next thing I know, I'm straddling West. My knees are pressed into the leather seat on either side of his hips as his dick slides through mine and Mason's combined juices.

Even though I've just come, I can feel the telltale clenching in my lower belly as I rock my hips and stare into his eyes. His thrusts are rough and demanding, but the look in his eyes is full of adoration. I forget about the others watching as I get lost in his touch, until I'm once again diving head-first off that cliff and into oblivion, collapsing against him as he reaches his own release.

I take a second to catch my breath before climbing off him and turning to face Cam in the front seat. He meets me with a hopeful expectation shining in his lust-blown eyes, and I smirk as I squeeze between the front seats and climb into his lap. His back is still resting against the dashboard, and his hips rock against mine as I settle over him.

"You don't have to, if you—"

I press my finger against his lips, cutting him off, and slide my other hand between our bodies until my fingers circle his dick. "I want to." Lifting myself up, I position him at my entrance and slowly slide down until he's fully seated inside me. His hands squeeze my hips and he leans forward, capturing my lips with his as I begin to move.

"Fuck," I hear Beck groan from beside me, drawing my attention.

"Think you can suck him off while I fuck you, baby?" Cam purrs in my ear.

I lick my lips and bite my bottom lip, which is all the consent Beck needs before he pushes his seat back and pulls out his dick. Cam lifts me off his lap, and I sit on my knees on the passenger seat, leaning over the center console toward Beck as Cam shifts so he's standing with one foot on the floorboard, his other perched on the seat cushion to give him some leverage. I can feel his chest against my back as he leans over me, positioning himself at my entrance before pushing inside me once again.

I moan as I grasp the base of Beck's cock in my hand and run my tongue along his length. His hands thread through my hair, pulling it away from my face so he can watch me bob up and down on his dick, while Cam slowly builds the momentum higher and higher with every thrust into my pussy.

I lick and suck on Beck's dick until I feel his hold tighten in my hair, letting me know he's about to come. I hollow out my cheeks, taking him as deep as I can, faintly aware of his spluttered curses as he spurts down my throat.

Using his grip on my hair, he gently pulls me upward, slamming his lips against mine and tasting himself on my tongue. I feel Cam's fingers circling my clit, and it's like a bomb detonates somewhere inside me. I come so hard I see stars, screaming into

Beck's kiss as I practically strangle Cam's dick, feeling when he finds his own release.

Sweaty and breathless, I collapse against Beck, and he strokes my hair, murmuring sweet nothings into my ear. I'm still coming down from my high when I'm lifted into the backseat, and Mason and West fix my clothes back in place. They wrap a blanket around me as I pass out in a post-orgasmic haze, surrounded by the four men I love.

CHAPTER 17

Hadley

After our day at the beach yesterday, it is jarring to come back to reality, but sadly the real world is calling; in the form of homework, studying, and Emilia banging on the front door.

"Do you have a death wish?" I hear Hawk snarl, and the threatening tone of his voice has me wriggling out beneath the manmeat I'm sandwiched between and rushing around in search of something decent to throw on.

"Please, Davenport, like you would do anything to me."

I groan at Emilia's comeback, and I hear someone snicker from the bed behind me.

"Why is she taunting him?" I grumble to no one in particular, finally finding a pair of shorts to pull on. Snatching up a random top, I launch myself out the door, barely getting it pulled over my head before I reach the pair of them.

Emilia has her finger shoved in Hawk's chest, and he looks about two seconds away from ripping her head off. *Jesus, help me.*

"Emilia," I exclaim brightly, hoping to diffuse the situation. "What's up?"

I had to cancel our study session at the library the other day, after my little *episode*, and with being at the beach yesterday, I haven't seen her in a couple of days. She looks slightly different than normal, but I can't put my finger on what it is. She seems more annoyed than usual, or maybe she's carrying less tension in her shoulders.

The two of them glare at each other for another moment before she turns her attention to me, and just like that, the pissed-off expression she was wearing morphs into one of excitement as she holds up a flyer.

"Look!" she squeals.

I cast my eyes over the flyer. "A graduation party?" I fail to see why a graduation party has her so excited, but, no doubt, she's about to explain it to me.

She huffs out a sigh like she has no idea what she's going to do with me. "It will be our final hoorah. The last time we get all dressed up and go to a party on campus."

"So?"

She rolls her eyes. "*So*, it's the end of an era! We have to go!"

"Ugh," I groan. "Do we really?"

"Yes! You're going. We need dresses."

"You have the dress you wore last time." I grimace, remembering what happened to mine—such a waste of money.

"You can't wear the same dress to two parties in a row! We need to go shopping. A new thrift store opened up in Liberty Point, we should check it out."

Hawk leans over and whispers in my ear, "Remember that money I mentioned before?" When I just look at him in confusion, he continues, "You deserve to have some fun. Go spoil yourself."

Emilia squeals, having apparently overheard him, and we make plans to go into town the weekend before the dance. It isn't for another couple of weeks. Unfortunately, we have final exams to get through first. Exams I am guaranteed to fail if I don't start logging more hours studying in the library.

The problem is, we have to deal with *my mother* before I can even think about studying and exams and typical school problems. So that evening, instead of heading to the library, where it seems like every other student on campus is going, I head to the guys' dorm room so we can all discuss our next move.

Mason grabs all of us some Thai from the dining hall for dinner, and we sit around the island as we tuck in.

"Any word from your dad?" I ask West.

"Nope, but my bank account is fatter than it was a few days ago, and I spoke to our family lawyer today, who confirmed the house and shares have been transferred into my name."

I absently nod my head, unsure what to say to that. I mean, it's good that he's now financially secure, but I don't like the thought of any of us having shares in our names or being tied to Nocturnal Mercenaries in any way. It's bad enough that our surnames are associated with it, never mind having legal documentation linking them as well.

"You should probably transfer your shares into my name," Hawk says, catching me by surprise. "I don't know what my mom might try to do if she finds out you have Wilbert's quarter of the company."

"And you don't think she will come after you when she finds out you have them?" I snap, scowling.

Hawk shrugs a shoulder. "I'm kinda hoping she draws the line at threatening or trying to kill her own son."

Somehow, I highly doubt that. "Well, why not put them in my name if that's the case?" I counter, calling his bluff.

He's shaking his head adamantly before I have even finished speaking. "Absolutely not. You just got rid of the target on your back, I'm not about to put a new one on it."

"But you're okay putting a target on your own back."

"It's a non-issue," Beck speaks up before Hawk can form some sort of comeback. "Right now, she doesn't know any of us have the shares." He looks at me and frowns, and I know I'm not going to like whatever he says next. "Hawk is right, though. He probably has the strongest relationship with her. If there is anyone she might soften toward, it's him." I go to open my mouth, but he cuts across me. "But for right now, we should focus on getting Frank's shares. We can sort out the rest once Maria is no longer breathing down our necks."

The others murmur their agreement, so I zip my mouth. It's not like I have a better plan anyway; I just don't like the feeling that we're getting dragged further into this mess rather than extricating ourselves from it.

Everyone looks at Mason, who sighs heavily. "I have a meeting with my father at the prison on Saturday. I'll get him to transfer the shares over then."

Not wanting to push him, knowing he hates talking about his father, the others silently agree. I don't miss that he never mentioned *how* he plans on getting his father to hand over his shares. It's not like he can just ask nicely and expect his father to comply. I drop the subject though, letting him enjoy his meal in peace as the conversation moves on to lighter topics.

***

AFTER SPENDING ALL DAY WITH MY ASS SUPERGLUED TO MY CHAIR IN the library, I'm practically vibrating with energy as I make my way through the forest to the clearing for this month's fight night. It's the first one since I got back, and I'm actually a little nervous about it. I usually live for the blood and violence, but with anything and everything triggering me these days, I can't be sure how I'll react, and that lack of control scares me.

The fights are already underway, and I can hear the faint sound of cheering as I get closer to the clearing, soon intertwined with the noise of a scuffle as two boys duke it out in the ring.

Moving to join the guys, Mason drapes his arm over my shoulder, pulling me in against him as one of the boys takes the other to the ground, and he quickly taps out. The two of them move to the side, joining the crowd again, and Mason and the guys scan their eyes over everyone, looking to see who will step forward next.

My eyebrows raise in surprise when Wilder steps forward, the threat of violence clear in his gaze as he grins psychotically at Deke.

"What the fuck did I ever do to you?" Deke snarls angrily before Wilder can call him out.

"You've been harassing Emilia." At Wilder's words, my gaze flits to Deke, and I feel Mason straighten beside me. What the fuck is he talking about? I know he approached Emilia that day in the dining hall, but as far as I'm aware, he hasn't bothered her since.

I open my mouth to demand answers, but Hawk beats me to it. "What the fuck do you mean by that?"

Wilder's scowl deepens. "He's suddenly started showing an interest in her, most likely because of her relationship with Hadley and the fact she's been seen hanging out with the *almighty Princes*. He's been cornering her when she's alone, pushing her to go on a date with him, and not accepting when she says no." He grits his teeth and glares at Deke with a look of death in his eyes, and I just know whatever he has to say next will make me want to kill Deke myself. "Last time, he left bruises on her."

Yup, I'm going to fucking murder this shithead!

I take a step forward, intending to do just that, except Mason's hold on my waist tightens, and Hawk's next words freeze me in place.

"Deke." His voice is as dark and deadly as Wilder's. "You better get in that fucking ring with Wilder, or you'll be facing all five of us, and you sure as fuck won't like that outcome."

Deke's pissed-off expression melts away, quickly replaced with a healthy dose of fear as he steps into the ring, but he still doesn't look fearful enough as he stands opposite Wilder, eyeing him up and assessing his likelihood of winning.

I can see it in his eyes. He thinks he can take on Wilder and walk out of this ring, and sure, Wilder is lean, and he doesn't have any of the muscle mass Mason or Hawk carry, but what he lacks in brawniness, he more than makes up for with his completely savage nature and lack of a moral compass.

Deke strips off his top, and Wilder follows, and I realize this is the first time I've seen Wilder topless. I'm not the only one who gasps as the beams from the flashlights illuminate his skin. Along one side of his torso, from under his arm to the top of his pants, and spreading out along his back, the skin is scarred and discolored in relation to the rest of his skin. The way the skin twists and undulates, it's obvious he's been burned badly in the past, and something he once said comes back to me—*Yeah, but I bet you didn't kill her.* What happened to him, and is that why he is the way he is?

Whatever he suffered in his past, I revel in his brutality as he attacks Deke with a ferocity I have only ever witnessed at the compound. It quickly becomes painfully apparent Deke never stood a chance.

The crowd watches on silently as Wilder batters him, delivering crushing blow after crushing blow until the sweat drips from his forehead and blood runs down his fingers and splatters his chest. He's heaving by the time he's finished, and Deke is unconscious, covered in blood, and definitely in need of a hospital visit—not that I give a shit about him to make sure he gets to one. Wilder loosens his hold, and Deke slumps to the ground. Standing up straight, Wilder's face is drawn tight, his pupils dilated, making him look beastly, as he surveys the crowd before storming off out of the clearing and into the trees.

Fucking hell, I think we just caught a glimpse of Wilder's monster.

"Ugh," I groan, dropping my forehead to rest on the wooden table in the library. "There's no way I can learn all of this in a week. I'm going to fail."

Emilia, the bitch, just cackles beside me.

"For the number of hissy fits you've thrown, you could have finished an entire subject by now."

I lift my head and glower at her but keep my mouth shut. She's probably right. Studying just isn't my thing. Especially with everything else hanging over my head right now, the guys insisted I come and get some work done. Cam had to go to swim practice anyway. The national championship is right around the corner, and even with everything else going on at the minute, he's intent on winning it.

Mason's been subdued the last few days, spending more time alone than usual in the gym. I think he's stressing about going to see his dad, not that I can blame him. He's never really opened up to me about his childhood or his dad, not that he really needs to. The emotional damage is plain to see for anyone who looks closely enough. As someone who's been through what he has, I know it's best not to push these things. He processes his feelings in his own way—at the gym—and clearly, that's been working for him. He had the patience to wait for me to finally come to my senses before confiding in the guys about what was going on in my head. So I can at least have the patience to wait for him.

West has also been flat-out keeping tabs on his dad and my mother. He practically sits glued to his computer screen, watching them every second of the day to make sure one of them doesn't make a move against us. I think it's safe to say we're all on edge, and none of us are making healthy choices right now. We need this fucking shit done with before it ends up killing us. We haven't come this far, fought this hard, to let fucking stress take us out.

Beck is the only one out of all of us who seems capable of looking toward the future at the minute. He keeps shoving college brochures under our noses and telling us to pick one, so he knows where to apply to for jobs, but I have no fucking clue which one to choose. Do I want to live by the beach? In a mountain state? Do I want to see snow in the winter? And that's just the weather and terrain. Then there's the type of colleges—community, regular, or fancy-as-fuck private ones. Not to mention, whatever we choose must have a reputable swim team, probably some sort of wrestling team or something for Mason and me, and it needs a good computer program for West. There are *so* many factors, and that's not including the most important one of all—Hawk. I haven't spoken to him about any of this, and I have no idea what his plans are. We've only just found each other, so I'm sure as shit not going anywhere he's not going to be.

The really fucking annoying voice in my head also keeps whispering Barton's name every time I think about it too, but surely, things are too up in the air when it comes to him to know whether or not he's a factor I need to consider. For all I know, he could be playing us, in which case, I see his death playing out in the near future—along with Maria's.

But yes, all the recent talk of the future and going to college is why I'm here, complaining for the eighteenth hundredth time about how I'm going to fail these exams—in which case, all this talk about college will be futile.

Wilder enters the library with a frown on his face and makes his way toward our table. "I've seen far too fucking much of this place," he grumbles, slumping into his chair. He doesn't make a move to pull out any textbooks or his tablet, however. He just sits there, sulking.

Emilia just frowns and rolls her eyes at the pair of us before returning to her work, and with a heavy sigh and zero enthusiasm, I do the same. I have made it through about half a page of notes before Emilia snaps, "Aren't you going to at least do some work?!"

Wilder looks completely horrified at her suggestion. "God, no, why would I do that?"

"Eh, so you can pass your exams and go to college or whatever it is you want to do once you graduate?"

Wilder waves off her words. "Pfft, I don't need good grades for any of that."

I scowl at him and grumble, "I wish I didn't," which earns me a bark of laughter from Wilder, one which is loud enough to draw annoyed looks from the surrounding tables.

"You don't, Sunshine. You've probably got more money than I do. You can buy your way into any college and future you want."

My mouth pops open. *Daaaamn, I'm that rich?*

"Seriously?" Emilia snarls, looking seriously fucking pissed, and I quickly close my mouth. She waves her hand over herself. "Do you *not* see the scholarship kid here actually *working* her ass off to get into college?!" She slams her textbook shut, and *holy crap,* I don't think I've ever seen her so pissed. She gets to her feet, all the while scowling furiously at Wilder. "Some of us don't have the fucking luxury of getting everything in life handed to us. Grow some fucking respect for the people around you, or keep your goddamn mouth shut next time."

Snatching up her belongings, she storms out of the library. Wilder's gaze follows her, not looking the slightest bit chastised. He doesn't look away from her retreating form until the library door closes behind her. When he does finally turn to look at me, I swear I see goddamn hearts in his eyes.

"I think I'm in love."

I snort. "You seriously pissed her off, you dumbass!"

"And I'll do it again if she throws that fire my way. Nothing hotter than having a girl blow a fucking fuse at you."

I shake my head, not knowing how to respond to that. "You should go apologize to her."

"That's an excellent idea!" He waggles his eyebrows suggestively. "Girl could do with some de-stressing, anyway."

He quickly grabs his still-packed backpack and rushes out of the library after her. *Fucking idiot's got no chance.* Emilia's more likely to tear him a new one than fall for his unique brand of charm.

After telling her off for not confiding in me that Deke was bothering her, I told Emilia all about what went down at the last fight night. She was shocked, but she also seemed furious with Wilder for what he'd done, and ever since, any time he's around, she gets unduly agitated. I can't figure out what that's all about.

I finally got the truth from her about what was going on with Deke, and it turns out that every time she was alone, the fuckface would approach her and demand she spends time with him. Every time she said no, he got more and more aggressive. Wilder noticed the bruises on her wrist one day—it infuriates me that I didn't—and cornered her about it until she told him the truth.

I'm not entirely sure what it means. Wilder cared enough to encourage her to open up to him and he went apeshit on Deke's ass—who is still in hospital, by the way, with a punctured lung and bruised spleen—and then the fact he was able to look out for my friend when I wasn't. He has his name permanently etched beside Emilia's in the *best friend* category for me.

Left alone, I focus back on my work, and with Emilia's words playing in my head, I actually try to focus. While the thought of just paying my way in somewhere sounds so fucking sweet right now, it's not how I want to get by—relying on money and the Davenport name. I want to make my own way in this world, and that starts with not completely failing these exams.

CHAPTER 18

Mason

THE DAY MY FATHER GOT LOCKED UP WAS SURREAL. IT WAS ONE OF those things I'd always wished for—that, or for him to just drop dead. Or better yet, die a slow, painful death. He deserves a fate far worse than rotting away in a prison cell. Although, honestly, so long as he's out of my life, I don't care where the fuck he is.

He turned my childhood home into a place of nightmares. Made me scared to go home at the end of the day, fearful of leaving my room, and terrified to be in his presence. His temper was so volatile the slightest thing would set him off—stuff like if the server dripped a single drop of red wine on the white linen, if I had the slightest scuff on my shoe, if my mother had a hair out of place. He looked for any excuse to unleash the horrific creature that resided inside of him.

My mother hid behind her specially produced makeup that covered the marks he left on her, and I hid behind excuses—a broken arm from skateboarding, a fractured eye socket from fighting. The only ones who knew the truth of what went on behind closed doors were Hawk, Cam, and West. They were the ones that would help clean me up when I was left bruised, bloody, and broken on the floor. They'd bandage up the lashes from his belt and provide me with the necessary excuse to spend the night elsewhere. They'd listen when I vented, be there when I cried, and spar with me when I needed an outlet. They were my saving grace when everything else around me seemed hopeless.

What was worse than the always present fear and the beatings though, was the blank expression my mother wore as she watched him break me into pieces. I don't know if she was just so immune to the violence that it didn't affect her or if she genuinely didn't care. Or perhaps she was just so broken herself. Whatever the reason, watching her sit there, unresponsive, while I cried out for her help… was what shattered me. It wasn't the physical pain, or the embarrassment, or the fear. It was knowing my mother was sitting *right there*, watching it all, and she did nothing. There was no pleading for my father to stop, no crying, no soothing me after he'd stormed off. Like the dutiful wife or manipulated puppet she was, she'd rush after him, apologizing and begging *him* to let her make it up to him. I understand that she was a victim too, but I just can't wrap my head around that level of detachment.

The clanging of the gate as it slides open jolts me out of my inner turmoil, and I step forward.

"Arms out to your side, legs apart," the guard barks.

I do as he says and wait for him to pat me down. When he's satisfied I'm not smuggling anything illegal into the prison, he waves me on, and I quickly join the back of the line at the reception desk.

My foot taps impatiently against the floor as the line slowly shuffles forward, and eventually it's my turn at the desk.

"Inmate's name," the woman behind the desk asks, not even bothering to look up from the clipboard in front of her.

"Frank Hayes."

"Relationship?"

"He's my father."

She ticks a box and points toward a small waiting area. "Take a seat. You'll be called when they're ready for you."

Doing as I'm told, I take the last empty seat beside a young woman with a crying infant in her arms. She's not paying the baby any attention, too busy on her phone to do anything more than bounce him up and down on her knee.

Mary, Mother of Joseph, please don't let me have to return to this hell hole again. Once is more than enough.

Hadley was incredibly persistent that she come with me today, but she's seen the inside of prison walls more than anyone should, so there was no way I was about to let her accompany me. I managed to talk Cam into distracting her while I slipped out this morning, and I'm sure she's blowing up my phone with all sorts of pissed-off texts, but I left it in the car, wanting to focus purely on what I came here to do.

Getting my dad to hand over his shares will be no small feat. He's a callous man, one who only ever gave a shit about his own wants and needs. He'll want to maintain control of his quarter of the company, but I placed a call to his lawyer before I came here today, and he explained that my dad is looking at a life sentence without parole. He hasn't had his trial yet, but with the extensive evidence against him, it's effectively a slam-dunk case. The lawyer has been pushing him to hand over power of attorney; the stubborn bastard just hasn't done it yet, so I'm hoping it shouldn't be a huge struggle to convince him.

Despite his lack of regard for anyone other than himself, he's a very traditional man. He's always believed in the eldest son taking over the responsibility of the company and stepping into the role as head of the family when the time came—I just don't think he expected that to be any time soon. His reasons for being so 'tough' on me—as he described it—was because he was building me into the man I'd need to be to continue on the family legacy. I have no doubt there was probably some element of truth to his thinking, knowing what I know now about Nocturnal Mercenaries. I'd well believe it's a cutthroat industry, something Barton already confirmed. But the thing is, I am *not* my father. It might be his blood in my veins, his genetic makeup in my DNA. Only that's where the similarities end.

Cam has struggled a lot these last few months, carrying the weight of his father's crimes, and I can understand where he's coming from, but it's not a burden I bear. I had to realize at a young age that the sins my father commits are not mine. The things he does, the person that he is—that's not me. Every time he beat on me and whipped me bloody, I didn't see how alike we were; I saw how *different* we were. Every whoosh of his belt through the air only strengthened my resolve that I would never, ever, end up like my father.

Of course, right now, sitting in this plastic chair with an expensive suit on, my hair slicked back as I appear more like a lawyer than a visitor, I—very fucking disturbingly—look like the spitting image of my father.

Nevertheless, going in there pissed off and demanding he hand over his shares to me isn't going to get me anywhere. I need to play this smart, and that's precisely what I'm doing. Even if every second I sit here, my skin itches, and the need to punch something ratchets higher.

"Mason Hayes," a guard calls, and I get to my feet, my heels tapping on the linoleum floor as I cross the waiting room toward a metal gate that the guard stands on the other side of.

"ID, please."

I lift up my driver's license to show him, and he looks at it for a long moment before lifting his eyes to run them over my face, ensuring I look like my photo. Eventually he nods his head, and I tuck the license away in my wallet as he opens the gate.

"Follow me."

He leads me down a corridor until we stop outside a door. "Visitation time is one hour. A guard will be stationed outside the door and your visit will be recorded. No touching the inmate. No passing anything to him or accepting anything from him. If you are caught breaking these rules, your visitation rights will be revoked, and you could incur a hefty fine. Understood?"

I readily agree, keen to get this over with, and he ushers me into the room. I hear the lock turn in the door behind me, the sound making my heart rate spike. The thought of being alone in the room with this monster makes my collar feel tighter than it did a second ago.

"Son, this is a surprise."

Looking at my father, he's sitting on the far side of a worn table that has been bolted to the floor. I breathe out a sigh of relief when I see he's handcuffed and chained to the table, restricting his movements. It's fucked up that I can't even be alone in the same room as my own dad without fearing what he might do to me. It's been a long time since I've received anything more than a black eye or split lip from him, but it still doesn't stop my long-ingrained reaction to his mere presence.

Puffing out my chest, I push back my shoulders and straighten my spine so I'm standing at my full six and a half feet, effectively towering over him.

Every ounce of hate I have toward him is tucked away in a box, tightly shut, and instead, I fix a nonplussed expression on my face.

"I needed to talk to you."

I stride confidently across the small space, pulling out the chair opposite him and sitting down, acting as though being this close to him doesn't make goosebumps pebble along my skin.

He quirks an eyebrow but doesn't say anything, waiting me out. He's always been good at that. The silent treatment. I guess that's where I've learned it from. Perhaps even why I'm such a reserved person. I've mastered the significance of silence. It unnerves most people, but having had it used on me my whole life, I'm immune to it by now. And I let him see that.

Leaning back in my chair, I watch him back, noting the new lines that have formed around his eyes and mouth. His hair is more disheveled than I have seen before, and his beard is longer than he would ever have worn. Along with the bags under his eyes, he looks years older than before he was arrested, and smug satisfaction warms my blood. I'm careful not to let it show, though.

"I've been stepping into your role at the company."

He mimics my position, leaning casually back in his chair and keeping his fingers linked as his arms rest on the table.

"I figured as much."

"I take it you've heard about the compound and Lawrence."

My father's lips flatten. "I have." He shakes his head before sneering, "I get arrested, and the whole place falls apart. Typical."

Of course, the self-centered asshole thinks he was the only one holding the company together.

Despite my inner scoff, I nod my head as though I agree with him.

"I need your help to get everything back up and running. We've been left in quite a predicament, and *Maria* has taken it upon herself to take charge."

My father's lip curls and his hands form fists on the table. I knew he would object to hearing Maria attempting to take the reins. The misogynistic bastard would have a heart attack at the thought of a woman running a company all by herself. Women are arm-candy, made for producing male heirs and beating your aggression out on—at least in his mind. Regardless of his prehistoric, misogynistic views, it works in my favor for now.

"Of course, that sniveling idiot, Barton, is letting his wife take control. The guy probably can't piss without her telling him how to do it. He's never had the balls it takes to succeed in this business. Lawrence and I were the only ones who had the guts to strive for more, to fight to be at the top of this industry."

The anger pouring off him is palpable, and it takes everything in me not to jump when he slams his fist down on the table. It's interesting to hear him speak so openly about the others, though. I had no idea there was this disputation between the families.

"Wilbert will be useless," he mutters, continuing to shake his head. "We can't let them run everything I have worked so hard to build into the ground."

"I agree." I most definitely do *not* agree. "They're going to destroy the Hayes legacy at the rate they're going. Look at how much we've already lost because of their incompetence."

My father sears me with a critical look, and I know he's trying to ascertain how genuine I am. I can sit here and pretend to be invested all I want, but at the end of the day, we both know there's no love lost between us. I'm not here for him, so he has to believe I'm here because I want to be. After all, *I'm* invested in the welfare of the company's future, in the progression of the Hayes legacy.

I meet his steely gaze with an unflinching one of my own and let him look his fill until he finds whatever it is he wants to see. At the end of the day, he's trapped in a corner. He's never going to see the light of day again. He'll never have the freedom to run the company the way he wants. He *has* to pick a proxy. I just have to give him whatever justification he needs to make that person me.

"What's your plan?"

Despite not wanting to be any closer to him than I currently am, I lean forward in my seat, resting my elbows on the table and interlocking my fingers. "There's no place for women in this industry. And you're right about Barton and Wilbert. They're useless. The guys and I have been talking, and we want to take control. We have big plans for the company now that we've been fully brought in. Not only do we want to rebuild the compound, but we want to expand. We want to build similar camps across the country and further afield."

I can see the hungry greed in his eyes at that idea, even as every word tastes like ash on my tongue.

"Cam already has Lawrence's shares, and West is confident he can get his hands on his father's. Hawk is in talks with his father to get his."

"And you're here for my portion of the shares," he astutely states, to which I nod.

"I am."

There's a long moment where he looks me over, before he asks, "Why should I hand them over to you?"

I take my time mulling over his question before responding—silence is more powerful than words, after all.

"I know as well as you do, you're never getting out of here. You might have the cutthroat personality for this business, but you can't run it from a prison cell. You need someone who can fill your shoes, who can not only carry on the Hayes legacy but can make it more prominent than it has ever been before."

"And you think you're the one to do that?"

The catch is, I'm the *only* one who could fucking do it. The idiot only had one son—me. My sister is too young to deal with any of this shit, not that my father would even consider a woman to continue on the Hayes legacy. So, there's no one else, and he fucking knows it. The sick fuck just wants to make me work for it.

With my expressionless mask in place, I curl my lip in a confident sneer. "I know I am."

THE SECOND I'M BACK IN THE DORM, I SHRUG OFF MY SUIT JACKET and pull the tie over my head, needing to divest myself of this fucking suit as soon as possible. I feel too much like my father, dressed like this, with the grimy air of the prison still stuck to my skin. Shucking off my trousers, I head straight for the shower, not wasting a second as I turn on the faucet and stand under the hot spray. Pressing my hand flat against the tile wall, I press my chin to my chest and let the water just wash over me.

Today was a win. My father agreed to sign over the shares, but it took a lot out of me to go toe-to-toe with him in that room, alone. Since I started Pac and moved out from under his roof, I've rarely had to spend time alone with him. And as much as I like to think I'm over what he did to me, when I'm face-to-face with him like I was today, it's challenging not to remember the way he made me feel as a little kid.

I feel a warm hand on my back, and I don't even have to turn around to know who it is. She stands on her tiptoes, wrapping her arms around my upper arms, clinging to my shoulders, and pressing a kiss to my shoulder blade. The two of us stay like that for a long while, and I just let her nearness take the edge off my jitteriness. Now more than ever, I can understand how Lawrence's presence had such a debilitating effect on her. It doesn't matter how much you tell yourself you've come to terms with your past, that you're bigger, stronger, more powerful now. When you come face-to-face with that one thing, that one person who has always gotten under your skin, it tears through every barrier you've ever constructed, breaks apart every positive thought you've repeated to yourself, and strips you bare of the armor you'd carefully placed around you.

It doesn't matter if you're five years old, twenty-five, or fifty. Trauma is trauma, and no matter how much you tell yourself you're over it, that you're tougher than the ghosts that haunt you, you will always be weakened in their presence. They are always going to have a hold over your inner psyche. This is why you need people around you, people you can rely on, lean on, and stand up beside you and remind you that you're not a weak kid anymore.

Hadley is my strength, just as I hope she can now see that I am hers, as are the others. Together, we can face any challenge and come out stronger.

I turn in her arms, pulling her in flush against me, and rest my head on her shoulder. She strokes her fingers through my wet hair, the gesture soothing, and I feel the last of the tension leave my body.

Eventually, she shuts off the shower and grabs towels for us, and quietly leads me to my bedroom for us to settle on the bed. I drag her into my arms, and she slots in perfectly against me.

"Tell me about today," she whispers. It's not a demand, and I know if I told her I didn't want to talk about it, she would let it be, but she deserves better than that, and honestly, now that it's done, I feel like I have gained some closure. Today drained me, but I feel stronger for having faced my father. I feel fucking great for having deceived him. He's going to be absolutely furious when he discovers the truth, but by then, it will be too late—not that he can do anything about it from behind bars.

I bury my nose in her hair, breathing in her vanilla and honey scent. "I got the shares."

She doesn't say anything, waiting me out. She doesn't care about the shares, not really, and that's not what she meant anyway.

I sigh, relishing in the feel of having her pressed up against me. It's not easy for me to talk about my feelings. It's not something I've ever had to do before, and it doesn't come naturally. But slowly, I open up to her, telling her how it felt seeing my dad again today, and once I start, the words flow out of me until I'm telling her all about my past and the dark cloud he shrouded our house with.

The whole time, she just lets me hold her and silently listens to me, and by the time I'm done, I feel lighter than I ever remember feeling. Huh, maybe there is something to be said for this whole *talking your feelings out.*

She's reticent for a bit before she speaks up, her voice husky and clogged with emotion. "You're never going back there."

Abso-fucking-lutely.

"Have you had any more, uh, episodes?" I ask her once I'm all talked out. I have no idea what to call those moments when she's not in the present, but finding her beating up that kid scared me. Not the fact she was attacking him, but the vacant look in her eye. It was obvious she wasn't aware of what she was doing.

"None like the day you and Hawk found me...but sometimes I struggle to remember I'm not back there. It's like, I can be here, in the present, then something small sets me off—a certain smell or noise—and suddenly, I'm trapped in that cell again. Usually, it's only for a second or two, but it's terrifying." Her admission is a quiet whisper, like it's something to be ashamed of. Only I can't begin to imagine how difficult that must be, to feel so out of control. It certainly explains her need to burn herself out in the gym.

I pull her in closer to me, feeling her snuggle into my side, and it's not long before we drift off to sleep.

CHAPTER 19

Hadley

For the third fucking time in as many weeks, we're all sequestered back in the boardroom at our parents' offices. Honestly, I've seen enough of this fucking building to last me a lifetime.

"Do you have the shares?" Maria asks as soon as she enters, skipping right over any pleasantries. Probably for the best. There's no point in pretending this is a civil meeting; this is a war between people that hate each other.

Barton and Wilbert enter behind her, and interestingly, Barton doesn't sit in his usual seat on her side of the table. Rather he pulls out the chair at the end of our row. Maria barely spares his change of seat a second's glance. Refusing to think about what it means that he's sitting on our side of the invisible war line running down the center of the long board table, I instead focus on Wilbert. The man himself is sitting beside Maria, looking loyal as ever…except he's sweating bullets and looks like he's about to pass out.

What the hell? He looks suspicious as fuck right now with the way his gaze bounces around the room, never settling on one place for too long. He shuffles in his seat and coughs to clear his throat, and I'm almost convinced he's about to give away what we've been planning. Still, thankfully, Maria doesn't seem to notice his suspicious behavior, too focused on the paperwork in Hawk's hand to give a shit about Wilbert or anything else going on in the room.

"We do." Hawk slides the documentation for Cam's and Mason's shares across the table, and Barton adds the documentation for his shares to the pile.

Maria looks positively gleeful as she hungrily snatches up the paperwork, meticulously checking through each page and ensuring it's correct.

"It's all there," Hawk assures her. "Just like you asked."

"Yes, it appears so," she finally agrees, setting the paperwork on the table in front of her. Resting her hands on top of it, her talon-like claws begin to tap impatiently against the paper.

"And you'll uphold your end of the bargain?" Barton clarifies. There's no fancy paperwork to sign or legal documentation to ensure she does, in fact, uphold her end. None of that will actually stop her from doing whatever the fuck she wants. We just have to hope, on a wing and a prayer, that, now she has what she wants, she will just leave us the fuck alone.

Not that that's good enough. I can't just silently sit back and live my life, knowing she will be rebuilding her empire here and, before long, be back to stealing more kids off the street and subjecting them to the harsh realities of the compound.

The problem is, I have no idea how to stop her. Okay, well, I have a few somewhat permanent ideas, but I'm not entirely sure her death is the desired outcome here. While personally, I have no issues with killing her, I don't think it's what Hawk wants. Despite her cold attitude, she's still his mother, and I can't just fucking kill her if he's not okay with it. It's not something we've talked about, but the fact he hasn't just suggested offing her himself is all the conversation we need to have.

"Yes, yes," she snaps, far too dismissively for my liking.

"You are going to let *all* of us lead our own lives without dragging us into the company," I say, spelling it out for her. "You're not going to threaten, bribe, or coerce any of us into doing your bidding, or anything for the company."

For the first time, possibly ever, she actually looks at me. Like, properly takes me in, and sees me as more than just some stranger in her house, some girl her son has brought home, or some pawn she can maneuver around a chessboard at her will. There's still no motherly love in her gaze, merely recognition that I've spoken and an assessment that I'm worthy of a response. She probably doesn't look at me for more than a minute, yet it's enough time for me to determine that I will never care to know this vapid, narcissistic woman in front of me. She's not a mother to me, and she never will be. And surprisingly, I'm okay with that. Sure, I grew up dreaming of the traditional family, but who the fuck wants traditional? The world is full of non-traditional families. I'd take non-traditional and happy, over traditional and miserable as fuck, any day.

"I said yes, didn't I."

Jesus, this woman's attitude is infuriating.

I smile tightly at her. "Just making sure you understand the terms."

"Yes, you all want to give up your legacies, like the entitled children you are, for the freedom you *think* it will gain you." She pins each of us with a serious look. "Just know, I won't be interested in taking any of you back when you come begging me to."

I can tell I'm not the only one holding back my snort. *Yeah, fat fucking chance of that happening.*

"Well, if we're done here," Hawk says tightly, wrapping up the meeting. Before he can get to his feet, Maria lifts a finger, indicating she's not yet done. *Great, now what?*

"Just one more thing." She focuses her gaze on Barton.

"You've handed over all of your shares, and as such, I think it's only fitting that you step down from your position."

"I intended to," Barton responds curtly.

Maria nods. "And I also want a divorce."

You could hear a pin drop; the silence is so intense. Surely this is not the appropriate place to have this conversation, in front of all of us? This is a private matter between the two of them. And yet, despite being painfully aware that we're intruding on an otherwise personal conversation, I can't tear my eyes away from Barton's face.

His eyebrows have lifted in surprise, except that's his only reaction. He clears his throat and fixes his suit jacket before responding, "I think that's for the best." With that, he gets to his feet, and we all follow, pushing back our chairs and standing. *Seriously? That's it?* Twenty-one years of marriage, and it ends just like that? I don't know if it's for the best or the saddest thing I've seen all day.

We all follow Barton out of the room and into the elevator, where we stand awkwardly. The others cast glances at Barton, as if waiting for him to have a meltdown. He just stands stoically as the lift descends, looking surprisingly unbothered by the events in the boardroom.

The awkwardness continues as we all shuffle out of the elevator and through the building's reception, onto the street.

"Uh, we'll see you back at campus in a bit," Beck says, looking between Hawk, Barton, and me before leaning in and pressing a kiss to my temple. The others give their own kisses and hugs goodbye and climb into Mason's SUV. Part of me wishes I could go with them and leave this awkwardness behind. I have no idea what to say to Barton. For all intents and purposes, it *appears* he's on our side. He handed over his shares, and he doesn't seem the slightest bit fazed by the end of his marriage, but none of his recent actions add up with his previous ones. Why, all of a sudden, is he putting us first? Above his wife and the company?

And yet, if what Hawk said about the wooden box is correct,

my father has perhaps been more affected by my disappearance than his actions dictate. Maybe he was telling the truth, and he thought he was doing what was best. I mean, it definitely wasn't for the best. There's no excusing his past behavior, but is it possible that this is him trying to make up for it? I don't know, and trying to work it out is just giving me a headache.

"Maybe we should go grab lunch and talk?" Hawk suggests, sounding unsure.

"Lunch sounds like a great idea." Barton's voice holds none of the hesitation or heaviness that Hawk's did. "There's a great little Italian place around the corner."

I quirk a brow at Hawk, who just shrugs, uselessly, and we follow Barton as he leads us to the Italian restaurant.

Once we've all ordered and the waiter has taken our menus, I look at Hawk expectantly. Barton doesn't appear to be in any rush to discuss today's meeting, but I, for one, need answers. I need to know if we really can trust him.

"Uh, so…" Hawk begins hesitantly, taking a sip of his water. "About today…"

Barton lifts a hand to cut him off. "Don't worry about it, son. It's been a long time coming. Honestly, I'd been planning on having the same discussion with her, just…in private. We're both after different things in life."

"And, uh, what is it you're after?" I question, confused.

The way Barton looks at me, it's as if he can't believe I even have to ask that question.

"Now that I've got you back, I want to get to know you, to spend time with you…" He looks away from me to focus on Hawk. "…with both of you."

Unsure what to make of his raw honesty, I look at Hawk, and I can see he wants to believe in his father, but he's just as unsure as I am.

"I know I have made bad decision after bad decision, and nothing I say or do can make up for that, but I'd really like it if we could start fresh and get to know one another."

I have so many questions, but I guess the answers don't matter. I probably wouldn't understand his reasoning for many of the things he did—like pushing me into the tradition at school or trying to marry me off to Wilder. At the end of the day, if he's willing to move forward and doesn't try to direct our lives any further, I guess we can see where this goes.

I can feel Hawk looking at me, and when I meet his gaze, he lifts his brows, wordlessly asking what I think. Honestly, I don't know. Does part of me want the chance to get to know my father? Yeah, of course, but I'm also so burned by people that I don't know if I have any more trust left to give.

"You won't have any say in our lives," I state, fixing Barton with a serious look. "You won't dictate what we do or force our hands on anything. If there is to be any hope of a relationship between us"—I hold up my hand, pointing my finger back and forth between us—"it's on *my* terms."

"I understand. I don't want to control you, or run your life for you, I just want to be a part of it—in whatever way you're comfortable with."

Not sure of what else to say, I nod and take a drink of my water, needing to quench my dry throat. I'm not entirely sure if I'm making a massive mistake by inviting him in or opening the door to a relationship I have always craved but never thought I'd have.

THE REST OF THE WEEK GOES BY IN A BLUR OF STUDYING, SPENDING time with the guys, Emilia and Wilder, studying, and did I mention studying? So. Much. Studying. If I never see the inside of a library or have to open another textbook again, I'll die happy. But exams start in a few days, and to say I've been slacking is an understatement.

Unfortunately, with all this studying, we haven't had a chance to sit down and discuss our next moves regarding Maria. She's off our backs for now, but apparently the next shareholder meeting is only a week away, and West will have to be there, which will ultimately reveal to Maria that the company is not all hers to do whatever the fuck she wants with.

There has been no more talk of putting the shares into Hawk's name; honestly, I don't know that it would make a difference. We're all a target, regardless of who has the shares. The only benefit to whoever owns the shares is that Maria isn't going to kill that person and risk losing them altogether. But that doesn't mean she won't have any qualms about killing the rest of us.

I'm not okay with her hurting any of us, which is why we need a plan in place, because there is no way she isn't going to be gunning for us when she discovers the truth. This is why I bring up the conversation on Thursday night, even though it's late and we're all already exhausted from our busy schedules.

"We need a plan in place before West has to go to this shareholder meeting next week."

My words are met with exhausted sighs and groans from everyone except Beck, who leans forward in his seat in the living room with a serious expression. He's been staying here every night since my little breakdown, and either all five of us crash in my bed or the others start off in their own rooms, but usually, at least one of them ends up in bed with Beck and I at some point during the night.

"I agree," he begins. "I know you've all been busy with studying for exams and everything, but we're running out of time, and there's no way West is going into that meeting without a plan in place."

His words have everyone else sitting up straight and paying attention, no one willing to put West's life at risk.

"Okay, does anyone have any ideas?" Mason asks, looking at each of us.

I have one idea, but I bite my tongue, unwilling to voice it. Killing her is obviously the best way to deal with this, but I'm not going to unless Hawk mentions it. I won't be responsible for putting him in that position; of making the decision whether or not his mom lives or dies.

Thankfully, Beck speaks up, "We need to focus on protecting ourselves. I've been wracking my brain, and honestly, the only plausible solution I can come up with is to"—he looks at Hawk and grimaces—"kill her."

Hawk's lips flatten as he presses them together, and he doesn't immediately respond to Beck's words.

After a long moment, he sighs, running his palm over his face. "I don't know," he groans. "I just—there must be another option."

"Are we really those people that resort to killing off their problems?" Cam pipes up with a shrug. "I mean, no offense, man, but your mom is a bitch. She's as bad as the rest of our parents, but I don't know how I feel about killing her. I know she's going to be furious with us, and maybe it's stupid not to consider it. Nevertheless, I just think if there's another option, we should take it."

I squeeze his hand reassuringly as my heart swells. This is why he could never be like his father. He's too good. Where I—or probably Beck—wouldn't hesitate to behead that bitch. He wants to be able to walk away from all of this with his soul still intact, and goddamn, if that doesn't make me love him even more.

After a second's hesitation, Beck nods and we swiftly move on as he continues. "Alright, then we need to try and cut her off at the knees, prevent her from coming after us."

"How do we do that?"

Beck looks at West. "Do you know how the company gets jobs to the mercenaries working for them—the adults that aren't being forced into this life?"

"Eh, yeah, they have a highly encrypted portal that they advertise jobs through, and whoever wants to take it, accepts and receives the details via an encrypted email."

"Do you think you'd be able to get into that system?"

"Yeah. There should be a backdoor through the company's mainframe, which I have access to."

Beck grins. "Good. Once you're in, crash it. That way, she

won't be able to reach out to any of them and get them to do her dirty work for her."

West nods and goes to grab his laptop.

"Okay, so that'll prevent her from sending any mercenaries after us, but there's still plenty more she could do. Even if we take measures to protect ourselves, we can't live on the defense for the rest of our lives."

Beck sighs, running his hand down his face in exhaustion or frustration. "I know, but that's all I've got for now."

Several hours later, West has successfully sent out a message to all the mercenaries for hire who are in our parents' employ, telling them that the company won't be taking on any new jobs for the foreseeable future, and crashed the system, so Maria can't gain access to it.

It won't solve our problem, but it's a start.

***

APPARENTLY, IMPENDING EXAMS DO NOT MEAN THE WEEKLY FRIDAY night Pacific Prep party is canceled. Actually, after spending all week staring at the bland walls of the library, trying to cram so much knowledge into my head that my brain is nothing but mush at this point, I'm kinda looking forward to sitting by the lake and just relaxing for the night.

"Ahh, it's been so long since we've had a night out," Emilia squeals in excitement when I answer the door to her on Friday night. She looks fantastic in booty shorts and a tube top, showing off her tanned skin and flat abdomen.

She pulls me in for a tight hug, and I can already smell the sickly-sweet odor of alcohol on her breath. She giggles as she pulls away, moving further into the apartment, and Wilder comes strolling behind her with a crazy-ass grin on his face.

"Sunshine." He nods his head and moves past me to the kitchen, lifting some beer and wine coolers out of a bag he's carrying and filling up the fridge.

"Can you believe it's the final party of the year?" Emilia exclaims when I join her on the sofa.

"We have the dance next week."

She shakes her head and rolls her eyes, like she doesn't know what to do with me. "That's different. This is the final *Friday night* party."

Yeah, I'm still not understanding the difference. Even if I did, it's all the same to me. A party by the lake in skimpy clothes or a dance in the dining hall with gowns and suits. Either way, people get drunk, sleep with inappropriate people, and regret their decisions in the morning.

Hawk strides in, wearing a dark green shirt and cream chinos, pausing on the threshold before he makes a beeline for the fridge. Lifting out a beer, he joins us in the living room. I notice his gaze linger on Emilia for a second, frown lines wrinkling his forehead before he looks away. I have to suppress my eye roll. The idiot needs to learn to get along with my best friend. She's not going anywhere, and neither is he, so to save all of us the headache, they need to learn to be in the same room without pitching a fit.

Emilia makes a point of ignoring him, talking my ear off about one thing and another, catching me up on the school gossip I couldn't care less about. Not long later, Cam walks in, looking fucking drool-worthy in a tight pale gray shirt and dark denim jeans. The way his eyes drop over me heats my skin, and I have to suppress a shiver of desire. He smirks, knowing just how much he affects me, and squeezes into the space beside me on the sofa, dragging me into his lap.

Leaning in, he bites my earlobe, making me squeeze my thighs together. His dark chuckle does nothing to abate the need coursing through me. "You look absolutely fuckable tonight."

Hoooly shit, someone get me a fan.

Thankfully, before I can self-combust, the others stroll in, and we keep the topic of conversation light as we all down a few predrinks.

The party is well underway by the time we make it down to

the lake, but regardless of the mass of bodies writhing in time to the music on the pebbly shore, the plastic chairs the Princes always sit in around the fire remain unoccupied.

I'd half expected someone to have claimed the seats. In fact, I'm surprised no one has tried to claim the title of Princes. It's not as though the guys have been all that present recently, but the threat of their wrath seems to be enough to keep people in line. As for the girls, there hasn't been the same uproar to the stopping of the tradition as there was last time. Maybe it's because the guys explained they're in a relationship—although somehow, I doubt that's the reason—or perhaps they've just gotten sick of all the drama. Now that I could understand. Whatever the reason, I'm not questioning it. We're down to the last couple of weeks of school, and everyone's thoughts seem to be on the summer and college. You can practically taste the excitement in the air as everyone looks toward their futures with the kind of optimism that only comes with youth.

We all take our seats, West pulling me into his lap, freeing up a chair for Emilia.

"What do you want to drink, babe?" Mason asks, flipping open the lid on the cooler, revealing a selection of beers, wine coolers, and water.

"Water, please."

He hands me the bottle, before moving on to dole out drinks for everyone else, and I inspect the lid, ensuring it's properly sealed before unscrewing it. It's become a habit ever since Michael managed to get one over on me. I still don't know how he managed to sneak something into my coffee without me noticing. It's not something I'll ever allow someone to achieve again, though. Now, unless I get the drink myself, I make sure it comes sealed, and I always double-check the seal and bottle for any signs of tampering. Of course, I trust Emilia, Wilder, Hawk, and my guys, but we didn't carry that cooler down here, meaning they got someone to do it for them, and who knows what the fuck some random asshole might have done to our drinks.

We all lapse into easy conversation, watching the party rage around us. It's honestly the best party I have been to all year. No one approaches us or tries to make conversation with the guys. While they still receive *come fuck me* looks from girls dancing nearby, none of them do more than that, and it's fucking bliss not having to watch desperate wannabe housewives grinding all over *my* guys.

As the night wears on, the music gets louder and louder, and I can feel sweat gathering at my temples and along my spine, even though I've done nothing but sit in West's lap. My heart rate starts to spike, and when the music switches to a new song and a loud bass starts up, I flinch.

It's just music. It's a party. You're outside. You're at school. You're safe.

I repeat the mantra over in my head, sucking down huge lungfuls of air as I try to breathe through it.

"Hey," West whispers in my ear. "Let's go for a walk."

Nodding, I climb to my feet, and he slips his hand in mine as we head down the shore, away from the loud music.

"Are you alright?"

"Yeah, I'm fine."

He quirks an eyebrow. *Right, saying* I'm fine *isn't an acceptable response.*

I huff out a chuckle. "It's like, I can be fine one minute, and the next, I can feel myself getting agitated, and I struggle to keep myself grounded in the present."

He mulls over my words for a second, before asking, "What happened back there?"

I chew on my bottom lip before sighing. I keep my gaze glued to the stony shore beneath my feet, unable to look at him as I say, "Sometimes they'd blast death metal music into my cell, for what felt like days on end. The constant noise and lack of sleep drove me crazy. It would get to the point that I would have done just about anything to get some peace."

He squeezes my hand, and I glance up at him. He smiles softly, pulling me to a stop as he wraps his arms around me. "Any time you start to feel yourself losing control, just tell one of us, and we'll distract you or go somewhere else with you. Whatever you need."

Returning his hug, I bury my nose in the crook of his neck. "I know. Beck showed me these really useful breathing exercises, and I've found if I repeat a mantra in my head, it helps to ground me."

"You're so strong, Firefly. Scarily so. Sometimes, I worry you don't need me," he confesses on a quiet whisper.

Leaning back, I lift my hand, running my fingers through his hair before cupping his cheek. "I'll always need you, West. You're so thoughtful and always thinking of me and my needs. You could see that I was getting stressed, and you fixed it. I could feel myself spiraling, and while I probably could have talked myself down, getting away from the party for a bit was exactly what I needed."

I press up onto my toes and place a soft kiss against his lips before we continue on our walk around the lake. Only when I'm feeling thoroughly relaxed and back in control do we return to the party.

As we approach the fire, Cam lopes over and purrs in my ear, "Dance with me, baby." I might have two left feet, but there's no way I'm about to deny him when he talks to me with that deep, gruff voice that has my lower belly clenching.

Taking my hand, he pulls me toward the writhing mass of bodies, careful to stick to the outskirts of the crowd and staying on the opposite side of the lake to the DJ. How he even knows to do that is beyond me.

His hands rest on my hips as I sway to the tune—some upbeat pop song—and wrap my arms around his neck. As the song continues, our bodies gravitate closer until we're pressed up against each other.

He rests his forehead against mine as his hands slide around to my lower back, somehow managing to pull me in even closer. His eyes never leave mine, and the rest of the party fades away as I get lost in his gaze. The mischievous glint in his eyes holds me captive. It was missing for so long, I worried I'd never get to see this side of him again, and now that he's found his way back to me, I want to capture every second of it.

"My life was nothing before you," he murmurs. We're standing so close that, even with the thudding of the base and the boom of the music being pushed out over the crowd from the large speakers, it would be impossible not to hear him. "I was lost, going through the motions. I didn't even realize how unhappy I was."

Our lips are a hairsbreadth apart, and I couldn't look away from him now, even if a meteorite flew by overhead.

"I thought I had all I needed in life, but you've shown me how much I was missing out on. I never thought I could feel this way." A shy yet awe-inspiring smile brightens his face. "For the first time in my life, I'm excited about the future. I can't wait to spend every day with you—to wake up together, go to sleep together, to argue over stupid things, and just revel in the mundane."

To most people, that might sound like nothing special. It's no grand gesture, but for me, it's the biggest gesture of all. Normal is all I've ever wanted—to live a normal life...with Cam, West, Mason, and Beck. I want Hawk to piss me off, and have Emilia make me laugh. I want to do crazy shit with Wilder, and at the end of the day, curl up with my guys and know that life can never get better than this.

I return his shy smile with one of my own and press up onto my toes, placing a chaste kiss to his lips. "Good, 'cause you're never getting rid of me. You're it for me; you're all I'll ever need. All four of you. I want everything you just mentioned. I want the mundane. I want to share every boring moment of my life with you."

He chuckles. "Oh, baby, absolutely nothing about our life will be boring."

He slants his lips over mine, stealing my breath with a

passionate kiss. Just as I'm getting lost in his touch, he pulls back only enough to whisper against my lips, "I love you."

"I love you too." He swallows my words with another kiss that has me forgetting about everything other than the parts of my body he's touching as my skin lights up like wildfire beneath him.

CHAPTER 20

Hadley

I link my fingers with Cam's and pull him away from the writhing mass of bodies in the direction of the boat house. His body is flush against mine, pushing me faster as we rush away from the party, the loud music quickly fading the farther we go. I glance back at him over my shoulder as I giggle, the hungry look in his eye making my vagina flutter with need.

Out of the corner of my eye, I notice the bonfire, and sparing it a glance, my gaze lands on West watching us run off into the night. His lip lifts in a half smile and he winks at me. There's no jealousy on his face, no anger that I'm spending time with Cam and not with him. He knows, just as I do, that I might be with Cam now, but I'll always have time for West. Just as I'll always have time for Beck and Mason too. I love when we all hang out as a group, but I also love my one-on-one time with each of them.

Once we reach the boat house, I slip around the side so we're hidden from the rest of the party and any nosey onlookers.

HE PUSHES ME AGAINST THE WALL, THE COARSE WOOD CHAFING against my peaked nipples as he pins me in place with his hips. His lips trail up the sensitive skin of my neck before he bites down on my earlobe, making me whimper and grind my ass back against his erection.

"I can never get enough of you," he murmurs against my ear. His voice is a seductive husk overflowing with hungry need. "I want to wake you up with my tongue in your pussy and make you come around my dick every night. I want to have lazy Sunday sex on the couch and be that annoying couple who can't keep their hands off each other when we're out in public."

Fuck me. I'm all for dirty talk, and what he's describing has me fucking gagging for him. I can't do anything but moan obscenely as he presses his hard cock between my asscheeks, demonstrating just how fucking much he wants all of that.

His hands slip under my top and skim over my ribs. He squeezes my tits, pinching the nipples and causing me to groan in delight.

"Do you want all of that too?" His husky voice and dirty words have me incapable of producing words.

"Mmmhmmm."

My skin burns everywhere he touches, and my breathing hitches, each breath nothing but a rapid pant. Trailing his fingers down my abdomen, he deftly unbuttons my shorts and pushes his way beneath my panties until his fingers are stroking over my sensitive nub. I jerk in his arms, throwing my head back against his shoulder and groaning.

He kisses the base of my neck. "I love how much I turn you on. Love how wet you get for me." His fingers slide lower, and he pushes his way inside me, teasing me mercilessly. "You feel it just as much as I do, don't you? That deep ache in your chest that only recedes when we're locked together."

His fingers sink deeper into my pussy, and I'm already so close to coming from his words alone. Is orgasm by dirty talk a thing? 'Cause I'm pretty sure I'm about to make it one.

"Yes," I pant. "I feel it. You burn me up inside and make me feel alive, and when you're not around, it's like something inside of me is missing."

He bites along my neck as he slowly pumps his fingers in and out of me, driving me wild. Just when I think I can't take it anymore, he pushes his thumb firmly against my clit, and I go off like a rocket, screaming my release into the night.

He doesn't give me a second to recover, spinning me around to face him. My shorts fall to the ground and he rips my panties clean off me. In the next second, he's hauled me up into his arms, his fingers digging into my asscheeks as my back smacks against the wood of the boathouse, and he slams into me in one swift thrust.

I spasm around him, my fingers clawing into his shoulders, as I lift my head to the sky and cry out. When I lower my gaze to look at him, I find him staring at me, mesmerized. "You're so beautiful," he murmurs. I lean in to kiss him, and it quickly turns wild as he sucks my tongue into his mouth, biting and sucking on my lower lip. He still hasn't moved, and I grind down on him, pushing him impossibly deeper in an attempt to get him going.

He groans into my mouth and pulls back, so only the head of his cock is resting inside me. In one forceful thrust, he slams into me and sets a fast pace that quickly has me climbing closer to the stars above us. Our kiss turns sloppy, and my pussy clenches around him as I cry out his name. He continues to hammer relentlessly into me, dragging out my orgasm and starting me back up that cliff again. It feels like I'm on a rollercoaster, being pushed impossibly higher, but I know once we reach the top, it's going to be a hell of a journey back down again.

My head is spinning, and my breaths are coming so quickly I'm not entirely sure I'm getting any oxygen into my body. My skin feels like it's about to burst apart as, with each thrust, Cam pushes me toward my third orgasm of the night.

"Cam." The word is nothing more than a half-plea, half-pant. I'm not even sure if I can come for a third time, but I know my body needs *something.* This chaotic ball of energy building within me needs some sort of release.

"I know, baby. I feel it too."

I'm delirious, out of my mind with need, but I register the feel of Cam's fingers on my chin as he tilts my head so I'm looking deep into his eyes. Once he's locked me in his gaze, it's impossible to look away, and I watch riveted as he drives himself toward his own release.

He picks up the pace, and his hand moves down between our bodies, until it's circling my clit. He pinches it, and I swear I must black out for a moment, as the next thing I know, I'm lying bone-less in his arms, panting like I have just run a marathon and feeling sated like a cat who just had a whole bowl of milk.

"Fuck," I breathe out against his neck, unable to even lift my head. He leans against the wall, steadying us, and I can feel the rapid rise and fall of his chest beneath me.

He chuckles breathlessly, planting a tender kiss on the crown of my head. We stay like that until our breathing has returned to normal, and I'm confident my legs aren't going to give out from under me when I put my weight on them. Then we get cleaned up and re-dressed before heading back to the party.

THE NEXT MORNING, I'M AWAKE BEFORE EVERYONE ELSE, INCLUDING Mason. I still don't sleep well at night, and usually by four a.m., I've given up trying. Mason will be up in an hour to go to the gym, so I typically use that time to get my caffeine fix and binge-watch TV.

There's this show where people buy old, rundown houses and renovate them. It's riveting to watch. I love how they take these buildings that other people have written off and turn them into something beautiful.

Still in my sleep shorts and hair like a rat's nest, I pull open my bedroom door and freeze. I blink rapidly, trying to clear my vision and make sure I'm actually seeing what I think I'm seeing.

"What are you doing?"

Emilia jumps a foot in the air and spins to face me with wide, panic-stricken eyes. I quickly drop my gaze, taking in what she's wearing—her outfit from last night. Returning to her face, I notice last night's makeup smudged around her eyes, and her hair hasn't been brushed yet.

My own eyes widen as understanding dawns, and my gaze bounces back and forth between her and the door behind her—the door to *my brother's* bedroom.

"Did you…Were you…Are you…" Words fail me as I struggle to comprehend what I'm seeing.

"Let me explain," she rushes out, but before she can say anything more, the door behind her opens, and none other than Wilder fucking Clearwater steps out, also wearing last night's clothes.

My jaw drops open as Emilia turns beet red. Wilder, cool as a fucking cucumber, glances between us, smiling. *Smiling.* Like absolutely nothing about this situation is entirely mind-altering.

"Coffee?"

Neither of us responds to him. Instead, I just gape at Emilia, who looks everywhere but at me.

Eventually, he must realize he isn't going to get a response. "Alright, I'll put on a pot."

Yeah, that might be best. God knows my brain needs coffee if I have any hope of wrapping my head around what I just witnessed.

Still not looking at me, Emilia makes a beeline for the bathroom.

Oh, no, she's not getting off the hook that easily.

I push open the bathroom door as it slowly closes behind her, and once I'm inside the bathroom, I flick the lock behind me and stand in front of the door with my arms crossed, waiting her out.

She takes her sweet time, splashing water over her face to

remove the last of her makeup before running her fingers through her hair in an attempt to flatten the bedhead look she's sporting.

"Eh, wanna tell me what's going on?" I eventually snark, when it becomes pretty apparent she's not going to bring it up on her own.

"Nope. Not really."

I roll my eyes. The girl who's always asking inappropriate questions about *my* sex life, and can never seem to shut up, suddenly has nothing to say? Ironic.

"Did you have sex with Wilder last night?" Her cheeks turn crimson. *So that's a yes, then.* "In my brother's bedroom?" My brows tug together in confusion. "Where is Hawk?"

If it's possible, her cheeks redden even more so. You could fry an egg on them at this point.

"Oh. My. God." My mouth drops open in shock. "You didn't." She looks at me through the mirror above the sink, and the guilt is written all over her face. "Emilia, please tell me you didn't sleep with my brother last night."

Her lips press together, and her eyes take on a pleading look.

"Oh my god, you did." I run my palm down my face. "You slept with my brother. And Wilder."

"It was an accident," she rushes out, spinning to face me.

"What, you just slipped and fell on their dicks?"

She grimaces. "Well, no, not exactly."

"What does this mean? Do you *like* like them? I thought you hated Hawk?"

"I do...hate him," she's quick to assure me, which only confuses me further, although I guess I don't have a leg to stand on. I was attracted to the guys even though I hated them. Hell, I slept with Cam and made out with Mason, even though they were actively trying to ruin my life.

She groans, running her hand over her face as she sinks to the floor. I sit down opposite her, resting my back against the door.

"It doesn't mean anything. I still hate him. I just had too much to drink last night, and...I don't know." She groans again.

There's a long moment of silence while I try to process everything, and I watch silently as Emilia beats herself up.

"It would be okay, you know…if you did like him, or Wilder…or both of them."

Emilia slowly looks up from the spot on the floor she was staring at, her eyebrows raised in surprise. "It would be? You'd be okay if I wanted to go out with your brother?"

I shrug a shoulder. "I mean, yeah. Why not? He'd be lucky to get a girl like you. God forbid he go out with one of the Pac skanks." I wrinkle my nose in disgust at that notion.

She chuckles weakly. There's a knock at the door before she can say anything more, and Wilder speaks, just as I'm about to tell him to go piss outside, "There's coffee at the door."

Huh, that's actually quite thoughtful of him. Once I have heard his footsteps fade away as he disappears back down the hall, I flick the lock and crack the door, peering out to check that the hall is empty. Snatching up the mugs, I quickly close the door and lock it again, passing a cup to Emilia before reclaiming my spot on the floor.

As soon as I'm comfortable, she shakes her head, picking up the conversation again. "It's not like that anyway. I don't like your brother that way. He *infuriates* me. Even just being around him has my blood pressure spiking."

"And yet, you slept with him."

She scowls. "I told you, it meant nothing. It was a drunken mistake. The scholarship kids don't talk to me, and I don't know whether it's because I'm a scholarship student or because I hang out with you guys now, but no one else in the school will talk to me. Pass it off as being horny and having limited options."

Having unfortunately just taken a sip of my coffee, I snort and quickly swipe at my nose, catching a few dribbles of coffee that went up the wrong pipe. Coughing, I take another few gulps, this time managing to get the coffee into my system.

"And what about Wilder?"

She frowns into her mug. "If it's possible, I'm even more confused about him. I mean, he was *your* fiancé, and I guess we were kinda friends before you, you know...disappeared. I don't know why, but when you were gone, he took it upon himself to check in with me and keep me company. He'd listen to me rant about the guys and freak out over you...he was, sweet, almost." She must see the completely flabbergasted look on my face as she says, "I know, I know. I can't believe I'm using Wilder and sweet in the same sentence."

She's silent for a moment before continuing, "Then he beat up Deke, and I was furious with him. I still am. I didn't ask him to do that or need him to. I can fight my own battles; I don't need him stomping in here like a neanderthal and pissing all over what isn't his."

I snort at her analogy, and we lapse into silence as I watch her glower at a spot in the floor, thinking something over.

"I've, uh, actually, been invited to go on tour with Death on a Matchstick this summer," she says hesitantly.

My mouth drops open. "No way, seriously? I didn't even know you kept in touch with them."

She shrugs casually. "They've sent me a few emails. Well, Axel and Jared have."

"I can't believe you're only telling me this now," I gape, faking outrage.

"I wasn't going to go, but..." she trails off with another shrug. "Now I think I should. I've done nothing but study and live in the small bubble that is Pacific Prep for the last four years, and I'm about to go to college and do the same thing. I think...I think I want to just enjoy life for a bit."

I nod, understanding what she's saying. "You should. It would be good for you, and besides, they're hot as fuck. No sane person would turn down a chance to spend the summer with a rock band."

She chuckles. "Right? I must have been crazy to question it."

Another moment of silence lapses as we both sip on our coffees. "So, you're not angry at me?" I can hear the nervousness in her voice, and without a second's thought, I put my mug on the floor and crawl over to her. I wrap my arms around her in a tight hug.

"Never!"

The two of us sit on the bathroom floor, drinking our coffee and chatting about the fantastic summer Emilia's about to embark on, until there's a hard thud against the door and Hawk's gruff voice interrupts our chit-chat. "Hadley, Jesus Christ, you can't occupy the bathroom all morning. Some of us need to fucking shower."

Emilia and I just burst out laughing, leaving him to huff for another half hour before we finally emerge.

Once we've showered and dressed, we catch the bus into town —much to the agitation of Hawk and the guys, who wanted to drive us—to pick out dresses for the dance.

I have the new bank card Barton left for me, burning a hole in my pocket, even though I'm still reluctant to spend any of it. I haven't even dared to look at how much is in the account. I'm reasonably certain that I will be shell-shocked no matter what the amount is, so I'm better off not knowing.

"Shall we try that new thrift shop?" Emilia suggests.

"Sounds good."

We make our way to the shop, and for the next hour, we try on a multitude of dresses before picking the ones each of us like. It might not be the fancy, designer dresses we had last time, but we have just as much fun laughing at each other and mucking around in the changing rooms, before going to the checkout with our purchases.

Thankfully, I can pay for the dress from my scholarship stipend instead of using the card. I know Hawk told me to treat myself, but it feels weird, especially considering my strained rela-tionship with Barton. However, I use the card to treat us to lunch afterward—somehow, it feels more acceptable if I spend the money on both Emilia and me, as opposed to buying myself something frivolous I don't need. I know it doesn't really make any sense, but that's how I feel.

We go to a sea-front cafe and order more food than the two of us could eat in a week, filling the table with various dishes, and laugh and enjoy ourselves as we gorge on the food until my stomach feels like it's about to tear apart at the seams.

"So the guys and I have decided we're going to go to college," I tell her, once I'm so full, I can hardly breathe.

"That's great. Do you know where?"

I shake my head. "Not yet. Obviously, we're too late to apply for anything this year, so we'll take some time once school is finished, and we've sorted out this crap with Maria and the company, to think over our options."

"I'm so happy for you." The smile drops off her face, and she sighs. "It's going to be so weird being away from you next year."

"I'll come visit you, and you can come to wherever we are anytime you want. Plus, there's the phone and video chat. West showed me how to set that up, so we can do that every week."

She grins and holds her hand out across the table. "I'm holding you to that, Davenport."

I laugh and shake her hand, ignoring the prickle of tears in my eyes. *Damn, I am going to miss this girl.*

IT'S LATE AFTERNOON BY THE TIME I LET MYSELF BACK INTO THE GUYS' dorm, finding all five of them huddled together in the living room, talking in low voices.

"What's wrong now?" I sigh, the good mood from my day out quickly evaporating.

Dropping my shopping bags, I plunk myself on the sofa between Beck and West, snuggling in against Beck when he drapes his arm over me.

"I found this on the cameras today," West says, pressing play on his tablet and holding it up for me to see.

Maria is sitting at her desk, when her cell starts ringing. Lifting it, she looks at the screen before answering.

"Everything in place?"

There's a moment of silence while whoever is on the other end responds.

"Good. I need everything to go smoothly. No hiccups."

Whoever she is speaking to says something and then Maria hangs up.

West pauses the video, and I glance from him to everyone else. "What does this mean? Does it mean anything?"

"That's the problem—we don't know. It could be something, or it might be nothing," Beck answers.

"Well, have you talked to your dad?" I ask, looking at West.

"Yeah, I phoned him earlier. He claimed he didn't know anything, but we can't trust him. Just because he transferred the shares and money, doesn't mean he's not in Maria's pocket."

He's right. I know he's been keeping eyes on him, just like he is with Maria, but we can't trust him.

"Maybe we should pay him another visit?" I suggest.

"Yeah, except we all have exams this week, and I'm not even sure it would do any good." I can hear the frustration in West's tone.

I chew on my bottom lip, thinking. "Can you track the call or something?"

"I tried that too, but it mustn't be her normal cell. There were no calls at that time registered to her number."

"So it's a burner phone. That's suspicious."

"Exactly."

"Well, let's see if she does anything else suspicious this week. We don't know enough to make a decision yet."

We all mumble our agreements, but I can tell none of us are happy with this development, and I'm unsettled for the rest of the evening, unable to focus on studying for my first exam on Monday morning.

CHAPTER 21

Hadley

The next week goes by in a blur of exams and studying, to the point that words lose all meaning, and just looking at math equations gives me a headache. More than once, I contemplate breaking my arm just to get out of doing these exams, but as Emilia wisely reasons, if I don't do them now, I'll have to do them when everyone else is enjoying their summer break. *Girl makes a lot of sense sometimes.*

So, instead, I knuckle down and do my best to not fail every subject.

"How do you think you did?" she asks as we step out of our last exam on Friday.

"Eh, I don't think it was a complete failure." I'm hoping it's at least a C. I'm not expecting top grades in any of my classes. I've barely scraped through the year, what with my lack of a formal education before now. Honestly, if I was still a scholarship student, I'm pretty sure I'd have been kicked out long ago. Anyone looking at my grades can see that my transcript is visibly fake. All A's to barely getting by? Yeah, that, or it's a cry for help, and the headmaster is doing a shit job of ensuring his students are thriving here at Pacific Prep.

"You?"

"Yeah, I think it went okay."

I have to suppress my eye roll. She's said that about every exam so far, but I know for a fact that in all her practice tests, she was scoring in the nineties every time. So it definitely went better than 'okay'.

"You've got that board meeting tomorrow?"

"Yup," I answer on a sigh. We have our first—and hopefully last—ever shareholders' meeting at Nocturnal Enterprises tomorrow to celebrate the end of exams. On the plus side, I get to see the look on Maria's face when we tell her we own the remaining shares, and give her a big, old, fuck you as we watch all of her future plans for the company go up in flames.

"Whatever you and the guys are planning, you're going to be safe, right?" she asks nervously, looking worried for me.

I haven't told her exactly what's happening—it's better if she doesn't know—but she knows shit's going to hit the fan tomorrow.

"We'll be fine," I reassure her. When she still doesn't look mollified, I tack on, "I promise. We've taken all the precautions we can." I sigh heavily. "I'll just be glad when this is all over, and we don't have to worry about insane parents trying to come after us."

She chuckles. "You won't know what to do with all that spare time. Although, I can think of a few things you could get up to." She waggles her eyebrows in a suggestive motion that makes me burst out a laugh.

"Have you worked out what your plans are yet? There's only a week left of school."

"I know," I groan. "But not yet. I need to talk to Hawk and find out what his plans are. I have a pile of college brochures on my desk, but no idea how to narrow it down to one. I can't even decide where I want to live, and besides, this isn't a decision that I can make alone."

"Well, you've still got several months before you need to be picking a college. I think as long as you work out where you're going to live after next week, you can go from there."

"That's true. Hawk says Barton has mentioned more than once that we're welcome to live with him." I give her a look, and she just laughs.

"Has he been making more of an effort recently?"

I nod my head, still unsure what to make of it all. "Yeah. Every day he texts, telling me something about himself. He hasn't pried for any information or asked any questions. I think he's waiting for me to reciprocate.

"And you haven't yet."

"No. I don't know what to say to him."

"Do you want a relationship with him?"

"I don't know…I mean, maybe."

"I never knew my dad, so I don't know what that's like, but I have a great relationship with my mom, and I couldn't imagine not having her in my life. If your dad is genuine about trying to be an actual father, I think you should give him a chance. You might regret it if you don't."

We part ways outside the girls' dorm, and I mull over what Emilia said as I continue on to the guys' dorm. She might have a point. As a kid, I would have jumped at this opportunity, but life has made me cynical, and even though the little girl in me still wants that relationship with her dad, I'm not sure if I can handle the possibility that this is all a scam.

I let myself into the apartment, drop my bag, and collapse into the chair. Pulling out my phone, I open the chat with Barton, looking at his message from today.

BARTON: WHEN I WAS IN COLLEGE, I HAD A MOTORCYCLE CALLED Shirley. Everyone thought I was referencing a girlfriend whenever I talked about her. In hindsight, it was pretty embarrassing having to explain that I did, in fact, have an unhealthy relationship with an inanimate object.

I BARK OUT A LAUGH, EVEN AS A SMALL VOICE IN MY HEAD TELLS ME not to let my guard down. But, dammit, I want to. I really fucking want to. It might be incredibly stupid of me, but I *want* to believe he could one day grow to be a father I could turn to and rely on.

With my heart in my throat, I type out an unsure reply, sticking with his theme of sharing stuff about each other.

HADLEY: I'M SLOWLY WORKING MY WAY THROUGH EVERY FLAVOR OF ICE cream, and this week, my favorite is butterscotch.

THE SOUND OF THE DOOR OPENING HAS ME LOOKING UP AS HAWK strides in.

"Hey, how was your exam?"

I shrug. "Fine, yours?"

"Same."

He moves to join me in the living room, and I chew on my bottom lip before blurting out, "What, uh, are your plans...for, like, the future?"

He gives a casual shrug. "I haven't given much thought to it. If you're asking what my plans are for after next week, when we're kicked out of here, then what are yours?"

I have to fight back the grin threatening to form at his words.

"I'm not sure. The others have talked about going to college, and I'm game to give it a try—assuming I get the grades to get in—but obviously, it would be next fall before we could go."

"Yeah, I think I want to go to college. Hard to say no to four years of keg parties and sleeping 'til midday."

I snort out a laugh.

He moves to sit beside me on the couch, nudging my shoulder. "Wherever you and the guys go, I'm going too. We always talked about going together if we could convince our parents to give us those four years before going to work for them. I'm not about to let you all go off and have the college experience without me now."

My lip lifts in a grin.

"As for right now, maybe we should stay here while we work out our next move. There's still stuff that needs to be sorted, and Cam, West, and Mason all have houses that they need to decide what they're doing with. Plus, it will give us a chance to spend some time together...and with Dad too, if that's something you want."

I nod my head thoughtfully. "Yeah, that works. I guess there's no need to have everything planned out right now."

"There's some excitement in not knowing."

"CAN I ASK YOU SOMETHING?"

When I look up from the book I'm reading, I find West standing beside me, chewing on his bottom lip nervously.

"Uh, sure."

He hesitates for a second longer, and I frown, trying to figure out what could be bothering him so much.

"I was, uh, wondering if you'd be able to help me with something."

"Of course. What is it?" Setting my book on the coffee table, I stand, expecting him to lead me to whatever he needs help with. Only he continues to stand there, looking unsure.

He frowns and huffs out a small breath before blurting out, "I was hoping you'd be able to teach me a few things, self-defense moves or whatever, just in case shit goes down with your mom tomorrow."

A weighted silence fills the space between us before he continues to ramble.

"I'm just sick of being the weak link among us. I couldn't help when the mercenaries attacked us at Christmas, and I wasn't of any use when we went to rescue you at the compound."

I stare at him incredulously. "What are you talking about? I would never have gotten out of there if it wasn't for you."

He frowns, and I don't like how it scrunches up his face or the way he's talking about himself, as though he doesn't have these exceptional qualities that are so wonderfully him.

"West, you have such a unique set of abilities. I'm envious of your skill with computers. Anyone can learn how to fight and defend themselves, but it takes a certain way of thinking to do what you do."

He still doesn't look convinced. "I still feel ridiculous asking you for help."

"Well, you shouldn't. You didn't think less of me when I asked you for help in computer class. Even though I *know* my stupid questions drove you mad." One side of my lip lifts in a smile. "But I am curious, why didn't you ask Mason or Hawk instead?"

"They've tried teaching me before, and, well, let's just say it never ended well. Usually, they'd get frustrated and storm off, or I'd get angry and snap at them."

I give him a rueful smile. "Well, I'd love to teach you. Let me grab a few things, and we can head out to the clearing. That way, no one will interrupt us."

"Sounds good, I'll grab some flashlights for us."

I dart down to my room, grabbing my boxing gloves and some

tape, and a couple of other items that might come in handy, and as West and I reconvene in the living room, Cam appears.

"Where are you two off to?"

I glance at West, not wanting to tell Cam anything if he doesn't want him to know, but instead of the uncomfortable look he sported when he asked me for help, he looks absolutely at ease.

"Firefly's going to show me some of her moves."

Cam's face lights up. "Ooh, can I come?"

Again, I hesitate, looking to West for direction. This is his thing, after all.

"Pleeeeeease," Cam pleads, batting his eyelashes like an imbecile and making me snort at his childish antics. I quirk a brow at West. It's his decision. If he doesn't want Cam to come, I know Cam will be okay with it, despite how he's currently acting.

Huffing out a breath, West rolls his eyes. "Fine."

"Ahh, yay! I get to watch my girl be a kickass ninja. Oooh, are you gonna go all Dominatrix on his ass?"

I have no idea what that means, nor do I get the chance to find out as West shoves Cam in the shoulder and ushers us out the door.

Once we reach the clearing, I drop everything I brought on the ground and walk West through a few exercises to limber him up while Cam places the flashlights in a circle around us, similar to the setup on fight nights. It's still early dusk, but it won't be long before it's too dark to clearly see each other. Once he's done, he sits beside my things and silently watches us as I walk West through a few basic self-defense moves.

He watches my movements diligently and quickly puts them into practice when I pretend to attack him. The advantage of what I'm teaching him is that you don't need brute strength to beat your opponent; you just need to keep a cool head and think your way out of the situation. It's about finding your attacker's weak points and using them to your advantage.

I start by showing him a few easy ways to deflect an attacker and how to get out of their grip, whether they're holding onto your wrist or have their hands wrapped around your throat. Once he's got that down, I show him some offense techniques so he can take down an attacker and escape.

"Okay," I start when he's gone through the motions a few times. "This time, we'll go through the whole thing. When I come at you, try to get out of my grip and take me to the ground."

"What? I'm not actually going to fight you back."

I huff out a breath. "Why not?"

He glances incredulously at Cam before returning his gaze to mine. "I don't want to hurt you."

I chuckle softly. "You won't, I promise."

"Still, it's one thing to go through the motions, but to actually fight you off…"

"Ooh me, pick me! I'll do it!" Cam exclaims, throwing his arm in the air like we're in class or some shit.

"Yeah, I'll practice on Cam."

I throw my arms up in the air in exasperation. *Boys! There's no fucking dealing with them.*

"Fine, tackle Cam then."

Cam jumps to his feet, looking far too excited about the prospect of ending up face-first in the dirt, and does some weird thing with his arms as he shakes them out before lowering into a crouch and grinning ruthlessly at West.

I quirk a brow at him. "Just go through what we've talked about, Cam."

"Sure thing, boss."

I roll my eyes and step to the side to see both of them clearly. "Alright, go."

Cam moves on lightning-quick feet, closing the distance between him and West. He grabs West's wrist and tries to pin it behind his back, but West does exactly as I taught him, enabling him to break free and use the momentum to twist Cam's arm. Cam hisses in pain as he's forced to bend over to prevent his arm from being dislocated. With Cam's balance off center, West easily pushes him to the ground, giving him ample time to escape.

"Good! That was really good." I grin proudly at him as he helps Cam to his feet.

"You alright, man?"

"All good," Cam assures him, rotating his shoulder and pumping his hand to get the blood flowing through his fingers again.

"Let's go again. This time, use a few offensive moves, West. Don't be afraid to really go for it. Cam will survive a few bruises."

"Ouch, baby! You really wanna mess up this handsome face?"

I roll my eyes, even while I suppress my laughter. He does have a gorgeous face, but that's not to say he wouldn't look any less handsome with a bit of bruising. It would totally give him that alluring bad-boy look.

They go again, and West holds nothing back, giving Cam a good dig in his ribs when he tries to tackle him and swiping his cheek to get him to back off.

Clapping starts behind me as West again manages to take Cam to the ground, and I spin to find Beck, Hawk, and Mason watching us.

"How did you guys know we were out here?" I ask as they move to join us.

"Cam sent us a video of you and West. We thought we'd come watch the show." Mason smirks.

"We're not here to entertain you, idiots. It's important that he —that all of us—knows this stuff."

"I know, babe." Mason leans in to kiss my temple. "I was only joking. It's good that you're able to show him some things. I must admit, I was never very good at explaining it."

"We'll just sit quietly over here and watch," Hawk assures me, moving to sit in Cam's vacated spot. Mason and Beck silently agree and move to join him, but when I focus back on West, he looks more nervous than before. Great, he's not going to be able to concentrate if he's too busy worrying about what they'll think of him.

Sighing, I spin toward the three intruders. "Hawk, up," I snap.

"What? I don't need any lessons. I'm good to watch."

At his cocky attitude, I place my hands on my hips. "Really? You don't think you could learn a thing or two?"

I see the second he realizes how his words could be misconstrued.

"No...uh, I didn't mean it that way. I just...I can handle myself."

Lifting a brow in challenge, I goad him. "Prove it." It's all I need to say to guarantee he's going to get up and do precisely that. Just as expected, with his perpetual scowl in place, he rises to his feet and stomps toward me.

"Right, I have been teaching West how to break out of an attacker's hold and take them to the ground, so when I come at you, try to do that."

He gives a sharp jerk of his head and focuses all of his attention on me. Quicker than he can blink, I rush him, darting around his side so I can wrap my arms around him from behind. This is a hold I taught West earlier. Although I don't spare him a glance, needing to keep my focus if I'm to make my point—which is basically that Hawk is wrong, as per usual—I'm confident he's already assessed the situation and ascertained the best way to get out of it.

Unfortunately for Hawk, he does not immediately suss out my weak points and instead tries to use his extra strength to shake me off. I simply tighten my hold around him, as if I'm giving him a giant bear hug from behind. He leans forward, and I can already tell what his next move will be. As my legs leave the ground, I don't hesitate to wrap them around his waist, only further securing my hold. Yeah, okay, unless my aim is to squeeze him to death, I'm not going to do any actual damage. It's not like I could drag him off somewhere like this, but the intent of this exercise is to shake off your opponent.

From his bent-over position, he tucks and rolls, and I ignore the shouts from the guys as the air is knocked out of my body and I suddenly find myself flat on my back, with the enormous fucking weight that is Hawk Davenport on my chest. It's a clever tactic, but I'm not about to give up that easily. With the way my arms and legs are wrapped around him, Hawk has no use of his arms, no matter how hard he tries to raise them and knock me off. That leaves him with just his legs, and now that we're both on the ground, he can't do anything more than shuffle around and wait me out until I run out of oxygen. However, now that my legs are pinning his arms, my hands are free to do whatever I need them to, like, place him in a headlock that will have him going unconscious long before I run out of air.

I do precisely that, making it clear exactly who is in control here—i.e., not him—before I let up, loosening my hold and letting my arms and legs go limp. Coughing, he quickly rolls off me, and the others rush over.

"Dude, you could have hurt her," Mason snaps, helping me to my feet. I give him a soft smile, letting him know I'm okay, as I brush the dust off my backside.

He continues to scowl at Hawk regardless, who promptly ignores him as he climbs unaided to his feet.

"Your turn," I tell Mason, who only stares wide-eyed at me. Before he can fob me off with some ridiculous excuse or say something that will only backfire on him, I jibe, "Show me what you've got."

Instead of backing out, he smirks at my challenge, and I quickly move in to tackle him. Having already watched me with Hawk, he's much harder to pin down, but eventually he gives up, unable to break my hold on him, and I turn to Beck with a smug look on my face.

He just chuckles and shakes his head, stepping up to the plate without protest. Beck's the only one of the three of them that I haven't fought before, so I don't know his fighting style, but he was able to take on Mason, so I know he's more than capable, and given his background, he'll most likely be scrappy.

He lets me get him into a chokehold—yeah, I'm bringing out the big guns—and the second my arm wraps around his neck in a tight hold, he sidesteps me, hitting at my groin and elbowing me in the chin. None of it is done with full force, but enough to let me know he knows exactly what he's doing. Distracted, my hold loosens, and he easily breaks free, but instead of stepping away from me, he spins, surprising me as he kicks my legs out from beneath me. His hand whips out, slowing my descent to the ground as he comes down on top of me, pinning me beneath him.

I gape up at him with wide eyes. "Is it completely inappropriate that I'm turned-on right now?" I mutter, making him laugh darkly. He grinds his pelvis against mine, letting me know I'm not the only one affected by that act of dominance, and I have to bite back my groan. *Now isn't the time, Hadley!*

He presses a quick kiss to my lips before lifting me off and helping pull me to my feet, and we all break into pairs to practice a few more valuable moves. I'm hoping none of them will ever need to know this, but everyone should at least be aware of it.

When it looks like they've got that all down, I move to grab the few other things I brought with me. I still remember Cam's bafflement over me carrying a knife, and I don't like the thought of him walking around unarmed, especially with the threat of Maria coming after us. After everything we've already survived, I know she's just one person, but just because she doesn't have any close connections with the mercenaries in her company doesn't mean she's incapable of finding someone who will do her bidding. We need to be prepared for every eventuality.

Palming my own knife in my hand, I hold the other two I brought in a loose grip at my side and turn to face the guys.

"Knives?" Cam exclaims, and I can't tell if he's excited by the prospect or nervous.

"Yup."

"We already have the guns Cain gave us," Hawk reasons, and I nod, knowing that.

"Guns are great and all, but they have limited use when your opponent is right up on you, whereas a knife can always be useful."

I hand a blade each to Cam and West, who both hesitate before accepting them, and I quickly run through how to handle them and point out the main things to aim for. Large arteries are the best. My personal favorite is the femoral artery. People seem to expect it less. The neck is an overrated, overused artery that any half-decent opponent can see coming a mile away. However people never seem to expect a dagger to the groin.

I also take each of them through the best places to wound an attacker. Injuries that won't kill them but will incapacitate them, and make it much easier to get the advantage, or escape.

Despite appearing unsure, each of them listens intently to what I have to say, and I watch as they each practice a few simple movements with the knife, attempting to jab it into an invisible opponent.

When we're done, I focus on West. "Does all of that make you feel a bit better, or is there anything else you wanted to know, or go over again?"

"No, that was great, Firefly. I'm a little scared of ever pissing you off, but what you've taught us tonight was amazing."

He presses a sweet kiss to my cheek and I blush under his praise. When he goes to hand back his knife, I hold up my hand. "You keep that. I have a bunch more. Besides, you should really keep something on you at all times. It astounds me that you don't."

I bend to tuck my own blade back in my boot, and when I stand up again, I catch Cam's expression. He's biting on his lower lip, his pupils dilated with lust as he stares at where I tucked the knife away. Catching me looking, he gives me a dirty wink before giving himself a once-over, debating where to store his blade only to realize he doesn't wear comfortable yet sensible combat boots like myself, and stuffing it in the pocket of his hoodie instead.

"There should be a couple of blades in my old room I can give you guys, unless you grabbed them when you got my stuff?" I tell them, directing the question at Hawk.

"I didn't even know you had knives in your room."

"Well, I don't want to remove the ones I have stashed around your dorm, and I don't have any others just lying around."

"You have knives placed around our dorm?" Hawk asks, sounding incredulous, yet I can't for the life of me understand why.

"Of course I do. And I have a couple at Beck's place too."

"What—Where? When? Why?" Cam stutters out, looking shocked, although I can't for the life of me work out why.

I shrug my shoulder. "I dunno, I started stashing them when I moved in, but I had one or two already hidden before then. You can never be too careful." I don't tell them that I have hidden a bunch more around the school since what happened with Michael. I've even strapped one to the underside of my chair in the dining hall and buried one in the ground down by the lake. It helped make me feel like I had more control over my surroundings, even if it's not really true. After all, I had my knife on me that day, which didn't do me any good. But just knowing I always have something nearby, should I need it, helps me sleep better at night.

Nobody seems to have anything to say to that, and we gather up the flashlights and head back to the dorm, stopping by my old room so I can retrieve my knives and give one each to Hawk, Mason, and Beck. A calmness settles over me as I hand them over. I hadn't even realized how stressed I was about each of them, but I'm glad West suggested this tonight. I feel so much more at ease knowing they're better prepared to face whatever is coming our way.

Beck, Mason, Cam, and I huddle around the computer screen, watching as West and Hawk walk into Nocturnal Enterprises. Unfortunately, only shareholders are invited to the meeting, so we couldn't all go—something I was most disappointed about. West had to go, but none of us were comfortable sending him alone, so

Hawk went with him for backup. We're hoping once Maria finds out that we've fucked her over, she'll be less likely to do something irrational and stupid if Hawk is there. We're relying on the fact she might give a bit of a shit about her son and not act out in her anger. Honestly, I'm not convinced she's capable of caring about anyone other than herself, nonetheless Hawk seems to think he might be able to get through to her if shit goes sideways.

However, we weren't about to sit around with our thumbs up our asses and wait for them to come back, so we attached a small camera and microphone to West's suit jacket so we could all watch. No fucking way was I about to miss the look of shock on Maria's face when she discovers we've screwed her over.

I hate the fact I'm not there in person, though. To say I'm nervous about them facing off against Maria alone is an understatement. Still, the guys have assured me there will be plenty of people in this meeting, so Maria won't be able to do anything to either West or Hawk when she finds out what we've done. Pretty much everyone else who attends these meetings is clueless as to what goes on behind the curtain at Nocturnal Enterprises. They are only involved in the legal side of our parents' operation, and as such, Maria won't be able to do or say anything that could raise suspicion.

The elevator pings as the guys arrive on the thirty-seventh floor and are escorted to the boardroom. I chew on my bottom lip and my leg bounces anxiously with every step they take, until Beck reaches out and squeezes my knee reassuringly.

As West pushes the door open to the boardroom, we're greeted with a nearly full table of businessmen and women, with Maria Davenport seated at the head of the table. Wilbert is sitting dutifully on her left and my eyes narrow on him. He's been suspiciously quiet since handing over his shares and half of his wealth, but West hasn't found anything in the cameras to suggest he's spilled the beans to Maria.

The woman herself looks up at the intrusion, and her lips flatten in disapproval as her brows scrunch together in confusion.

"Hawk, what are you doing here?"

There's a sharpness to her tone, and it's obvious she's all business right now. She's about to inform the board that she's the majority shareholder and that she will be taking over the running of the company, so no doubt she's keen to get on with her one-woman show.

I can hear the smugness in Hawk's voice, and damn, do I wish I could see his arrogant expression, but I know him well enough by now to picture it in my mind's eye. "Why, we're here for the shareholders' meeting, Mother."

He strolls toward one of the spare seats at the top end of the table, next to her, which I imagine were the seats Barton and the others occupied at previous meetings. He's careful to keep a seat between himself and her at the head of the table, and West claims the empty seat on his other side.

"This meeting is for shareholders only, *dear*. Of which, neither of you are." Her gaze darts back and forth between Hawk and West, and I can see the anger radiating in her blue depths.

"Actually, I have recently acquired shares to the amount of 25% of the company," West states, lifting the necessary documentation out of his inner pocket and placing it on the table in front of him. His tone lacks the same smugness as Hawk's, but it's no less victorious.

My gaze is transfixed on Maria's as she glowers at where West's hand rests possessively on top of the paperwork, and I can see her jaw working in agitation. Her lips are pressed so firmly together they're nothing more than a thin pink line.

After a long moment, she tears her gaze away from West's hand, sparing a glance around the rest of the table as she works her face into an impassive mask. Focusing back on West, she manages to sound indifferent as she asks, "Where did you acquire those?"

By now, Wilbert is a bucket of sweat beside her. I can see the pit stains from here, and his hair is sticking to his forehead. On the other hand, West sounds cool as a cucumber as he casually states,

"Father here decided it was time to hand them over to the next generation."

With trembling hands, Wilbert lifts a handkerchief out of his jacket pocket and dabs at the sweat lining his temple. He's going to need a lot more than one measly square of cotton to mop up all that perspiration, however.

Like something out of a horror movie, Maria's head slowly swivels to fix Wilbert in place with a Davenport special glower. *So that's where Hawk learned it from.* He shifts uncomfortably in his chair, deliberately avoiding eye contact, and I can tell he's resisting the urge to bolt. I'm actually a little impressed. I have seen kids all but crumble when Hawk has turned that look on them.

He doesn't say anything, and she quickly dismisses him then focuses back on West, before fixing Hawk in her sights. "And what are you doing here, son?"

I notice the sleeve of Hawk's suit shift as he shrugs. "Moral support."

She could easily tell him to get out since he's not a shareholder —it's honestly what we expected—but instead, she dismisses him, huffing out a frustrated breath before calling the meeting to start.

She takes her time, her gaze slowly drifting over every member at the table and making it perfectly fucking clear who is in charge here.

"Who is everyone else?" I whisper to Mason.

"Heads of departments, people on the board of directors. Honestly, I'm not entirely sure. None of them are aware of Nocturnal Mercenaries, though. They all only work for the legitimate side of the business."

"How do you know that?"

"West did background checks on them all—on everyone in the company—when we first found out what our parents were really up to. As far as we can tell, everyone inside that building is clueless as to who they really work for."

"So the only people who know the truth are our parents and the guards at the compound?"

"Seems so. I guess the fewer people who know, the better. Between the four families, they were able to ensure all aspects related to Nocturnal Mercenaries were managed by themselves. Frank laundered any cash, so it looked like it came from legitimate sources, and he was able to justify the purchase of the compound by claiming it was a training facility for the men they recruited to protect their clients. With Barton and Maria in charge of security, they would have been able to keep an eye on things and make sure no employees were snooping anywhere they shouldn't. While Lawrence was in charge of the day-to-day running of the compound, those at Nocturnal Enterprises believed he was responsible for overseeing the running of the training facilities and private security personnel, and I doubt anyone would question Wilbert's client meetings."

Maria's voice interrupts us, and I focus my attention back on the screen. "To start us off, I'd like to update you all on a few changes regarding leadership." She side-eyes Hawk and West. "West has already—rather unprofessionally—informed us of the change of ownership of the Warren quarter of the shares, but given the unfortunate situation Frank has found himself in and Lawrence's untimely death, I have absorbed their responsibilities, along with their control in the company. With the unexpected return of our daughter, my husband has also decided to step down. All of this is to say that from now on, I'll be running things.

"I, of course, will be looking to fill the positions within the company that have been left vacant by the sudden absence of my fellow colleagues…"

For the next hour, they drone on about company-related things, most of which go over my head, but *finally*, everyone gets up to leave. Not waiting to hang around for Maria to catch up to them, Hawk and West are the first two out the door, and the elevator doors slide shut before anyone else can filter into the small space with them.

They descend in silence and make their way onto the street. With the meeting now over and the two of them out of harm's way, Mason leans forward to close the lid of the laptop, when the screen suddenly goes black.

"What the hell just happened?" I question, looking puzzled at the laptop. "Did the camera just cut out?"

"Maybe West turned it off?" Cam suggests.

Maybe.

"Shush, do you hear that?" With his brows tugged together in confusion, Beck leans in closer to the laptop, turning the volume up full. Whatever is covering the camera must be muffling the sound as well, but with the volume turned up, we can hear what sounds like a scuffle and the unmistakable sound of West grunting, followed by what sounds like a car door slamming.

"What the actual fuck is going on?" I snap. "Are they being kidnapped?"

I look desperately to the others, but Beck is the only one who looks away from the screen to meet my gaze.

"I think so."

CHAPTER 22

Hawk

I GROAN, AND IT TAKES A SECOND FOR ME TO RECALL WHAT happened. I distinctly remember something hard smashing across my temple. The second I remember that, the rest of my memories flood back like a tsunami, not that I remember much of use. I remember exiting Nocturnal Enterprises after the meeting. Of course, we knew we were putting a target on our backs by turning up today, but I didn't expect a retaliation so soon. The second our feet hit the pavement outside the building, someone threw a bag over my head, and two or three people must have surrounded me. When I hit out at one of the fucktards—and I know my hit landed well, causing some damage—someone else closed in behind me, pinning my arms.

I could hear West struggling beside me, but it wasn't long before we were both neutralized and thrown into the back of some sort of van. I was screaming obscenities at the fucking shit-heads, vividly painting their deaths with my words, when something hard whipped me across the head. The next thing I knew, the darkness was calling my name.

THE HOOD IS STILL DRAWN OVER MY HEAD, BUT I DRAW ON MY OTHER senses, noting that I'm tied to some sort of a chair with my arms tied behind my back. I try to move my legs but find them equally restrained. *Fuck.* I'm only left contemplating my options for a moment before I hear a faint groan from my left. I immediately recognize it as West's, and I hiss out his name. I've no idea if anyone is around to hear us, but I have to know he's okay. Fuck, Hadley will have my balls if he isn't.

"West," I hiss again when he doesn't respond.

"Uuuugggghhh." It's the only response I get. *Better than nothing, I guess.*

"Dude, wake the fuck up," I rasp more urgently, trying to keep my tone low in case anyone is nearby.

There's a long pause before he finally responds, and I breathe out a sigh of relief. "Fucking hell, I'm awake, asshole."

"Are you okay?"

"I'll survive, you?"

"Same. Do you know where we are?"

"No. They knocked me out."

Fuck. Neither of us mentions it aloud, but I know he's as perceptive, if not more so than I am, so without having to say it, I know he's hoping the others will have seen through the camera what happened and be able to track us somehow.

"Cough," he tells me, and without questioning him, I start hacking up like I'm having a fucking asthma attack. Over the sound of my own wheezing, I can faintly hear him talking, and I know he's speaking into his mic, likely reassuring the others that we're okay and relaying any information he can. I just hope we have reception and they actually hear what he's saying, but it's not like we have any better options at this point.

When he's finished, we lapse into silence, both of us lost in our own thoughts. The fact we were lifted right outside Nocturnal Enterprises means this has to be my mother's doing. Does that mean she knew about the transfer of shares before we arrived today? There's no way she would have had time to arrange for us to be kidnapped during the meeting. I watched her every move the entire time we were in that room.

That only leaves one option—that we were double-crossed. And there's only one person who would have gone running to Maria. Wilbert Warren. That limp dicked, pathetic sack of shit. I'm going to fucking carve out his insides for this.

Time has no meaning as we sit, both of us restrained to our chairs, and wait for whatever the fuck is to come next. We make a point of not talking much, not wanting to draw any unwanted attention, but we confirm that we're both tied to chairs and that neither of us saw who kidnapped us. The consensus seems clear, though—my mother is behind this act. Who else could it be?

I'm bored out of my fucking mind and dying to piss when the hood is finally pulled off my head in a dramatic flair that is completely lost on me, and I stare into the frosty eyes of my mother. The apathetic look in her eye makes me pause, but regardless of her expression, I carefully rearrange my face and give her a bland, unsurprised response. "Mother, about time."

She doesn't need to know my heart is racing in my chest and that my palms are sweating. Despite my outward appearance, I've never been held fucking captive, and to say I'm a little unsettled would be an understatement.

One side of her lip curls up in a cruel smirk. "You never did have any patience."

Her gaze drifts to my left, and I know she's eyeing up West. If I thought she looked at me with a cool gaze, it's nothing compared to how she is staring at him. My best friend. My brother, for all intents and purposes. To her, he's nothing more than a bargaining chip. Someone she can use to manipulate and threaten her way to achieve what she wants. It only makes me hate her more. She's my mother, and despite her callous attitude, I want to believe she wouldn't hurt me, but I'd be a fool to think that leniency would extend to anyone else.

I'm not even sure she would show Hadley any laxity. I have seen the way she looks at her own daughter. The detachment in her eyes. It's not normal, but then nothing about our situation is normal. Barton has made excuses for her, saying removing herself from the situation and focusing on work is her way of coping with everything that happened, but is that really true? At what point does she stop hiding and just accept that she's not that sort of mother? Does she care? Did she ever?

I made sure I was the one to come with West today, hoping Maria would listen to me, but honestly, I'm not sure she will. I want to believe that deep down inside, she doesn't mean me any harm, except the harsh reality is that I'm not entirely sure that's accurate. Yeah, she and Dad didn't treat me with the same distant callousness as West's dad or inflict the same judgement on me as Cam's. They definitely never beat me like Mason's dad did to him, but does that mean they cared? Barton is making a point of proving himself, but Maria...well, I'm still unsure about her. Regardless of how skeptical I am, the little boy inside me wants to believe his mother isn't capable of hurting him.

She moves to pull West's hood off, and regardless of the fear I can see shining in his eyes, he glowers defiantly back at her. Looking away from him, I focus on the threat in front of us. "What do you want?"

She takes her time, fixing me in her sight and tilting her head. "Why, son, I want what's mine. I want my company. *All* of it."

I shake my head. "We can't let you rebuild."

She laughs, this empty sound that lacks any sort of humor. Any emotion at all, really.

"What you're doing is wrong!" I snap, getting angry. "You're stealing kids!"

Her face transforms before my eyes into this heinous thing, and she snarls, stepping close to me and squeezing my cheeks in her hand. "I'm giving these children a future they wouldn't otherwise have. They should be fucking grateful! Without me, they'd have no prospects. They'd be dead in a gutter, high out of their minds, or shot in a gang war before they were even old enough to vote."

The longer I look into her eyes, I realize she believes the shit she's spouting. She truly believes she's saving these kids. And maybe she would be, if she wasn't subjecting them to a childhood of torture and forcing them into a life they might not want. But as it stands, what she's offering these kids isn't some sort of safe house. The compound isn't a haven. It's one of the levels of hell, and there's no escaping it once you're taken captive. It's not a place fit for children. No one should be subjected to the fucked-up shit that goes on in there.

Hadley has so many strengths, and I envy her tenacity; her ability to keep going in the face of adversity. Even so I can't help but wonder how she would have turned out if she'd led a normal childhood. If she'd grown up with the rest of us. I know she's fighting her own demons, and some days her PTSD wins, but the point is she shouldn't have to deal with any of it. No eighteen-year-old should have to go through what she's experiencing, what she's had to live through. She should have grown up with a mom and dad who loved her; and with a brother who drove her crazy. She should have attended sleepovers, where she gossiped with her friends about her latest crush and experienced the typical awkward teen moments at school that are essentially a rite of passage. She should have sent Valentine's cards and received flirty texts. She should have gone on first dates and gotten all dressed up for school dances.

She should have had it all.

Instead, she wakes up screaming at night, has trust issues, jumps to the worst-case scenario, and can't relax unless she's got her knife nearby. It's not a life I would have ever wished for her, and if I could do it over, I'd trade places with her in a heartbeat. Unfortunately, life doesn't work that way. We don't get a do-over. We must live with the choices we make…but that doesn't mean we can't avenge past mistakes.

"And what about your daughter?" I snarl, that ever-present anger I feel burning beneath the surface, sparking to life and flaring up at the thought of all the injustice. "What was she being saved from when she was kidnapped and hidden away in the compound? From you? From Dad?"

Mom tenses, and a flicker of surprise crosses her features before she masks it. "I didn't know you knew that."

Eh, what? That was *not* the response I was expecting!

I frown, scrutinizing her impassive expression. "*You* knew?"

Her lips purse and she gives a small shake of her head, but she doesn't answer me. A desperate need to know what she knows builds within me, and I glance at West, finding the same confused, questioning look on his face.

"Did you know where she was all this time?" I demand, my voice coming out strained yet insistent.

As if I asked her what's for dinner, she waves away my question like it means nothing, spinning in her high heels and striding away from us.

After several steps, she turns back to face me, and I can see what I didn't before. The malevolence marring her face. "She was *supposed* to be fucking dead," she spits out the words, her lip curling in a sneer. I honestly can't do anything but stare at her. I fucking gape, wondering how I ever thought I knew this woman. Wondering how I ever called her *mom*, 'cause at this moment, she is more reminiscent of a nightmare than any mother I know. "That fucking asshole screwed me over. He couldn't even keep a *child*" —she sneers out the word—"under control."

She huffs out a humorless laugh. "The fact she was able to escape under his command is laughable. It's a testament to the wayward nonsense he was running in that compound. Under my leadership, such shirking of responsibility will *not* be tolerated."

My mind races as I try to process what she's saying, only West beats me to it as he croaks out, "You knew? All this time, you knew where she was?"

"Don't be ridiculous," she snaps irritably, gesturing to me. "I had no idea she was even alive until you brought her home and told me who she was. She was supposed to be dead or buried so deep in the foster care system no one would ever find her. She was *not* supposed to be right under our noses, on our own goddamn property."

My head is spinning now. "So you did play a hand in her disappearance?"

She stops in front of me, her gaze hardening. "We're not here to talk about *her*. She won't be a problem for much longer." What the fuck does that mean?! It takes everything in me to not struggle against my restraints, but it's hard to fight past that clawing need to get to Hadley. She's been through so much, and I *refuse* to let anything else happen to her. Not under my watch. No fucking way. I don't give a damn what it takes, I will protect my sister with my life. With every fiber of my being, I will ensure she leads a long and happy life.

"What I want is the shares you stole from me." Maria's next words cement me back in the present though and remind me I can't just storm out of here to go to Hadley's aid. I want to be the one to save her, but I'm fully aware of the fact she's capable of looking after herself. We didn't expect my mother to come after us this quickly, but we *are* prepared for this, and I try to take some comfort in that knowledge; in the fact that Hadley can take care of herself, and she has Beck, Mason, and Cam to look out for her. I'd trust them with my life, so I know I can entrust them with hers too.

"I'm not just going to hand them over to you," West sneers, lifting his chin.

The condescending look Maria throws his way stalls the breath in my lungs. "Nor did I expect you to." Lifting her hand, she raises two fingers in a *come here* gesture, and from somewhere behind us, two men dressed in black appear. No further instruction is needed as they lay into West.

"NO! STOP!"

I fight against my restraints, screaming for them to leave West alone, but it's futile. It's only a minute or so, but as I watch, I feel like they beat on my best friend for fucking ages before they eventually relent. They're not even breathless as they move to stand in a soldier-like fashion, their hands clasped behind their backs and their legs hip-width apart. Their expressions are blank as if they weren't just beating on a kid a second ago.

I gape at them in shock, before focusing on West. His head is dropped against his chest, and a string of blood-tinged drool hangs from his lips, but his chest rises and falls in exerted breaths. He lets out a pained groan, reassuring me that he's still with me.

"What the fuck?!" I snarl furiously at my mom. I'm not surprised by her actions, but I am taken aback by the display of violence and the apathetic way she just stood by and watched.

Ignoring me, she approaches West, tugging on his hair until he's looking up at her. She smiles at him, and it almost looks gentle, reassuring, if it wasn't for the cruel gleam in her eyes. The longer I sit and watch her, the more I wonder if I ever really knew her. It's a question I've been asking myself on repeat all year, ever since I found out the truth about my parents. I have been going back through old memories, trying to put together the pieces and see the truth behind their facade, but everything is so murky it's impossible to tell what was real and what was all for show. Nevertheless, observing her now, I can't help but think *this* is the real her. Maria Davenport without her fake socialite mask on.

"Was any of it real?" I ask, drawing her attention my way.

She removes her tight grip from West's hair and his head flops forward as he groans. She doesn't spare him a glance as she stands upright again and turns to face me.

"Any of what real?"

"The time both of you spent with me? When you'd come to my football games and cheer me on, or when you showed up at my middle school graduation with a smile on your face and clapped like you were proud parents...was it all for show? Did you ever care?"

She tilts her head to the side, a pitying look on her face that confirms what I thought. Knowing I'm right doesn't make me feel any better, and I can feel something inside me shrivel up at the knowledge.

She pushes her lips out in a pout. "Aww, sweetie, did you want your mommy to love you?"

My lip curls back in a snarl as I go into my default protection mode. "What the fuck is wrong with you?"

The mocking look on her face drops off, quickly replaced with one of fury, and her hand flies out to smack me across the face. My head whips to the side, and I can feel the sting in my cheeks, but I use that pain to fuel my own rage, glowering at her with so much hatred I can feel it burning through my veins and turning my insides to charcoal.

"What is wrong with *me?*" she snarls furiously. Her lip curls back, making her features appear grotesque. "Just because I never wanted children, that means something must be *wrong* with me? Your father is the one who couldn't accept living a life without sniveling, snot-nosed gremlins running around—although I can't for the life of me work out why. Not once have you disproved me, and now that you've finally started to serve a purpose, you fuck *everything* up."

I can't do anything but gape at her as she rants. The disguise she's been hiding behind all these years is long gone now, and for the first time, I'm getting a glimpse at the despicable human being that lies beneath. Growing up, I spent so much time wishing my parents were present more, that they gave enough of a shit to be around, but now, as I look into the eyes of the monster that birthed me, I'm seriously fucking glad she played a minimal part in my life.

"Everything was fine until *she* came back." I watch as my mother visibly unravels before me, and I cast a quick glance at West out of the corner of my eye, finding the same *what the fuck* expression on his face. "She was meant to be DEAD!"

My eyes snap to her face. That's the second time she's said that, and the thought that she had anything to do with Hadley's disappearance only adds fuel to the burning fire of rage building within me.

"What did you do to her?!" I yell. My harsh words pull her

back into the here and now, and her gaze snaps to mine. Fire burns in her eyes, and rage pours off of her.

"I gave her life a purpose. Since I was forced to carry her around for nine months, giving up my size zero figure and dealing with fucking cankles, I was going to make goddamn sure I got something out of it."

"What the fuck does that mean?" I snap furiously, needing to know and simultaneously dreading the answer.

A cruel smirk stretches across her face, and the gleam of pride at what she's done is sickening. "I got rid of her to break your father. He was such a fucking sucker for you two. I knew losing his *little girl* would send him over the edge. The pathetic waste of space all but gave up after her disappearance, leaving me to take control. Between Lawrence, Frank, and I, we pushed the company to new heights. We made Nocturnal Mercenaries number one, the go-to organization."

She sounds so fucking proud of her achievement, and I sneer at her, not even recognizing this conniving bitch standing in front of me. Why was I so hesitant to kill her? It's all I can fucking think about as she glowers at me.

"But, Lawrence…"

"Lawrence was obsessed with me. He would have done anything I wanted for the chance to get me back—he *did* do everything I asked of him." She laughs humorlessly. "And the pathetic sap thought it was all his idea. A dropped hint here, a subtle nudge there. He loved fucking me while we spitballed ideas for how to destroy Barton."

Her insinuation is more than enough for me to gather she and Lawrence were working together back then. However, I'm guessing once Maria got him to do her bidding, she was done with him. Over time, as he became increasingly infatuated with Hadley at the compound, he became less interested in pursuing Maria, instead seeing Hadley as his second chance to start over. It's all incredibly fucked up.

My mother's expression turns sour. "Of course, I didn't expect him to double-cross me. To keep that little whore all for himself and use her against me." I can tell her focus is lost in the past as her eyes cloud over. "It makes so much sense now. How accepting he was when I broke things off with him. I had no other purpose for him. He was useless to me, just like Barton. All I have ever wanted is the company." Her gaze hardens as she snaps her attention back to me. "Now, enough of this nonsense. Give me the goddamn shares!"

She starts to stomp toward West, ready to pick up where she left off, but I call out, "You can't kill him."

She pauses mid-stride, looking at me with a feral look in her eye. "Who said anything about killing him?" My shoulders sag in relief, not realizing the prematurity of my actions. "That's what I have you here for."

Fuck.

A malicious grin curves up her botoxed lips, and without hesitation, she changes direction, striding over to one of the men dressed in black. He doesn't even move as she lifts the gun out of the holster on his belt and, flicking off the safety, she turns to face me. There is no emotion in her eyes as she lifts her arm and points the barrel at my head.

"Now, West," she says in a sickly-sweet voice, "give me the shares, or Hawk here, dies."

Fucking shit. I grit my teeth and glower at her, even as sweat forms along my back and my heart hammers against my chest. Until now, I never thought she was capable of it, but if all the shit she spouted in the last few minutes isn't proof enough, then the unwavering set to her face is definitely all the confirmation I need. My mother won't hesitate to kill me.

My tongue flicks out to run along my bottom lip, and I glance briefly at West, seeing the same *oh shit* look on his face before I return my focus back to the gun pointed in my face.

He opens his mouth to speak, and I know he's about to offer her anything she wants, but he doesn't get the chance. I jump as a blaring alarm goes off, delaying my execution...for now.

CHAPTER 23

Hadley

The four of us sit in silence, listening to the sound of a vehicle driving away, with my brother and boyfriend inside it.

"We need to go after them," I insist, jumping to my feet. "We need to go *now!*" I push more urgency into my tone when no one else moves. *What the fuck are they waiting for?*

"They'll be long gone by now, babe." Mason sighs, his brows furrowed as he thinks.

"So what, we just sit here and do nothing? We have to do *something!*"

"We can track their phones…assuming they're still on," Cam suggests, and my ears perk up. I knew I loved that gorgeous man for a reason.

He pulls his phone out, and I lean in to watch over his shoulder as he pulls up an app.

"What's that?"

"Fam Finder. You can add people to it, and so long as they have their phone on them, and it's turned on, you can track where they are."

"Handy," I mutter, watching as each of our names come up on a list on the side of the screen.

"Yeah, we added you and Beck to it after you disappeared." He maintains his focus on the screen, clicking on Hawk's name. An image of a map comes up with a flashing green dot in the middle. I lean in to get a closer look.

"It's moving."

"Yeah, they're heading West on Greenwich Street. It looks like they're trying to get out of the city."

"Where do you think they're taking them? The compound?"

I notice Beck shake his head and turn to look at him. "I'd doubt it. That place will be in ruins by now. The company probably owns other property—they could be taking them there."

"It doesn't matter where they're going," Mason says. "If we leave now, we can follow them."

We rush around, gathering bits and pieces. I shove on my combat boots, checking that my trusty knife is there, and with purposeful feet, I stride into the living room. Bending down, I reach under the coffee table and retrieve the knife I'd taped to the underside. Moving to the kitchen, I do the same with the knife taped to the top of the undercounter cabinet.

I'm faintly aware of the others watching me. Cam has made a game out of trying to find all of them. So far, he's found the one I had under the coffee table, but that's it. Idiot didn't even think to check the cistern behind the toilet or under his own damn mattress.

"You've still got your knives?" I ask, and everyone nods.

"Here's a gun, too," Beck says, holding one out to me. I notice each of them has one tucked in the back of their pants as well. Taking it from his outstretched hand, I do the same, and we all share a final look—a fierce determination burns in their eyes, which I imagine is reflected in my own.

With a sharp jerk of my head, I bark out, "Let's do this," and turn on my heel, striding out of the dorm without a backward glance. I don't need to. I know each of them is behind me. I can hear the promise of retribution in every thud of their boots as we make our way down the stairwell and out of the building.

WE WASTE NO TIME GETTING TO MASON'S CAR, AND WE ALL PILE IN. Cam, who's sitting shotgun, pulls up the map on his phone. "It's stopped," he exclaims, zooming in. He rhymes off directions to Mason, who doesn't hesitate to put his foot down on the accelerator and gun it down the road. "Looks like the industrial part of the city on the outskirts on the West side."

"Nocturnal Enterprises probably owns property out that way," Mason muses absently, most of his focus on the road in front of him.

I turn my attention to Beck beside me as he works away on his phone, before a video feed showing some sort of warehouse appears on his screen. Leaning in, I frown at the screen.

"It's West's camera," he explains.

I scan the image for clues as to where they are, but it's just a large, generic-looking room. It could be any warehouse owned by anyone, anywhere in or outside the city.

As I watch, someone moves into view, and I gasp when I recognize my own mother. I mean, I suspected she was behind this—who else could it really be? But I didn't expect her to show up to do the dirty work herself.

Her mouth moves, saying something.

"Turn it up!" I bark, staring wide-eyed at the screen as I desperately try to read her lips.

"What do you want?"

I let out a sigh of relief at hearing the strength in Hawk's voice.

"Why, son, I want what's mine. I want my company. All of it."

I watch, agape, as right before my eyes, Maria turns into something inhuman. Any pretense she had before is discarded as her hatred and rage rise to the surface and overflow. My hand flies to cover my gasp when two brutes come into view and start beating on West. I can feel Beck vibrating with anger beside me, and my heart clenches as all I can hear is his heavy breathing and pained groans.

"Hurry up!" I cry in earnest to Mason. "We have to get there *now!*"

He pushes the car faster, and I know we're going well above the speed limit, but my eyes remain transfixed on the phone in Beck's hand as the horrifying show continues to play out before us. I mentally store away the implication that my own mother was involved in my kidnapping. I don't understand how. Lawrence made it sound like he took me to get back at her and Barton, so it makes no sense how she would have been involved, but I don't have the time now to think about it.

"How long?" I cry, glancing out the front windscreen, and watching as large industrial warehouses fly by at breakneck speed.

"We're nearly there. Five minutes." Cam's voice is tense, and I know everyone is freaking out as much as I am right now.

Focusing back on the screen, I watch in horror as my mother strides toward one of the guards and lifts out a gun.

"Oh god," I gasp. I can feel vomit rise up the back of my throat as she points the handgun at Hawk, and says, "Now, West. Give me the shares, or Hawk here, dies."

"This is it! Up here on the left!" Cam shouts, already unbuckling his seatbelt, ready to dive out as soon as Mason pulls into the lot and slams on the brakes. Not hesitating, the second the car stops, I hurtle myself out of the backseat and run toward the warehouse, desperate to reach Hawk before it's too late, all the while straining to listen over the high-pitched blaring of an alarm for the sound of a gunshot that may as well be aimed at my own heart.

I mentally chastise myself for not considering the possibility of the warehouse having a perimeter alarm. We must have triggered it when we drove into the lot, and no doubt guards will be on the lookout for us now, so we need to move quickly.

My senses are alert to everything around me as we approach the warehouse. Annoyingly, the loud noise from the alarm makes it difficult to communicate with the others, preventing me from hearing if anyone tries to sneak up on us. On the camera, Maria has two guards in the warehouse with her, but she could have more lurking around out here.

How did she even amass people to help her so quickly? She shouldn't have the connections or the necessary pull with any of the guards to get them to do her bidding. Nor does she have access to the server to contact the mercenaries, and yet, she clearly has help. The gut-wrenching feeling in my stomach tells me we've greatly underestimated Maria Davenport.

Keeping low as I approach the warehouse, I wait for the others to catch up and signal for them to keep quiet before I ease the steel door and peer through the crack. I do my best to treat this like any job and go into work mode, but knowing my brother and West are in there make it infinitely more challenging. I've never had an emotional connection with anyone I worked with, so I have never had to deal with this. Suddenly, the way the compound raises us, tearing apart our humanity and teaching us not to care about anyone other than ourselves, makes sense. It's the only way to focus completely on your objective and not let emotions cloud your judgment.

Finding the room beyond empty, I pull the door open fully and enter the room, the guys closely behind me. It appears to be some sort of storage room we're in, consisting of nothing more than a few large crates. I make a move toward the door on the far side of the room, my objective single-minded, when the alarm cuts out, and the space seems to fall deathly silent as we all share a look. As I start toward the door again, a hand latches onto my wrist, and Beck hisses, "Hold on."

Frowning, I look over my shoulder at him. Not put off by the look I'm giving him, he states, "We need a game plan. We can't all just go barging in there."

"I agree," Mason pipes up, and I purse my lips, knowing

they're right.

Sighing, I nod. "Alright." I mull it over for a second. "We should split up. Mason and I will continue on this way"—I point to the door behind me—"you two go around the back of the building and see if you can find another entrance."

Cam looks between Beck and me. "Maybe we should call the police?"

I don't even need to think it over, shaking my head. "They won't get here in time. She had a gun pointed at Hawk's head. Even if they did get here before she did something, I'm not satisfied with her just going to prison. After everything she's done, everything she's doing, and everything she wants to do"—I shake my head again—"she's not leaving here alive."

The deadpan tone of my voice leaves no room for argument, and after a tense moment of silence, Beck sighs. "Okay. We'll go around back but be careful."

He and Cam don't hang around, moving back toward the outer door and slipping out of the room. Glancing at Mason, I silently check if he's good to continue. With a grim expression and a determined set to his jaw, he jerks his head, and I continue moving across the room to the door on the far side.

As I approach, I hear muffled voices on the other side, and I bring my finger to my lips before pointing at the door. Indicating that he hears the voices too, we both remain still as we listen. More muffled words that are impossible to make out, nor can I tell who's talking. Mason doesn't seem able to discern the voices either, based on the concentrated frown on his face.

I guess there's nothing else for it. Carefully, I reach out and pull down the handle, slowly inching the door open until I can peer in. The room beyond looks like the central part of the warehouse, consisting of an ample, open space. There's a giant metal shutter on the far wall that looks like it can roll up to allow forklifts to move easily in and out, with another steel door to the side of it.

I hear the voices again, drawing my attention to the middle of the room. *What the fuck?* I ease the door open further so Mason can see, and the two of us stare at Maria, standing in the middle of the room, with her gun aimed at…my father? Why is he here? Two guards are standing behind her, like a wall of muscle, while another two are manhandling Barton. Tied to the chairs in front of them are West and Hawk. Their backs are to us, so I can't see their faces, but other than West slumping a little in his chair, they appear to be unharmed. Hawk doesn't look dead, and the sheer relief I feel at receiving that confirmation has my knees nearly buckling.

I quickly scan the room for any other entrances or exits, noting none. *Okay, so Beck and Cam will have to make their entrance via the steel door beside the roll-up shutters.* Once again searching the room, there is a stack of crates near the back wall.

"Do you think you could get over to them?" I whisper to Mason, pointing out the crates.

He takes a moment to work it out, assessing the distance and cover points and weighing up how likely he is to be caught by Maria or one of her goons.

"Yeah, that should be doable. What are you thinking?"

"I'm not sure yet, but Beck and Cam are going to have to come through that door,"—I point out the only other door on the opposite side of the room to us—"so if you come from there, and I approach Maria from here, we would have them pretty well surrounded."

He mulls it over before nodding, and I step back so he can slip out. He shifts toward the door, but before he leaves, he spins around. His hand comes to rest on the back of my neck, pulling me in as his lips find mine in a searing kiss. "Be careful," he murmurs, slipping out of the room and stealthily making his way across to the crates at the far back corner.

I don't breathe again until he's hidden behind the crates, giving me a thumbs-up to let me know he's okay. As my heart rate settles back to a normal rhythm, I focus back on Maria and Barton.

"How did you even know we were here?" Maria asks him suspiciously.

"You forget, dear, I was the head of security. You might have been running the illegitimate side of things, but I still have access to anything associated with Nocturnal Enterprises. I was alerted to unusual activity here, and imagine my surprise when I signed into the system and saw my own son tied to a chair." He loses his cool by the end, snarling furiously at Maria and pulling against the two guards holding him in place.

From what I heard of Maria's speech earlier, it sounds like Barton, out of the two of them, has been the only one to give a damn about our well-being all these years. If what she said is true, she was the one that never wanted kids, but it sounded like Barton did. Is it possible he was the one that dragged her to Hawk's sports games and school events, wanting to have a more active part in his son's life? Regardless of the reason, he wouldn't be here now, trying to help his son, if he didn't care on some level. For that, I have to respect him, but it does complicate the situation somewhat.

I notice a small movement on the far side of the room, and my gaze snaps to the steel door, seeing it's ajar. I can just about make out Beck, who catches my eye, and I signal toward where Hawk and West are being held. He purses his lips, nodding, and I see his mouth move, likely relaying what he sees to Cam.

When he looks back at me, I do my best to tell him where Mason is, but he doesn't speak shorthand, and I end up huffing out a breath in frustration. It takes me a second to wrack my brain before realizing I can just send him a text.

Pulling my phone out of my back pocket, I notice Mason already sent one to a new group chat he set up that doesn't have Hawk or West in it—probably not wanting to accidentally set their phones off in case Maria or one of her gorillas reads the messages. Quickly scanning through the message, he's already described the warehouse layout to Beck and Cam and has informed them where he's hiding.

As I finish reading his message, a new one pops up.

BECK: WHAT'S THE PLAN?

HADLEY: YOU TWO REVEAL YOURSELVES AND DISTRACT THEM. I'LL sneak up behind Maria and catch her off guard. Mason, you stand by in case things go sideways.

BECK: OK. BE CAREFUL.

*MASON: *THUMBS-UP EMOJI**

PUTTING MY PHONE AWAY, MY PALMS SWEAT AS I WAIT FOR BECK AND Cam to reveal themselves. I have done plenty of jobs not dissimilar to this before where me or my teammates have been at risk. However, I've never put anyone I care about in danger like this, and my stomach is threatening to revolt as I second-guess my decision. I can't afford to lose any of them. I have no idea how I'd survive if I was responsible for any harm coming to any of them.

I don't get the chance to spiral any further as the door Beck and Cam were hiding behind is whipped open, daylight flooding the room and casting them in shadow as they step in, guns raised and pointed at Maria.

Maria turns slightly, and the guards shift to stand in front of her, protecting her from the new threat and giving me the advantage while their backs are turned to sneak into the room. On silent feet, I hurry toward a small collection of large wooden barrels and duck down behind them.

Peering my head around the side, no one has spotted me, and everyone is still focused on the new threat Beck and Cam have presented. I'm not paying attention to the conversation going on as I work out my next move and then quickly sprint toward the next item I can hide behind.

I continue to do this until I'm within firing distance of Maria. With the guards standing in front of her, blocking her from Beck and Cam's shot, her back is exposed to the unknown threat lurking behind her—me.

As I lift the gun out and flick off the safety, the voices start to escalate, and for the first time since Beck and Cam stepped into the warehouse, I actually focus on what's being said.

"It doesn't matter where your friends are hiding, you're outnumbered. This is your final warning. Give me the shares!"

The confidence in Maria's tone has me narrowing my eyes on her. She's so fucking sure that she's on the winning side here. That her goons are enough to protect her. Well, she has seriously underestimated us.

She swings the gun, pointing it at Hawk, and I see red. Her face is in profile, but even from here, I can see the intent in her eyes. She has no qualms about killing her son. If I was unsure about it before, the last of my hesitation disappears as I get to my feet.

I'm a trained killer. I know that once you decide and start down that path, you have to see it through to the end. So my decision was made the second I stood up. Which is why, as soon as I have my feet planted firmly beneath me, I pull on the trigger, and the sound of a gunshot rings out around the room.

Time seems to slow as the bullet shoots out of the chamber, and several things happen simultaneously. Maria must see my movement out of the corner of her eye as she turns her head, but keeps her gun focused on Hawk. Her eyes widen in surprise. At the same time, the two guards holding Barton spot me, and they drop their hold on him to reach for their weapons. No longer restrained, Barton dives forward in front of his son just as the sound of a gun goes off.

That one was definitely not mine.

CHAPTER 24

Hadley

Chaos erupts around me, but I don't pay attention, swinging to point my gun at the guards going for their weapons. I'm faintly aware of the sound of more gunshots, and the other two men blocking Maria hit the floor.

My ears ring with the aftershock of the shots and the rapid pounding of rushing blood, and as I look away from the dead bodies of the guards and Maria, the world comes to a standstill. It takes me a second to process what I'm seeing, unable to tear my eyes away from the blood spatter on Hawk's face.

"Dad!" he screams, and the tremble of fear in his voice is what breaks through my trance. As I blink back to the present, the reality of what I'm seeing crashes into me. Hawk is thrashing in his chair, trying desperately to get to Barton, who is lying unmoving in front of him, blood seeping out from a gunshot wound to his abdomen.

Beck rushes toward Barton, tugging off his top and pressing it to the wound. Barton's face scrunches, and he groans, the only indication he's still alive as Beck keeps putting pressure on the wound, attempting to stem the blood.

Mason moves to quickly tear through the bonds holding Hawk in place, and he falls to his knees beside his father. "Dad." The word sounds more broken this time, and it fractures something inside me. My heart breaks for Hawk, for what he's about to lose, but it also bleeds for myself, for the relationship I never had the chance to foster. I have been going back and forth for weeks, but suddenly I realize how right Emilia was. I *want* to know the man who's my father. And now I might never get that chance.

My feet are glued to the floor as I watch on in horror. The feel of Cam's warm palm slipping into mine is the only thing grounding me right now.

"We need to get him to a hospital!" Beck yells.

Now free, West drops onto the ground beside Hawk, and Mason moves to Beck's side and asks, "What can I do?" His expression is tight as his gaze darts over Barton's supine form.

"Eliz—Hadley." Barton's weak croak has all of them pausing, and the way his eyes dart unseeingly back and forth, trying to find me, makes my heart hammer in my chest. My feet feel like they've been laid in cement as I watch helplessly, unable to move closer.

Cam places his hand on my lower back, applying gentle pressure to get me moving. "Go see him," he whispers in my ear, his voice full of heartache.

With his support, I move over to where Barton is lying, and West shuffles out of the way as I collapse to my knees beside Hawk.

"I'm here."

I hadn't even realized tears were coursing down my face until Barton lifts a shaky hand to swipe them away.

"I'm sorry." His words are a weak rasp, followed by a

coughing fit that sounds horrendous and leaves him looking paler.

"Shush, it's okay. Just rest." I can't look away from his face as the life seems to drain out of him, and he smiles feebly. I'm faintly aware of the guys' hushed whispers around me, but I can't seem to concentrate on what they're saying. All my focus is on memorizing every crease and line of my father's face, wanting—needing—something to remember him by.

"I wish I had the chance to know you better."

The tears are flowing freely now, and Hawk wraps an arm around my shoulders as I sob. "Don't say that. You will. We'll get you help."

He manages another small smile, though I can see it in his eyes. He knows he's not getting out of here alive, but I refuse to accept that reality. I refuse to believe my luck is so fucking shitty that, just when I'm handed the opportunity to get to know my father, fate—the psychotic bitch that she is—is going to come and take it all away from me.

"Hawk." The urgency in Beck's voice has my gaze snapping up to his. "We need to move him."

"Did you phone an ambulance?" Hawk asks.

Pursing his lips, Beck shakes his head. "They won't be here in time. Mason can drive him to the hospital faster."

Hawk gives a sharp jerk of his head, and between the five of them, they sort out how to lift and maneuver Barton out of the warehouse.

"Hadley, I need you to keep this pressed firmly against the wound. Can you do that?"

My voice wobbles as I respond. "Y-yeah." Beck holds my gaze for another moment before confirming I'm present enough to follow his commands.

"Mason, go bring the car around. Park it as close as you can get it, and be ready to fly out of here as soon as we've got him in the backseat."

Nodding, Mason rushes off to do just that, and between them, the rest of the guys get Barton to his feet with his arms slung over Hawk and Beck's shoulders. The second he's upright, I press the shirt against the bullet wound.

Awkwardly, the three of us move toward the door as Beck and Cam come through. Glancing over my shoulder, Cam is helping West, who is looking worse for wear, with a black eye forming and blood trickling from a cut to his brow. As we approach the outer door, Cam runs ahead, propping it open as we shuffle through it, finding Mason pulling the car up.

Cam yanks open the door to the backseat, and Hawk and Beck carefully ease Barton into the car so he's lying across the seats. His eyes are closed, and his breathing has this god-awful rasp that doesn't sound good.

My hands are shaking like crazy when Beck clamps his hands over mine, taking the blood-soaked shirt from me. "You did good, sweetheart. I'll take it from here." He gently kisses my temple and climbs into the backseat, careful not to jostle Barton as he checks his vitals and continues tamping the wound. "We've gotta go!" he shouts.

"Hadley, get in!" Hawk barks urgently.

"What? No. You get in! We'll get a cab and meet you there," I insist, pushing Hawk toward the front passenger seat.

"No. I'm not leaving you." Without waiting for me to argue with him, he pins West with a look. "West, get in. You need to be checked out anyway."

West's mouth opens in protest, but Beck has had enough of our shit. "West," he snarls. "Get in the fucking car."

Huffing out a breath, West glances at me with what looks like an apology in his eyes, but I'm not sure why, before he climbs into the passenger seat. He hasn't even closed the door before Mason is gunning it out of the lot and down the road, out of sight.

When they've disappeared, I look to Hawk, seeing the despair in his eyes. Despite the lack of hope I see there, I ask, "Do you think he's going to make it?"

He wraps his arms around me, and I bury my head in his top,

stealing some of his strength. I don't miss the fact that he doesn't answer my question, and the sick feeling in my stomach solidifies.

When he pulls back, I run my eyes over him. I take him in for the first time since everything went down. He's got a split lip that looks like it's scabbed over. Other than red marks around his wrists, he seems relatively unharmed. He's definitely in better condition than West.

"Are you okay?" I ask quietly, scanning him over for any injuries I may have missed.

"I'll be fine. Let's just get to the hospital."

"I've booked a cab," Cam pipes up helpfully. "It'll be here in fifteen."

I look over my shoulder to the warehouse behind us. "What, uh, are we going to do about the mess in there?"

Hawk grimaces. "I'm not sure. Maybe Beck can see if Cain knows anyone who could sort it out?"

"Maybe."

It's not the best of plans, but I'm too concerned about Barton to try and figure out a better solution.

The three of us make our way toward the main road to wait for the taxi. Hawk all but collapses onto the sidewalk, placing his elbows on his knees and sighing heavily as he goes to bury his face in his hands before realizing they're covered in blood.

Pausing, he stops and stares at the blood on his hands, like he can't recall how it got there, before he frowns and crosses his arms instead while hanging his head.

I move to join him, suddenly feeling exhausted, but as I bend down, I notice the absence of my gun from the back of my pants. I quickly straighten and pat myself down.

"What's wrong?" Cam asks, watching me closely.

"My gun, I don't have it."

"Does it matter? You probably can't take it to the hospital anyway," Hawk mumbles, looking up at me.

"My fingerprints are on it. I don't want to leave it behind."

I start back toward the warehouse, but Cam's arm snaps out, his fingers wrapping around my upper arm. "I'll go get it."

I give him a small smile. "It's okay, I'll get it. I can't just sit here and wait anyway."

His lips flatten, but he lets go of me. I don't waste any time jogging back to the warehouse, not wanting to hold us up if the cab arrives while I'm gone.

Pulling open the side door, I scan the floor, my gaze bouncing over the dead bodies as I search for my gun. Spotting it lying on the ground, I swallow around the sudden lump in my throat as my eyes bounce to the puddle of blood beside it. I can't think about what might happen to Barton right now. One thing at a time. Retrieve the gun. Get in the cab. Go to the hospital. *Then* I can think about him.

My footfalls reverberate around the large space as I move to retrieve my gun, yet as I go to bend down, the sound of stiff boots on the concrete behind me has me spinning around, crouching and raising my fists in preparation for whatever shitstain tried to sneak up on me.

My eyes widen as I come face to face with Bowen, pointing his gun in my motherfucking face, like I haven't already had the day from hell.

"Ah-ah." He waves his gun, indicating for me to step away from mine, which is uselessly lying on the floor at my feet. Keeping my eyes trained on him, I slowly sidestep until the gun is out of my reach, holding my hands out to my sides, making it clear I don't have any other weapons within reach.

I watch him closely, on alert for any sudden movements, as I try to work out where the fuck he came from. Was he here this whole time? Hiding out? Why?

"You couldn't have made this easier for me, D," he purrs, his beady eyes eating me up. The way they flare in excitement at having me trapped, sickens me, and I struggle to regulate my breathing as my pulse spikes and my palms begin to sweat. "I thought I'd have to chase you down, but here you are." His lips curl up in a cold smirk that sends a shiver down my spine. "It's almost like you missed me…did you miss me, D?"

I can hardly focus on his words as images flash before my eyes. One second I'm standing opposite him in the warehouse, and the next, I'm chained to the wall in his torture room back at the compound.

In my distraction, he manages to get closer to me, and when I blink back to the present and find him towering over me, I scurry backward on shaky legs, desperate to maintain some distance between us while I talk myself out of my panic attack. *Now is not the fucking time to be having traumatic flashbacks!*

I take a second to give myself a mental reprimand. I have been doing well since I opened up to the guys. Sure, there have been the odd moments when I've struggled or woken up from a nightmare, but talking to the guys and opening up to them has really helped me adjust. Knowing that we have been systematically working on bringing down our parents and the company has been an enormous help too. I can't let this sick fuck destroy all that progress.

Thoughts flitter across my mind of Hawk and how fucking grief-stricken he will be if he loses his dad. Or if I allow this asshole to destroy me, along with what losing me might do to the guys. Would West and Beck's relationship survive if something happened to me? I know it wouldn't take much for Cam to break. He might appear like he's back to his normal self, but his wounds are still healing. One strong pull on the stitches, and he would fall apart. And Mason…he's only started to poke his head out of his shell and feel confident enough to be himself. I don't want him to go back to the cold, impassive person he was when I first met him.

Those thoughts bolster me, and I straighten my spine, glowering at Bowen as I refuse to let him intimidate me. My little act of defiance has one side of his mouth lifting, excitement for the chase flaring in his eyes.

"I always knew there was more fight in you than Lawrence believed. You wouldn't have survived all those years if there wasn't." He chuckles malevolently, like we're sharing some sort of joke. "You had him fooled, in any case. He thought he had you broken and reliant on him, ready to do just about anything he asked of you." He tilts his head to the side ever so slightly. "But that wasn't the case, was it? You've been deceiving him—all of us —all these years, planning your little escape." He shakes his head and sighs as though he's disappointed. "But, D, you should have known you could never have a normal life." His mocking laugh echoes in my head, along with his next words. "Who would want to be with someone who can't bear children, after all? Face it, you can never escape your fate."

Instead of shrinking back from his words, which terrify me more than he could ever know, I match his smirk with one of my own, loving how a little line forms between his eyes as he tries to make sense of my reaction. "Maybe not, but neither can you."

The gun goes off as I dive to the left, sliding along the gritty concrete floor, ignoring the pain that flares along my side as I reach for my gun. Quickly flipping onto my back, I point the barrel at Bowen as he spins, glowering at Hawk in outrage, adrenaline masking the pain he must be feeling from the bullet wound to his shoulder.

"For Meena, and for me," I whisper as I fire off a shot straight into the side of his head before he can raise the gun at my brother. Enough fucking people have shoved a gun in his face today. I won't let one more piece-of-shit scumbag get the chance.

His eyes widen comically before he crumples to the ground in a heap. I stare at him as if expecting him to come back to life and attack us again, as I try to wrap my mind around the fact the man who killed my best friend, who tortured me relentlessly over the years, is dead. It almost feels too easy. I'm waiting for the other shoe to drop...but it never comes.

Instead, I feel the warmth of Hawk's presence at my back as he pulls me into his arms.

"Are you okay? Hadley! You're bleeding."

I have to blink several times, but as the adrenaline wears off, the sting of torn flesh along my arm cements me in my reality—one where Bowen truly is dead.

Looking down at my arm, the long Henley I was wearing has been ripped open, and the underlying skin scraped off from where I slid across the ground, leaving it red and raw looking, with bits of blood forming where the grit has broken the skin.

"I'm fine," I assure him, not that he listens, lifting my arm to inspect it himself. Seeming satisfied, he lets me go, helping me to my feet. My side aches a little, but it's nothing I can't live with.

"Where did you get the gun from?" I ask, brushing the dust off myself.

"When you didn't come right back, I got a weird feeling. Something was just telling me I needed to get in here, so I grabbed it from Cam and came to find you…although it looked like you had everything handled." One corner of his lip lifts, and I can see the proud gleam in his eyes.

I scoff. "I don't know about that. He definitely got the better of me for a second there. I-I kept remembering what it felt like to be back in that compound, chained to his wall."

Hawk's eyes darken, and he places a hand on my shoulder. "You'll never be back there again. And look at how far you've come. You were able to work through the trauma and fight back. I'm so proud of you, Hadley."

Tears prick my eyes. "I couldn't have done it if you hadn't come looking for me."

He smiles placatingly. "I'm pretty sure you'd have found a way. Now let's get out of here. The cab should be here, and Cam will be wondering where we are."

I glance around at the dead bodies strewn over the ground, noticing Hawk's gaze linger on the unmoving form of his mother, and a look I can't place passes over him.

I nudge my shoulder against his. "I'm sorry about your mom. I know you wanted to believe the best in her."

He lets out a long, exhausted-sounding sigh. "Yeah, I did." He shakes his head, as though he's annoyed at himself. "But she was never the mother I wanted." When he looks at me, lines mar his forehead. "Did you hear what she said?"

"About how she got rid of me and that I'm supposed to be dead?" I snort. "Yeah…I just don't understand how she was involved."

He shrugs his shoulders. "I don't know."

"Lawrence told me he and Maria were meant to get married until Barton came along. Do you think they were working together?"

Hawk wraps an arm around my shoulders, pulling me in against him. "It sounded that way, but whatever their plan was, it doesn't matter now. They're both gone, and we're still here."

"Did you hear gunshots?" Cam shouts, rushing into the warehouse. He freezes when he spots Bowen lying on the floor, and his expression darkens. "What the fuck was *he* doing here?" he snarls.

"It doesn't matter," I say, repeating Hawk's words. "Let's just get the fuck out of here."

Cam continues to stare at Bowen's body until Hawk's phone goes off, drawing each of our attention.

Pulling it out of his pocket, he puts it on speaker before he answers, "Yeah?"

"They've just taken your dad into surgery," Beck says, his voice sounding grim. "They weren't able to tell me anything more."

"Thanks, man. We'll be there soon."

"Don't worry about the warehouse. I've spoken to Cain, he knows someone. He'll get it sorted."

Before any more assholes can crawl out of the woodwork and attack us, we leave the warehouse behind and head to the hospital. With every passing mile, I pray to god that Barton makes it through his surgery. I have lost so much, I can't lose him too.

CHAPTER 25

Hadley

Hours go by as the six of us wait anxiously in the waiting room for news on Barton's progress. All we know is he's still alive, but that's not much comfort considering he's been in surgery for the last four hours and could still die at any moment.

The only positive is that West has no lasting damage, just some bruising that will heal in a few days.

Beck's phone buzzes, and he looks at the screen before showing it to me. There's a picture of a building being ravaged by flames, and it takes me a second to realize it's the warehouse from earlier.

I guess Cain's man came through. At least that's one less thing to worry about. I smile at Beck. "Thanks for taking care of that."

He wraps his arm around my shoulder and kisses my temple. "You know it."

WE LAPSE INTO SILENCE. HAWK'S FOOT TAPPING INCESSANTLY against the linoleum tiles is slowly driving me insane. He's had a scowl on his face since he sat down, and he's only gotten increasingly more worked up the longer we've been sitting here. I can't tell if he's just worried about Barton or if something else is bothering him.

Eventually, he lets out a long, frustrated sigh and runs his hand through his hair. "What did Bowen mean when he said you can't have children?"

My throat is dry as I stare wide-eyed at him. *Shit.* I didn't know he had heard that.

He stares at me with a look I can't quite place—a half-plead, half-blood-thirsty rage. I'm incapable of forming any sort of response as I swallow around the lump in my throat.

I can feel the others looking between Hawk and I, but I cannot look away from the maelstrom of emotions flittering across his face. His stare holds me captive, practically pulling the dark secret out of me.

I lick my dry lips and chew on my lower lip. "He—" Fuck, how do I even explain this to everyone. Tearing my gaze from Hawk's bewitching ones, I glance at each of my guys, hoping this final secret won't be the one that breaks us. We've already survived so much, but this is...different. While I'm not sure if I want children in the future, that doesn't mean the guys are willing to attach themselves to someone who will *never* bear children and are ready to accept the possibility of never having their own kids.

My face crumples as I sigh, turning my gaze back to Hawk. "Several years ago, I was, uh, sterilized."

My words are met with a deafening silence, which feels like it lasts a lifetime, and I swear I see something break in Hawk's eyes as he stares at me with such a profound sadness it constricts the air in my lungs.

"I don't—" Beck begins, and when I finally look at him, lines form across his forehead as he tries to process what I'm saying. "They performed surgery on you?"

I nod my head. Leaning back in my chair, I push down my pants enough to show them the barely visible scars on my lower hips. They're just tiny white lines, and in comparison to the marks on my back, they're nothing.

They all lean forward to see where I'm pointing, and the second Hawk sees the marks, he storms off, looking ready to punch someone. I watch him go with concern, but Mason's hand on my thigh draws my attention back to the guys and where he is crouched in front of me.

"Let him go," he says, giving my thigh a reassuring squeeze. "Talk to me."

I give a small shrug of my shoulder. "What is there to say? I can never have kids." Unable to look into his blue eyes and see the concern there, I drop my gaze to my lap. "If you stay with me, you won't ever have your own children." I can feel the tears welling in my eyes, the guilt of robbing the guys of that opportunity riding me hard.

"Baby." Mason presses his finger under my chin, forcing me to look at him. "Has a doctor ever told you that? Or is that just what Bowen or someone at the compound told you?"

My brows scrunch together, and I respond in a quiet, unsure voice, "Some guy at the compound told me."

A small smile graces his lips. "Then let's talk to a doctor and get a second opinion before we make any decisions, yeah?"

I give a hesitant nod. "But, what if…"

"If it's true, then we'll deal with it like we have everything else." He strokes his thumb down my cheek, and how he looks at me with such earnest devotion leaves me speechless. "Nothing you say or do will ever scare us off." He must be able to see the doubt in my eyes, as he continues, "If you can't have children, then, if and when we decide we're ready for kids, we can adopt. Or look into surrogacy, or…I don't know, but we will work it out. As a team. The five of us."

A small grin lifts one side of his lips. "You're stuck with us, Little Warrior. It's you and me. Always."

I glance up at Beck, West, and Cam, and the three of them move to surround me. Beck clasps one of my hands in his, and West takes the other. Mason scooches to the side so Cam can kneel beside him in front of me.

"Always," Beck promises as Cam and West nod their agreement, all of them looking at me with impassioned gazes. The amount of love pouring off them has tears overflowing and running down my cheeks.

"I love you, all of you."

Beck presses a kiss to my forehead as each of them murmurs loving sentiments.

Mason and Cam eventually pull up chairs, so we're all huddled together, which is how Hawk finds us when he finally returns. As soon as he steps into the doorframe, my head snaps up, and the anguish in his eyes has me standing up, moving toward him as he steps into the room.

His arms wrap around me as mine wind around his neck, pulling him in for a hug. He whispers apologies into my ear, and I run my hand up and down his back as I soothe him. None of this is his fault, and he shouldn't have to bear any of the pain.

"We'll talk to a doctor and find out for sure. We will do whatever it takes to fix this, if that's what you want." I smile into his hug, loving how this grumpy brother of mine who hates everyone except his family is always ready to fight my battles with me. He always has my back, and I know he always will.

We pull apart as a man dressed in scrubs walks into the waiting room. "Davenport family?"

"That's us," Hawk rushes out, turning to face him.

"I'm Dr. Gallaher, can we, eh, talk in private?" The doctor glances at everyone else crowded around us.

"It's okay, you can tell us in front of them. How's my dad?" Hawk asks, desperate for answers.

I feel Cam slip his hand into mine, and I hold on tightly, terrified to hear the doctor's next words.

Nodding, he looks down at the clipboard in his hands. "Your

father was shot in the abdomen. The bullet nicked his aorta, causing massive internal bleeding. He lost a lot of blood, and it was touch-and-go a few times during the surgery, but we managed to stop the bleeding, and he's currently in recovery."

"He's alive?" My voice is a harsh croak as tears overwhelm me.

"He is. He's still under anesthesia, and it will probably be a while before he starts to come around, but he's alive. He's currently getting a blood transfusion and will require careful monitoring for the next twenty-four hours, but after that, he should be out of the woods."

I practically keel over with relief and feel someone's arms around my waist, holding me upright.

"Can we see him?" Hawk asks anxiously.

"Immediate family only for now," the doctor explains, glancing behind us to the others.

"We're his children," I clarify.

"Then the two of you can sit with him, but no other visitors for now."

We both nod in understanding, and I glance over my shoulder at the guys, who all wave me on before I follow after the doctor and Hawk.

He leads us into a room, and I'm taken aback by how frail Barton looks in the bed. Monitors are hooked up all over the place, and he looks as white as the sheets draped over him.

"As I said, it will be a while before he's awake. I'll come back to check on him in a bit."

I murmur a thanks, unable to take my eyes off Barton as Hawk moves to the bedside. His gaze runs over him, stopping on the various tubes and wires attached to him before he glances up at the machines.

We pull up chairs and sit beside him, both of us watching him closely for any signs of movement. We rarely talk, only passing a few remarks back and forth.

I lose all track of time, but at some point, a nurse pops her head in. "Visiting hours are over. Why don't you kids go home and get some rest. We'll let you know if there's any change in his condition overnight."

I can see the reluctance in Hawk's expression, but before he can argue, I speak up, "Thanks. We'll leave in a few and come back tomorrow."

Nodding, the nurse closes the door, once again leaving us alone.

"We need to get some rest ourselves. They'll call if anything happens," I assure Hawk, taking in the bags under his eyes. We all had one hell of a day, and I still haven't updated the others on what happened at the warehouse with Bowen after they left.

Sighing, Hawk nods his head in agreement, and we mutter our goodbyes to a still-unconscious Barton before we leave.

Cam wraps me in a bear hug when we return to the waiting room, and I sink into his embrace.

"You didn't have to wait for us," I say as Mason does some sort of bro-hug thing with Hawk.

"We wanted to wait in case you needed anything. How's your dad?" Beck asks. He looks exhausted, and glancing at the others, I see the same weariness tugging at their features.

"He's stable. We'll know more tomorrow," Hawk answers with a small smile as Cam pulls me in for another hug, not yet ready to let me go.

Extricating myself from his embrace, I link my fingers with his. "It's been a crazy long day. Let's go home."

ONCE WE'VE ALL SHOWERED AND THROWN AWAY OUR BLOODIED clothes from today, we all collapse onto the sofas in the living room, and Cam hands out beers to everyone. I can already feel my eyelids drooping, exhaustion from today's drama taking its toll.

"Can we all just take a second to talk about what a complete and utter psychotic bitch your mom is," Cam states with absolutely zero tact as he drops down into the only remaining empty seat. "I never thought she'd have it in her to off her own kids."

I notice Hawk rub his eyes before pressing his face into his hands and sighing wearily, and I turn to look at him. "I didn't think she had it in her to actually kill me...but I saw the resolve in her eyes when she pointed that gun at me." He lifts his head, and there's a sadness in his eyes. "Never mind what she said about you." He shakes his head. "I don't understand how any parent could do that to their child. To a harmless baby."

Neither do I, but I don't see the point in dwelling on it. "Me neither, but it doesn't matter. She's dead, and Barton's going to be okay. We're free and clear."

"Yeah, except for my father," West grumbles from beside me.

I squeeze his thigh in reassurance. "We'll deal with him...tomorrow. You need to get some rest."

"I'm fine, Firefly," he assures me, lifting his arm so I can cuddle into him, being extra careful not to jostle him or press on any of the bruising around his ribs or abdomen. Even sitting here must be painful for him.

Just as I'm getting comfortable pressed up against him, Cam's next words have me groaning. "So, guess who showed up at the warehouse after you left."

Mason, Beck, and West all look at Cam before their gazes bounce to Hawk and me.

"Motherfucking *Bowen*," Cam continues, knowing damn well his words are going to get the other three all riled up.

"What the fuck? What happened?" Mason exclaims, running his gaze over me, inspecting me for any injuries.

Bar a little road rash, I'm fine. I have kept my arms covered all day though, first with Cam's hoodie at the hospital and now with one of West's long-sleeved sweatshirts, wanting to put off any questions that were sure to arise from the others at the state of my arm.

"Nothing. I'm not sure what his angle was—maybe to try and take me." I shrug my shoulders, not sure what Bowen thought was going to happen when he snuck up on me. "Not that I was ever going to let him do that. He's only ever seen me in the compound when I was weak, and even though he knew the training I'd received and what I'm capable of, I think he thought he'd be able to cower me. He's always been the one in charge, the one in control, yet outside the confines of the compound, he doesn't have that same power over me."

"And your PTSD?" Beck questions. "Were you okay?"

"Not at first," I mumble quietly, ashamed of how I panicked when he first approached me. "But I was able to work through it."

"She was amazing," Hawk speaks up, a proud note in his voice and a prideful glint in his eye. "Took him out with one shot."

I blush under his compliment, returning his heart-warming smile with a shy one of my own.

The six of us sit and chat for a while longer before everyone starts to yawn, and we call it a night. Hawk makes his escape down the hall, and I kiss the others goodnight.

"I'm going to stay with West tonight, and make sure he's okay."

"Of course, Little Warrior. I'll see you at breakfast." Mason places a searing kiss to my lips before heading to his room, and Cam takes his turn before following after him.

"You can stay in my room tonight," I tell Beck, who nods and glances at West.

"Look after him." With a kiss, he heads for my room, and I turn to West.

"Come on," I say, taking his hand. "You need painkillers and to go to bed."

He doesn't argue, letting me get him a glass of water and tablets before leading him to his bedroom.

As the door closes behind me, I trail my hand down the front of his t-shirt before tugging it up. He raises his arms so I can pull it off over his head, revealing his chest and abdomen. He watches my every movement with a keen eye, so I'm sure he doesn't miss the way my face scrunches in annoyance as the dark bruises that are beginning to form on his skin are revealed.

I lightly stroke my thumb over one, feeling that familiar spark of anger flare to life. He tucks his finger under my chin, lifting my head until I'm looking him in the eye.

"I'm fine," he assures me. "I'm here. You're here. Forget about today."

Closing the distance between us, his lips brush mine, stealing my breath and setting my skin on fire. I run my hands over his firm pecs, and he tugs on my hoodie. I pull it off as he steps out of his sweatpants. We discard the last of our clothes, and I can feel the sheer need pouring off him as he drinks me in.

He reaches out a hand, grasping my arm and turning it so he can see the abrasion better. "It's nothing," I promise him. His lips pinch, but he thankfully lets the topic go as I step into him. My nipples brush against his chest, hardening at the contact, as my hand moves to cup his balls, giving them a gentle squeeze that has him groaning before I wrap my fingers around his length to work him up just the way he likes.

"Fuck, Firefly," he groans, staring mesmerized at where my hand is wrapped around him. "Lick me." The words are a husky demand, and when I glance up at him through my lashes, his pupils are dilated with lust.

Slowly, I get to my knees before him, flicking out my tongue to run around his head, catching a bead of pre-cum and relishing the salty taste on my tongue before licking along his shaft. I pump him slowly as I suction my lips around him, giving another swipe of my tongue over his tip that has a low growl rumbling in his chest. The noise has me clenching my thighs together with need.

"Touch yourself," he orders, and I don't hesitate to press my fingers against my swollen nub as I suck him deeper into my mouth.

He lets me have control for a moment, but when I sink my fingers knuckle-deep inside my pussy, and moan around his thick shaft, his restraint snaps and his fingers pull my hair out of its hair tie, tangling in my messy strands as he thrusts into my mouth, and hits the back of my throat as he takes control.

I circle my fingers in tandem with his hard thrusts, and just as I feel the telltale tingle of an impending orgasm, West pulls back and I release him with a pop.

"Ah-ah," he chastises when I whimper with need. "All of your pleasure will be at my hands tonight."

All of my guys are different when it comes to sex. Beck fucks me like the process is an exorcism, ridding him of his demons. Mason can be surprisingly sweet and soft but no less dominant. Cam is all about making sure I come as many times as possible—he's definitely a giver in the bedroom. But West…it's not enough for him to make me come. He has to own every second of my pleasure.

In a move that must have his muscles screaming in pain after today, he sweeps me into his arms and carries me to the bed, dropping me onto it with a bounce before he wraps his arms around my thighs and pulls me to the edge of the mattress. Getting on his knees between my spread thighs, he doesn't waste any time before diving in and lapping at me. My back arches as I fist the bedsheets, already breathless and desperate for release.

All I can think about is the spiral of lust unraveling within me when I feel his finger, coated in my juices, press against the tight ring of muscle at my ass before pushing in. I tense for a second before relaxing, letting him slide in further. He begins to thrust shallowly in time to the movement of his tongue, and I quickly fall apart, crying out his name.

He doesn't give me a second to recover as he maneuvers me up the bed and hovers over me. In one swift move, he sinks inside me until his pubic bone grinds against my sensitive clit. My mouth drops on a gasp as I stare into his wild, lust-hazed eyes.

"Arms above your head," he murmurs in a deep husk that has my lower belly clenching with need, already forgetting that I just had an earth-shattering orgasm.

Doing as he asks, he leans over and pulls a satin tie out of his bedside table, tying it around my wrists. The material is soft against my skin as he pulls my arms further up the bed, securing them to the railings on his headboard.

He trails his fingers over the sensitive skin of my inner arm as he slowly works his way back down my body. His shallow thrusts drive me wild, tempting and teasing me.

He pulls back until just the tip of his dick is inside me, and towering above me, he takes his time to look over my blushed, heaving chest and peaked nipples before his gaze rests on my face.

"Now, no moving," he orders in a serious tone that brokers no argument, spearing me with a stern look before he slams inside me in one quick motion that has me crying out.

His eyes never leave mine as he continues his relentless pace, pushing me back up that peak until I swear I can taste my orgasm on my tongue. My hips involuntarily buck, and he draws back as soon as I move, slowing to a stop as his eyes narrow in disapproval.

He holds himself still above me, lifting a hand to press it flat against my sternum. I can see the question in his eyes, feel the hesitation in his movements, but I know I'm safe with him. Despite being tied to the bed, I know he won't ever go too far or do anything I don't want him to do.

If anything, handing over control to him like this has provided me with moments of relief over the last few weeks. I spend so much of my day trying to gain control that there's something ulti-mately freeing about being with West and handing all of that control over to him.

"It's okay," I assure him. "Do it." I tilt my head back, exposing my neck to him, and he stares into my eyes for a long moment before he slides his hand up my chest, wrapping his fingers around my neck. I'm sure he can feel my pulse as it thuds rapidly beneath his hand. My response isn't one of fear but excitement.

He flexes his fingers, testing his grip before he again sinks inside me. I feel his hold tighten around my throat, limiting my breathing just enough to add to the heady sensation that comes from being slowly driven toward ecstasy.

I'm truly held captive beneath him, my body wound tight as I try not to writhe, my breaths coming in pants the higher he pushes me.

"West," I moan needily, lost to his ministrations. "Please."

"I love it when you beg," he rasps, picking up his pace.

"I can't take any more," I cry, half delirious.

"You'll take what I give you," he growls in a demanding tone that leaves no room for argument. It only ratchets up my need for him.

His fingers tighten further, but it's still not enough to have me panicking. If anything, the entire world seems to fall away until I'm aware of nothing but his tight hold on my throat and the way my pussy clenches around him with every thrust, as I stare up into his deep green eyes that watch me in wonder.

"Come for me, Firefly," he growls in a breathless pant, rutting into me until he finds his release. The feel of him swelling inside me pushes me over the edge into an orgasm that feels like it goes on forever until I'm left lying limp on the bed.

West kisses me gently as he reaches above me to undo the ties and rub soothingly at my wrists before he flops over onto his back, taking me with him.

I curl into his side, careful not to put any pressure on his bruises, and as my eyes drift shut, I feel him press a kiss to the top of my head.

"Go to sleep, baby." His fingers stroke through my hair, and I feel sleep tugging me under as he murmurs, "Everything's going to be okay from here on out. I'm going to give you everything you've always wanted."

CHAPTER 26

Hadley

I JERK AWAKE AT SOME POINT LATER IN THE NIGHT AND LIFT MY HEAD, looking around to see what woke me. I'm just about to pass it off as a nightmare when I hear a floorboard creak in the hallway.

Careful to keep quiet, I slip out of bed, grab a pair of West's sweats and a top, and pull them on before stuffing my feet into my boots and cracking the door open to peer out into the darkened hall. I can make out a dim light and hear the sound of movement coming from the kitchen. Slipping the knife out of my boot, I move on silent feet out of the bedroom.

Slowly, placing one foot in front of the other, I close in on the kitchen. As I approach, I tighten my hold on the handle, ready to drive it into whatever asshole broke into our dorm, but as I step into the kitchen, I stutter to a stop when I come face-to-face with Beck.

"What are you doing?" I hiss, dropping the knife to my side.

He glances down at the steel blade in my hand, and instead of seeming surprised—you know, a *normal* reaction—his pupils seem to dilate, and one side of his lips lifts up in a smirk. "Were you about to stab me, sweetheart?"

"You're not supposed to find that a turn-on," I grouse, tucking the knife back in my boot. "What are you doing up?"

He steps back to grab something from the island, and I take in what he's wearing—He's dressed head-to-toe in black. "Or maybe I should be asking *where* you're going."

When he turns back to look at me with a black backpack in his hand, his expression is tight, his lips pressed flat.

"Where are you going?" I repeat more insistently, tilting my head slightly and quirking a brow as I wait him out.

After a moment of silence, he huffs out a breath. "To deal with Wilbert."

"Alone?" I'm already shaking my head. "I don't think so. Give me a couple of minutes to change."

"No, sweetheart." He reaches out to snag my wrist as I turn away, forcing me to turn back to face him. "Go back to West. I'll sort out this last hurdle for us."

"I'm not letting you go alone," I insist. "I'll be your backup in case you need it."

My wrist is still held captive in his as he stares at me for a long moment before relenting. "Fine, but no stabbing people unless it's necessary."

"No promises," I mutter under my breath as I turn away from him and scurry back down the hall to my bedroom, grabbing some appropriate clothes and throwing them on as quickly as possible in case the asshole so much as thinks about trying to sneak out while I'm changing.

I'm relieved to find him still standing where I left him when I return to the kitchen. "Ready?" I ask, and he nods, throwing his backpack over his shoulder and heading toward the front door.

The campus is quiet as we walk through it to where Beck's car is parked in the staff lot. His car is an eyesore, parked amongst various brand-new Audis and Mercedes, but he doesn't seem to give a shit as he strides toward it.

Inserting the key in the door, he unlocks the car, and we climb in. It takes a few tries before the ignition starts, and I side-eye him, wordlessly hoping the car doesn't break down halfway there.

He pats the wheel in some sort of weird, loving gesture before putting it in gear and driving us away from the campus. Neither of us talks, comfortable in the silence as we make our way along the seafront and up the cliff to our parents' residence—although all but Barton's house belongs to the guys now, so I guess it's their residence. *Weird.*

We pull up to the gate and Beck enters the code, waiting for the gates to open before driving through them and parking at the entrance to Wilbert's driveway.

"You have a plan in mind?" I question before we get out of the car.

"Not really. I'm fairly confident we can wing it. He probably doesn't know about Maria yet, and if he was in on her plan, the last thing he would expect tonight is a visit from us."

Nodding my head in response, I push open the car door and get out, careful to close it quietly behind me. With a knife in my boot and another in my hoodie pocket, I'm more than prepared as we stealthily move toward the darkened house. At this late hour, he's probably sound asleep, giving us the element of surprise.

I follow Beck as he enters the house and, without making a sound, begins to climb the stairs. He stops at a bedroom door, glancing over his shoulder at me. I give him a quick nod, letting him know I'm ready when he is, and he slides a gun out of his pocket before easing the door open.

The second he does, I can hear the sound of a machine whirring. Nevertheless. Beck pays it no attention, so he must have heard it before, when he was here with West.

He pushes the door open further, until we can step into the darkened room, and I can just about make out the outline of the bed. Before I can determine whether or not Wilbert is lying in it though, I hear the recognizable click of a gun being cocked from the far side of the room. The loud noise has both Beck and I spinning, raising our weapons in anticipation of an attack.

"Stop right there," Wilbert growls angrily, pointing what looks like a fucking shotgun at us. We both freeze. "Weapons on the ground." Slowly I lower my knife to the floor, and Beck does the same with his gun before we both stand upright and raise our hands in the air.

Wilbert reaches out to turn on the light on the table beside where he's sitting, lighting up the room. Now that I'm not having to squint through the darkness, I can see pillows or clothes or something have been stuffed underneath the duvet to make it appear like there's a body lying in bed and then there is some sort of device sitting on his bedside table making the annoying whirring noise. All of it was set up to make us think he was asleep in the bed. *Sly, Wilbert. Didn't know you had it in you, you fat fuck.*

"I set the gate alarm to alert me whenever it was opened. Didn't want to be caught unaware again."

At his words, I return my focus to him, and the large gun pointed straight at Beck, obviously deeming him to be the greater threat out of the two of us.

Glancing at Beck, he looks utterly unperturbed by the gun pointed in his face.

"Gotta give you some credit, old man. We didn't think you had it in you to deceive us."

Wilbert's face reddens in anger at Beck's words.

"You think I was about to let some *children* take everything I have worked for?"

I quirk an eyebrow. "Doesn't sound like you've really contributed much. You just leave all the decisions up to everyone else and reap the rewards."

His gun stays pointed at Beck, but Wilbert's furious gaze bounces to me, and his lip curls up in a snarl. "Stay out of it, girlie. You have no business sticking your nose where it doesn't belong." His gaze darts back and forth between Beck and me.

"Maria's the one you should be chasing anyway. She's got your brothers."

So the piece of shit knew that.

"And you don't even give a shit that she could be doing god knows what to West?" Beck snarls furiously.

"He shouldn't have come after me or tried to win one over on her. We weren't about to let him get away with that."

"So you let Maria do all the heavy lifting," I begin, shifting slightly so I can move closer to him. "You let her organize his kidnapping." Another small shuffle. "Let her have her goons beat him up. Let her threaten him." I let the monster inside me rise to the surface and shine through so he can see exactly who the fuck he's messing with.

I relish as the sneer drops from his face, quickly replaced by fear and astonishment.

"H-how do you know that?"

I grin savagely at him. "Because we killed her." I don't give him any time to process that information, taking a large, deliberate step toward him. My sudden movement has him swinging the gun in my direction, but this is the thing I *hate* about guns, especially huge, long-barreled shotguns—they just don't work in small spaces, and I'm far too close for him to get any sort of a decent shot.

The second the barrel swings in my direction, I reach out and grab a hold of it, fighting him for control. With him distracted, Beck quickly rushes to his other side, and in a move that turns me on *way* more than it should, he pulls a knife out of his fucking boot and holds it to Wilbert's carotid.

The fat shitstain stops struggling, immediately falling still at the press of cold steel against his neck and letting me rip the gun from his hands. Flicking on the safety, I chuck the stupid thing on the bed and turn back to grin manically at the look of utter terror on Wilbert's face.

"Is it inappropriate if I tell you how much I want to fuck you right now?" I ask Beck, ignoring Wilbert's splutters.

Beck laughs darkly, his own monster stirring just below the surface. When he looks up at me from where he's crouched behind Wilbert, I swear, I fucking gush for him. That titillating combination of darkness and lust brims in his eyes, and I am so fucking here for it. "Not at all, sweetheart. If only you could see the boner I'm sporting for you right now."

My grin turns genuine as Wilbert's wide-eyed gaze darts between us.

"What the—"

"Shut the fuck up," Beck snarls, focusing back on his scumbag father. "I think we've heard just about enough from you."

"Definitely," I mutter in agreement.

Wilbert's breaths come in rapid, panicked pants, and sweat coats his forehead.

"Now," Beck muses, glancing up at me with an excited gleam in his eyes, "what are we to do with you?"

I lift my finger to my lips as I mull over our options. I'm all for gutting him here and now, but given Maria's death earlier, we probably shouldn't be drawing any more unwanted attention our way.

An idea comes to mind, and Beck quirks an eyebrow when I grin at him. "I have an idea." He waits patiently for me to continue. "It involves a cliff and a long, *long* fall to the bottom."

"What? Wait—"

"Sounds perfect," Beck agrees, his fucked up grin matching my own. "Come on, fatty, let's get some fresh air."

"What?! No!" Wilbert insists, pushing himself further into the chair and gripping on tightly to the arms as if that will save him. It's fucking laughable.

Beck seems to think the same as he chuckles, digging his blade deeper into Wilbert's neck, nicking the skin. "It wasn't a suggestion," he barks.

With much pushing, Wilbert eventually gets to his feet. His knees are practically quaking as Beck shoves him in the back, causing him to stumble as he takes a step toward the door.

I retrieve the gun and knife from the floor, handing the weapon back to Beck before I open the bedroom door. Keeping ahead of them, we make our way at a painfully slow speed along the landing and down the stairs. Wilbert blubbers and cries and protests with every fucking step, but Beck and I pay him no attention.

It feels like it takes fucking forever before we finally reach the doors leading out the back of the property. I've never ventured close to the edge of the cliffs, but I remember West telling me about them, and somehow it feels like a fitting end to all of this.

Opening the back door, there's a slight breeze in an otherwise still evening, which swirls the sea air around me. I take a deep breath, and I don't know if it's the sea salt or how close to being finished we are, but damn, the taste of freedom is so fucking sweet.

"Please don't," Wilbert pleads for like the fiftieth time as Beck shoves the end of the gun in Wilbert's back, rolling his eyes at me. I laugh, and Wilbert looks at me like I'm crazy.

"You're both sick," he snarls. "What normal person would do this to someone?"

The laughter drops off my face, and in the next second, I'm standing in front of him, so close I can feel his disgusting breath on my cheek. "What sort of person turns children into monsters for a living? What sort of person makes his son feel like shit and pretends the other doesn't exist until he has a need for him? What sort of person forces his children to do what you've made Beck do?"

Stepping away from him, I shrug, letting my anger at his words bleed out into the night air. "Besides, we never claimed to be normal. We are what you made us. We're a product of our environment. *You* turned us into who we are, and now it's time for your reckoning."

He just looks confused, and I'm pretty sure he's got no fucking idea what I'm on about. Not that I give a shit.

"Now come on, Beck and I have better things to be doing with our night."

Beck shoves Wilbert forward again, and he begins to sob like the pathetic waste of life he is. Slowly, we make our way toward the cliff edge, the sound of the waves crashing far below getting louder with every step, and the smell of sea salt in the air grows stronger.

There's something so peaceful about it all, and this unusual sense of calm settles over me as we approach the cliff. When we're a few feet away, Wilbert collapses to his knees.

Beck and I both huff out a breath of frustration. This is taking so fucking long.

"Jesus Christ, be a fucking man about it," I snarl angrily.

"I can't," he sobs. "Please."

"Please, what? Show you mercy? Spare your life?" I wrap my hand around the hair on the top of his head and wrench his head back, so he's staring up at me, not that he can see me through the tears streaming from his eyes. "Where was your mercy when you were killing kids? When Meena was being beaten to death? When you stripped us of our fucking humanity to line your own pockets?" Letting go of my hold on his hair, his head flops forward until his chin meets his chest.

"I didn't—" he blubbers, and maybe he's right. He didn't pull the trigger. It wasn't his boot that kept driving into Meena. But it *was* done under his purview. Whether or not he was directly involved isn't the fucking point. It was *his* company. He is just as much to blame as Lawrence, Frank, Maria, and even Barton to some extent.

Unfortunately, I wasn't lucky enough to be able to throw Lawrence, Frank, or Maria off the side of a cliff. Regardless of how each of them met their demise, it was more than deserved.

The sound of a gunshot going off makes Wilbert scream before he breaks down in a fresh round of tears.

"On your fucking feet," Beck snaps, having reached the limit of what he's willing to tolerate. Knowing his father isn't going to stand up on his own, he grabs him by the back of his pajama top, and I help yank him to his feet.

With the gun shoved deep into the middle of his spine, he stumbles forward another few feet, until he's hovering at the cliff edge.

I can see his entire body shaking with fear now, and Beck and I make sure to stay a few feet back from the edge to be safe.

"Please," Wilbert continues, his words falling on deaf ears.

"Go on, over you go," I encourage him, but he shakes his head furtively, continuing to plead for mercy.

"Fucking hell," I grouse. "Get it through your thick skull, you're not getting out of this. This is the end of the line for you. The only decision you get to make is whether you go out like a man or the bawling baby you're acting like."

An ominous crack follows my words, and in the next second, the ground beneath Wilbert's feet gives way, and he and the ground he was standing on disappear. My mouth drops open as I lean forward, not daring to step any closer to the edge. Not that I need to since his screams float on the air until there's a crash of waves below, followed by a reverent silence.

We both listen intently for another moment or so, almost expecting to hear him crying for help, but when we hear nothing but the sea hitting the rocks far below us, I turn to Beck, a disbelieving chuckle bursting out of me.

He returns my smile with a dark grin of his own, wrapping his arms around me. "Damn, that felt good." He chuckles.

"I just wish all of them could have met the same gruesome death."

He tucks a stray strand of hair behind my ears, cupping my cheek. "I know, but it's over. That's all that matters."

I nod my head, but then I pause. "Actually, not quite. Do you think Cain would be able to get someone inside Ashfield Prison to take care of Frank?"

Beck's eyebrow lifts in surprise. "He's going to be sentenced to life in prison."

"I know, but I'm not willing to risk him ever getting released. After the things he's done to Mason, he doesn't deserve to live."

Nodding, Beck pulls me in for another hug. "I'll reach out to him and see what he can do."

We stand on top of the cliff behind West's house for a long time, and the faint pink and red of the sunrise is gracing the horizon by the time we head back to campus.

When we return to the dorm, I pull him into West's bedroom with me, and we quickly strip off our clothes before climbing into bed.

As Beck slides in behind me, I can feel his erection pressing between my asscheeks, and I push back against him.

He nibbles on my earlobe. "What is it about killing off the last of your enemies that is such a fucking turn-on?" he whispers in a low growl into my ear.

I turn my head, capturing his lips with mine in a heated, sloppy kiss, full of tongue and teeth. "Fuck me," I half-plead, half-demand.

He smirks into my kiss, shifting us so I'm on all fours. "Climb on top of West," he orders. "See how many times I can make you come before he wakes up."

Doing as he says, I place a knee on either side of West's hips and press my hands into the mattress on either side of his shoulders. Beck lines himself up behind me, and after checking that I'm more than ready for him, he pushes all the way into me until his balls slap against my clit, making me moan.

He sets a slow pace, taking his time building up our climax, and I shift my weight to one arm so that I can stroke my other hand down West's gorgeously naked body. Trailing down the center of his chest, I stroke over his happy trail, holding back my giggle when his dick twitches under my touch.

Wrapping my fingers around his length, I pump him slowly, in time with Beck's thrusts, and my focus is so intent on watching him grow in my hands that I don't initially realize he's woken up, until he lifts his hands to press his fingers against my clit.

"What do you think you're doing, Firefly?" he questions, his voice thick with sleep and lust.

Lifting his head, he kisses me before I can answer, and between his fingers and Beck's dick, my orgasm hits me, and I moan into his mouth. Beck continues with his thrusts, dragging out my climax, and when I finally come down, he pulls out. I don't get a second to miss him though, as West pushes his dick into my pussy instead, and as soon as he's fully seated inside me, I feel Beck pressing against my ass. *Fuck yes, a hot brother sandwich!*

Inch by achingly slow inch, he pushes into me, until I'm so full I can hardly breathe. "Is that good, baby?" he asks, his voice dripping with need.

"Mmmhmmm." It's the only semi-coherent response I can form as the two of them start to move in tandem, one sliding out as the other pushes in, so I constantly feel full. I can feel their hands roaming over my body, setting my skin on fire as I rush toward an even more explosive orgasm.

"Oh fuck," I pant, as my skin begins to feel like it's about to rip apart at the seams. "I'm going to come."

Beck's fingers dig into my hips, and West's hand slides up my chest to wrap lightly around my throat, and the combination of their possessive touches pushes me over the edge as I scream out my release, faintly aware of their grunting as they find their own.

After we clean up, the three of us collapse into the bed, and I quickly drift back into a deep sleep filled with all my happy thoughts for the future that I've never let myself dwell on for too long...until now.

CHAPTER 27

Cam

I SHAKE OUT MY ARMS, DOING A FEW STRETCHES TO LOOSEN THE muscles as I step up to the side of the pool. The last few days, since Hadley and Beck snuck out to kill Wilbert, have been strangely quiet. I could get used to the peace, though. To carefree breakfasts and afternoons spent lying on the lawn. To movie nights and climbing into bed with the only girl I'll ever need.

Of course, there has also been a lot of time spent at the hospital over the last few days, but thankfully, Barton has woken up and seems to be recovering well. There have also been many conversations about the future and everyone's plans for after graduation. We're down to the final days of school, and this time next week, we will have packed our bags and said our goodbyes to this place. Today is the last school competition of the year—nationals—and we should receive our exam results this afternoon. Tomorrow is the final dance of the year, then graduation is next week, and after that, we're officially done with all things school related.

Barton should hopefully be discharged next week, and Hadley and Hawk have discussed at length about staying here for the next year so that she can foster a relationship with him. I think it would be good for her, and I'm all for hanging around here for a bit longer. Besides, just because we live here, doesn't mean we can't take the year to go on a few sex-crazed adventures of our own. We have the money and means to go wherever the fuck we want on vacation, and I've been encouraging Hadley to make a list of everything she wants to see and do. I want her to experience everything, and I know the others do too.

I push thoughts of the future to the back of my mind as the whistle goes off, and I dive into the pool, intent on making this my best performance yet. Without the weight of the company and our parents' bullshit hanging over my head, I put everything I have into every stroke, kicking my legs as hard as possible. Reaching the far end, I flip and push off the edge of the pool, gliding through the water. Nothing exists except the sound of my heart racing in my ears and the cool water as it laps at my sides. I don't hear the noise of the crowd, nor do I register the movements of my competitors on either side of me. No, these moments of peace are all about me, and I give every second of it my all.

The whistle blasts as I slam my hand down on the tile, lifting my head to check the time. A new personal best. *Fuck, yes!*

The next hour is a whirlwind of handshakes and congratulations.

"And this year's national swimming champion for the freestyle is Cameron Rutherford," the chairman announces, a round of applause going up from around the pool. I hear a wolf whistle from the stands behind me and turn to grin at Hadley and the guys, all of whom are on their feet, cheering and clapping, before climbing the steps to shake the chairman's hand and accept my trophy.

There's another round of applause and handshaking before I'm free to go shower and change.

Before I can make it that far, though, I'm accosted outside the changing room.

"You were fucking incredible, man!" Mason exclaims as Hawk smacks me on the back and Hadley pulls me in for a hug.

"You were amazing out there," she says, smiling brightly at me.

I give her a quick kiss, unable to get carried away and celebrate the way I want with her brother standing right beside me. *Cockblocker.*

"Hurry up and change, Emilia messaged saying the exam results were up."

I can see the nervousness in her eyes, and I know she's been anxious about the results. Given the lack of formal education she has received until now, I can understand why she would be nervous, but she's worked hard this year—which is saying something, considering all the other shit we've had going on. If anyone deserves passing grades, it's Hadley. She might not be the smartest, but she tries the hardest, and no one else I know deserves a fresh start more than her. Not that she needs good grades to do that. None of us gives a shit what college we go to. In fact, the less prestigious, the better. Sure, all of us could just buy our way into whatever school we wanted, but I know Hadley intends to earn her place wherever we go next. Something that I both respect and admire about her. I don't give a flying fuck if we're at some community college or fucking Crestmore—the most prestigious college in the country—so long as we're all together.

"Cameron." I turn around as a well-dressed middle-aged man approaches us. "My name is Richard, and I'm a scout for Ridgeway College. I appreciate that it is a little late in the year to be asking this, but what are your college plans for next year?"

"Ehh, I don't have any. My friends and I are taking a gap year. I intend to apply in the fall for next year."

Richard beams. "Fantastic. Let me give you my card. When it comes time to fill in your application, give me a call. If you can keep up your swimming training next year, I think you would make an excellent addition to the Ridgeway swim team."

He reaches into his pocket and produces a card, and I take it from him, completely flabbergasted.

"Uhh, thanks."

"No, thank you. It's been a long time since I've seen such talent and determination in a young athlete. You could have a bright future ahead of you, young man."

Tilting his head in goodbye, he walks away, leaving me gaping after him and trying to work out if that was real or if I imagined the whole thing.

"Holy shit, Cam," Hawk gasps. "That was insane! Did you hear him? He said you have a bright future!"

"And that you'd make an excellent addition to their swim team," West tacks on.

"Yeah." I stare at the card in my hand. "I mean, it could all be bullshit. For all I know, he's a sexual predator who likes to hang out at high school swimming meets and try to lure kids into his car with fake cover stories."

Even as I say it though, I run my thumb over the very real business card in my hand.

Richard Steltzer, athletic scout for Ridgeway College.

He didn't seem like a perv.

I hear someone snort, and I tear my gaze away from the card in my hand.

"Go on," Hadley encourages, shoving me toward the changing room. "Get changed so we can get our results and start celebrating." She's got a massive grin on her face, and she looks fucking amazing right now. Brighter than she has in a long time, like she's no longer carrying the weight of the world on her shoulders anymore.

"Yes, boss." I wink at her as the door swings shut behind me, cutting off her tinkling laughter.

"Ahh, oh my god," Hadley squeals, flinging her arms around me. "I only failed one subject."

I laugh, wrapping my arms around her. "What one?"

"History." She chuckles. "But who cares about that?"

After my swim meet, we all returned to the dorm and pulled out our tablets to check our results, although I don't think the rest of us give a shit about our grades, so long as Hadley is happy with hers.

Mason, Beck, West, and Hawk all take their turn congratulating her, and I don't think she could wipe the stupid grin off her face if she tries. It's fucking adorable.

"I'm so proud of you, little sis," Hawk murmurs quietly when he wraps her in a bear hug. A soft blush forms on her cheeks as she faces the rest of us.

"How did everyone else do?" She gnaws on her bottom lip as she looks between each of us.

"All good, Little Warrior," Mason assures her.

"Same," I pipe up. I have a healthy mix of letters, mostly B's, so I'm good. I've never been much of an academic person, and so long as I didn't flunk, I didn't really care about my grades. The only time I put in any effort was when I was paired up with Hadley for our English assignments. I guess I wanted her to see me as more than the guy who gets by on his good looks and parents' money. I wanted her to see when I put my mind to something and how I gave it my all. At that time, all of my focus was on getting Hadley. Of course, there was a fuckton of unexpected road bumps along the way, but now I've got her, and everything is finally looking up. She might not know it, but I'll dedicate the rest of my life to making her happy.

"West?"

He grins at her. "Second in the year. I can probably guess who came first, so I'm happy with that."

Right on cue, there's a peppy knock at the door that can only belong to one person.

"Open up, biatch," Emilia calls through the door, following it up with another round of knocking, which persists until Hadley opens the door, and the little black-haired girl flings herself into Hadley's arms.

"I came first!" she squeals in a high-pitched tone that only dogs should be able to hear. "In the whole year! The. Whole. Year! Can you believe that? I never thought...I just wanted to do well enough to get into Halston."

I hide my snort of laughter behind a cough. She must be the only one out of all of us who didn't think she would be Valedictorian. She and West have vied for the top place for all four years at Pac. If she had been up against Hawk or Mason, she would have come to blows with us years ago, but West never gave a shit about his ranking. He just enjoyed studying—although I can't fathom why. Dude clearly needed to get laid. Although, he's been getting plenty of sex this year, and still beat everyone else's ass.

Anyway, with the amount of hours Emilia has been logging in the library, and dragging our girl along, there was no doubt in anyone's mind she would be top of the year.

I obviously missed part of the conversation, as the next thing I hear is Hadley saying, "Give me a sec, I just need to grab my dress," before she rushes off down to her bedroom. She and Emilia had agreed to get ready in Emilia's room before the dance tonight, and we'll pick her up on our way there. The two have been trying to spend as much time together as possible the last few days before school ends. I've no idea where Emilia is from or where she will be spending her summer, but I can tell Hadley's going to miss her terribly when she leaves. I guess I'll just have to treat my girl to a few weekends in Halston so that she can have herself some girl time...and I can definitely get some mind-blowing thank you sex afterward.

Hadley enters the room with her dress slung over her shoulder and waves a quick goodbye, saying she'll see us later, before rushing out the door with Emilia, a grin plastered on her face. It's been kind of jarring seeing her so happy, but I fucking love it.

"Guess it's just us guys for the rest of the afternoon," I say with a shrug, grabbing beers for all of us.

"Here's to the end of school," Mason says, raising his bottle.

"And to finding lost siblings," West adds, smiling fondly at Beck, who returns it with one of his own.

"Cheers!" We all clink our beers together and drink from them before moving over to comfier seats in the living room.

"Bet you can't wait 'til school's over and you don't have to hide your relationship with Hadley anymore," I say to Beck as I plunk my ass on one of the couch cushions.

"Fuck, I can't wait. It's been driving me mad, especially since you guys announced to the school that you were dating her."

I grimace, not having given any thought to how that might affect him. "Sorry," I mutter, but it's a pointless apology. He waves it away.

"Don't be. It had to be done. I'll just be glad when I no longer have to hide what she means to me."

We all sip on our beers for a bit before Mason speaks up, "So Ridgeway college? That's not too far from here. We should go check out the campus."

I shrug my shoulders. "It's just a card. Doesn't mean anything."

"Don't sell yourself short like that. You were on fire today. They'd be lucky to have you on their team." Beck sounds sincere, and when I look his way, he's wearing his serious 'school counselor' expression.

His confidence bolsters me, and I straighten my shoulders. "Yeah," I say, turning back to Mason. "It would be cool to go look around."

There's a knock at the door, and we all share a knowing look. I roll my eyes as I get up to answer the door, knowing who will be on the other side before I even open it. Since Emilia has just left, only one other person would dare knock on our door.

Wilder comes bouncing into the dorm like a two-year-old on a sugar high. "I just bumped into the girls, and they said something about a guys' afternoon."

I don't think I'm the only one who stifles their groan, but when Wilder lifts his hand and says he brought beers for everyone, I decide I can put up with an afternoon of his craziness.

I know Hadley likes him, and I must admit, despite his unhinged personality, he's really stepped up. He was dumped in this school, not knowing anyone, and expected to marry a girl he'd never met. Most guys would have cowered when they discovered their fiancé came with four pissed-off boyfriends and an overprotective brother, but not Wilder. I have to respect the balls on the guy—so long as he never sticks them anywhere near Hadley!

I think letting something happen to Hadley on his watch messed with him slightly—not that he'd ever let on—but he accepted responsibility and insisted on coming with us to rescue her, even though he didn't have to. And I know he kept a close eye on Emilia when Hadley wasn't around. The rest of us were too concerned with bringing Hadley home to even think about Emilia. Still, Wilder, without having to be asked, immediately thought about what Hadley would want, and was there for Emilia at a time that I'm sure was confusing for her. If nothing else, I know that meant a hell of a lot to Hadley, however her weird friendship with him is more than just that. They seem to get each other in a way we can't understand. Whenever I tried asking Hadley about it before, she just shrugged it off, claiming something about his darkness being similar to hers—whatever the fuck that means.

Regardless of what it is, I guess he's kinda wormed his way into our friendship group, and thankfully has stopped flirting with Hadley—although he still insists on calling her fucking Sunshine—ever since we told the school we were dating her.

When I tried to broach the subject with Hadley about whether or not she was interested in dating him, or adding him to the harem or whatever, she nearly pissed herself laughing, and looked at me as if *I* was the crazy one. It had seemed like a genuine question at the time before the shit hit the fan and my fucking scumbag of a father got his grimy hands on her again, but I can see her friendship with Wilder for what it is now. He's a genuine, albeit slightly psychotic, friend, and Hadley needs more of those in her life. Michael—even thinking his name has me wanting to beat the shit out of him again—battered her already very limited trust in people, so it's good to see her letting Wilder in. He's actually worthy of her friendship.

"Did you hear the good news?" Wilder asks, flopping down on the couch beside Hawk and dropping his arm over his shoulder, which Hawk quickly shoves off. "We've upgraded from bros-in-law to pussy brothers."

"Dude, what the fuck?" Hawk snarls, glaring at him with such fury. Any normal person would be backpedaling at this point, climbing over the back of the sofa to get away from him, but not Wilder. He just grins like a fucking loon.

My nose wrinkles in disgust before what he said registers with me. "Wait, what? You banged the same girl? Who?" I can't think of a single girl on campus Hawk would willingly go near, except, maybe...no. Surely not.

"Fuck me," Mason groans, glowering at Hawk. "Tell me you didn't."

My mouth drops open and I gape at Hawk. "You both fucked Emilia?!"

Hawk buries his head in his hands, mumbling curses under his breath as Wilder bobs his head like a puppy looking for a treat.

"Dude, why the fuck would you do that?" West snorts, trying and failing miserably to keep a straight face when Hawk scowls at him.

"Hadley's going to skin you alive when she finds out." I chuckle. Damn, I need some popcorn and a comfy seat for that show.

"Oh, she already knows," Wilder states casually. "She ran into Emilia and I the next morning."

If it's possible, my mouth drops open even further. *Fuck, I bet that was awkward as fuck.*

Hawk groans into his hands, obviously not having realized that little tidbit.

"Emilia?" I'm still struggling to wrap my head around the whole thing. "But, why? Out of all the girls on campus, you had to fuck Hadley's best friend?"

"I don't know," Hawk groans.

"Does it mean anything?" Beck asks, leaning forward in his seat, his gaze bouncing between Hawk and Wilder.

"God, no." Hawk's quick response and vehement 'no' has my eyebrows rising in surprise. "It was just sex. I can't go near any other girl at Pac without them expecting a fucking ring at the end of the year...and Emilia was just there."

I kinda get what he's saying, but still...Emilia? He's such a fucking idiot for crossing that line. I'm beyond shocked Hadley hasn't handed him his ass for it.

"What about you?" Beck asks, jerking his head at Wilder, who just shrugs.

"Dunno yet."

Jeez, what a response. I can hardly restrain my eye roll.

We drop the subject after that. I'd well believe, to Hawk, it was just a one-night stand, although, with Wilder? Fuck, never thought I'd see the day he'd be down for sharing a girl, let alone with a dude he hardly knows. He must have been drunk off his ass at the time.

"What are your plans after graduation?" I ask Wilder instead.

He gives another one of those infuriating shrugs. "Haven't decided yet. Thought I'd hang around here for a bit."

Well, that's vague, but then, I guess so are our post-graduation plans.

We drink and chat for the rest of the afternoon until we have to get ready for the dance.

"Don't we clean up well," Wilder preens, checking himself out in the mirror as he fixes his canary yellow bow-tie that matches his yellow sneakers. Along with his black suit, he looks like some sort of deformed wasp. "Come on, pussy brother, let's go check out the Pac sluts one last time."

"Don't call me that," Hawk grumbles, but he follows him out of the apartment nonetheless, leaving me alone with West and Mason. Beck had to leave earlier as he offered to supervise the dance tonight—basically, he just wants to torture himself all night by watching us grind all over Hadley.

Checking my outfit in the mirror one final time, I turn to the others. "We ready to go get our girl and give her the best dance of her life?"

CHAPTER 28

Hadley

Emilia left a couple of minutes ago, and I'm smoothing out the creases on my forest-green dress when there's a knock at the door. Giving myself a final once-over, I move in my kitten heels to answer it, the skirt of my dress flaring out and swishing around my thighs.

Pulling open the door, I couldn't keep the grin off my face even if I tried, as I run my gaze over the three handsome men, all dressed up in suits, standing in the doorway—*my* men. My stomach is a bundle of nerves and excitement. The last dance I attended was a disaster, and I want tonight to go better, so we can all end the year on a high.

My skin heats as each of them roam their eyes over my outfit. "Wow, Firefly, you're stunning," West praises, stepping forward to plant a kiss on my lips.

"Absolutely gorgeous," Mason murmurs, when West steps aside, staking his claim with a heated kiss of his own. I melt under the softness in his sky-blue eyes, and a blush forms on my cheeks as Cam shoves him out of the way so he can stand in front of me, a dirty smirk curling his lips and a wicked glint in his eyes. Before he even opens his mouth, I know whatever he's going to say would be inappropriate, so I shut him up with a dirty kiss that I have to break off before we both get carried away and don't make it to the dance at all. I'm all for stripping each of them out of their suits and spending the night licking every part of them, but Emilia will never let me live it down if I miss out on tonight.

Pulling away from Cam, I look up at each of my guys. "Should we go?" No one misses the breathiness of my tone, but thankfully they overlook it.

"Oh, hold on," Cam says, digging in his suit pocket. "I wanna get a photo of all of us."

Pulling out his phone, he puts it on selfie mode and lifts his arm as we all huddle in for a photo. I'm grinning at the camera like a loon, with a blush still coating my cheeks, and Cam is making some stupid face. West looks stoic as ever, and Mason is staring at me instead of the camera. When I turn to ask him about it, he captures my lips with his, his hand resting possessively on my neck as he kisses all the sense out of me. I'm nothing but a puddle of hormones when he pulls away, whispering against my lips, "I love you, Little Warrior."

I can see the sheer honesty in his eyes, his words warming me from the inside out as I murmur my response, "I love you, Mason Hayes."

Cam ushers all of us out of the room, and we can hear the music and sounds of partying coming from the dining hall as soon as we step out of the dorm and make our way over.

The hall is packed with what looks like every student enrolled at Pac squished into the hall. Unlike last time, with the exception of a drinks table set up along the far one, the rest of the room is basically one giant dance floor, already packed with students dancing with one another and in large groups. I spotted tables and chairs set up under a string of fairy lights on the lawn outside the hall, the fairer weather enabling students to go outside if they wanted to sit or get some fresh air.

I'm looking around for Emilia, when my gaze meets Beck's on the other side of the room, his lips quirking up in a barely-there smile of acknowledgement that he sees me. His gaze drops, taking in what he can see of my outfit—which is basically just the way it pushes my boobs together and makes them look pretty damn good—and I can see the flare of heat in his eyes all the way over here, before a teacher nudges his shoulder, gaining his attention as he breaks eye contact with me.

I continue my search of the room for Emilia, and spotting me, she comes bounding toward me.

"Come dance." Without waiting for a response, she grabs my hand and drags me into the crowd, toward where Wilder is being his usual brand of insane with some weird-ass dance moves. He grins when he spots me.

"Sunshine!"

Returning his grin with a smile of my own, Emilia lifts my arm in the air, tugging my body in rhythm with the beat. Laughing, I move my hips, getting into the swing of it as the three of us dance our hearts out, until we're all panting and breathless.

"Need a drink," Emilia pants.

Wilder nods his head in agreement. "Same."

We start to push our way through the throng of people, but a hand clasping onto my wrist has me spinning around.

Coming face-to-face with Mason, a smile graces my lips as I quickly forget about my need for a drink and get lost in his pearly blue depths. A dirty smirk curls up one side of his lips as he pulls me into his arms, placing his large hands on my hips and grinding against me to encourage me to move.

I wind my arms around his neck, unable to look anywhere but at him as another song starts.

"Are you doing okay?"

I know he's talking about the fact I'm in the middle of a densely crowded room with loud music, and you know what...I'm actually not freaking out. I felt sweat coating my palms when we first walked in here, and the heat hit me, but somewhere along the way, I got lost in having fun with my friends and just living in the moment. Not to mention, there's something about not having obsessed psychos chasing after you, and not having deranged parents controlling your every movement that has me walking taller and breathing easier these days.

A soft, genuine grin spreads across my face. "I'm fantastic."

He matches my expression with one of his own, and the relief in his features has me leaning in, pressing my lips to his, and I drown in the taste of him. He slips his leg between my thighs, and I grind shamelessly against it. His body is perfection and presses against mine in all the right places.

Pulling back, he bites his lower lip before spinning me around. With swollen lips and love-drunk eyes, it takes me a second to compute the gorgeous hunk of man-meat standing in front of me.

"Cam," I purr as he places his hands on my waist, just above where Mason is holding possessively onto my hips.

"Baby, you're a sight for sore eyes." His words come out in a seductive husk that goes straight to my greedy pussy, and I fist the tie hanging loosely around his neck, pulling him into me, so I'm wedged between his lean, athletic body and Mason's huge, muscular one.

The three of us move in tandem, swaying and grinding to the music, and I feel Mason's hands slide down my sides, over my hips, until he reaches the hem of my skirt, and his fingers dance along my bare skin.

Arching my back, I press my ass against his hard erection, loving the deep groan that escapes his lips. Cam's hands slowly work their way to join Mason's, his fingers stroking along my inner thighs and making my breath hitch. As his hands slide under my skirt, Mason slides his up my body until his large palms are spread across my ribs, his thumbs brushing the side of my breasts.

My head falls back to rest against Mason's chest as Cam's fingers get closer to discovering just how fucking soaked my panties are for him—for the two of them. Mason ducks his head, running his nose up the column of my neck and occasionally flicking his tongue to taste me.

My hands cling desperately to Cam's shoulders in a vain attempt to hold me upright, but let's face it, Mason's solid body and firm hold on my waist are really what's holding me up, because my legs are fucking quivering under their ministrations.

Cam's fingers *finally* brush along my damp panties, and the glint in his eyes is positively wicked as his tongue runs along his lower lip. His dilated pupils bore into mine, the carnal need in his eyes holding me captive as Mason sucks and bites along my throat.

My lungs empty of all air when his finger presses firmly against my nub, making my hips buck. Mason chuckles into the crook of my neck, the noise sounding more like a rumble reverberating from his chest. He subtly brushes the pad of his thumbs over my nipples, most likely able to feel their hard peaks, even through the fabric of my dress.

A shiver of desire courses up my spine, and my cheeks are flushed from both heat and the wicked things these boys are doing to my body. I fall apart under their touch, my breaths coming in rapid pants as Cam's fingers slip beneath the thin fabric of my panties and easily push their way into my wet core.

My eyes drift shut as the two of them send me rushing toward a climax. Just as I feel my core tightening, my eyes pop open and looking over Cam's shoulder, my eyes meet Beck's lust-addled gaze.

Knowing he's been watching us get hot and heavy in the middle of the dance floor is my undoing, and Cam slams his lips down on mine as I come on his fingers and moan into his mouth.

"So fucking sexy," he murmurs against my lips when I come back to reality.

"Mmmhmmm," Mason agrees, still nibbling on the sensitive skin along my collarbone. "The sexiest."

I snort out a laugh as West, Hawk, Emilia, and Wilder join us, and the seven of us form one large group, dancing the rest of the night away. At one point, West and I break away from the others to get some fresh air, and when we come back in, I notice Wilder and Emilia arguing at the side of the room. Emilia's brows are drawn in confusion as her arms gesticulate wildly, and Wilder scowls at her before he snaps something out and storms our way, not sparing us a glance as he skirts past us and storms out the door.

Looking back at Emilia, her shoulders drop on a sigh, before she shakes her head and turns to grab a drink from the table. I worry my bottom lip, trying to decide if I should check on her or give her time to cool down, when West drags me back onto the dance floor. I decide I'll wait for her to tell me, in case she doesn't want to talk about whatever that was.

An hour later, Wilder returns, his usual grin plastered on his face, except I can tell it's sharper, more forced, and he watches Emilia with a weird expression. Emilia ignores his presence, but other than that little awkwardness, all of us have a great night. The sun is gracing the horizon by the time we all fall into our beds, and even though my feet hurt and my jaw is sore from laughing so hard, I don't remember ever having so much fun.

DRESSED IN A BLACK GOWN, I FIX MY HAT ON MY HEAD, FLATTENING my curls beneath it.

"We're gonna be late. Come on!" Hawk gripes, his own graduation gown billowing out behind him as he strides into the kitchen, just as there's a knock on the door, and Emilia shouts through it, "Open up! It's graduation day!"

The sheer excitement in her voice has me laughing as Hawk scowls at the door, refusing to move to open it.

Rolling my eyes, I shove my way past him and open the door. Emilia's eyes glisten with excitement, and she can't keep the grin off her face.

"They have everything set up on the lawn. It looks like they're getting ready to start soon," she says, bouncing up and down on her toes.

"Is your mom here?"

Her face falls. "Someone called into work, sick, last minute, and she had to cover for them."

"I'm sorry," I murmur, pulling her in for a hug. "We'll take loads of photographs to send to her, though."

She nods her head, fixing her smile back in place. I know having her mom here would have meant a lot to her, but I get the impression Emilia has gotten used to her mom not being able to make important events in her life because she has to work. It's sad, but she understands her mom is only trying to provide for both of them, and I know when they do get to spend time together, they both appreciate it much more.

"Let's go graduate!" Wilder calls out. There's still some weird tension between him and Emilia, but for the most part, they seem to both be ignoring whatever happened at the dance. Emilia hasn't mentioned their spat, and I haven't asked her, so I'm assuming it was nothing significant.

We all file out of the dorm and make our way down to the lawn, where they've set up a stage, with rows of chairs lined up in front of it that are quickly filling with students. Surrounding the stage and chairs are stands which are already overflowing with parents here to celebrate their children's achievements—or what is more likely, here to socialize and connect with other entitled, elitist assholes.

There's an excited thrum of energy in the air, along with a constant buzz of conversation and girly squeals as students meet up with each other and find their seats.

The rows seem to be set out in alphabetical order, and grinning at the others, Hawk, Wilder, and I move to find our seats near the stage while the others go in search of theirs further back in the rows. As Valedictorian, Emilia has to make a speech, so she has to sit up on the stage, along with the Heads of Departments and the headmaster.

I'm wedged between Hawk and Wilder when Mr. Phister stands up and moves to the podium. The noise settles down to a quiet hum as he speaks into the microphone.

"Ladies and gentlemen, I am honored to be here with you all today, to celebrate the Class of 2021. A graduation is always such a special occasion..."

He rambles on for a good few minutes about the bright future ahead of us and makes a point to remind us that it was Pacific Prep that set us up with the necessary foundations to achieve success—seriously, dude, is getting donations all you think about?

Glancing at Wilder out of the corner of my eye, I see him frowning at Emilia on the stage, and I lean in to whisper in his ear. "Are you okay?"

Tearing his gaze from her, he meets my eye, still frowning. "She's going on tour with some band." His lip curls in disgust.

Tilting my head, I try to get a read on him, but as usual, it's impossible. "Yeah, I know."

He doesn't elaborate on his thoughts, just shakes his head and returns his focus to the stage. Does Wilder like Emilia? Or does he just not approve of her summer plans? I can't work him out, and after a moment, I give up, returning my attention to the stage as Mr. Phister finishes his speech, and Emilia stands.

As she approaches the podium, I nudge Hawk. "Record this so she can send it to her mom," I whisper in his ear. He huffs but does as I say, lifting his phone out to start recording.

After thanking the headmaster and faculty, Emilia looks out over the sea of assembled students. Her gaze latches on to mine, and she smiles timidly before she glances down at her page of notes.

"Fellow students, today is both the end of everything we have known for the last four years, and the beginning of something new and exciting. After today, our futures are up to us to do with as we please. Whether you're going off to college, starting work, or heading off to find yourself, the future is yours to grab ahold of. Life is an adventure, and every opportunity to do something is a chance to learn more about yourself and push yourself to new limits. So make the most of this opportunity you have been given. Do something that scares you. Take the trip you keep putting off. Talk to the guy you have a crush on." She glances my way, one side of her mouth lifting in a grin, and I can see the tears forming in her eyes. "Take a chance on the new girl. Because you never know, she might just turn out to be the best thing to ever happen to you." I grin back at her, blinking away my own tears. "Live your life with no regrets, because every misstep is a chance to learn. Every mistake enables you to make the necessary changes and do better next time."

The guy in front of me turns to the girl beside him and rolls his eyes. Leaning forward, I smack him around the back of the head. His head whips round to glower at me, but seeing my furious expression, combined with Hawk's looming presence beside me, the pissed-off look on his face drops right off, and he mumbles an apology before turning around and paying attention again.

I glower at him for a second longer, making sure he's going to sit there and shut the fuck up before I focus back on Emilia's speech. "Pacific Prep has given me so much, and I'm not just talking about a high-quality education. It is here that I discovered myself, that I met my best friend and found a group of people who accept me for who I am, where I was pushed to stand up for myself and for what I believe in. No doubt, my time here came with challenges and low points, but even those I look back on with renewed clarity and know they helped to prepare me for what's to come. So, as we all, together, take that step out into the real world, let's remember the lessons we've learned here, appreciate the friendships we formed, and embrace whatever challenges we may face in this next unknown phase of our lives." With a bright grin lighting up her face, she finishes off her speech. "Congratulations, Class of 2021!"

I jump to my feet, clapping and grinning like an idiot, closely followed by Hawk and Wilder. I'm pretty sure I hear Mason whistling from somewhere behind us, and, more slowly, the rest of the year get to their feet, applauding.

With a final look my way, Emilia reclaims her seat, and the headmaster steps up to the podium again and begins calling out student names. Each student walks across the stage, accepting their certificate and shaking his hand before descending the steps, and the next one goes up, until the headmaster calls out, "Hadley Davenport."

Emilia grins at me, and I hear several whoops and whistles from my guys as I laugh and walk across the stage. Accepting my diploma, I glance first at Hawk, standing at the side of the stage, fist-pumping the air and grinning as brightly as I am, before I turn to face the sea of students in front of me to seek out West, Mason, and Cam. I then search the stands for Beck, and my mouth drops open when I find him standing front and center, clapping and smiling harder than anyone else. Standing right beside him, looking worse for wear, is my father—who is supposed to still be in the goddamn hospital. He's got tears in his eyes and an equally blinding grin on his face.

I walk off the stage as Hawk's name is called, and when he returns to his seat beside me, I lean in to whisper in his ear. "Did you know Barton would be here?"

He shakes his head. "No. He's not supposed to be released until later this week."

The headmaster continues through the list of names, and I clap equally as hard for all of my guys, until *finally*, the ceremony is over. Once we're released, I go in search of Beck and Barton.

Spotting him in the mass of students and parents, I push my way through the crowd toward Beck, and when he sees me, his face lights up. As I approach him, I jump into his arms, winding my arms around his neck as I plant a kiss on his lips, no longer giving a shit who sees us. Beck handed in his resignation a couple of weeks ago, and school is officially over. Now is our time, and I'm never going to hide my relationship with Beck, or the others, from anyone ever again.

He returns my kiss with a passionate one of his own, and when we break away, I can see the same happiness in his eyes that he can no doubt see in mine. He slides his fingers through mine, holding my hand, and I turn to look at Barton, taking in the way he's hunched over slightly and leaning on a walking stick for support. He's pale looking, with bags under his eyes, but the fact he's even up and walking about is a vast improvement. Hawk and I have visited him nearly every day, and with each day, he looks healthier and healthier.

"What are you doing here? We thought you didn't get released until the end of the week."

"I managed to talk them into letting me go early. I couldn't miss your graduation." He gets a nostalgic look in his eye. "I have missed so much of both yours and Hawk's life. I wasn't about to add this occasion to the list."

I smile appreciatively. We've been talking a lot recently, all three of us spending time together, getting to know one another, and establishing some sort of family unit. Given how he dove in front of that bullet for Hawk, not giving a damn about his own well-being, more than solidified the fact Barton had turned over a new leaf and wanted to put Hawk and me first. I feel nauseous whenever I think about how things could have ended differently that day.

Given his heroic actions, I have been making a concentrated effort to open up to him, and we've had some in-depth conversations about Maria's involvement in my kidnapping, and I've shared some of my time in the compound with him. Mostly, though, I've just talked to him about Pacific Prep and everything I have experienced this year.

"Dad!" Hawk has a wide grin on his face as he comes toward

us and hugs Barton, careful to keep it light and brief so as not to hurt him. "I wasn't expecting to see you here."

"Wild horses couldn't keep me away," Barton jokes.

We spend the next hour or so getting various photographs taken, until Barton holds up his camera. "Okay, one last one of all of you, then dinner is on me."

He herds us all into the shot, Emilia on one side of me and Hawk on my other, with Mason, Beck, West, Cam, and Wilder surrounding us.

"Say Princes," Cam shouts out.

Emilia and I share a wicked look, and as they all say *Princes,* we call out, "Pricks," and cackle our heads off as Barton takes the photo and the guys start up a protest.

EPILOGUE

Hadley

Local prominent businessman, Frank Hayes, who was recently arrested for the homicide of Lauree Hamilton, was found stabbed to death in his cell yesterday morning. There were no witnesses to the crime, and the prison hasn't reported any suspects at this time…

I set down the newspaper, snorting out a laugh. Of course, Mason got a phone call from the prison yesterday, not that it came as a surprise to him. Once Cain confirmed he could get the job done, I told Mason what I had planned. The way his shoulders lifted and he pulled me in for a bear hug, made me kick myself for not thinking of it sooner.

He would never have burdened us with his fears, but he was obviously worried about what his father might do in retaliation for us destroying Nocturnal Mercenaries.

"What are you laughing at?" Beck asks, walking into the kitchen carrying a large box. He sets it on the table and looks over my shoulder at the paper in front of me.

"Ah. It's always nice to see the news reporting happy stories, isn't it?"

He kisses my temple as I nod. "It definitely is."

"What are you up to?" I ask, eyeing up the box.

"Just helping the guys move the last of their stuff in. Who knew the lot of them had so much shit—I thought it was only girls who got sentimental about every belonging they own."

I laugh and shake my head. The five of us agreed to move into West's house, opposite my dad's, for the year. Of course, we've closed the door on the main bedroom suite and won't be setting foot in there until it's been completely gutted and redone. Moving in here seemed like a weird choice at first, and I wasn't sure how I felt about it, but none of the guys seemed bothered about coming back to live on the little cliff they grew up on. Understandably, Mason didn't want to live in his old house, and there was no way we were moving into Cam's, so that just left West's house. It's only for a year anyway, before we head off to college, and this way, we are close by to help Barton if he needs it over the next few weeks—although he's recovering well.

Cain has been struggling to find homes for some of the kids he rescued from the compound, and Barton offered to take some of them in. He's got this huge mansion all to himself, and I think a mixture of guilt and not wanting to be alone encouraged him to offer up his home. So he's got four teenagers living in the house now, and he says there's more life about it than there has been in years. He seems happier too, and I think most of that is down to him having both Hawk and I nearby.

Hawk, after much arguing, agreed to live in Cam's house, and the three of us make time for family dinner once a week, and I'm learning so much about both of them. It's amazing how much I actually enjoy our weekly dinners. My relationship with both of them has come a long way. It's crazy to think that not even a year ago, Hawk would glare daggers at me in the hallway, and Barton couldn't even stand to look at me. Now we hug and laugh, and I know without a doubt that Hawk would jump on a grenade to save me—just like I would for him. We're a family. A large, dysfunctional, perfect family.

Hawk also reluctantly agreed to take on an unexpected room-mate. Wilder had no plans after graduation, and he looked so down after Emilia left, I didn't want him to be alone. It just made sense that he lives with Hawk. It's such a big house for one person, although I did question my decision when I told Wilder, and he responded with some fucked up shit about living with his pussy brother? Nope. I do not *ever* need to hear those two words used in a sentence together, especially not in reference to my brother. *Fucking gross!*

We've only been living here for a week, and there have already been more shouting matches than I can count between the two. I've stocked an entire kitchen cupboard with popcorn bags so I can munch on something while I watch the blow-ups between them. It's more entertaining than TV, and since Beck and I only had a fraction of everyone else's belongings, I have had a lot of time to sit and watch The Hawk and Wilder show.

Sitting on the stool beside me, Beck asks, "How are you feeling after yesterday?"

"I'm okay. It was what I expected, although I'm a little over-whelmed with all the options we have. I don't know which one is right for us."

I had an appointment with a gynecologist the other day to find out for sure if I truly was sterilized at the compound. It turns out, I was. It was a nice thought for a moment, that perhaps it was all a ploy to make me think I couldn't have children, but of course, Bowen doesn't like to take risks. There's no way he would just say he sterilized us. It was still a shock—having it confirmed—but the biggest surprise was that this didn't mean I could never have chil-dren. I admit, it's not something I have ever given much thought to. Why would I, given the upbringing I've had?

The prospect of having a family of my own one day was never one I allowed myself to dream of...until now. Now that it's an option, I have no idea if it's even something I want. The good news is, we don't have to make any decisions right away. The gynecologist gave me a whole bunch of leaflets on my options.

Everything from having surgery to undo the sterilization—but apparently, it has a horrendously low success rate—to IVF, to surrogacy, and to adoption. The five of us need to decide what we think is the best option for us, but there's no rush. For now, we just want to live our lives. We want to go to college, travel, learn to live together as a family, and get to know one another better. We have more than enough to keep us occupied.

Beck kisses the top of my head. "The good thing is, it's not a decision you have to make alone. When the time is right, we'll make it together."

I smile warmly up at him, taking some peace from his words. They've all said similar things to me since the appointment, and I know that, regardless of what happens, nothing will send any of the guys running for the hills. No matter what the future brings, all of them will be there for me, and that unwavering support calms me whenever I get anxious about it.

The others filter into the kitchen, carrying their own boxes of belongings, and I slip out of my chair to put the newspaper in the recycling bin before Mason can see it. He already knows; he doesn't need to see any reminders of his dad. He got what he deserved, and that's that.

We're all starting a new phase of our lives, and no parents will interfere with our plans. This is our time—our time to do what we want, to live the lives we've talked about, and enjoy the newfound freedom none of us thought we would have.

Thick, muscular arms wrap around my waist. "What has that smile on your face?"

I turn in Mason's arms, pressing my hand flat against his chest. "I'm just thinking about our futures."

"Oh, yeah, what about them?"

Tilting my head back, I look up into his eyes. "How amazing they're going to be."

I feel the others close in around me. West on one side, Cam on the other, and Beck at my back. I look up at each of them with the same love in my eyes that I can see shining in theirs. Yup, so long as we have each other, the future can throw anything it wants at us. No obstacle is too hard, no challenge too big. Don't they say love conquers all? Well, our love is a force to be reckoned with.

365

EXTENDED EPILOGUE

Beck

Six Months Later

"IT'S SO GOOD TO HAVE THE CREW BACK TOGETHER," CAIN SAYS FROM beside me, sipping his beer. I lean back in my chair and survey the room with a smile on my face. We're gathered in the new premises—a rundown apartment complex—that Cain has acquired for his vastly expanding gang. West, Cam, Mason, Hawk, and Hadley are spread out around the small hall that's in the process of being turned into a bar for Cain and his growing army of men, chatting with various people.

We're all here today to celebrate Oliver's homecoming. He was released from prison several months ago but has been living in a halfway house until now. He accepted Cain's offer to stay here once he was released and has agreed to help him get set up in his new headquarters. I'm not sure what his long-term plans are; I'm not even sure *he* knows what they are yet, but I have to say, it's fucking great to see him again.

THE MAN HIMSELF CLAPS THE GUY HE'S TALKING TO ON THE shoulder. Oliver introduced him earlier—Aiden, I think his name is—when he was catching me up on what he's been up to these last ten years. Cain had already told me he'd fallen in with The Feral Beasts, a gang of ruthless thugs who used to control Black Creek when we were growing up, but the shit he's been through that resulted in him ending up in prison? Holy crap, it sounds insane. Not a far stretch from what we've managed to survive. Oliver walks our way, snatching a bottle of beer from the bar on his way past, before collapsing into a chair on my other side.

"What's it like to be a free man?" I ask.

He chuckles. "It feels fucking great. I forgot how much I missed just chilling with a beer and good company."

I scan the room once again. It's packed with Black Creek men that Cain has recruited, plus the recruits he saved from the compound. I see Reaper Reject tattoos on the ones who have decided to stay and help Cain, but some of the kids are far too young to be getting involved in any of this. They should be growing up in houses with parents and a backyard to play in. They should be going to school and complaining about homework. Cain is still trying to find their families or suitable homes if they have no families. It's a slow process, but he's getting there. I think after not being able to save his sister, it gives him a sense of accomplishment to be able to help these kids.

I even spotted the guard Hadley said was Meena's brother earlier—Marcus. Apparently, now that he'd found out what happened to his sister and gotten his revenge on the people who had killed her, he wanted to help Cain get revenge for Evie.

"I like Hadley," Oliver states. His words have my eyes drifting toward her, not even having to search her out in the crowd. I'm attuned to her every movement. After everything we've just survived, there's no way I'm ever letting her out of my sight again. She's currently standing on the far side of the room, chatting to a dark-haired girl, Oliver introduced as Sophie, and Aiden has moved to join them, pulling the girl into his chest. He looks wholly besotted as he just stands and listens to the two girls talking.

I can't help the sappy-as-fuck smile that lights up my face. She looks so at ease here, mingling with others. She and Sophie seem to be hitting it off, and I noticed her earlier talking to some of the kids from the compound. I wonder if being able to talk to people who have been through the same as her helps.

Cain chuckles beside me. "I still can't believe you're sharing a girl with three other guys. No way I could do that shit."

"It's the same sort of relationship Aiden and Ty are in with Sophie," Oliver explains. "It was a bit of a shitshow at the beginning. The other two guys, Preston and Barrett"—he points them out to us—"couldn't be any further from us. Preppy, trust fund kids, but they really stepped up when Sophie needed them, and they all seem pretty happy together."

"You'll understand when you find the right girl, man. I didn't think it was my thing either, but Hadley has a habit of getting herself in trouble." I laugh. "Let me tell you, it takes the four of us to wrangle that girl sometimes."

"I'll take your word for it, man. I just don't think it's for me. I'm all for sharing a girl for a night, but long term?" He shakes his head and scrunches his nose. "I don't think it's even the sharing. I'm just not a relationship person." Even as he says it, one of the slutty girls who have been hanging around, mostly bothering with the mass of new recruits milling about, makes her way toward us. Everything about her screams *come fuck me*, from the seductive sway of her hips to the heated look in her eye, and the way she bites on her lower lip.

"Hi, handsome," she purrs, running a long red-painted fingernail along Cain's massive bicep. "You were looking awfully lonely over here."

Cain emits a dark, throaty chuckle as his eyes drop over her scantily clad body. I'd forgotten how few clothes the girls in Black Creek wear. Girls who hang around gangs are even worse. Something I'm struggling to get used to, but clearly Cain has no such issues, as he eyes the girl like she's his next meal.

"Let me talk to my boys, but come find me later, okay?"

She smiles coyly. "You got it."

With a cocky grin, he turns to us. "See? Why would I give all that up for some chick?"

I just shake my head and roll my eyes.

"How is everyone settling in?" I ask instead, changing the subject.

"Good, I think. It's been a bit of an adjustment." He sighs. "Some of them were so fucked in the head when they first got here."

So far, Cain has found homes for most of the younger kids he rescued from the compound, but there's still a surprising number of recruits here. You can still identify who in the room came from the compound. They all have that look about them, the same one I still see on Hadley at times—that wariness. Even now, at a party, they're the ones that frequently dart their gaze around the room. They don't fully relax, albeit they do seem at ease around their fellow Reaper Reject members.

"So, what's your plan now?"

I notice Cain's hand tighten around his beer bottle, and there's a sharpness to his voice that wasn't there before. "Our numbers are growing every day. You know what my game plan has always been—it's the reason I've built all of this." He waves his arm around the room. "I won't let what happened to Evie be in vain. This town has gone to shit the last few years, and I'm fucking sick of it." He pins me with a dead serious look. "I'm claiming Black Creek as mine, and I'm taking down every single one of the fuckers that played a part in that day."

THE END

ACKNOWLEDGMENTS

This series would not have been been possible, or even half as successful, if it wasn't for the amazing team I have around me. You all play such an important role, and without each and every one of you, I'd be lost! To my friend and PA, Nikki, who puts up with me every day and keeps me in check. From creating the covers to alphaing and spending the last six months living and breathing these characters, she's as deep in the world of Pacific Prep as I am. I love you, girl, thank you so much for all that you do!!

A shout out to Nikki number 2, AKA UK Nikki, who is always available to help me out, and even though she loves to throw wrenches in my scenes when I think they're done, without her critical eye, this series would not be half as good.

A massive thanks to Shawna for beta reading and helping to make this book the best it can be, and to Zainab for her thorough editing and fine tuning. And a huge thanks to my street team and those who signed up with affinity to read and review this book. I appreciate all your hard work promoting every week and I've absolutely loved reading your reviews and seeing your edits.

Lastly, thank you to all of you, the readers, for picking up this book and reading it. Without you none of this would be possible!! If you loved this book, please help me spread the word by leaving a quick review.

ALSO BY R.A. SMYTH

Crescentwood Series

A dark, high school bully reverse harem with a stalker and gang element.

Pacific Prep Series

A dark, academy bully reverse harem with a taboo relationship.

Black Creek Series

A rival gang-mafia reverse harem with a vigilante FMC. Contains MM.

The Ruthless Boys of Ridgeway

A college, friends-enemies-lovers, second chance reverse harem with a stalker and secret society elements.

ABOUT THE AUTHOR

R.A. Smyth is best known for writing contemporary dark romance filled with unexpected twists, mystery, and plenty of steam. Rachel lives in the UK with her husband and two golden retrievers, and when she's not busy thinking up crazy cliffhangers to drive her readers insane, she enjoys inflicting the same torture on herself by reading incomplete series.

She has always been an avid reader, starting from the Harry Potter books as a kid. It's an interest that has grown into an obsession over the years and becoming an author has been a secret lifelong dream of hers.

* 9 7 8 1 9 1 5 4 5 6 1 1 3 *